The Best American
Mystery Stories 1998

The Best American Mystery Stories 1998

Edited and with an Introduction
by Sue Grafton

Otto Penzler, *Series Editor*

HOUGHTON MIFFLIN COMPANY
BOSTON NEW YORK 1998

ISSN 1094-8384
ISBN 0-395-83586-0
ISBN 0-395-83585-2 (pbk.)

Printed in the United States of America

QUM 10 9 8 7 6 5 4 3 2 1

"Child Support" by David Ballard. First published in *New Mystery*, Vol. V, number 2, Fall 1997. Copyright © 1997 by David Ballard. Reprinted by permission of Charles Raisch.

"Swear Not by the Moon" by Scott Bartels. First published in *Tamaqua*, Vol. VI, Issue II, Fall 1997 (Parkland College, Champaign, Illinois). Copyright © 1997 by Scott Bartels. Reprinted by permission of the author.

"Keller on the Spot" by Lawrence Block. First published in *Playboy*, Nov. 1997. Copyright © 1997 by Lawrence Block. Reprinted by permission of Knox Burger Associates, Ltd.

"The Man Next Door" by Mary Higgins Clark. First published in *The Plot Thickens* (Pocket Books, Nov. 1997). Copyright © 1997 by Mary Higgins Clark. Reprinted by permission of the author.

"This Is a Voice from Your Past" by Merrill Joan Gerber. First published in *The Chattahoochee Review*, Vol. XVII, number 4, Summer 1997. Copyright © 1997 by Merrill Joan Gerber. Reprinted by permission of the author.

"The Old Spies Club" by Edward D. Hoch. First published in *Ellery Queen's Mystery Magazine*, May 1997. Copyright © 1997 by Edward D. Hoch. Reprinted by permission of the author.

"Beyond Dog" by Pat Jordan. First published in *Playboy*, August 1997. Copyright © 1997 by Pat Jordan. Reprinted by permission of the author.

"Find Miriam" by Stuart Kaminsky. First published in *New Mystery*, Volume V, number 1, Summer 1997. Copyright © 1997 by Stuart Kaminsky. Reprinted by permission of Charles Raisch.

Contents

Foreword · ix
Introduction by Sue Grafton · xii

DAVID BALLARD
Child Support · 1

SCOTT BARTELS
Swear Not by the Moon · 17

LAWRENCE BLOCK
Keller on the Spot · 39

MARY HIGGINS CLARK
The Man Next Door · 58

MERRILL JOAN GERBER
This Is a Voice from Your Past · 84

EDWARD D. HOCH
The Old Spies Club · 96

PAT JORDAN
Beyond Dog · 113

STUART M. KAMINSKY
Find Miriam · 134

JANICE LAW
Secrets · 152

JOHN T. LESCROART
The Adventure of the Giant Rat of Sumatra · 163

JOHN LUTZ
    Night Crawlers · 179

MARGARET MARON
    Prayer for Judgment · 200

JAY MCINERNEY
    Con Doctor · 214

WALTER MOSLEY
    Black Dog · 224

JOYCE CAROL OATES
    Faithless · 238

PETER ROBINSON
    The Two Ladies of Rose Cottage · 262

DAVE SHAW
    Twelve Days Out of Traction · 277

HELEN TUCKER
    The Power of Suggestion · 284

DONALD E. WESTLAKE
    Take It Away · 299

STEVE YARBROUGH
    The Rest of Her Life · 309

Contributors' Notes · 333
Other Distinguished Mystery Stories of 1997 · 344

Foreword

FOR JUST HOW MANY years have we heard the publishing axiom that short story collections don't sell? When I was too young, too naive, to know this truth, I filled shelf after shelf with short story collections, unaware of my deviant behavior for engaging in this apparently unusual, if not outright bizarre, act.

Having continued down this awkwardly antisocial path for more years than it would be polite for anyone to enumerate to me, I am now struck by the fact that I have never had difficulty finding enough excellent collections (the work of a single author) and even more anthologies (stories by a variety of contributors) to satisfy my unending thirst. Can there be such generosity, such out-and-out *charity*, on the part of publishing houses to continue to publish these money-losing projects? If we are reading the same newspapers and magazines, with their endless lamentations about the strangulation of publishing houses by their new leaders, all accountants and lawyers still awaiting their first actual reading experience, that seems unlikely. Or — could it be? — short stories *do* sell.

When I consider the number of periodicals, anthologies, and collections I read to accumulate the best stories of the year, I cannot help but be cheered by the many markets open to short story writers. Nothing like the golden age before television, of course, but enough to ensure that any worthwhile piece of fiction will find a home.

While there are too few magazines specializing exclusively in the type of fiction contained in this volume, there are many mainstream consumer publications that use some mystery fiction, just as there are many small literary magazines that might be a trifle too blue-blooded ever to consider a mere mystery story but are happy to feature a tale of passion, fear, violence, suspense, or revenge that results in murder or its attempt or its aftermath. Finally, recent years have seen a dramatic increase in anthologies of original mystery fiction. Adding it all up, we counted nearly six hundred mystery-crime-suspense stories published in the calendar year 1997.

It has always been my practice to define mystery fiction broadly as any story in which a crime, or the threat of a crime, is central to the theme or plot. This definition opens the door to much that is not structured as a classic detective story.

In the United States, the professional organization of authors who produce this type of fiction is called the Mystery Writers of America. Its English counterpart is the Crime Writers Association. The members of both organizations are writers of mysteries, or stories essentially told from the point of view of the detective in which an attempt is made to discover who committed a crime or, more often nowadays, why the crime was committed. Both also count among their members writers of crime fiction, which is largely told from the point of view of the criminal: we see the crime committed, generally understand why it has been done, and then wait to discover how or why it all unravels.

As Sue Grafton points out in her introduction, there seems to be a preponderance of crime stories in this volume. It has, it seems to me, become more and more difficult for detective story writers to find new motives, or new clues, with which to fool readers. Agatha Christie consumed more than her share of original plot notions, leaving a pretty skimpy carcass for those who followed. On the whole, there seems a wider range of opportunity in the areas of suspense and crime than in the tightly plotted story of observation and deduction, so it cannot be a surprise that the output of contemporary authors reflects that shift of direction.

As is the custom in the Houghton Mifflin series of distinguished anthologies, the series editor (in this case, me) does the preliminary reading and passes along the best fifty stories to the guest editor (in this case, Sue Grafton), who selects the twenty stories to be published, with the remaining thirty listed in an honor roll at the end of the volume. To further enhance the reading experience, each author is invited to provide notes about his or her story and its genesis or other pertinent anecdotal material.

Happily, *The Best American Mystery Stories* enjoyed success with its initial volume in 1997 and gives the appearance of a series that will have a nice long run. It would be a shame to miss any eligible stories, so if you are an American or Canadian author of a mystery story published for the first time in the calendar year 1998, or if you have read one in a source that I am unlikely to have discovered, I would be happy to hear of it. Please write to Otto Penzler, Mysterious Bookshop, 129 West 56th St., New York, N.Y. 10019.

O. P.

Introduction

THIS COLLECTION of short fiction might more properly be labeled the "Best American *Crime* Stories of 1998." Regardless of the angle of attack, all of these stories feature crime in some form, either as the central driving force or as the anchor for other, sometimes disparate, elements. Certainly, the mix includes many stories constructed along the lines of the classic mystery, but there are unconventional approaches to the subject as well. In reviewing the many fine submissions, we were impressed with the ingenuity employed by writers whose styles and stratagems ranged from the formal to the offbeat. Almost without exception, crime here is the metaphor for human beings in distress, and violence, whether actual or implied, provides the compression chamber for the resolution of interpersonal hostilities.

These stories are exquisite studies in the complexity of human nature. Whether told from the point of view of the criminal, the victim, or representatives of law enforcement, each story touches on a facet of evil and, by implication, sheds light on its counterpart, good. Stanley Ellin has defined the mystery story as "short prose fiction that is, in some way, concerned with crime." This definition, while serviceable, scarcely speaks to the varied techniques these writers utilize to achieve their effects.

The construction of the crime story requires the establishment of a world easily recognizable to the reader. Whatever the parameters of this fictional universe, the reader must, early on, accept its reality, regardless of how alien it may seem to the reader's own. From the moment of this connection, the reader is led through a dark and tangled wood to the light of revelation on the other side. At the end of the journey, the reader has experienced a shift in perception . . . the *ahh!* of understanding that gives a story its impact. It is the marvel of the short story that it can accomplish so much in so few words.

Ross Macdonald once said: "An unstable balance between reason and more primitive human qualities is characteristic of the detective story. For both writer and reader it is an imaginative arena where such conflicts can be worked out safely, under artistic controls." Crime is the battering ram that breaches our defenses, forcing us to acknowledge how vulnerable we are. Given the daily newspaper accounts of crimes committed in cities across America, we're forced to construct a wall of denial around us in order to keep functioning. How else could we dare to venture forth from day to day? Murder, assault, robbery, gang violence, muggings, random freeway shootings . . . these are the threats to our personal safety, dangers we must somehow find a way to keep at arm's length.

Crime fiction is the periscope that permits us to peer over the wall without having to deal directly with the horror beyond. The crime story allows us to scrutinize the very peril we're afraid to face. At the same time, crime fiction seduces us into acknowledging aspects of ourselves that we might prefer to repudiate. Through crime stories, we can wear the mask of the killer without risking arrest and conviction. Through crime stories, we can experience the helplessness of the victim without suffering real harm. Thus, the writer's imagination authorizes an examination of the felonious outer world and our own concomitant emotional transgressions without compromising our humanity or surrendering our staunchly held moral views.

The stories in this collection serve as a seismograph, charting the effects of violence on the world around us. Sometimes what's recorded is a brutal upheaval of the visible landscape, sometimes a subtle tremor occurring far below the surface. With the crime narrative, there is always the tension of not quite knowing when the next eruption will occur. Where suspense is created, we find ourselves subject to a heightened awareness, our comprehension of events distinctly sharpened by dread. Ordinary people are seen with extraordinary clarity. Extraordinary events are reduced to their baser components: greed, rage, jealousy, hatred, and revenge.

Since the biblical moment in which Cain killed his brother, Abel, we've seen the reflection of our Shadow side in the stories we tell. What can be darker than the taking of human life? What more illuminating than such a tale brought to consciousness? We've always been attracted to the sly charms of the crime story. Look at the list of best-sellers in any given week. Of the top ten best-selling books, close to half are devoted to crime and mystery. The form may vary from the legal thriller to romantic suspense, from the hard-boiled private eye to the police procedural, but the appeal is the same.

"Crime doesn't pay," or so the old saying goes, yet watching a fictional character violate the law is irresistible, not necessarily because we wish such misfortunes on our fellow humans, but because, through reading, we can watch the perpetrator's destiny unfold without penalty to ourselves. Watching others get caught gives us the delicious sensation of our own safe delivery from our inner lawlessness. Crime fiction, like a report of political chicanery, allows us to identify with evildoers while we cling to our innocence, stoutly maintaining our disapproval of such behaviors. We can safely condemn offenses we might (with sufficient temptation or provocation) be capable of committing ourselves, staying a comfortable distance away from our own blacker aspects. A crime story allows us to plead "not guilty" to the sins of any given character. *He* was caught, and we weren't. *She* crossed the line, while we remained on the side of right. Fiction points the finger at someone other than ourselves, and we feel giddy with relief. How else can we explain the universal fascination with trials and public executions? We want to see justice done . . . to someone else. We like to see the system work as long as it isn't operating at our expense.

From the lowliest of criminals to the loftiest of public figures, retribution seems to catch up with every miscreant eventually. And nowhere is iniquity, wrongdoing, and reparation more satisfying to behold than in the well-crafted yarns spun by the writers represented here. While we're plunged into the darkness by their skill and imagination, we're simultaneously reassured that we are safe . . . from ourselves.

SUE GRAFTON

The Best American
Mystery Stories 1998

DAVID BALLARD

Child Support

FROM *New Mystery*

DEXTER HARRISON CURSED the biting wind as he pushed the blue baby carriage up the park path with one gloved hand and struggled to hold onto the tugging dog leash with the other.

It was even colder at the top of the hill, and Harrison growled a curse at Lex, his black Lab, for refusing to drop his chewed red Frisbee as Harrison tried to free the dog from his choker collar. As he locked the carriage brake and handed a baby bottle to his son, Adam, Harrison clenched his teeth and swore at his soon-to-be-ex-wife and her idiot attorney for withholding the promised cash settlement until Friday, when Harrison desperately needed $16,000 today.

After shaking the Frisbee overhead like a tambourine to get the dog revved up, Harrison shouted, "Here we go, boy! Come on! Bet you can't catch this one!" Harrison whipped the Frisbee so hard into the wind it sailed toward an abandoned soccer goal at the north end of the park. Lex bolted after it. He caught it easily with an airborne lunge, ending with the enamel *crunch* of sharp teeth clamped into plastic. As Lex trotted back with the Frisbee, Adam waved a mittened hand from within the baby carriage and squealed, "Dog-geee!"

From behind, Harrison heard the muffled *whump-whump* of two car doors slamming far away. He turned and saw a black Mercedes with darkened windows parked at the curb. Two figures leaned into the wind as they walked up the hill toward him.

Pretending not to notice, Harrison glanced around the deserted park. The overhead lamps down by the tennis courts were not yet lit, despite the gloomy overcast sky. The gunmetal gray playground equipment — the slide, a row of swings, and a tilted merry-go-round — sat neglected off to the east. The closest house with a porch light burning was across the street at the other end of the park, at least five hundred yards away. In front of him, Lex danced in anticipation, alert for another throw.

Without hesitating, Harrison threw the Frisbee again, and Lex flew after it, following the crimson arc of the Frisbee's flight as the wind angled it toward the merry-go-round. Like a pro, the dog timed the approach perfectly, caught the Frisbee inches from the ground without breaking stride, and rushed back for another throw.

Harrison glanced sideways at the two men slowly walking toward him. One was tall and skinny, while the other was broad and immense. They both wore long black coats tied at their waists, and their attention seemed focused on Harrison the whole time.

This must be it, then, thought Harrison. Time to pay the piper.

Harrison looked at his son in the baby carriage, bundled in his little blue parka. "You're my little rabbit's foot, Adam," he whispered as he bent down to take the Frisbee from Lex. "My lucky horseshoe. Nothing bad will happen. They only want to talk to Daddy. I'll just explain the delay. They'll understand."

Adam beamed up at his father and grinned. He was a magnificent eighteen-month-old little boy — bright and inquisitive, with round blue eyes and hair the texture of cornsilk. Harrison treasured his son more than any of his possessions, and so far Adam represented the only profit resulting from Dexter Harrison's dull and dreary marriage to Dr. Lynn Harrison.

As an attorney himself, Harrison had deftly whisked away temporary custody of their son from his wife. While he had been pondering a divorce, Harrison had spent months preparing a detailed and somewhat exaggerated chronology of all the abilities that made him a wonderful parent, while at the same time embellishing accounts of all of Lynn's shortcomings, lapses in judgment, and blunders. When Harrison filed for divorce, his attorney obtained an *ex parte* order from the judge granting Harrison temporary custody of Adam, all before any of the divorce papers were even served on Lynn. Harrison had capitalized on the fact that, while Adam spent weekdays in the most expensive day care in town, Lynn could arrange no baby-sitting for the evenings and weekends she was on call at the hospital, especially on such short notice.

Harrison had supported his wife financially while she was in medical school, and now she earned almost ten times what he did with his floundering personal injury practice. The property settlement had already been reached in principle, with Harrison to receive a large part of it in cash this morning. Lynn's attorney, however, had deliberately withheld the paperwork until Friday, probably out of spite.

I'll get even at the custody hearing tomorrow, thought Harrison. His own attorney had assured him that all of their witnesses were lined up and that preliminary signs were good that Harrison would win permanent custody of Adam. Harrison smiled at this thought as he regarded his son. The ultimate prize.

The wind carried the steady sound of boot heels slowly approaching. The two men were thirty feet away.

Still composed, Harrison took the Frisbee from his dog's mouth and let loose with a mighty throw. Lex pounded the ground after it as if his life depended on it. The dog's head bobbed like a greyhound's as he raced to get under the Frisbee before it floated to the ground.

That dog sure loved to run. As a sporting dog, Lex understood and appreciated the thrill of the chase, the electrifying rush of pursuit. He savored the hunt and the kill, even though his target may be only a softball, or a piece of flying plastic.

Lynn, on the other hand, simply had no imagination, no sense of adventure. She preferred her heavy medical books and mildewed chess manuals to the frenzied excitement of a race or the wild exhilaration of a home game.

Chess was boring. It was static, monotonous and simply uninteresting. Harrison would rather invest his leisure time tackling a high stakes poker game or watching a small fortune build at the track. The promise of the big payoff surged through Harrison like adrenaline. Although it was sometimes painful to lose money — and yes, a lot of it on rare occasion, Harrison insured against loss by placing only intelligent and calculated bets.

How was he supposed to know that last year's Super Bowl champion would lose on Sunday to an expansion team?

Lex returned with the Frisbee just as the two men stopped in front of the baby carriage.

The tall one had the sunken sockets and bulging eyes of a fish, as if he spent days in the dark staring into a television screen. As he peered into the baby carriage and smiled, decayed yellow teeth seemed to burst from his mouth. His lips were circled by an untrimmed goatee that made Harrison's own face itch when he looked at it.

Harrison gripped the vinyl handle of the baby carriage, trying to appear casual. Just keep breathing, he thought to himself. This is just like being in court.

"Cute little boy you got there, Mr. Harrison. Never seen a finer lookin' little kid. Wouldn't you agree with me, Mr. Corillian?"

The shorter man said nothing. He was massive and squat, like a sumo wrestler sizing up an opponent. Thick arms, thick neck — even his eyelids were thick slabs of flesh almost squeezing shut his eyes in a menacing squint. Tight ridges of chocolate skin rippled down the back of his scalp and into a blue turtleneck as he looked first to his right, and then left in smooth, fluid movements, checking out the surroundings.

"Yes," the taller man concluded, as he clapped moist hands together for emphasis. "This is one snapper of a lad."

Watching out of the corners of both eyes, Harrison quietly said, "Yes, I know."

"That is a boy in there, ain't it?" the tall man continued. "Kinda hard to tell when they're that little, you know? Boys, girls, they're more or less the same at that age, don'tcha think?"

Harrison suddenly felt crowded as he gripped the carriage handle tighter. "Who the hell are you guys? What do you want?"

"Ooooh, hey! Calm down, Sport. Don't get all stimulated. By all means, introductions are most certainly in order. This, as you now know, is Mr. Corillian. He's not very sociable, so I wouldn't expect him to hold out his hand and shake."

The taller man thrust out his own blistered hand to compensate, his naked wrist and forearm jutting out from inside the leather sleeve. "Call me 'Fish-Hook.' Pleased to meetcha, Mr. Harrison."

As if to punctuate his introduction, he produced a long, rusty fish-hook from inside his sleeve after Harrison refused the handshake, and began teasing at lacerations in his palm with it.

Harrison swallowed. This definitely was not developing well.

"What did I tell you, Mr. Corillian, we would find our Sport out here playing games. What sort of games do you like to play, Mr. Harrison? I'll bet Hide-and-Seek is one of your favorite games."

Harrison's legs felt like bee hives. He looked over hopefully at Lex, still wagging his tail and waiting for someone to throw the Frisbee. No help there.

Harrison swallowed his initial panic and continued to pace his breathing, gaining control. He could take charge of this situation, with the right approach. He had done it a thousand times before, with a reluctant witness on the stand, or a suspicious client unsure of legal procedure. It was just a matter of setting the tone, controlling the conversation, directing the course of negotiations, and maintaining superiority over these opponents.

"I take it," Harrison opened, "that you two are here representing the interests of Mr. Shaw."

"You take it very well," said Fish-Hook, who then savagely punched Harrison in the stomach.

Harrison's grip on the carriage handle withered as he folded over and sucked wind. Lex whined in confusion and dropped the Frisbee, but he kept wagging his tail, ready to resume play.

"I don't have the sixteen thousand," Harrison managed after a moment with his hands on his knees. "Look, I expect to get at least ten times that much in my divorce settlement. It's just that the papers haven't come through yet."

Fish-Hook arched one eyebrow and glanced down at Mr. Corillian, who shook his head.

"This is very bad, Mr. Harrison," Fish-Hook said, "but such is not our concern. You will have to talk to our employer."

"But I can't —"

Harrison stopped as he noticed for the first time another figure walking up the park path. The man was huge.

Where Mr. Corillian was thick and massive, this man was all fat. His face was pink and completely hairless, with splashes of red stinging his cheeks. His gray eyes were intelligent and playful, and his blubbery smile was impish. A hearing aid was virtually lost in the expansive folds of one ear, and his face ended in an abundance of chins overlapping like snow drifts into his buttoned overcoat. He waddled as he walked, with his right hand poised out in front of him, as if he were carrying a phantom cane.

When the fat man spoke, his voice was gruff, but friendly. "Mr. Harrison. We had an agreement. I am somewhat disappointed."

"Look, I thought I would have the sixteen thousand this morning, but I know I will have it for sure by Friday. You just have to give me a little more time."

"Ahhh, Mr. Harrison, it appears you fail to grasp an essential truth here. By Friday, the amount you owe will no longer be $16,000. It will be $128,000. Compound interest, my friend. Compound interest." At this he began to chuckle, a throaty, rumbling laugh that rocked his whole body. "Someone once asked Albert Einstein what he believed to be the most powerful force in the universe, and do you know what he responded? 'Compound interest.' In your case, my friend, it may also prove to be the most destructive."

The fat man then bent down toward Lex and picked up the Frisbee. Lex sprang up in anticipation.

"A beautiful animal you have here, Sir. I have always loved a good sporting dog. You love sports, do you not, Mr. Harrison?"

The fat man then swung his arm forward to throw, but the Frisbee merely fluttered to the ground as soon as it left his hand. Lex scooped it up anyway, and brought it back.

"I propose a solution to our dilemma," the fat man said, with a twinkle in his eye. "I am prepared to forgive your debt and wager you $100,000." From within his broad overcoat, the fat man withdrew five thick stacks of cash, tightly banded, with hundred dollar bills visible under the rubber bands. He tossed all five stacks into the baby carriage.

At the sight of the money, Harrison tasted warm silver in his mouth. "What's the bet?"

The fat man chuckled, as he picked up the Frisbee again. "Oh, that is very good, Mr. Harrison. I see you are interested. Very good, indeed. I have been watching you throw this device to your beautiful animal. How graceful he is. He is in his element here, is he not? This is what they were bred to do, and I see you have treated him well."

The fat man looked Harrison directly in the eyes, his pupils like pinpricks. "I am prepared to wager $100,000 on whether this beautiful dog can catch this saucer eight times in a row."

Harrison flinched only slightly, assuring himself that he heard the fat man correctly. "He could catch that thing a hundred times in a row!"

"Very well, then! Let's make it a hundred —"

"No! . . . no," interrupted Harrison. "Eight is good. I'm sure he can manage eight."

"Very good, Sir. Eight times in a row, throwing from this walkway. Let's say the throws have to go as far as that trash can. That's approximately fifty yards. Does that seem fair to you?"

Harrison chewed on his thumbnail and considered it. The further the better, actually.

"All he has to do is catch it, right?"

"That is correct. Eight times in a row, without letting the saucer touch the ground. You win two thousand dollars per catch, and you can stop at any time."

"And if he drops it?"

"Well, then," the fat man began, and he reached into the baby carriage and softly stroked Adam's tiny exposed hand. "How exactly did Rumpelstiltskin phrase it? 'Living things are more important to me than all the treasures in the world.'"

Harrison's stomach lurched — it felt worse than the punch Fish-Hook had given him. He grabbed the carriage handle and wrenched it away from the fat man. "You're crazy!"

"Perhaps, for as you say, your lovely animal could catch many more throws than that on which I am prepared to wager."

"Pick something else! I'm not betting on my son's life!"

"Now, Mr. Harrison, you are committed to nothing. If at any point during the wager you wish to quit, you simply pocket your cash and walk away. At which point my associates will take it from you and remove one of your eyes as collateral for the balance owed. I do not believe you will enjoy their method."

Harrison's mouth went dry.

"Hang on a second," rasped Harrison. He looked again at the trash can. "Say I accepted your wager. What's to keep me from just running away with Adam if I lose? There are houses all around here. If I scream loud enough that my son is being kidnapped, someone should come out."

The fat man smiled, a cold eel grin that showed no teeth. "That is true, Mr. Harrison, you could. We do not have to claim such a fine prize tonight. We have many means at our disposal. For example, please gaze at what Mr. Corillian is holding."

Harrison had not even seen the silent hulk move. In a hand as broad as a tablet, Mr. Corillian held a laminated security card from the Little Treasures Day Care Center, with Adam's picture on it, the I.D. needed to enter the Center's front door.

My God, thought Harrison. They only give those cards to parents!

"How the hell did you get —"

Mr. Corillian snapped his hand shut and tucked the card into his coat pocket.

"So you see, Mr. Harrison," chortled the fat man, "we have our means. This is only one potential avenue of collection. We are very resourceful, would you not agree?"

Harrison looked over at Lex, still wagging his tail, still full of energy. They had been playing only five minutes, and Lex looked like he could go another fifteen. The trash can wasn't that far. Lex had done this a million times.

"You will find that I am a fair man, Mr. Harrison. You win, you walk away a rich man. You lose, you will pay the price, believe me."

Harrison looked at Adam bundled in his carriage, but Adam's attention was focused on the money. The stacks of money looked like heavy green bricks. Harrison took the one Adam was playing with and riffled the corners of the bills — they were all hundreds. The numbers danced in awkward animation as he thumbed through the stack, and then thumbed through it again. He lifted the stack and smelled it. He pressed it against his cheek. It felt scratchy and cool.

"I think we have a player, boys," whispered the fat man. "Please give him room."

Eight times. Harrison picked up the Frisbee and hefted it. Eight times. The Frisbee weighed 140 grams. It felt like a 14-pound brick. Eight times. Only eight. Eight is nothing. He pantomimed some throws with it, practicing his wrist flick. Eight. He looked at Lex, and Lex was eager. He was very eager. He was ready.

Eight times.

The wind swirled around Harrison, and it felt vigorous.

Eight times.

Eight.

Eight-eight-eight-eight-eight.

"Are you ready, Mr. Harrison?"

"I don't see that I have much choice, do I?"

"You always have a choice, Mr. Harrison. That's what makes life exciting, would you not agree?"

Harrison turned his back on the fat man and shook the Frisbee overhead again to re-ignite Lex, but it was hardly necessary. The dog had been standing at attention and staring at the Frisbee in Harrison's hand with a single-minded focus, waiting for him to renew the game.

Harrison threw it, and the dog left tufts of grass flying behind him as he bounded after it. The Frisbee sailed well past the trash can, and for a second Harrison thought he may have thrown it too far. It seemed to hang in the air for a long time, until Lex arched up gracefully like a swordfish from the sea, bringing the Frisbee back down with a satisfying *crunch*.

Suddenly it felt to Harrison like eight was an eternity away.

"That's one, Mr. Harrison," said the fat man, who chuckled his throaty rumble again, shaking his entire body.

Without hesitating, without giving himself a chance to back out, Harrison took the Frisbee from Lex and threw it again. As soon as he released it, the wind gusted and blew the Frisbee so high that it careened in a vertical plunge toward the playground. The Frisbee fell like an arrow, gaining speed. For a moment Harrison forgot about the dog. The Frisbee was now a knife, plummeting toward Adam's tiny heart.

Lex caught it again, smoothly, with fluid grace. He returned quietly with the Frisbee, and placed it in Harrison's hand.

"That's two. Excellent, Mr. Harrison. Would you like to up the wager?"

"No! I've got nothing left to bet. And stop that counting, would you? This is hard enough as it is."

Amazingly, this brought no rebuke from the fat man or his assistants, and Harrison felt his confidence return. He cocked back to throw the Frisbee again, this time waiting for the wind to die down a little before releasing. As Harrison swung the Frisbee forward, Adam called out, "Dog-gee! Daddy — Daddy — Dog-geeeee!"

The Frisbee wobbled as soon as Harrison released it. Lex had already run out past it, unaware that Harrison had botched the throw. The Frisbee headed straight toward the trash can, barely three feet in the air, and Lex wasn't going to see it.

"Lex! Oh, Jesus! LEX!"

Instantly, the dog slammed on the brakes, turned his head back, and miraculously reversed his momentum to charge toward the trash can. The Frisbee barely cleared the top of it, and Lex caught it low, with his chin brushing the grass.

"That's three."

"I quit, you son of a bitch. Give me my six thousand now and I'll take my chances. I've got until the end of the day to get the rest anyway, don't I?"

The fat man looked over at his two assistants and smiled. Fish-Hook and Mr. Corillian walked forward, their hands in their coat pockets. The fat man turned his attention back to Harrison.

"You do have a point, Mr. Harrison, but I am disappointed in you. I thought you had more steel in you. But as I told you, I am a fair man. I will even give you a five-minute head start before my associates begin looking for you again, for I do not believe you will accumulate the rest of the money so quickly."

"Just give me the money."

"Ah, yes. The money."

The fat man reached into the carriage and withdrew one of the stacks of cash. He tossed it to Harrison.

"Please be so kind as to count out sixty of those bills for me. I would hate for my count to be off."

Harrison bobbled the stack like a hot potato, managing to un-loop the rubber band. The crisp bills poured into his hands like a newly-opened deck of cards, cascading over his fingers. He counted out ten bills, then twenty, and lost count. The stack was so thick he could barely enclose it with one hand. Again he counted out ten, then twenty, and then he put those in his mouth. As he breathed through his nose, he inhaled the splendid perfume of green wagered and won. He counted out ten more bills, but the stack in his hand seemed boundless, like it would keep coming, as if it multiplied in his hands the more he handled it.

As he counted the fourth thousand the money seemed almost to talk to him. *I could be all yours,* it said, *so much of me you could take a bath in hundred dollar bills tonight. You'll be a winner tonight. On top. I know you will. You'll win, and you'll beat everyone. You're almost there.*

Harrison clenched the cool bills in his hand and knelt down to talk to his son.

"Adam, listen to me. I'm not going to lose. I can't. Lex never misses. You've seen him. We're going to win, Adam, just watch

Daddy. In just five minutes we will be rich, I guarantee it. I feel it. I know it. This is the big payoff, Son, the one we've been waiting for."

Feeling confident and justified, Harrison threw the bills back into the carriage, picked up the Frisbee, and threw. It climbed and lifted with another gust of wind, and the dog hustled after it. Lex jumped, and Harrison's stomach lurched as he heard the crocodile *click!* of hard teeth snapping on empty air.

No!

Lex had only bounced the Frisbee further in the air, to his left. He stayed with it, and after cutting at a right angle, he caught the Frisbee and kept it from hitting the ground.

"Spectacular, Mr. Harrison! Your animal is simply amazing." After a pause, the fat man added with a sly grin, "That's four."

When Lex returned, it was with shaky hands that Harrison took the Frisbee from him. The fifth throw sailed straight and solid, unaffected by the wind, and Lex caught it easily. The sixth angled a bit, but Lex understood the idiosyncrasies of the Frisbee, and recognized the physical forces affecting it. He compensated marvelously. The fat man continued to count out loud.

Harrison noticed the dog's tongue lolling from the side of his mouth, sticking out from under the Frisbee. "Lex, lie down," he said. The dog immediately dropped to the ground, apparently grateful for the break. It was getting colder, however, and Harrison was anxious to have all of this finished. Only two more catches. Two more catches and they were home free.

Fish-Hook walked over to Lex and knelt.

"Get away from him," Harrison snarled. "I only need two more catches."

"Take it easy, Sport. I just might help you out and buy this mutt off'a you when you lose. He would look good on film, yes, I believe he would. Quite a virile specimen. I just happen to operate a side venture in the video industry." Fish-Hook turned to Harrison and flashed a rotted grin. "Special orders, you might say."

Good God, thought Harrison, as his hands turned to ice.

"Besides," Fish-Hook continued, as he left the dog and touched Adam's carriage, "I have some exciting plans for my new star here. Believe me, such young talent is in demand, and *extremely* difficult to obtain these days."

Blood sank from Harrison's face as he turned toward the fat man and croaked, "You can't be serious."

"My associate is quite serious, Mr. Harrison. He has become quite the enterprising producer."

Fish-Hook knelt down and peered in at Adam, flicking his chalky tongue rapidly in and out at the boy. He then looked back at Harrison and shrugged. "Boys, girls, they're more or less the same at that age, don'tcha think?"

Revulsion erupted inside Harrison as he lunged at Fish-Hook. "You bastard, you get away from —"

Again, Harrison never saw the thick man move a muscle. Before Harrison could reach his son, Mr. Corillian's right arm was around Harrison's neck. His left hand held a black device inches from Harrison's face. It looked like an electric razor, but with two points protruding like silver mandibles from the face. Once Harrison stopped struggling, the strong hand gently squeezed the device, and a blue arc of electricity sizzled between the two probes.

"What was that you were saying, Mr. Harrison?" asked Fish-Hook, as he bounced on his toes. "I wouldn't try that again, if I was you. Two hundred thousand volts would turn you to jelly for at least an hour. In fact, I think we should zap you right now, and just take the kid."

"No, no," interrupted the fat man. "I made a wager with the man. So far he has performed admirably." Mr. Corillian released Harrison and resumed a quiet stance. "You do intend to finish, do you not, Mr. Harrison?"

"Just two more throws and you guys will leave me, and my son, alone?"

"Of course, Mr. Harrison. I am a man of my word."

"And I get to walk away from here with the cash. No strings attached."

"No strings attached. Absolutely."

"You guys won't come after me as soon as I turn around?"

"Mr. Harrison, you watch too much television. Do you plan to continue?"

Lex was standing already, refreshed from his rest, and Harrison picked up the Frisbee. This time, it felt weightless, and Harrison gripped it tight until the chewed plastic edge bit into the sides of his fingers. Two more times, he thought to himself. Take it easy, just two more. Please, Lex, don't screw this up.

He felt numb as he threw the Frisbee, and once again it fell short and looked like it might not even reach the trash can. Like a bowler trying to will the ball to move left with body language to pick up that spare, Harrison swung both arms low and thrust them upwards, trying to create an updraft that might lift the Frisbee. Magically, a burst of wind did appear, pitching the Frisbee up high as if it were a small boat struggling to stay afloat in a storm. Lex watched it, waited for it to drop, and then stabbed out and caught the Frisbee before it hit the ground. Harrison cheered and dropped to his knees, his fists still up in the air, his mouth opened wide as he screamed with the surge of victory. When Lex returned, Harrison vigorously ruffled his fur and scratched at his neck in hearty celebration.

"That's seven, Mr. Harrison."

Yes, thought Harrison, that's seven and there's only one more to go and then it's payday.

"Come on, boy," he urged, "you can do this. Just one more, champ. Let's go, boy, let's do it. Let's win."

Harrison looked over at the fat man before the final throw, to see if he showed any sign of concern. To see if he was sweating as the final card was being dealt. If they had intended to cheat him all along, thought Harrison, they would probably look unconcerned, even bored.

The fat man's eyes were fixed on the Frisbee in Harrison's hands. Those eyes revealed intense interest. At least this appears to matter to him.

The fat man's two assistants also stared at the Frisbee in Harrison's hand.

So did Lex.

Harrison looked over at the baby carriage, and at the stacks of cold cash piled inside. This could finally be the big score.

It was getting darker, and Harrison looked out over the park and where he needed to throw the Frisbee. Just an easy toss, no need for anything fancy. He scraped the edge of the Frisbee with his fingernail as he wound back. Lex perked up, ready to take off. The Frisbee felt normal, finally. All he had to do was toss it. All he had to do was let go. Throw it like he had a trillion times before.

After what seemed like two days, Harrison finally swung his arm forward, and flicked the Frisbee into the air.

It sailed clear of the trash can, out in the open, with a slight arc to the right. Lex kept up with it easily, his dog tags jangling as he ran under it to position himself for its descent. Finally, he reached up to grab it, and Harrison heard the satisfyingly familiar *crunch.*

Except Lex missed it. The Frisbee looped from his mouth and rolled to the ground.

Harrison froze.

He stared at the Frisbee resting in the grass.

He could not breathe. His lungs had collapsed. His circulatory system immediately flushed as antifreeze surged through his veins. All he could do was turn his head toward his baby boy, toward the three men now hovering over him like crows over carrion.

With pain branching throughout his chest, Harrison saw that somehow he had crept at least twenty feet away from Adam — unconsciously, he had been hedging closer to the trash can with the last two throws. Suddenly he felt as if he were in a free falling elevator, whooshing away from his baby boy. As in every dream he had ever had where he had been chased by mobsters, Harrison's feet felt like cement blocks trudging across hot sand as he struggled to reach his son.

The fat man, however, was not looking at Harrison, nor at Adam. He was looking at nothing, with his left index finger pressed into his hearing aid. Suddenly the fat man lifted the lapel of his jacket and began talking to it.

"Did you get all of that?"

Harrison stopped, numb.

"Good," the fat man continued. "Good . . . Excellent! Oh, this is better than we hoped for. Mr. Harrison, I'm told that your expression just now came out wonderfully on the monitor. Dr. Harrison just informed us she will pay a bonus for a copy of the videotape alone! Oh, this is marvelous!"

Harrison stared, dumbstruck, as the fat man shook with laughter.

All three men then reached into their jackets, and it occurred to Harrison that they might just shoot him right there. Instead of pistols, however, each pulled out a business card, and held it out. Harrison took the one from the fat man and read:

Leonard Y. Piper
Private Investigator
221–2121

"What —"

"Mr. Harrison," the fat man began, "our client, Dr. Lynn Harrison, has been somewhat concerned with . . . oh, how should we put it, your fitness to be the custodial parent of young Master Adam here. With the custody hearing coming up tomorrow, I'm sure you can appreciate her need for a demonstration of your . . . concern toward your son's welfare. Please direct your attention down the lane, toward our car."

Harrison looked to where the fat man pointed, and the rear door of the black Mercedes opened. Out stepped Lynn, wearing a white sweater and tan skirt he had not seen before, and also holding a finger to her left ear.

"I don't believe you."

"Oh, believe me, Mr. Harrison," Leonard Piper continued, "both the video and the audio portion came out extraordinarily well, as I understand both are being reviewed just this moment for clarity. Would you like to hear?"

Piper plucked the earpiece out by the cord with a *pop!* and held it out. Harrison saw a small dab of wax dangling from the rubbery insert.

"Get that thing out of my face! Even if you do have this on tape, none of it is admissible in court. You people deliberately set me up!"

"Ahhh, but it is admissible, and quite desirably so, as you should very well expect, Mr. Harrison, in matters central to the moral fitness of a custodial parent. How do you think the news agencies will react to your acceptance of and participation in our little wager? Or perhaps the bar association?"

Piper withdrew a stack of papers and a pen from inside his jacket.

"We are no longer recording, Mr. Harrison. Please sign this consent decree. It indicates your desire to award permanent custody of Adam to Dr. Harrison, thus obviating the need for the hearing tomorrow. I'm sure you will find that everything is properly addressed within the document."

Harrison grabbed the papers and scanned them. After a long moment, he took the pen. As he signed, he saw Piper replace the earphone and listen. Harrison looked back down the hill toward Lynn. The white sweater accentuated her long dark hair blowing in the wind. She held a small microphone with a cord trailing into the car, and Harrison could see her lips move as she spoke into it.

"What is she saying, as if I really need to know?"

Piper clasped both hands together on his chest and chuckled

again, his gelatinous body jiggling as he tried to find breath to
speak. "Just this, Mr. Harrison," Piper managed between snorts.
"Checkmate."

Harrison let loose with a string of profanities shouted at his wife,
angry spittle flying from his mouth. Piper roared with laughter, but
then interrupted Harrison suddenly with an outstretched hand.
Piper touched his finger to his ear again, listening.

"I've just been instructed to make you a cash settlement offer, Mr.
Harrison. Apparently, Dr. Harrison does not wish for the boy to be
fatherless, nor for you to lose the ability to contribute child support. She has authorized me to present you with enough cash to pay
off whatever stake there is against you. In exchange for the dog."

Piper thumbed through a stack of cash and pulled out a chunk
of bills. "Please count these," he instructed as he tossed the still-
banded remainder to Harrison. "I would hate for my count to be
off."

Two minutes later, Dexter Harrison stood alone in the park, the
wind now colder in the twilight. He quietly cursed as Piper pushed
the blue baby carriage down the park path with one chubby hand
and struggled to hold onto the tugging dog leash with the other.

SCOTT BARTELS

Swear Not by the Moon

FROM *Tamaqua*

I WAS ONLY nine the first time I was on fire. It was during a family
vacation, or as close to one as we ever got seeing as Momma and
Daddy gave up tryin' to travel together since before I can remember. Winter break Momma would take us to Granny's farm in Verde
Pointe (good to wash the sin of the city out from under our nails,
Daddy would say as he helped us pack the car). Summertime, me
and him and David would strike for the beach in Mobile, or as near
a beach as Alabama gulf coast comes. One time I asked him why we
never went nowhere all together (except Carnival every February,
and that just to shout "Repent!" at the revelers) and he just smiled
that crooked smile of his — the one I later suspected he gleaned
from Elvis and practiced in the cracked bathroom mirror all through
high school — and said they always would fuss and fight over sched-
ules and directions and all that shit. Not that Daddy ever said "shit"
in his life. That glib hound-dog grin was as raucous as he ever got.

But that ain't here nor there. It was during a summer trip and
we had the tent up and the lines still in the water and a camp fire
going under a new moon sky. A sky like that always makes me
wonder how the shepherds made up all those constellations; sky
like that has so many stars so close together, what you ought to do is
make pictures out of the black spaces between them. Sayin' shit like
that always got David to raggin' on me. Three years older and four
years dumber and it was easier to bully and humiliate me than be
overshadowed by my imagination. So while I was staring up at the
rivulets of black creases between distant suns teeming with potential, David pushed me ass over teakettle into that camp fire.

I howled and rolled around in the sand long after the flames
from my clothes and hair and eyelashes were out, trying to worm
my way into the soft, gritty earth and save everyone the trouble of a
decent burial. Daddy was in the tent and didn't come out 'til I was
screamin' and writhing. My brother told him I was lookin' up and
musta got dizzy and fallen in. And later, after I got done floppin' in
the moist granules and spent shells; after I ran down to the ocean,
refusing to heed my Daddy's shouts; after I learned just how salt
water feels on a fresh burn; after all that, I said: Yeah, Daddy, that's
just how it happened.

He tried to help me take my mind off the pain, joked about how
I'd been "bathed in fire." "Speak us some tongues, Esau," he egged
me. (And yeah, that really is my given name, so now you know why I
tell everyone to call me Creole, even though I ain't one.) Didn't
take me to no doctor, though. Didn't see no doctor 'til the day we
got home and Momma took one look at my singed face and mostly
scarred skull and that was the only time I ever *saw* my folks have it
out. I remember Momma sayin' something about Daddy bein' stupid to think God would heal *this* one and I remember the slap
("Don't doubt Him and don't *never* doubt *me*") and two hours later
at Sisters of Mercy I remember me and Momma both getting bandages. To this day I still got no eyelashes and the crown of my bald
spot is crinkly like pudding you left in the fridge for two weeks.

I said all that just to say this: the second time I was on fire was two
weeks ago. Chase, this guy I'd been buying from, swore to me he
had some China White. Got it right cheap, he said, and me being a
regular, he'd lay some off to me discount. So I got me a big idea that
if I could buy low and sell high I'd be on the road to redemption.
And deep down, Faith always wanted a stock broker. So I got a big
stash from Chase on credit. Figured to peddle some and pay back
inside a week. Only I sampled a little before I sold the first gram. It
cooked up nice and I had visions of sugarplums dancing in my head
as I loaded up the needle. Dreamin' about showin' up at Faith's
doorstep with about ten grand in my pocket. Dream didn't last long
after the spike though, and this damn sure wasn't China White.

If this were the movies, I'd tell you I knew the smack was bad the
second I pushed the plunger. But that wasn't the case. I watched the
little pink cloud float into the liquid, like crimson fingers reaching

from my veins to grab hold of the fix and draw it inside. I love that moment, when you know the high is coming and nothing that's happened up to that very second has any bearing and everything in front of you is going to be fine as wine, right as rain and all that shit. People who don't get it will ask: who would do that, stick himself in the arm with a needle. But *I* ask *you:* a moment when absolutely your whole prior existence is (as Daddy would say) washed away and all your tomorrows are sunshine and peppermint — man, who *wouldn't* do that? I hear smack use is at an all time high, but I maintain it's still the best kept secret in sanity.

So it was maybe four, five minutes after I sunk the spike before I knew I was in trouble. I was just drifting along but I could hear a buzzing, like a mosquito you can't quite find who keeps whispering: "Here I come; gonna get you; won't feel me 'til I slide out your skin and skit away, taking a piece of you with me and poisoning you in the bargain." Heard them kind of skeeters plenty of times on Daddy's summertime beach retreats.

Then the buzzing was like the muted roar of a teakettle just coming to boil, only instead of roiling, my blood began to simmer and spit, like fatty meat on a bonfire. I know I tossed my head to and fro a good bit — shaking a condemned madman's no no no this can't happen to *me* — because my neck muscles still hurt. And then the fire was there.

I wish I could describe it as an unfolding flower, the bloom of pestilence reeking revenge or a black blossom tinged red with wrath, yawning in rage. It would be much more poetic than the truth, which is that one moment I was in the void, the next I heard the buzz, and then I had porcupines rampaging through my veins. Porcupines wielding rusty, gas-powered chainsaws. They started from everywhere, spontaneously filling my world, commandeering every nerve ending in my body so that even blinking seemed to slice my eyeballs open with acidic papercuts. You would think a pain like that would have an epicenter, but it was like Daddy talked about God: there was the void, and then the void was filled, and if you blinked you missed it, and if you hadn't blinked you'd missed it anyway, but just because you didn't see it happen didn't mean it hadn't.

It was a hell of a thing to have my subconscious manning the controls while my body was begging for some action — *any* action

— that would end the turmoil. Call 911, slit my wrists — the latter seemed a better option since the relief would come faster. I love my subconscious; I love its view of the world and the way it's able to draw analogies between vastly segregated and seemingly incongruous events; I love its detached realization and the way it fails to marvel at its most striking discoveries, its passive and uncaring genius for observation. But as the captain of the sinking ship that was my body's pyre, it sucked. It convinced me that the smack had intelligence, was contriving to wrest control of my body, poppies become animate. And so in the heat of battle, I shook my stash into the toilet and flushed it away, a $4,500 turd.

Chase showed up four days later (the day after Fat Tuesday, or what we in the Quarter call I-Did-*What*-Wednesday) looking churlish and victorious, like he'd just done the head cheerleader in the back seat of her boyfriend's car. He wanted his money. I told him how I'd spent fourteen hours doing my best Joan of Arc and another twenty-four cramped up like a diver shot from the abyss to the surface by a nuclear cannon. How I could not have sold that smack to anyone and lived. Accused him of cutting it with Drano when the accusations got to flying.

"Yes, that's very interesting," Chase conceded. "But if I thought you were sincerely accusing me of intentionally misrepresenting product, I'd cut your balls off and serve them in your famous paella. Geoffery could make it Macanudo's house special, or sell it as a take-out dish — sack in a sack." And he spat on my floor. On the carpet.

"Hey, Chase, that's great." I was surprised by something I hadn't felt in a very long time, I think since that camping trip when I survived my post-torching weekend on nothing but raw determination. After that, I figured I was pretty damn close to invincible. But I recognized the feeling right off anyway: I was scared. A man who will spit on your DuPont Plush-Lite is liable to do anything. "Only I lost my job when I was too racked to even pick up the phone to call in sick for two days." You no-show at a restaurant in New Orleans during Carnival, you pretty much forget about asking for your back pay, much less your job.

"Damn, Creole, that's a fucking pity. I will so miss that blackened mustard chicken." He tisked at me the way the bad guy always mocks James Bond when he's got 007 chained to the wall and the laser aimed at his pecker. Only I didn't have no belt buckle grenade launcher to counter with. "Now what we gonna do, huh?"

He was on me so quickly, the knife blade fat against my throat so fast, that when I recovered enough to compose a thought, it was: Damn, let me see you do that again in slo-mo. I never saw the knife come out, or actually felt the blade under the plump of my adam's apple. Too much adrenaline to feel anything but the air pumping in and out of my lungs. But I heard the telltale click of a butterfly being flicked open and the finger holes secured. There is no more menacing sound, not even a gun being cocked or a round sent home in the chamber. Any pussy can point a pistol at you and play chicken. But a man who'll put a blade to your throat so tight that a hard pulse in your vein will slice you open for him, that's a man who means business. That's a man who's ready to get dirty.

"Let me lay it out for you, Creole," he whispered. It was an intimate sound, the tone of voice I'd use only with a woman I'd already seduced, the sound of a man rounding third and heading for home knowing full well the center fielder has booted the ball to the wall. "I owe Lazarus for that stash, you owe me for that stash. I don't pay Lazarus back tonight — To-Fucking-Night — and you'll be finding pieces of my teeth and fingernails in your *andouille*. Well, I'm not about to be sausage fodder, so you better stop fucking around and tell me you laid the shit off at the restaurant, or at Carnival or at your fucking grandmother's nursing home." His hands were shaking so wildly I could hear the cold steel clatter of the butterfly handle as it rattled between his fingers.

I kept waiting for my life to flash before my eyes, but all I got were non-sequential glimpses, like someone had tossed a couple photo albums into the air and I was watching them randomly float down. I saw Faith, and Emily our daughter, but not as we were bringing her home, or the way her little fingers encircled mine the first time I held her, or the way Faith's soft lullaby voice used to greet me when I stumbled home at the two A.M. feeding, smelling like hickory with crawfish guts still under my nails and the raucous combination of reds and smack coursing through my brain. No, instead I saw them leaving me for Faith's mother in Baltimore. I saw myself in the kitchen at Macanudo, but not stuffing bell peppers with trout and jambalaya, or being called out to visit so many tables the first night

I introduced my black seared catfish in a pecan crust. Instead, I saw myself being initiated in uppers and rush and crystal-meth — anything to keep the energy flowing — by Geoffery, head chef to my sous-chef, Eve to my Adam. And I saw my brother, who pushed me into the fire and without a word convinced me to blame my own clumsy stupidity. My mother, who would later die at the hands of my father. My father, who would later die at the hands of his fellow inmates, held down and beaten to death in the shower with bars of soap cradled in towels, slings like the one David used to slay Goliath. These pictures floated by me in only a second. Failures all, except for my mother, who had dedicated her life to seeing after her children until they were big enough to see after themselves, and who had made it — though only just. And it was most likely her memory that saved my life. Her, and the way she'd stayed my father when he was in a temper.

"Chase," I said, but I had to say it twice because the first time my voice was gravel dry and choked with the fear that if I strained my vocal cords too hard I'd slice my own throat. "Chase, I can't pay you what I don't have. That stash was shit. Damn near wiped me, swear to God, and I flushed it. Let me find work, the Columbia or even Antoine's if I have to stoop to that, but I'll pay it off. I'll even explain it to Lazarus if you want. But Christ, Chase, you kill me and you'll never get your money." An appeal to logic that would have done Momma proud. She'd talked Daddy down from many a rage with that kind of thinking.

And praise the Lord and pass the pipe and all that shit if Chase didn't back off with the blade. He shook his head and laughed the way Eva Braun must have after completing her vows, knowing how futile the whole arrangement was. "Shit, Creole. You've fucked me and didn't even give me the reach around." He got up off the floor and paced a bit, and after a minute, when he hadn't spat again, I collected myself and tried to do the same. I stumbled a bit moving from horizontal to vertical, and suddenly was aware how badly I was jonesing. I hadn't fixed since my smack inferno and was so badly in need that I briefly considered asking Chase to raise my credit limit.

"Look, Creole, you're a good customer, and I can't get blood from a stone. I'll talk to Lazarus. We'll work something out. You'll pay me back and you'll cater me a party or something and we'll call it square. Eh?"

He offered his hand and I took it, two whores bequesting their words of honor. He pumped firmly and locked my eyes with his as he added: "And one more thing."

In my relief I'd felt like the kingfish who dives deep enough to outrun the line on the reel, so relieved that I'd lost track of the knife. Our eyes stayed locked as I felt the blade glide through the oft-burned skin and gristly sinew of my little finger. My mouth widened in a shocked O as I heard the blade crack into bone and wind its way around the knuckle, like a seasoned butcher's knife carving tender baby back ribs away from tougher, more muscular meat. His free hand dropped the bloody blade and held up my own pinky finger for my examination, his other hand still pumping my remaining four fingers in some perverse gentlemen's agreement.

"I'll give this to Lazarus, a token of your sincere intentions, eh? Come see me tomorrow at the Quad. Don't disappoint." He stuffed my finger in his shirt pocket and left me a man bleeding from so many different wounds that, had I a needle to do up with, the spike would have simply deflated me, releasing only air from my veins.

There was one other snapshot I saw floating non-sequentially from the heavens while waiting for Chase to make me Isaac to his Abraham. I wasn't going to tell you about it, but what the hell; ain't no way out but through and all that shit. It was the fight I had with Faith the night she was packing to leave. I told her that if this is what it came down to, I would quit. Cold turkey, no rehab required, the thought of her taking my little daughter away was all the therapy I needed thank you very much.

"No, Creole, you won't, not if we stay. That's just it."

"Bullshit," I tried to rage, but by then the only wind in my sails was fueled by reds and opium and three hours sleep. It was hard to sound convincing, even to myself. "You're all that matters to me."

She stopped packing long enough to cradle my face in her hands just so. It was a melancholy, sympathetic gesture full of the sorrow of what could have been. Should have been. "If I threaten to leave, you'll quit for a day, maybe even a week. But then when I'm still here, it will be too easy to go back to it. You keep thinking you aren't hooked because if someone put a gun to your head and said 'quit' you *could*. But that's never going to happen. Life is the *little* decisions that you make, the choices that keep you from becoming so divided against yourself that someone *has* to put a gun to your head. So choose for yourself, not for Emily, not for me. Choose for yourself the same way you'd pick out breakfast cereal. And maybe we can work from there."

She was right only to the extent that there was a weapon involved, though it was a knife and not a gun. The rest of the scenario she had dead wrong, including, sadly, the path I'd choose.

The Quad was the Student Union courtyard at Loyola where I'd first met Chase and the sympathetic poison he pedaled. By then I'd been designing specials at Macanudo for two months, doing the sous-chef's job while the sous-chef was doing Geoffery's wife, burning seventy, sometimes eighty hours a week and serving hickory grilled shrimp Chippewa over jambalaya cakes with crowder peas and artichoke Monte Cristo while everyone else was just doubling up the saffron in their crab bisque and gouging tourists like stuck pigs. Geoffery was so fired up over the reviews he was getting, he kept springing for meth and tear drops and anything that would keep me going. And me with a new baby in the house on St. Philip Street needing a new roof or a new slab every six months, I was willing to sell my soul for way less than thirty pieces of silver.

One of the busboys at the restaurant knew what hopped-up shape I was in and said he knew a guy who had something that was good for what ailed me. Despite spending ninety percent of my waking hours inside Geoffery's kitchen, I was still enough in touch with the outside world to know that taking a second pill to cancel the first was stupider than forgoing the first one altogether. But by then Geoffery had busted his wife and the sous-chef job was wide open and Emily was graduating from four ounces six times a day to eight ounces sixty times a day. Most men believe that chefs are pussies, complimenting each other's fairy hats and tasting one another's sauce, if you know what I mean. But the restaurant business — especially the New Orleans Jackson Square restaurant business — is cut-throat. You put that many cut-throat guys in that small a space around that many knives and that much fire, it gets easy to understand why stimulants are a major food group.

I wish I could believe that my habit was Geoffery's fault, or Chase's, or even Faith's. God knows I told all three that plenty of times. Even more — for whatever this says about me — I wish *you* would believe it. But I would have found my way there somehow, like it was written in my genes, always coursing through the very veins it would later pollute. I came to drink early — I can remember sharing a flagon of filched communion wine with my brother, hiding behind the Cornstalk Fence on Royal and goofing on the tourists; I think I was eleven — and I smoked my share of grass in high school. Probably smoked several people's shares. About the time Daddy's inmates were revoking his sentence I got into psychedelics and became real acquainted with the subconscious that would betray me so miserably just a few days ago. Met Faith at a Michael Doucet and Beausoleil show at Tulane where we shared a sugar cube communion. I guess you can follow the line of progression from there.

But many times in the past few months, ever since Faith lost hope and took Emily with her, I've wondered why I was unable to right the ship when I knew I was navigating not by the stars but by the black spaces in between. My wife, never shy to be third on a quaalude, gave it all up. Geoffery pumped me full of speed but never touched the stuff. Even Chase claimed never to sample his wares. My only answer is: sometimes a man quits trusting his strengths and starts trusting his weaknesses. His weaknesses are more apt to be dependable.

I met Chase at the Quad the next day, a heavy rouge gauze wrapped around my right hand. My filleting hand, it occurred to me. I was in a bad way. Weak from blood loss, jonesing to kill all after almost five days (holy shit, five goddamn days and it was getting worse? Who *ever* beats this shit?) without doing up. Fuck sleepless in Seattle, I was Neurotic Needing Narcotic in New Orleans.

We went for a coffee in this beatnik coffee shop where my hand was the only thing not dressed in black. I tried to feel Chase out by saying: "Hope you're buying. As you know I'm in poor shape financially." Which was true to the extent that I had no money (I told Faith to clean out the checking account when she left; never knew so much money could assuage so little guilt; rationalizations are the most expensive commodity on earth) and no income. I did, however, still have my house. A street-level pastel stucco right on St. Philip Street, between Bourbon and Royal. Great sub-tropical hanging garden on the front porch and a friendly courtyard in the back.

Paid in full, courtesy of the Great State of Louisiana, which would rather settle a wrongful death case than have the security procedures of its penal institutions scrutinized by the courts and the media. Half a mil for me, half for the ambulance chaser, instant French Quarter. God bless Mommy and God bless Daddy.

Over his double espresso, Chase told me: "Your debt has been cleared." He kept glancing around and smoking so fast that he'd light a new cigarette before the last one was half gone, even though it was obvious the clientele were all deep into their Kerouac and having narcissistic, homoerotic fantasies about Neal Cassidy. I waited as he sipped, knowing — as a man who trusts his weaknesses must know — that I had merely exchanged one debt for another. "Lazarus was not happy, not at first. This is a pretty liquid business, you know? IOU's don't buy shit from the Haitians, and little fingers are funny but they don't pay bills. Yours went in his garbage disposal by the way." He puffed heavily and glanced about, letting me take that in. I tried not to react, but I was five days sober and easy to read.

"There's a ship in Biloxi," he continued. "*Finnegan,* ever heard of it?" I shook my head and felt the drawn skin of my cheeks tight against my face. "Gambling boat, big business. Lazarus tried to buy a big stake in it and got cut out, guy by the name of Gabriel Arentino, ever heard of him?" I shook my head again and looked at my chicory mug. "Well, that deal's not closed. If Gabriel Arentino were to suddenly rescind his offer, Lazarus would be the high man. Lazarus badly wants to be the high man. For forgiving your debt, Lazarus wants you to convince Gabriel Arentino to have a change of heart."

"Change of heart how?" I croaked dryly, not sure how a cook with a high school diploma was supposed to argue asset allocation with an apparently large-living financier, afraid maybe I knew the answer.

"Change of heart, you know." His eyes worked the room again while he blew as much smoke as he could, as though the clouds of tobacco would render him inaudible. "Like change from beating to still."

"Jesus, Chase," I moaned. "I'm bad off. I'm battered and I need a fix. I can't do that shit, I can't even believe I've come to the point that someone would ask me. I'll just sell my house and pay you off. Gimmee a couple weeks." And to be honest, I felt good. I'd heard former rummies talk about hitting rock bottom, how only then did they truly *want* to stop. And I thought maybe I'd actually gone *deeper* than rock bottom, that I was at mantle bottom and would have to ascend to get to rock bottom. But I was wrong; I was still in free fall.

"It's much too late for that, my friend," Chase grinned, and I saw something I'd never seen before. He claimed not to use what he sold, and that was obviously true of smack. But his yellow toothed, fangy, triumphant expression was the overconfident ecstasy of a speed freak. In a flash of recognition I saw how he'd overplayed my role in his debt to Lazarus, how I owed not only my soul but Chase's as well to a small time gangster with delusions of grandeur.

Chase said: "Lazarus knows about Faith. About Faith and about Emily. About Baltimore." And my subconscious created a new picture to float past me, even though by this time the process had become like something out of *Clockwork Orange*. I saw a monster I'd never met grinding my baby in his garbage disposal, and laughing as his champagne kitchen counter top and his peach and bone checkerboard linoleum were bathed in her blood.

I walked all the away home from the Quad, heading up Royal to the Quarter so I'd pass the LaBranche House. I stood on the corner and tried to take in the enormity of the front gate, which twisted halfway down St. Peter into the late February dusk. I wondered about the people who'd built it originally, New Orleans patriarchy and all that shit. A family home that had been passed from father to son for almost two centuries. How could that be when I couldn't even hold my family together for three years? How could Henri LaBranche run a plantation and an export business and raise a family close enough to erect two cathedrals and preserve their name through a war with England, a war with Lincoln, and all the wars any family fights against itself? What a fucked-up proposition a family is. How can one man be a father, a husband, a worker, a creator? It isn't possible to fill all the roles everyone expects of you without losing yourself in the process. You keep giving away pieces of yourself until all you have left are the parts no one wants, not even you.

I spat on the sidewalk in front of the grand mansion — not as cool as spitting on the carpet, but as close as I was likely to get — and moved up Royal toward home. I had never imagined it possible to feel as hopeless as I felt and keep going on anyway. Who is weaker, the man who gives up in the face of defeat or the man who marches into that defeat hoping to lose anyway, just to get it all over with? Chase had convinced me that my estranged family would truly be in danger if I didn't kill Gabriel Arentino. Having them killed wouldn't get him his gambling ship, but at least the word would get around: Don't cross Lazarus! Damn Chase for lying about my debt. Lazarus no doubt thought I'd brought down a small savings and loan fronting for horse I couldn't afford. Nevertheless, having accepted the bargain, I'd talked Chase into giving me two syringes worth. And then I promised to pay him back for them.

With the sun down, I packed a gym bag with what I thought I'd need to kill a guy. I was a little bit proud of myself for holding out against the heroin. Two needles under my roof and I hadn't used either. I got everything ready first, knowing that despite how badly my brain was squirming without the drug, I'd be much more useless once I'd scratched the itch.

When I had it all together, I went into the bathroom to do up. It was an old habit from the days when Faith knew but didn't want to know and I sure didn't want my daughter to see. Guilt is the great inhibitor, they ought to use it instead of those silly government warning signs. We could all smoke "Your Kids Are Watching" menthols and drink "Little Timmy Junior Sees This" lite. And speaking of light, the one in the bathroom just couldn't make the grade, not as jittery as I was and as drawn in as my veins were. It was as though they knew they were on the verge of a victory; another week in hiding and they would never be invaded by the liquid devil again. So I tied up in the bathroom and then walked to the breakfast nook where I fixed under the ten-bulb chandelier, best spot in the house.

Finished studying the map of veins in my arm, I commenced to studying the map Chase had given me. We'd done the whole exchange right there in the Quad coffee shop, Chase passing his wares to me inside a hollow book. It was his way of out irony-ing the ironic students whose seriousness made their self-righteousness an annoyingly convenient foil. Just another dude in black sharing some Sartre or Kant.

While I was high, my subconscious conjured an alternate future in which I got aboard the *Finnegan* and gambled the house so broke that Gabriel Arentino couldn't pay me. In a supremely satirical moment, I cashed in the favor that I owed Lazarus via Chase and forced Gabriel Arentino to kill himself.

Chase made mention of a firearm he possessed — untraceable, he claimed — but I declined. Daddy's Colt was secure in my top nightstand drawer. There ain't many places you can pay a third of a mil for a one-story flat and still need a pistol by your head to sleep soundly, but the Quarter is one of them. I remember how Daddy loved to hunt, how he took me to the woods near DeSoto National Forest when I was eight to track deer (this would have been a year before David did his John the Baptist on me). I remember how we made camp and roasted weenies over a fire belching with knotted pine and Daddy taught me how to count points on a buck. And I remember how, so early the next morning it may as well have still been last night, an eight pointer crossed our path while we were calling turkeys.

"There he is, Esau," Daddy mouthed to me, his breath sweet with venison jerky. He smiled that crooked hound-dog grin and motioned with his rifle. The buck was looking the other way, but I believe I could have stared at his innocent, pure-souled face and popped the trigger anyway, Bambi eyes or no. All I saw was Daddy smoking a pipe in the den and pointing to the antlers on the wall and saying "my youngest brought that one down, summer seventy-eight." My volley was high, probably wide too but I took no notice. My first thought was that the gun had misfired and the round had exploded in the chamber. I dropped the rifle in shock at the sting of my hands while the echo of the shot — BLAM — bounced inside my brain from lobe to lobe.

"Dern," said Daddy soon as he realized I'd dropped my weapon. He took a bead on the deer but by then it had discerned its circumstances and begun to bolt for cover. David, who had set up a 45-degree triangle of crossfire (something he'd learned as a child watching coverage of Vietnam without realizing it, he of the unexplored, deaf-mute subconscious), damn near felled the animal, but it spun on a dime, hind quarters twisting grotesquely before it camouflaged itself.

"David!" Daddy screamed. "You ever risk ruining a rump like that again, I'll heat you up good!" He had nary a word for my high shot, and to this day I don't know what to make of it. Did he think I could not take a licking like my brother? Did he think the poor shot simply bad luck? If David had failed to follow up an easy mark like that, there would have been hell to pay. Sometimes, at night when my brain won't slow to my body's fatigue level, when six espressos and three double shifts converge, I ask my Daddy why he was so light on me that day, so easy on David after he lit me afire. Sometimes I suppose he wanted us to grow up confident, be secure that our actions would meet with approval. But then I have to chastise myself for presupposing such courageous intentions upon the man who killed my own Momma.

I said all that just to say this: I didn't take Chase's gun for the same reason I didn't take my rifle — too goddamn noisy. Daddy's Colt had a silencer, the one he'd bought after that trip; bought it so I'd practice my shooting and not shit my drawers in the process.

Oil cans, stop signs, empty beer bottles, it made no difference. Sundown meant Daddy would walk the mile and a quarter home and I'd be expected to obliterate some still life. Once Daddy figured out it was the noise spooking me high and saw what I could do with some focus and a quiet piece, he bought me the silencer and the Colt was effectively mine. Among the many thoughts shaken loose in my brain as I tumbled into that camp fire a year later was: if David could still outshoot me, I'd be making him a smore right now.

I tossed the pistol nonchalantly into the trunk along with my cheap nylon gym bag which held a change of clothes and a loaded syringe. When this was all over, I wanted to be able to medicate A.S.A.FuckingP. Chase's play-by-play told me that Gabriel Arentino would be watching the Mississippi State Bulldogs most of the night as they tanked to the U.K. Wildcats. Chase told me where and when I should be able to find my prey alone, and how I'd be able to slip out without a trace. His generous details helped fuel my suspicion that this was supposed to be his mission. The smack made me calm, and I at least felt confident that although I had obviously been set up, I hadn't been set up to fail. After all, if I got busted, the trail led clearly back to Chase. I felt the code of the woods would let me trust him: don't shit where you eat.

Most people who have never been there think New Orleans is

fairly isolated by the Mississippi, cut off from civilization like Walton mountain before the telegraph. But the truth is that I-10, running west to east, cuts through the heart of the city, providing easily two-thirds of the nation's drug trade. Too many convenient entry points, too few patrols. I was less than ninety minutes from my sacrificial lamb, who was at this very moment most likely pressing with three sevens and a four-hand losing streak taunting him.

I had an hour to burn before I was supposed to light out, but I didn't want to spend it at home. The horse was already starting to wear off, or else my body was so primed by the first sip it had in days that the well seemed to dry up awful early. Either way, I didn't want to be home and sobering up and contemplating a murder. There'd been too much death associated with that house already: the fall of my honesty with Faith; the decay of my pride when I did up while watching Emily alone for the evening; the collapse of my marriage — hell, the place was paid for with blood money.

So instead I drove Dauphine to Esplanade to Ten East. I remember the first time I drove on heroin I thought it should be required medication for the elderly. I saw the other lanes, the other cars, the signals — everything — so clearly. It was too easy to understand how every vehicle operated as a component of the infrastructure, each little tin auto playing its role like tiny corpuscles in a massive cardiovascular system. You know those people on the road who anticipate changing conditions like Bobby Fischer, always four moves ahead? That's us, baby, the hop heads, guardians of the three-seconds rule, purveyors of the stale green light.

I drove about half an hour, hoping maybe traffic would be heavy, what with it being two days after Carnival. But everyone had either bugged out broke and hung-over or they were still hanging on to the party after it should have been over, like Elvis at the end. You hear about how heroin makes you numb to the world around you, but I had never experienced that before now. Yeah sure it cost me my wife and my kid and all that shit, but through it all I was still Creole. I knew who was president and who led the NFC West and how to play Six Degrees of Kevin Bacon. Heroin was just a way to unwind, okay? But now, driving along a lonely stretch of increasingly rural Louisiana, I realized I'd missed the Mardi Gras, had no idea if there'd been calm or the cops had been uptight or the tips

good or the ta-tas plentiful or any damn thing about it other than
that it had been two days ago, which meant Sunday was Lent.

I could hear the second syringe calling me from the trunk. It's
odd how much honor this drug has. It could taunt you, call you a
cock-sucking mother-fucker and cut a two-inch notch in your pee
hole and you'd thank it politely and invite it into your home and
not even ask it to wipe its feet. But it doesn't. It just gently reminds you — doesn't even nag, just nudges a recollection — that
you need it. And then it goes to work. Heroin is the June Cleaver of
narcotics.

I didn't want to answer that call, not 'til the deed was done, and
since I was still way ahead of schedule, I pulled off at a truck stop in
Alton. The sign from the highway said simply "Gas" but I knew that
on Ten, outside the city limits "gas" meant "Diner."

I expected three or four greasy spoons duking it out by the town's
only red light, where every night the people gave thanks that the
state legislature had seen fit to bless their small marsh with an exit.
But I was disappointed to find only one truck stop and it was beside
only a flashing yellow. It didn't have a name, or not one that was
posted. But in a tiny Southeast borough off the interstate, the only
sign you need is a couple of rigs in your lot and a red and white
"OPEN" in your glass door. Even the parking lot was paved, not dirt,
so the stereotypical dust failed to envelop my car as I braked and
lumbered out.

Inside, the rebellion continued. Couldn't these people see I was
a junkie just off a jones about to commit an abominably immoral
act; didn't they know I needed a little stability from the outside
world while the chaotic vortex of my inner one whirled destruc-
tively faster? No tin sounding radio playing Merle Haggard tunes in
mono, no stuffed armadillos on the counter tops, and the waitress
neither had high-hair nor chewed gum. And her name tag had the
audacity to read "Patricia." Not Linda Lou or Tammi with an i, just
plain vanilla, waspy Patricia. I immediately dubbed her "Patsy" and
felt a little better about the situation.

The chalkboard propped behind her was lettered in bright pink:
"TODAY'S SPECIAL — MEAN ASS RED BEAN CHILI." Beneath
the words, someone had drawn a chalky blue bowl with the handle
of a spoon poking out, and wavy red squiggles above to simulate
heat. A not-so-fine layer of dust covered the whole thing, and I

could tell "today's special" had been "today's special" since the nameless "diner" had been (red and white letter) "open."

"What you want ta drink, honey?" Patsy asked without turning around, breaking me out of my wry meditation. Her accent was fifth generation Cajun, but somehow her unwillingness to face me seemed to stem from shyness not apathy. Then I saw that she *was* looking at me, in the angled mirror high above the back counter. And I saw myself as she saw me, or as I would have seen me had I been her. And I didn't blame her for not facing me.

By looking upwards to look down upon me, she had a prime view of the crown of scar tissue David had blessed me with. It was a cross I bore without frequent thought; after all, chefs can wear hats in the kitchen, and whenever the weather permitted I wore a light trench and fedora in the streets. The Quarter is full of freaks who cleave to and rely upon one another like ants in the mound, defending resolutely against outsiders who damn near sample the local culture into extinction. Nevertheless, I would be reminded now and again of my butchered cranium and if it wasn't exactly a freshly cut wound, it was certainly a handful of salt ground vigorously into the oozy pus of an old one. It was like having your defining moment pinned to the breast of your shirt — I didn't so much mind other people staring as I did being forced to realize that it *was* my defining moment.

I ignored the question. "About that special," I announced loudly, trying to distract Patsy — and anyone else x-raying my soul through my nugget — with a little levity. "What kind of man — knowing he's gonna be locked up in the ten-square-foot cab of a truck for the next six hours — orders anything with the words 'mean ass' in the title?" I grinned Daddy's crooked smile, and would have arched my eyebrows had they not both been burnt off sixteen years ago.

"The kind what's hungry, sugar," Patsy answered sweetly, finally turning to make direct eye contact. "You hungry?" The question and her stare were pregnant with meaning, as though by sighting my Achilles heel so early in our encounter she had been able to discern both its source and its effects on the chain of happenstance that had become my meager existence.

Yes, I should have cried out, Yes I hunger to be loved, or at least to be worthy of love. I long to feel that good things can last, that something gold *can* stay, and that I don't have to prove myself every single day. That the people I love recognize and remember my intrinsic value from one moment to the next. I hunger to be sitting home right now with my little girl, watching *Lamb Chop's Play-Along* and singing "The Song That Doesn't End" instead of venturing across state lines to kill a man I don't know, all so I can keep alive within my arteries a slowly growing cancer (a process which gives a whole new meaning to chemotherapy).

But I held onto all that and shook my head, said "No, just a mug of chicory, if you don't mind." Said it to the counter top rather than face Patsy, knowing full well that by refusing to look up I was giving her another dead-on shot of my Daddy's son's hellish baptism. It was still better than looking the cunt in the eye. Either way, she was gonna know all about me — she had the knack, it flowed around her like vapor trails when you got too much strychnine — but facing her straight ahead would have forced me to see what she saw. And I already knew what she saw, knew I didn't want to see the stretched-thin junkie sitting at her counter wearing out an already threadbare joke about her menu. It was like algebra when the teacher would squeak an especially tough problem on the board and we'd all look down so he wouldn't call on us to answer; if we couldn't see him, he couldn't see us. That was my approach with Patsy now because it had always worked in the past: with Faith, with Daddy, with God.

"No appetite, huh?" she joshed, sloshing thick liquid as she slid the mug across the counter and into my hands until we each cradled a half as though it were a chalice and not a nicked enamel crock with loose grounds swimming at the bottom. "The only men I ever seen in here not hungry was love sick," she teased, making the word *love* into a several-syllable abortion, drawing out "you love sick?" the same singsong way she'd called out "you hungry?" Yep, saw right through me. Like when you told the man at the deli "thin, for sandwiches," and he held up the first slice and you could see his questioning glance through it and you had to backtrack and say "uh, not quite that thin, Tex." Patsy must have come to work every night and built a Dagwood from the little glimpses she stole from her patrons.

"You know how Karl Marx summed up capitalism's inherent shortcoming?" I asked, knowing full well she'd be trying to puzzle out whether Karl was the one who carried the bicycle horn and never spoke. "He said your employer will never pay you the true value of your work because he keeps more for himself." I took a mouthful of the rich chicory and swallowed bitterly, even though the liquid was syrupy sweet. "I think love works the same way."

In retrospect, stopping and chatting was the worst thing I could have done. My stoned intentions were good: be invisible by being brazen. Like an art thief defiantly hanging his booty in the foyer, I gambled that no one would suspect a *Das Kapital*–quoting would-be trucker of murdering a drug-importing riverboat casino operator. It was naked foolishness, a rash thing that I should believe will bring about my capture. But somehow I don't. Something about the way Patsy asked her patrons "you hungry?" No, not so much how she asked, or even *that* she asked, but that having drawn out the confession she already took for granted, she set about satisfying the need.

An hour later I abandoned I-10 for 49, figuring to run south to Gulfport and catch 90 east to Biloxi. My craving was hitting hard and I thought a slightly slower road might ease my anxiety. The distance on 49 between the off-ramp from 10 and the on-ramp to 90 is so short that you couldn't even play football on it; you'd have to play Arena Ball. Nevertheless, having rounded the spaghetti circle that officially welcomed me to sixty yards of due southerly travel, I managed to incur such a withdrawal-induced cramp that I whirled the car hard onto the soft shoulder, picked up a piece of nail-infected lumber, and spun 180 degrees trying to control the blowout. Facing north on the sideline of a due south highway, I listened to my heart beat out Babalu for a couple minutes before popping the trunk to free the donut. It was sad, really, how badly I was going to limp into Biloxi — strung out, on three-and-a-half wheels, shooting a twenty-year-old pistol — just so I could crawl back home with enough room on my available credit limit to start the process all over again. Once I had the jack on and was working the lug nuts loose, I realized that I could not go on repeating the cycle indefinitely: eventually I would run out of fingers. Maybe next time, I thought ruefully, I could convince Lazarus to settle for a toe.

Mulling such thoughts took what little of my concentration wasn't incessantly chanting *smack smack smack* and I never even saw the trooper's car approach until the nose of his cruiser was head-lamp to headlamp with my Jetta. He popped his lamps to bright, and when he opened the door I could hear the faint hum remind-

ing him his keys were in the ignition. It was close to the sound
Chase's nightmare opium had buzzed me with and for a moment I
felt certain I would flash back and begin writhing in turmoil. But
for once my subconscious was just that — sub — and I was able to
endure the rattlesnake hum by focusing on what to say, what to do
to end the conversation quickly.

I heard the trooper's boot crunch the loose asphalt as he took his
first step toward me. Far away, a lone rig approached us, barely seen
and as yet unheard. I imagined the conversation in my head. Very
simple. Picked up a tar tack. Need help? No sir, I can manage, good
to do a little work during a long drive anyway, clear the head. Long
haul, eh? Yes sir, clear to Tallahassee. Well, see you get that tire
patched and keep it under fifty with that spare on. Yes sir.

The rig finished rounding the off-ramp and approached, its
whine slowly eating into the buzz of the cop's Chrysler. I practiced
the conversation again, head down, thinking in rhythm with the
crunching of his boots. The third time through the script I saw the
fatal error, but it was too late. Parked nose to nose, with my left rear
wheel blown, the cop would have to come around the trunk of my
car to get to my side, to get to "need help?" Come around the *open*
trunk. The one with the bag holding a loaded syringe, the one with
an uncovered Colt pistol lying plainly in sight.

He was a step away from rounding my Jetta's back side when the
rig roared by. My subconscious burst on the scene and my mind
splintered eighteen different ways at once. I saw the cop spotting
the firearm, cuffing me and taking me in, and getting a bust for
possession in the bargain; I saw Lazarus getting the word to someone on the inside who owed him; I saw myself getting a tracheot-
omy with a toothbrush in the hoser at the Mississippi state pen —
like father, like son. I saw Faith raising Emily to believe "Daddy was
killed when the mine collapsed, before you were born," not wanting to admit to her brood, much less to herself, that her judgement
could have been so flawed.

A defiant scream erupted as the rig blew past, knocking the
trooper's hat off. "Goddammit," he insisted and bent to pick it up,
even as the tail end of the trailer completed its "woosh," leaving
only a vacuum of receding yellow reflectors. When the trooper
replaced his hat and turned to finally check on me, I crushed him
square in the jaw with my tire iron.

The sound was anticlimactic. Bones don't "crunch" as advertised, nor do they crack or splinter. I heard a dense wet thud, as though I were splitting logs that had just come in from a three day drizzle. Blood exploded from his mouth and his tongue protruded dumbly, forked by a deep gash running from tip to root. I swung again, then again, mesmerized by the soggy, absorbing slap of the blows and the off-beat metallic ping that preceded each one. Only later did I discover that each back-swing had cost my Jetta a tail light, a trunk lip, a dinged fender.

His eyes stayed open throughout. I kept waiting for oncoming cars but the only time in my life when things went my way happened to be the time I bludgeoned a police officer to death. You have no idea how resilient the human spirit is until you are forced to extinguish one. To pound a man's skull with a two-foot piece of steel and have him continue to gawk at you: why, it's all the proof of the existence of the human soul you can ever need. It took me ninety seconds to spill enough of his brains on the hardpan to ensure my escape, and then I had to scrape the pieces of his scalp from my tool so I could finish applying the spare.

And now it is a day-and-a-half later and I-90 (and I-10 for that matter) is just a memory since I hit 95 north in Jacksonville. There's no point in fulfilling my vision quest after doing one of Mississippi's finest. A dead cop and a dead gambler inside an hour would only help draw a line through the big red dots I left behind. A line that would form an arrow pointing straight to good old Creole. It comes down to fight or flight and I've done my share of the former. It's time to do some of the latter, or more accurately to do some of the latter by doing some more of the former. And maybe not alone either. Not if I can help it.

Charlotte is an hour away and I'll make my true destination by nightfall. It's been a long sobering drive in the dark and I have very little reason for hope. I left the cop's dead body in the short grass by the side of the road, his car door still open, brights still blazing. No doubt I left a breadbox full of forensic evidence as well. That rig driver could remember spotting us. Patsy probably doesn't get Marx quoted to her all that often. Yet, very little reason or no, I remain hopeful.

For one thing, what I said to Patsy was honest, and that's a start. If

I can confess my horrific concept of love as a house-rules gamble to a stranger, how hard can it be to do the same with my wife? And once I tell her, maybe she can help me find my way back to seeing it as I did when I first fell in love with her. For another, if I can write all this down for you — *you* who've never even set eyes on me and have every right, every *reason* to believe me a monster — if I can set all this down for *you,* what *do* I have to hide from Faith? And still another: I saw that cop coming and saw my future and fought back. Inherent in that slaying must be the conviction that a better, alternate future is possible. For the second time in as many days, I had a gun at my head, but this time I chose a new path.

So all signs point to a trust my subconscious has yet to make public but might. Maybe I can beat heroin. Maybe I can find my wife and my daughter in Baltimore, a scant ten hours away, and convince them I — we — deserve another chance. Maybe we can dodge Lazarus long enough for him to lose interest, get a job in San Luis Obispo, or Cincinnati, or Canada. Maybe we can live happily ever after and all that shit.

LAWRENCE BLOCK

Keller on the Spot

FROM *Playboy*

KELLER, DRINK IN HAND, agreed with the woman in the pink dress that it was indeed a lovely evening. He threaded his way through a crowd of young marrieds on what he supposed you would call the patio. A waitress passed carrying a tray of drinks in stemmed glasses and he traded in his own for a fresh one. He sipped as he walked along, wondering what he was drinking. Some sort of vodka sour, he decided, and decided as well that he didn't need to narrow it down any further than that. He figured he'd have this one and one more, but he could have ten more if he wanted, because he wasn't working tonight. He could relax and cut loose and have a good time.

Well, almost. He couldn't relax completely, couldn't cut loose altogether. Because, while this might not be work, neither was it entirely recreational. The garden party this evening was a heaven-sent opportunity for reconnaissance, and he would use it to get a close look at his quarry. He had been handed a picture back in White Plains, and he had brought that picture with him to Dallas, but even the best photo wasn't the same as a glimpse of the fellow in the flesh, and in his native habitat.

And a lush habitat it was. Keller hadn't been inside the house yet, but it was clearly immense, a sprawling multilevel affair of innumerable large rooms. The grounds sprawled as well, covering an acre or two, with enough plants and shrubbery to stock an arboretum. Keller didn't know anything about flowers, but five minutes in a garden like this one had him thinking he ought to know more about the subject. Maybe they had evening classes at Hunter or

NYU; maybe they'd take you on field trips to the Brooklyn Botani-
cal Gardens.

He walked along a brick path, smiling at this stranger, nodding at
that one, and wound up standing alongside the swimming pool.
Some 12 or 15 people sat at poolside tables, talking and drinking,
the volume of their conversations rising as they drank. In the enormous pool, a young boy swam back and forth, back and forth.

Keller felt a curious kinship with the kid. He was standing instead
of swimming, but he felt as distant as the kid from everybody else
around. There were two parties going on, he decided. There was
the hearty social whirl, and there was the solitude he felt in the
midst of it all, akin to the solitude of the swimming boy.

Huge pool. The boy was swimming its width, but that dimension
was still greater than the length of your typical backyard pool.
Keller wasn't sure if this was an Olympic-size pool, but he figured
you could just call it enormous and let it go at that.

Ages ago he'd heard about some college-boy stunt, filling a swimming pool with Jell-O, and he'd wondered how many little boxes of
the gelatin dessert it would have required, and how the college boys
could have afforded it. It would cost a fortune, he decided, to fill
this pool with Jell-O, but if you could afford the pool in the first
place, he supposed the Jell-O would be the least of your worries.

There were cut flowers on all the tables, and the blooms looked
like ones Keller had seen in the garden. It stood to reason. If you
grew all these flowers, you wouldn't have to order from the florist.
You could cut your own.

What good would it do, he wondered, to know the names of all
the shrubs and flowers? Wouldn't it just leave you wanting to dig in
the soil and grow your own? And he didn't want to get into all that,
for God's sake.

So maybe he'd just forget about evening classes at Hunter, and
field trips to Brooklyn. If he wanted to get close to nature he could
walk in Central Park, and if he didn't know the names of the flowers
he would just hold off on introducing himself to them. And if —

Where was the kid?

The boy, the swimmer. Keller's companion in solitude. Where
the hell did he go? The pool was empty, its surface still. Keller saw a
ripple toward the far end, saw bubbles break the surface.

He didn't react without thinking. That was how he'd always
heard that sort of thing described, but that wasn't what happened,

because the thoughts were there, loud and clear. *He's down there.
He's in trouble. He's drowning.* And, echoing in his head in a voice
sour with exasperation: *Keller, for Christ's sake, do something!*

He set his glass on a table, shucked his coat, kicked off his shoes,
dropped his pants and stepped out of them. Ages ago he'd earned
a Red Cross lifesaving certificate, and the first thing they taught you
was to strip before you hit the water. The six or seven seconds you
spent peeling off your clothes would be repaid many times over in
quickness and mobility.

But the strip show did not go unnoticed. Everybody at poolside
had a comment, one more hilarious than the next. He barely heard
them. In no time at all he was down to his underwear. Then he was
out of range of their cleverness, hitting the water in a flat racing
dive, churning the water till he reached the spot where he'd seen
the bubbles, then diving, eyes wide, barely noticing the burn of the
chlorine.

Searching for the boy. Groping, searching, then finding him,
reaching to grab hold of him. And pushing off against the bottom,
lungs bursting, racing to the surface.

People were saying things to Keller, thanking him, congratulating
him, but it wasn't really registering. A man clapped him on the
back, a woman handed him a glass of brandy. He heard the word
hero and realized people were saying it all over the place, and
applying it to him.

Hell of a note.

Keller sipped the brandy. It gave him heartburn, which assured
him of its quality; good cognac always gave him heartburn. He
turned to look at the boy. He was a little fellow, 12 or 13 years old,
his hair lightened and his skin bronzed by the summer sun. He was
sitting up now, Keller saw, and looking none the worse for his
near-death experience.

"Timothy," a woman said, "this is the man who saved your life. Do
you have something to say to him?"

"Thanks," Timothy said, predictably.

"Is that all you have to say, young man?" the woman asked.

"It's enough," Keller said, and smiled. To the boy he said,
"There's something I've always wondered. Did your life actually
flash before your eyes?"

Timothy shook his head. "I got this cramp," he said, "and it was like my whole body turned into one big knot, and there wasn't anything I could do to untie it. And I didn't even think about drowning. I was just fighting the cramp, 'cause it hurt, and about the next thing I knew I was up here, coughing and puking up water." He made a face. "I must have swallowed half the pool. All I have to do is think about it and I can taste vomit and chlorine."

"Timothy," the woman said, rolling her eyes.

"Something to be said for plain speech," an older man said. He had a mane of white hair and prominent white eyebrows, and his eyes were a vivid blue. He was holding a glass of brandy in one hand and a bottle in the other, and he reached with the bottle to fill Keller's glass to the brim. "'Claret for boys and port for men,'" he said. "'But he who aspires to be a hero must drink brandy.' That's Samuel Johnson, though I may have gotten a word wrong."

The woman patted his hand. "If you did, Daddy, I'm sure you just improved Mr. Johnson's wording."

"Dr. Johnson," he said, "and one could hardly do that. Improve the man's wording, that is. 'Being in a ship is like being in a jail, with the chance of being drowned.' He said that as well, and I defy anyone to comment more trenchantly on the experience, or to say it better." He beamed at Keller. "I owe you more than a glass of brandy and a well-turned Johnsonian phrase. This little rascal whose life you've saved is my grandson, and the apple — nay, sir, the very nectarine — of my eye. And we'd have all stood around drinking and laughing while he drowned. You observed, and you acted, and God bless you for it."

What did you say to that, Keller wondered. *It was nothing? Well, shucks?* There had to be some sort of apt phrase, and maybe Samuel Johnson could have found it, but Keller couldn't. So he said nothing, and tried not to look po-faced.

"I don't even know your name," the white-haired man went on. "That's not remarkable in and of itself. I don't know half the people here, and I'm content to remain in my ignorance. But I ought to know your name, wouldn't you agree?"

Keller might have picked a name out of the air, but the one that leaped to mind was Boswell, and he couldn't say that to a man who quoted Samuel Johnson. So he supplied the name he'd traveled under, the one he'd signed when he checked into the hotel, the one on the driver's license and credit cards in his wallet.

"It's Michael Soderholm," he said, "and I can't even tell you the name of the fellow who brought me here. We met over drinks in the hotel bar, and he said he was going to a party and it would be perfectly all right if I came along. I felt a little funny about it, but —"

"Please," the man said. "You can't possibly propose to apologize for your presence here. It has kept my grandson from a watery if chlorinated grave. And I've just told you I don't know half my guests, but that doesn't make them any the less welcome." He took a deep drink of his brandy and topped up both glasses. "Michael Soderholm," he said. "Swedish?"

"A mixture of everything," Keller said, improvising. "My great-grandfather Soderholm came over from Sweden, but my other ancestors came from all over Europe, plus I'm something like a sixteenth American Indian."

"Oh? Which tribe?"

"Cherokee," Keller said, thinking of the jazz tune.

"I'm an eighth Comanche," the man said. "So I'm afraid we're not tribal blood brothers. The rest's British Isles, a mix of Scots and Irish and English. Old Texas stock. But you're not Texan yourself."

"No."

"Well, it can't be helped, as the saying goes. Unless you decide to move here, and who's to say you won't? It's a fine place for a man to live."

"Daddy thinks that everybody should love Texas the same way he does," the woman said.

"Everybody should," her father said. "The only thing wrong with Texans is we're a long-winded lot. Look at the time it's taking me to introduce myself! Mr. Soderholm, Mr. Michael Soderholm, my name's Garrity, Wallace Penrose Garrity, and I'm your grateful host this evening."

No kidding, thought Keller.

The party, lifesaving and all, took place on Saturday night. The next day Keller sat in his hotel room and watched the Cowboys beat the Vikings with a field goal in the last three minutes of double overtime. The game seesawed back and forth, with interceptions and runbacks, and the announcers kept telling each other what a great game it was.

Keller supposed they were right. It had all the ingredients, and it wasn't the players' fault that he was entirely unmoved by their performance. He could watch sports, and often did, but he almost never got caught up in it. He had occasionally wondered if his work might have something to do with it. On one level, when your job involved dealing regularly with life and death, how could you care if some overpaid steroid abuser had a touchdown run called back? And, on another level, you saw unorthodox solutions to a team's problems on the field. When Emmitt Smith kept crashing through the Minnesota line, Keller wondered why they didn't deputize someone to shoot the son of a bitch in the back of the neck, right below his star-covered helmet.

Still, it was better than watching golf, say, which had to be better than playing golf. And he couldn't get out and work, because there was nothing for him to do. Last night's reconnaissance mission had been both better and worse than he could have hoped, and what was he supposed to do now? Park his rented Ford across the street from the Garrity mansion and clock the comings and goings?

No need for that. He could bide his time, just so he got there in time for Sunday dinner.

"More potatoes, Mr. Soderholm?"

"They are delicious," Keller said. "But I'm full. Really."

"And we can't keep calling you 'Mr. Soderholm,'" Garrity said. "I've only held off this long for not knowing whether you prefer Mike or Michael."

"Mike's fine," Keller said.

"Then Mike it is. And I'm Wally, Mike, or W.P., though there are those who call me the Walrus."

Timmy laughed and clapped both hands over his mouth.

"Though never to his face," said the woman who had offered Keller more potatoes. She was Ellen Garrity, Timmy's aunt and Garrity's daughter-in-law, and Keller was now instructed to call her Ellie. Her husband, a big-shouldered fellow who seemed to be smiling bravely through the heartbreak of male-pattern baldness, was Garrity's son, Hank.

Keller remembered Timothy's mother from the night before, but hadn't caught her name, or her relationship to Garrity. She was Rhonda Sue Butler, as it turned out, and everybody called her

Rhonda Sue, except for her husband, who called her Ronnie. His name was Doak Butler, and he looked like a college jock who'd been too light for pro ball, though he now seemed to be closing the gap.

Hank and Ellie, Doak and Rhonda Sue. And, at the far end of the table, Vanessa, who was married to Wally but who was clearly not the mother of Hank or Rhonda Sue, or anyone else. Keller supposed you could describe her as Wally's trophy wife, a sign of his success. She was no older than Wally's kids, and she looked to be well bred and elegant, and she even had the good grace to hide the boredom Keller was sure she felt.

And that was the lot of them. Wally and Vanessa, Hank and Ellen, Doak and Rhonda Sue. And Timothy, who had been swimming that very afternoon, the aquatic equivalent of getting right back on the horse. He'd had no cramps this time, but he'd had an attentive eye kept on him throughout.

Seven of them, then. And Keller . . . also known as Mike.

"So you're here on business," Wally said. "And stuck here over the weekend, which is the worst part of a business trip, as far as I'm concerned. More trouble than it's worth to fly back to Chicago?"

The two of them were in Wally's den, a fine room paneled in knotty pecan and trimmed in red leather, with Western doodads on the walls — here a branding iron, there a longhorn skull. Keller had accepted a brandy and declined a cigar, but the aroma of Wally's Havana was giving him second thoughts. Keller didn't smoke, but from the smell of it the cigar wasn't smoking. It was more along the lines of a religious experience.

"Seemed that way," Keller said. He had supplied Chicago as Michael Soderholm's home base, even though Soderholm's license placed him in southern California. "By the time I fly there and back —"

"You've spent your weekend on airplanes. Well, it's our good fortune you decided to stay. Now what I'd like to do is find a way to make it your good fortune as well."

"You've already done that," Keller told him. "I crashed a great party last night and actually got to feel like a hero for a few minutes. And tonight I get a fine dinner with nice people and get to top it off with a glass of outstanding brandy."

The heartburn told him how outstanding it was.

"What I had in mind," Wally said smoothly, "was to get you to work for me."

Who did he want him to kill? Keller almost blurted out the question until he remembered that Garrity didn't know what he did for a living.

"You won't say who you work for?" Garrity went on.

"I can't."

"Because the job's hush-hush for now. Well, I can respect that, and from the hints you've dropped I gather you're here scouting out something in the way of mergers and acquisitions."

"That's close."

"And I'm sure it's well paid, and you must like the work or I don't think you'd stay with it. So what do I have to do to get you to switch horses and come work for me? I'll tell you one thing — Chicago's a nice place, but nobody who ever moved from there to Big D went around with a sour face about it. I don't know you well yet, but I can tell you're our kind of people and Dallas will be your kind of town. I don't know what they're paying you, but I suspect I can top it and offer you a stake in a growing company with all sorts of attractive possibilities."

Keller listened, nodded judiciously, sipped a little brandy. It was amazing, he thought, the way things came along when you weren't looking for them. It was straight out of Horatio Alger, for God's sake — Ragged Dick stops the runaway horse and saves the daughter of the captain of industry, and the next thing you know he's president of IBM with rising expectations.

"Maybe I'll have that cigar after all," Keller said.

"Now come on, Keller," Dot said. "You know the rules. I can't give you that information."

"It's sort of important," he said.

"One of the things the client buys," she said, "is confidentiality. That's what he wants and it's what we provide. Even if the agent in place —"

"The agent in place?"

"That's you," she said. "You're the agent, and Dallas is the place. Even if you get caught red-handed, the confidentiality of the client remains uncompromised. And do you know why?"

"Because the agent in place knows how to keep mum."

"Mum's the word," she agreed, "and there's no question you're the strong, silent type. But even if your lip loosens, you can't sink a ship if you don't know when it's sailing."

Keller thought that over. "You lost me," he said.

"Yeah, it came out a little abstruse, didn't it? Point is, you can't tell what you don't know, Keller, which is why the agent doesn't get to know the client's name."

"Dot," he said, trying to sound injured, "how long have you known me?"

"Ages, Keller. Many lifetimes."

"Many lifetimes?"

"We were in Atlantis together. Look, I know nobody's going to catch you red-handed, and I know you wouldn't blab if they did. But I can't tell what I don't know."

"Oh."

"Right. I think the spies call it a double cutout. The client made arrangements with somebody we know, and that person called us. But he didn't give us the client's name, and why should he? Come to think of it, Keller, why do you have to know, anyway?"

He had his answer ready. "It might not be a single," he said.

"Oh?"

"The target's always got people around him," he said, "and the best way to do it might be a sort of group plan, if you follow me."

"Two for the price of one."

"Or three or four," he said. "But if one of those innocent bystanders turned out to be the client, it might make things a little awkward."

"Well, I can see where we might have trouble collecting the final payment."

"If we knew for a fact that the client was fishing for trout in Montana," he said, "it would be no problem. But if he's here in Dallas . . ."

"It would help to know his name." Dot sighed. "Give me an hour or two, huh? Then call me back."

If Keller knew who the client was, the client could have an accident.

It would have to be an artful accident, too. It would have to look good not only to the police but also to whoever was aware of the client's intentions. The local go-between, the helpful fellow who had hooked up the client to the old man in White Plains — and, thus, to Keller — could be expected to cast a cold eye on any suspicious death. So it would have to be a damn good accident, but Keller had managed a few of those in his day. It took a little planning, but it wasn't brain surgery. You just figured out a method and took your best shot.

If, as he rather hoped, the client was some business rival in Houston or Denver or San Diego, he'd have to slip off to that city without anyone noting his absence. Then, having induced a quick attack of accidental death, he'd fly back to Dallas and hang around until someone called him off the case. He'd need a different ID for Houston or Denver or San Diego — it wouldn't do to overexpose Michael Soderholm — and he'd need to mask his actions from all concerned: Garrity, his homicidal rival and, perhaps most important, Dot and the old man.

All told, it was a great deal more complicated (if easier to stomach) than the alternative.

Which was to carry out the assignment professionally and kill Wallace Penrose Garrity the first good chance he got.

And he really didn't want to do that. He'd eaten at the man's table, he'd drunk the man's brandy, he'd smoked the man's cigars. He'd been offered not merely a job but a well-paid executive position with a future, and, later that night, light-headed from alcohol and nicotine, he'd had fantasies of taking Wally up on it.

Hell, why not? He could live out his days as Michael Soderholm, doing whatever unspecified tasks Garrity was hiring him to perform. He probably lacked the requisite experience, but how hard could it be to pick up the skills he needed as he went along? Whatever he had to do, it would be easier than flying from town to town killing people. He could learn on the job. He could pull it off.

The fantasy had about as much substance as a dream, and, like a dream, it was gone when he awoke the next morning. No one would put him on the payroll without some sort of background check, and the most cursory scan would knock him out of the box. Michael Soderholm had no more substance than the fake ID in Keller's wallet.

Even if he somehow finessed a background check, even if the old man in White Plains let him walk out of one life and into another, he knew he couldn't really make it work. He already had a life. Misshapen though it was, it fit him like a glove.

He went out for a sandwich and a cup of coffee. He got back in his car and drove around for a while. Then he found a pay phone and called White Plains.

"Do a single," Dot said.

"How's that?"

"No added extras, no free dividends. Just do what they signed on for."

"Because the client's here in town," he said. "Well, I could work around that if I knew his name. I could make sure he was out of it."

"Forget it," Dot said. "The client wants a long and happy life for everybody but the designated vic. Maybe the DV's close associates are near and dear to the client. That's just a guess, but all that really matters is that nobody else gets hurt. *Capisce?*"

"*Capisce?*"

"It's Italian, it means —"

"I know what it means. It just sounded odd from your lips, that's all. But yes, I understand." He took a breath. "Whole thing may take a little time," he said.

"Then here comes the good news," she said. "Time's not of the essence. They don't care how long it takes, just so you get it right."

"I understand W.P. offered you a job," Vanessa said. "I know he hopes you'll take him up on it."

"I think he was just being generous," Keller told her. "I was in the right place at the right time, and he'd like to do me a favor. But I don't think he really expects me to come to work for him."

"He'd like it if you did," she said, "or he never would have made the offer. He'd have just given you money, or a car, or something like that. And as far as what he expects, well, W.P. generally expects to get whatever he wants. Because that's the way things usually work out."

And had she been saving up her pennies to get things to work out a little differently? You had to wonder. Was she truly under Garrity's spell, in awe of his power, as she seemed to be? Or was she in it only for the money, and was there a sharp edge of irony under her worshipful remarks?

Hard to say. Hard to tell about any of them. Was Hank the loyal son he appeared to be, content to live in the old man's shadow and take what got tossed his way? Or was he secretly resentful and ambitious?

What about the son-in-law, Doak? On the surface, he looked to be delighted with the aftermath of his college football career — his work for his father-in-law consisted largely of playing golf with business associates and drinking with them afterward. But did he seethe inside, sure he was fit for greater things?

How about Hank's wife, Ellie? She struck Keller as an unlikely Lady Macbeth. Keller could fabricate scenarios in which she or Rhonda Sue had a reason for wanting Wally dead, but they were the sort of thing you dreamed up watching reruns of *Dallas* and trying to guess who shot J.R. Maybe one of their marriages was in trouble. Maybe Garrity had put the moves on his daughter-in-law, or maybe a little too much brandy had led him into his daughter's bedroom now and then. Maybe Doak or Hank was playing footsie with Vanessa. Maybe. . . .

Pointless to speculate, he decided. You could go around and around like that, but it didn't get you anywhere. Even if he managed to dope out which of them was the client, then what? Having saved young Timothy, and thus feeling obligated to spare his doting grandfather, what was he going to do? Kill the boy's father? Or mother or aunt or uncle?

Of course he could just go home. He could explain the situation to the old man. Nobody loved it when you took yourself off a contract for personal reasons, but it wasn't something they could talk you out of, either. If you made a habit of that sort of thing, well, that was different, but that wasn't the case with Keller. He was a solid pro. Quirky perhaps, even whimsical, but a pro all the way. Tell him what to do and he does it.

So, if he had a personal reason to bow out, you honored it. You let him come home and sit on the porch and drink iced tea with Dot.

And you picked up the phone and sent somebody else to Dallas.

Because, either way, the job was going to be done. If a hit man had a change of heart, it would be followed in short order by a change of hit man. If Keller didn't pull the trigger, somebody else would.

His mistake, Keller thought savagely, was that he had jumped into the goddamn pool in the first place. All he'd have had to do was look the other way and let the little bastard drown. A few days later he could have taken Garrity out, possibly making it look like suicide, a natural consequence of despondency over the boy's tragic accident.

But no, he thought, glaring at himself in the mirror. No, you had to go and get involved. You had to be a hero, for God's sake. Had to strip down to your skivvies and prove you deserved that lifesaving certificate the Red Cross had given you all those years ago.

He wondered what had happened to that certificate.

It was gone, of course, like everything he'd owned in his childhood and youth. Gone like his high school diploma, like his Boy Scout merit badge sash, like his sack of marbles and his stack of baseball cards. He didn't mind that these things were gone, didn't waste time wishing he had them any more than he wanted those years back.

The certificate, when all was said and done, was only a piece of paper. What was important was the skill itself, and what was truly remarkable was that he'd retained it. Because of it, Timothy Butler was alive. Which was all well and good for the boy, but a great big headache for Keller.

Later, sitting with a cup of coffee, Keller thought some more about Wallace Penrose Garrity, a man who seemed to have not an enemy in the world.

Suppose Keller had let the kid drown. Suppose he just plain hadn't noticed the boy's disappearance beneath the water, just as everyone else had failed to notice it. Garrity would have been despondent. It was his party, his pool, his failure to provide supervision. He'd probably have blamed himself for the boy's death.

When Keller took him out, it would have been the kindest thing he could have done for him.

He caught the waiter's eye and signaled for more coffee.

"Mike," Garrity said, with a hand outstretched. "Sorry to keep you waiting. Had a call from a fellow with a hankering to buy a little five-acre lot of mine on the south edge of town. Thing is, I don't want to sell it to him."

"I see."

"There's ten acres on the other side of town I'd be perfectly happy to sell to him, but he'll only want it if he thinks of it himself. So that left me on the phone longer than I would have liked. Now then, what would you say to a glass of brandy?"

"Maybe a small one."

Garrity led the way to the den, poured drinks for both of them. "You should have come earlier," he said. "In time for dinner. I hope you know you don't need an invitation. There'll always be a place for you at our table."

"Well," Keller said.

"I know you can't talk about it," Garrity said, "but I hope your project here in town is shaping up nicely."

"Slow but sure," Keller said.

"Some things can't be hurried," Garrity allowed, and sipped brandy and winced. If Keller hadn't been looking for it, he might have missed the shadow that crossed his host's face.

Gently he asked, "Is the pain bad, Wally?"

"How's that, Mike?"

Keller put his glass on the table. "I spoke to Dr. Jacklin," he said. "I know what you're going through."

"That son of a bitch," Garrity said, "was supposed to keep his mouth shut."

"Well, he thought it was all right to talk to me," Keller said. "He thought I was Dr. Edward Fishman from the Mayo Clinic."

"Calling for a consultation."

"Something like that."

"I did go to Mayo," Garrity said, "but they didn't need to call Harold Jacklin to double-check their results. They just confirmed his diagnosis and told me not to buy any long-playing records." He looked to one side. "They said they couldn't say for sure how much time I had left, but that the pain would be manageable for a while. And then it wouldn't."

"I see."

"And I'd have all my faculties for a while," he said. "And then I wouldn't."

Keller didn't say anything.

"Well, hell," Garrity said. "A man wants to take the bull by the horns, doesn't he? I decided I'd go out for a walk with a shotgun and have a little hunting accident. Or I'd be cleaning a handgun here at my desk and have it go off. But it turned out I just couldn't tolerate the idea of killing myself. Don't know why, can't explain it, but that seems to be the way I'm made."

He picked up his glass and looked at the brandy. "Funny how we hang on to life," he said. "Something else I think Sam Johnson said, that there wasn't a week of his life he would voluntarily live through again. I've had more good times than bad, Mike, and even the bad times haven't been that god-awful. But I think I know what he was getting at. I wouldn't want to repeat any of it, but that doesn't mean there's a minute of it I'd have been willing to miss. I don't want to miss whatever's coming next, and I don't guess Dr. Johnson did either. That's what keeps us going, isn't it? Wanting to find out what's around the next bend in the river?"

"I guess so."

"I thought that would make the end easier to face," he said, "not knowing when it was coming, or how or where. And I recalled that years ago a fellow told me to let him know if I ever needed to have somebody killed. 'You just let me know,' he had said, and I laughed, and that was the last said on the subject. A month or so ago I looked up his number and called him, and he gave me another number to call."

"And you put out a contract."

"Is that the expression? Then that's what I did."

"Suicide by proxy," Keller said.

"And I guess you're holding my proxy," Garrity said, and drank some brandy. "You know, the thought flashed across my mind that first night, talking with you after you pulled my grandson out of the pool. I got this little glimmer, but I told myself I was being ridiculous. A hired killer doesn't turn up and save somebody's life."

"It's out of character," Keller agreed.

"Besides, what would you be doing at the party in the first place? Wouldn't you stay out of sight and wait until you could get me alone?"

"If I'd been thinking straight," Keller said. "I told myself it wouldn't hurt to have a look around. And this joker from the hotel bar assured me I had nothing to worry about. 'Half the town will be at Wally's tonight,' he said."

"Half the town was. You wouldn't have tried anything that night, would you?"

"God, no."

"I remember thinking, I hope he's not here. I hope it's not tonight. Because I was enjoying the party and I didn't want to miss anything. But you *were* there, and a good thing, wasn't it?"

"Yes."

"Saved the boy from drowning. According to the Chinese, you save somebody's life, you're responsible for him for the rest of your life. Because you've interfered with the natural order of things. That make sense to you?"

"Not really."

"Or me either. You can't beat them for whipping up a meal or laundering a shirt, but they've got some queer ideas on other subjects. Of course, they'd probably say the same for some of my notions."

"Probably."

Garrity looked at his glass. "You called my doctor," he said. "Must have been to confirm a suspicion you had. What tipped you off? Is it starting to show in my face, or how I move around?"

Keller shook his head. "I couldn't find anybody else with a motive," he said, "or a grudge against you. You were the only one left. And then I saw you wince once or twice and try to hide it. I barely noticed at the time, but then I started to think about it."

"I thought it would be easier than doing it myself," Garrity said. "I thought I'd just let a professional take me by surprise. I'd be like an old bull elk on a hillside, never expecting the bullet that takes him out in his prime."

"It makes sense."

"No, it doesn't. Because the elk didn't arrange for the hunter to be there. Far as the elk knows, he's all alone. He's not wondering every damn day if today's the day. He's not bracing himself, trying to sense the crosshairs centering on his shoulder."

"I never thought of that."

"Neither did I," said Garrity. "Or I never would have called that fellow in the first place. Mike, what the hell are you doing here tonight? Don't tell me you came over to kill me."

"I came to tell you I can't."

"Because we've come to know each other."

Keller nodded.

"I grew up on a farm," Garrity said. "One of those vanishing family farms you hear about, and of course it's vanished, and I say good riddance. But we raised our own beef and pork, and we kept a milk cow and a flock of laying hens. And we never named the animals we were going to wind up eating. The cow had a name, but not the bull calf she dropped. The breeder sow's name was Elsie, but we never named her piglets."

"Makes sense," Keller said.

"I guess it doesn't take a Chinaman to see how you can't kill me once you've hauled Timmy out of the drink. Let alone after you've sat at my table and smoked my cigars. Reminds me, care for a cigar?"

"No, thank you."

"Well, where do we go from here, Mike? I have to say I'm relieved. I feel like I've been bracing myself for a bullet for weeks now. All of a sudden I've got a new lease on life. I'd say this calls for a drink, except we're already having one and you've scarcely touched yours."

"There is one thing," Keller said.

He left the den while Garrity made his phone call. Timothy was in the living room, puzzling over a chessboard. Keller played a game with him and lost badly. "Can't win 'em all," he said, and tipped over his king.

"I was going to checkmate you," the boy said, "in a few more moves."

"I could see it coming," Keller told him.

He went back to the den. Garrity was selecting a cigar from his humidor. "Sit down," he said. "I'm fixing to smoke one of these things. If you won't kill me, maybe it will."

"You never know."

"I made the call, Mike, and it's all taken care of. Be a while before the word filters through the chain of command, but sooner or later they'll call you and tell you the client changed his mind. He paid in full and called off the job."

They talked some, then sat awhile in silence. At length Keller said he ought to get going. "I should be at my hotel," he said, "in case they call."

"Be a couple of days, won't it?"

"Probably," he said, "but you never know. If everyone involved makes a phone call right away, the word could get to me in a couple of hours."

"Calling you off, telling you to come home. Be glad to get home, I bet."

"It's nice here," he said, "but yes, I'll be glad to get home."

"Wherever it is, they say there's no place like it." Garrity leaned back, then allowed himself to wince at the pain that came over him. "If it never hurts worse than this," he said, "then I can stand it. But of course it will get worse. And I'll decide I can stand *that,* and then it'll get worse again."

There was nothing to say to that.

"I guess I'll know when it's time to do something," Garrity said. "And who knows? Maybe my heart will cut out on me out of the blue. Or I'll get hit by a bus, or I don't know what. Struck by lightning?"

"It could happen."

"Anything can happen," Garrity agreed. He got to his feet. "Mike," he said, "I guess we won't be seeing any more of each other, and I have to say I'm a little bit sorry about that. I've truly enjoyed our time together."

"So have I, Wally."

"I wondered, you know, what he'd be like. The man they'd send to do this kind of work. I don't know what I expected, but you're not it."

He stuck out his hand, and Keller gripped it. "Take care," Garrity said. "Be well, Mike."

Back at his hotel, Keller took a hot bath and got a good night's sleep. In the morning he went out for breakfast, and when he got back there was a message at the desk for him: *Mr. Soderholm — Please call your office.*

He called from a pay phone, even though it didn't matter, and was careful not to overreact when Dot told him to come home, the mission was aborted.

"You told me I had all the time in the world," he said. "If I'd known the guy was in such a rush —"

"Keller," she said, "it's a good thing you waited. What he did, he changed his mind."

"He changed his mind?"

"It used to be a woman's prerogative," Dot said, "but now we've got equality between the sexes, so that means anyone can do it. It works out fine because we're getting paid in full. So kick the dust of Texas off your feet and come on home."

"I'll do that," he said, "but I may hang out here for a few more days."

"Oh?"

"Or even a week," he said. "It's a pretty nice town."

"Don't tell me you're itching to move there, Keller. We've been through this before."

"Nothing like that," he said. "But there's this girl I met."

"Oh, Keller."

"Well, she's nice," he said. "And if I'm off the job there's no reason not to have a date or two with her, is there?"

"Not as long as you don't decide to move in."

"She's not that nice," he said, and Dot laughed and told him not to change.

He hung up and drove around and found a movie he'd been meaning to see. The next morning he packed and checked out of his hotel.

He drove across town and got a room on the motel strip, paying cash in advance for four nights and registering as J. D. Smith from Los Angeles.

There was no girl he'd met, no girl he wanted to meet. But it wasn't time to go home yet.

He had unfinished business, and four days should give him time to do it. Time for Wallace Garrity to get used to the idea of not feeling those imaginary crosshairs on his shoulder blade.

But not so much time that the pain would be too much to bear.

And, sometime in those four days, Keller would deliver a gift. If he could, he'd make it look natural — a heart attack, say, or an accident. In any event it would be swift and without warning, and as close as he could make it to painless.

And it would be unexpected. Garrity would never see it coming.

Keller frowned, trying to figure out how he would manage it. It would be a lot trickier than the task that had drawn him to town originally, but he'd brought it on himself. Getting involved, fishing the boy out of the pool. He'd interfered in the natural order of things. He was under an obligation.

It was the least he could do.

The Man Next Door

FROM *The Plot Thickens*

THE MAN NEXT DOOR had known for weeks that it was time to invite another guest to the secret place, the space he had fashioned out of the utility room in the basement. It had been six months since Tiffany, the last one. She had lasted twenty days, longer than most of the others.

He had tried to put Bree Matthews out of his mind. It didn't make sense to invite her, he knew that. Every morning as he followed his routine, washing the windows, polishing the furniture, vacuuming the carpets, sweeping and washing the walk from the steps to the sidewalk, he reminded himself that it was dangerous to choose a next-door neighbor. *Much* too dangerous.

But he couldn't help it. Bree Matthews was never out of his mind for an instant. Ever since the day she had rung his bell and he had invited her in, he had known. That was when his growing need to have her with him became uncontrollable. She had stood in his foyer, dressed in a loose sweater and jeans, her arms folded, one high-arched foot unconsciously tapping the polished floor as she told him that the leak in her adjoining town house was originating from *his* roof.

"When I bought this place I never thought I'd have so much trouble," she had snapped. "The contractor could have redone Buckingham Palace for what I paid him to renovate, but whenever it rains hard, you'd think I lived under Niagara Falls. Anyway, he *insists* that whoever did your work caused the problem."

Her anger had thrilled him. She was beautiful, in a bold, Celtic way, with midnight blue eyes, fair skin, and blue-black hair. And beneath that she had a slim athlete's body. He guessed her to be in her late twenties, older than the women he usually favored, but still so very appealing.

He had known that even though it was a warm spring afternoon, there was no excuse for the way perspiration began to pour from him as he stood a few inches from her. He wanted so much to reach out and touch her, to push the door closed, to lock her in.

He had blushed and stammered as he explained that there was absolutely no possibility that the leak was coming from his roof, that he'd done all the repairs himself. He suggested she call another contractor for an opinion.

He had almost explained that he had worked for a builder for fifteen years and knew that the guy she had hired was doing a shoddy job, but he managed to stop himself. He didn't want to admit that he had any interest in her or her home, didn't want her to know that he had even noticed, didn't want to give anything about himself away. . . .

A few days later she came up the street as he was outside planting impatiens along the driveway, and stopped to apologize. Following his advice, she had called in a different contractor who confirmed what she had suspected: the first one had done a sloppy job. "He'll hear from me in court," she vowed. "I've had a summons issued for him."

Then, emboldened by her friendliness, he did something foolish. As he stood with her, he was facing their semidetached town houses and once again noticed the lopsided venetian blind on her front window, the one nearest his place. Every time he saw it, it drove him crazy. The vertical blinds on his front windows and those on hers lined up perfectly, which made the sight of that lopsided one bother him as much as hearing a fingernail screech across a blackboard.

So he offered to fix it for her. She turned and looked at the offending blind as if she had never seen it before, then she replied, "Thanks, but why bother? The decorator has window treatments ready to put in as soon as the damage caused by the leaks is repaired. It'll get fixed then."

"Then," of course, could be months from now, but still he was glad she had said no. He had definitely decided to invite her to be his next guest, and when she disappeared there would be questions. The police would ring his bell, make inquiries. "Mr. Mensch, did you see Miss Matthews leave with anyone?" they would ask. "Did you notice anyone visiting her lately? How friendly were you with her?"

He could answer truthfully: "We only spoke casually on the street if we ran into each other. She has a young man she seems to be dating. I've exchanged a few words with him from time to time. Tall, brown hair, about thirty or so. Believe he said his name is Carter. Kevin Carter."

The police would probably already know about Carter. When Matthews disappeared they would talk to her close friends first.

He had never even been questioned about Tiffany. There had been no connection between them, no reason for anyone to ask. Occasionally they ran into each other at museums — he had found several of his young women in museums. The third or fourth time they met he made it a point to ask Tiffany her impression of a painting she was looking at.

He had liked her instantly. Beautiful Tiffany, so appealing, so intelligent. She believed that because he claimed to share her enthusiasm for Gustav Klimt, he was a kindred spirit, a man to be trusted. She had been grateful for his offer of a ride back to Georgetown on a rainy day. He had picked her up as she was walking to the Metro.

She had scarcely felt the prick of the needle that knocked her out. She slumped at his feet in the car, and he drove her back to his place. Matthews was just leaving her house as he pulled into the driveway; he even nodded to her as he clicked the garage door opener. At that time he had no idea that Matthews would be next, of course.

Every morning for the next three weeks, he had spent all his time with Tiffany. He loved having her there. The secret place was bright and cheerful. The floor had a thick yellow pad, like a comfortable mattress, and he had filled the room with books and games.

He had even painted the windowless bathroom adjacent to it a cheery red and yellow, and he had installed a portable shower. Every morning he would lock her in the bathroom, and while she was showering he would vacuum and scrub the secret place. He kept it immaculate. As he did everything in his life. He couldn't abide untidiness. He laid out clean clothes for her every day too. He also washed and ironed the clothes she came in, just as he had with the others. He had even had her jacket cleaned, that silly jacket with the names of cities all over the world. He didn't want to have it cleaned, but noticing that spot on the sleeve drove him crazy. He couldn't get it out of his head. Finally he gave in.

He spent a lot of money cleaning his own clothes as well. Sometimes when he woke up, he would find himself trying to brush away crumbs from the sheets. Was that because he remembered having to do that? There were a lot of questions from his childhood, things he couldn't fully remember. But maybe it was best that way.

He knew he was fortunate. He was able to spend all his time with the women he chose because he didn't have to work. He didn't need the money. His father had never spent a cent on anything besides bare essentials. After high school, when he began working for the builder, his father demanded he turn over his paycheck to him. "I'm saving for you, August," he had said. "It's wasteful to spend money on women. They're all like your mother. Taking everything you have and leaving with another man for California. Said she was too young when we got married, that nineteen was too young to have a baby. Not too young for *my* mother, I told her."

Ten years ago his father died suddenly, and he had been astonished to find that during all those years of penny-pinching, his father had invested in stocks. At thirty-four, he, August Mensch, was worth over a million dollars. Suddenly he could afford to travel and to live the way he wanted to, the way he had dreamed about during all those years of sitting at home at night, listening to his father tell him how his mother neglected him when he was a baby. "She left you in the playpen for hours. When you cried, she'd throw a bottle or some crackers to you. You were her prisoner, not her baby. I bought baby books, but she wouldn't even read to you. I'd come home from work and find you sitting in spilled milk and crumbs, cold and neglected."

August had moved to this place last year, rented this furnished and run-down town house cheaply, and made the necessary repairs himself. He had painted it and scrubbed the kitchen and bathrooms until they shone, and he cleaned the furniture and polished the floors daily. His lease ran out on May first, only twenty days from now. He had already told the owner he was planning to leave. By then he would have had Matthews and it would be time to move on. He would be leaving the place greatly improved. The only thing he would have to take care of was to whitewash all the improvements he had made to the secret place, so no one would ever guess what had happened there.

How many cities had he lived in during the last ten years? he wondered. He had lost track. Seven? Eight? More? Starting with finding his mother in San Diego. He liked Washington, would have stayed there longer. But he knew that after Bree Matthews it wouldn't be a good idea.

What kind of guest would she be? he wondered. Tiffany had been both frightened and angry. She ridiculed the books he bought for her, refusing to read to him. She told him her family had no money, as if that was what he wanted. She told him she wanted to paint. He even bought an easel and art supplies for her.

She actually started one painting while she was visiting, a painting of a man and woman kissing. It was going to be a copy of Klimt's *The Kiss*. He tore it off the easel and told her to copy one of the nice illustrations in the children's books he had given her. That was when she had picked up an open jar of paint and thrown it at him.

August Mensch didn't quite remember the next minutes, just that when he looked down at the sticky mess on his jacket and trousers, he had lunged at her.

When her body was pulled out of a Washington canal the next day, they questioned her ex-boyfriends. The papers were full of the case. He laughed at the speculation about where she had been the three weeks she was missing.

Mensch sighed. He didn't want to think of Tiffany now. He wanted to dust and polish the room again to make it ready for Matthews. Then he had to finish chiseling mortar from the cinder blocks in the wall that separated his basement from hers.

He would remove enough of those blocks to gain entry into Matthews' basement. He would bring her back the same way. He knew she had installed a security system, but this way it wouldn't do her any good. Then he would replace the cinder blocks and carefully re-cement.

It was Sunday night. He had watched her house all day. She hadn't gone out at all. Lately she had stayed in on Sundays, since Carter stopped coming around. He had seen him there last a couple of weeks ago.

He brushed away an invisible piece of dust. Tomorrow at this time she would be with him; she'd be his companion. He had bought a stack of Dr. Seuss books for her to read to him. He had thrown out all the other books. Some had been splattered with red paint. All of them reminded him how Tiffany had refused to read to him.

Over the years, he had always tried to make his guests comfortable. It wasn't his fault that they were always ungrateful. He remembered how the one in Kansas City told him she wanted a steak. He had bought a thick one, the thickest he could find. When he came back he could see that she had used the time he was out to try to escape. She hadn't wanted the steak at all. He'd lost his temper. He couldn't remember exactly what happened after that.

He hoped Bree would be nicer.

He'd soon know. Tomorrow morning he would make his move.

"What is *that?*" Bree muttered to herself as she stood at the head of the stairs leading to her basement. She could hear a faint scraping sound emanating from the basement of the adjacent town house.

She shook her head. What did it matter? She couldn't sleep anyway. It was irritating, though. Only six o'clock on a Monday morning, and Mensch was already on some do-it-yourself project. Some neat-as-a-pin improvement, no doubt, she said to herself, already in a bad temper.

She sighed. What a rotten day it was going to be. She had a lousy cold. There was no point getting up so early, but she wasn't sleepy. She had felt miserable yesterday and had stayed in bed all day, dozing. She hadn't even bothered to pick up the phone, just listened to messages. Her folks were away. Gran didn't call, and a certain Mr. Kevin Carter never put his finger on the touch tone.

Now cold or no cold, she was due in court at nine A.M. to try to make that first contractor pay for the repairs she had to do to the roof he was supposed to have fixed. To say nothing of getting him to pay for the damage inside caused by the leaks. She closed the basement door decisively and went into the kitchen, squeezed a grapefruit, made coffee, toasted an English muffin, settled at the breakfast bar.

She had begun to refer to this town house as the dwelling-from-hell, but once all the damage was repaired she had to admit it would be lovely.

She tried to eat her breakfast, but found she couldn't. I've never testified in court, she thought. That's why I'm nervous and down.

But I'm sure the judge will side with me, she reassured herself. No judge would put up with having his or her house ruined.

Bree — short for Bridget — Matthews, thirty, single, blue-eyed and dark-haired, with porcelain skin that wouldn't tolerate the sun, was admittedly jumpy by nature. Buying this place last year had so far been an expensive mistake. For once I should *not* have listened to Granny, she thought, then smiled unconsciously thinking of how from her retirement community in Connecticut her grandmother still burned up the wires giving her good advice.

Eight years ago she was the one who told me I should take the job in Washington working for our congressman even though she thought he was a dope, Bree remembered as she forced herself to eat half of the English muffin. Then she advised me to grab the chance to join Douglas Public Relations when I got that offer. She's been right about everything except about buying this place and renovating it, Bree thought. "Real estate's a good way to make money, Bree," she had said, "especially in Georgetown."

Wrong! Bree frowned grimly as she sipped coffee. My Pierre Deux wallhangings are stained and peeling. And it's not wall*paper,* mind you, not when you spring for seventy dollars a yard. At that price the stuff becomes wall*hanging.* She frowned as she remembered explaining that to Kevin, who had said, "Now, that's what I call pretentious." Just what she needed to hear!

Mentally she reviewed everything she would tell the judge: "The Persian carpet that Granny proudly put on the floor of her first house is rolled and wrapped in plastic to be sure no new leaks can damage it further, and the polish on the parquet floors is dull and stained. I've got pictures to show just how bad my home looks. I wish you'd look at them, your honor. Now I'm waiting for the painter and floor guy to come back to charge a fortune to redo what they did perfectly well four months ago.

"I asked, pleaded, begged, even snarled at that contractor, trying to get him to take care of the leak. Then when he finally did show up, he told me that the water was coming from my neighbor's roof, and I believed him. I made a dope of myself ringing his bell, accusing poor Mr. Mensch of causing all the problems. You see, your honor, we share a common wall, and the contractor said the water was getting in that way. I, of course, believed him. He is supposed to be the expert."

Bree thought of her next-door neighbor, the balding guy with the graying ponytail who looked embarrassed just to say hello if they ran into each other on the street. The day that she had gone storming over, he had invited her in. At first he had listened to her rant with calm, unblinking eyes, his face thoughtful — as she imagined a priest would look during confession, if she could see through the screen, of course. Then he had suddenly started blushing and perspiring and almost whispered his protest that it couldn't be his roof, because surely he would have a leak too. She should call another contractor, he said.

"I scared the poor guy out of his wits," she had told Kevin that night. "I should have known the minute I saw the way he keeps his place that he'd never tolerate a leaking roof. The polish on the floor in his foyer almost blinded me. I bet when he was a kid he got a medal for being the neatest boy in camp."

Kevin. That was something else. Try as she might, she couldn't keep him from coming to mind. She would be seeing him this morning, the first time in a while. He had insisted on meeting her in court even though they were no longer dating.

I've never brought anyone to court, she thought, and going there is definitely not my idea of a good time, particularly since I absolutely do not want to see Kevin. Pouring herself a second cup of coffee, she settled back at the breakfast bar. Just because Kev helped me file the complaint, she thought, he's going to be Johnny-on-the-spot in court today, which thank you very much I don't need. I do not want to see him. At all. And it's such a gloomy day all around. Bree looked out the window at the thick fog. She shook her head, her mouth set in a hard line. In fact, her irritation with Kevin had become so pronounced she practically blamed him for the leaking roof. He no longer called every morning, or sent flowers on the seventeenth of every month, the seventeenth being the day on which they had their first date. That was ten months ago, just after Bree had moved in to the town house. Bree felt the hard line of her mouth turning down at the corners, and she shook her head again. I love being independent, she thought ruefully, but sometimes I hate being alone.

Bree knew she had to get over all this. She realized that she was getting in the habit of regularly rearguing her quarrel with Kevin Carter. She also realized that when she missed him most — like this past Saturday, when she had moped around, going to a movie and having dinner alone, or yesterday when she stayed in bed feeling lonely and lousy — she needed to reinforce her sense of being in the right.

Bree remembered their fight, which like most had started out small and soon took on epic, life-changing proportions. Kev said I was foolish not to accept the settlement the contractor offered me, she recalled, that I probably won't get much more by going to court, but I wouldn't think of it. I'm pigheaded and love a fight and always shoot from the hip. Telling me that I was becoming irrational about this, he said that, for example, I had no business storming next door after that shy little guy. I reminded him that I apologized profusely, and Mr. Mensch was so sweet about it that he even offered to fix that broken blind in the living room window.

Somewhat uncomfortably, Bree remembered that there had been a pause in their exchange, but instead of letting it go, she had then told Kevin that he seemed to be the one who loved a fight, and why did he have to always take everybody else's side? That was when he said maybe we should step back and examine our relationship. And I said that if it has to be examined, then it didn't exist, so good-bye.

She sighed. It had been a very long two weeks.

I really wish Mensch would stop that damn tinkering or whatever he's doing in his basement, she thought, hearing the noise again. Lately he had been giving her the creeps. She had seen him watching her when she got out of the car, and she had felt his eyes following her whenever she moved about her yard. Maybe he did take offense that day and is brooding about it, she reasoned. She had been thinking about telling Kevin that Mensch was making her nervous — but then they had the quarrel, and she never got the chance. Anyway, Mensch seemed harmless enough.

Bree shrugged, then got up, still holding her coffee cup. I'm just all around jumpy, she thought, but in a couple of hours this will be behind me, one way or the other. Tonight I'll come home early, go to bed and sleep off this damn cold, and tomorrow I'll start to get the house in shipshape again.

Again the scraping sound came from the basement. Knock it off, she almost said aloud. Briefly debating going down to see what was causing the noise, she decided against it. So Mensch has a do-it-yourself project going, she thought. It's none of my business.

Then the scraping noise stopped, followed by hollow silence. Was that a footstep on the basement stairs? Impossible. The basement door that led outside was bolted and armed. Then what was causing it? . . .

She whirled around to see her next-door neighbor standing behind her, a hypodermic needle in his hand.

As she dropped the coffee cup, he plunged the needle deep into her arm.

Kevin Carter, J.D., felt the level of his irritability hit the danger zone. This was just another example of Bree's total inability to listen to reason, he thought. She's pigheaded. Strong-willed. Impulsive. So where in hell was she?

The contractor, Richie Ombert, had shown up on time. A surly-looking guy, he kept looking at his watch and mumbling about being due on a job. He raised his voice as he reiterated his position to his lawyer: "I offered to fix the leak, but by then she'd had it done at six times what I coulda done it for. Twice I'd sent someone to look at it and she wasn't home. Once the guy who inspected it said he thought it was coming from the next roof, said there hasta be a leak there. Guess that little squirt who rented next door fixed it. Anyhow, I offered to pay what it woulda cost me."

Bree had been due in court at nine o'clock. When she hadn't shown up by ten, the judge dismissed the complaint.

A furious Kevin Carter went to his job at the State Department. He did not call Bridget Matthews at Douglas Public Relations where she worked, nor did he attempt to call her at home. The next call between them was going to come from her. She owed him an apology. He tried not to remember that after she had gotten her day in court, he had planned to tell her that he missed her like hell and please, let's make up.

Mensch dragged Bree's limp body through the kitchen to the hallway that led to the basement stairs. He slid her down, step by step, until he reached the bottom; then he bent down and picked her up. Clearly she hadn't bothered to do anything with her basement. The cinder-block walls were gray and dreary, the floor tiles were clean but shabby. He had made the opening in the wall in the boiler room where it would be least noticed. He had pulled the cinder blocks into his basement, so now all he had to do was to secure her in the secret place, come back to get her clothing, then replace and re-mortar the blocks.

The opening he had made was just large enough to slide her body through and then crawl in after her. In his basement he picked her up again and carried her to the secret place. She was still knocked out, so there was no resistance as he attached the restraints to her wrists and ankles, and, as a precaution, tied the scarf loosely around her mouth. He could tell from her breathing that she had a cold. He certainly didn't want her to suffocate.

For a moment he reveled in the sight of her, limp and lovely, her hair tumbling onto the mattress, her body relaxed and peaceful. He straightened her terry-cloth robe and tucked it around her.

Now that she was here, he felt so strong, so calm. He had been shocked to find her in the kitchen so early in the morning. Now he had to move quickly: to get her clothes and her purse, to wipe up that spilled coffee. It had to look as if she disappeared after she left the house.

He looked at the answering machine in her kitchen, the blinking light indicating there had been seven calls. That was odd, he thought. He knew she hadn't gone out at all yesterday. Was it possible she didn't bother to answer the phone all day?

He played the messages back. All calls from friends. "How are you?" "Let's get together." "Good luck in court." "Hope you make that contractor pay." The last message was from the same person as the first: "Guess you're still out. I'll try you tomorrow."

Mensch took a moment to sit down at the breakfast bar. It was very important that he think all this through. Matthews had not gone out at all yesterday. It seemed as though she also hadn't answered her phone all day. Suppose instead of just taking her clothes to make it look as though she'd left for work, I tidied up the house so that people would think she hadn't reached home at all on Saturday night. After all, he had seen her come up the block alone at around eleven, the newspaper under her arm. Who was there to say she had arrived safely?

Mensch got up. He already had his Latex gloves on. He started looking about. The garbage container under the kitchen sink was empty. He took a fresh disposable bag from the drawer and put in it the squeezed grapefruit, coffee grinds, and pieces of the cup Bree had dropped.

Working methodically, he cleaned the kitchen, even taking time to scour the pot she had left on the stove. How careless of her to let it get burned, he thought.

Upstairs in her bedroom, he made the bed and picked up the Sunday edition of the *Washington Post* that was on the floor next to it. He put the paper in the garbage bag. She had left a suit on the bed. He hung it up in the closet where she kept that kind of clothing.

Next he cleaned the bathroom. Her washer and dryer were in the bathroom, concealed by louvered doors. On top of the washer he found the jeans and sweater he had seen her wearing on Saturday. It hadn't started raining at the time, but she had also had on her yellow raincoat. He collected the sweater and jeans and her undergarments and sneakers and socks. Then from her dresser he selected more undergarments. From her closets he took a few pairs of slacks and sweaters. They were basically nondescript, and he knew they would never be missed.

He found her raincoat and shoulder bag in the foyer by the front door. Mensch looked at his watch. It was seven thirty, time to go. He had to replace and re-mortar the cinder blocks.

He looked around to be sure he had missed nothing. His eye fell on the lopsided venetian blind in the front window. A knifelike pain went through his skull; his gorge rose. He felt almost physically ill. He couldn't stand to look at it.

Mensch put the clothing and purse and garbage bag on the floor. In quick, determined steps he reached the window and put his gloved hand on the blind.

The cord was broken, but there was enough slack to tie it and still level the blind.

He breathed a long sigh of relief when he finished the task. It now stopped at exactly the same level as the other two and as his, just grazing the sill.

He felt much better now. With neat, compact movements he gathered up Bree's coat, shoulder bag, clothing, and the garbage bag.

Two minutes later he was in his own basement, replacing the cinder blocks.

At first Bree thought she was having a nightmare — a Disney World nightmare. When she woke up she opened her eyes to see cinderblock walls painted with evenly spaced brown slats. The space was small, not much more than six by nine feet, and she was lying on a bright yellow plastic mattress of some sort. It was soft, as though it had quilts inside it. About three feet from the ceiling a band of yellow paint connected the slats at the top to resemble a railing. Above the band, decals lined the walls: Mickey Mouse. Cinderella. Kermit the Frog. Miss Piggy. Sleeping Beauty. Pocahontas.

She suddenly realized that there was a gag over her face, and she tried to push it away, but could only move her arm a few inches. Her arms and legs were held in some kind of restraints.

The grogginess was lifting now. Where was she? What had happened? Panic overwhelmed her as she remembered turning to see Mensch, her neighbor, standing behind her in the kitchen. Where had he taken her? Where was he now?

She looked around slowly, then her eyes widened. This room, wherever it was, resembled an oversized playpen. Stacked nearby were a series of children's books, all with thin spines except for the thick volume at the bottom. She could read the lettering: *Grimm's Fairy Tales.*

How had she gotten here? She remembered she had been about to get dressed to go to court. She had tossed the suit she had planned to wear across the bed. It was new. She wanted to look good, and in truth, more for Kevin than for the judge. Now she admitted that much to herself.

Kevin. Of course he would come looking for her when she didn't show up in court. He'd know something had happened to her.

Ica, her housekeeper, would look for her too. She came in on Mondays. She'd know something was wrong. Bree remembered dropping the coffee cup she was holding. It shattered on the kitchen floor as Mensch grabbed her and stuck the needle in her arm. Ica would know that she wouldn't leave spilled coffee and a broken cup for her to clean up.

As her head cleared, Bree remembered that just before she had turned and seen Mensch, she had heard a footstep on the basement stairs. Her mouth went dry at the thought that somehow he had come in through the basement. But how? Her basement door was bolted and armed, the window barred.

Then sheer panic swept through her. Clearly this hadn't just "happened"; this had been carefully planned. She tried to scream, but could only make a muffled gasping cry. She tried to pray, a single sentence that in her soul she repeated over and over: *"Please, God, let Kevin find me."*

Late Tuesday afternoon Kevin received a worried phone call from the agency where Bree worked. Had he heard from her? She never showed up for work on Monday, and she hadn't phoned. They thought she might have been stuck in court all day yesterday, but now they were concerned.

Fifteen minutes later, August Mensch watched through a slit in his front window drapery as Kevin Carter held his finger on the doorbell to Bree Matthews' town house.

He watched as Carter stood on the front lawn and looked in the living room window. He half expected that Carter would ring his doorbell, but that didn't happen. Instead he stood for a few minutes looking irresolute, then looked in the window of the garage. Mensch knew her car was there. In a way he wished he could have gotten rid of it, but that had been impossible.

He watched until Carter, his shoulders slumped, walked slowly back to his car and drove away.

With a satisfied smile, Mensch walked down the foyer to the basement steps. Savoring the sight that would greet him, he descended slowly, then walked across the basement, as always admiring his tools and paints and polishes, all placed in perfect order on shelves, or hanging in precise rows from neatly squared pegboard.

Snow shovels hung over the cinder blocks that he had removed to gain entry into Matthews' basement. Beneath them the mortar had dried, and he had carefully smeared it with the dry flakes he had kept when he separated the blocks. Now nothing showed, either here or on Bridget Matthews' side. He was sure of that.

Then he crossed through the boiler room, and beyond it, to the secret place.

Matthews was lying on the mat, the restraints still on her arms and legs. She looked up at him and he could see that underneath the anger, fear was beginning to take hold. That was smart of her.

She was wearing a sweater and slacks, things he had taken from her closet.

He knelt before her and removed the gag from her mouth. It was a silk scarf, tied so that it was neither too tight nor caused a mark. "Your boyfriend was just looking for you," he told her. "He's gone now."

He loosened the restraints on her left arm and leg. "What book would you like to read to me today, Mommy?" he asked, his voice suddenly childlike and begging.

On Thursday morning Kevin sat in the office of FBI agent Lou Ferroni. The nation's capital was awash with cherry blossoms, but as he stared out the window he was unaware of them. Everything seemed a blur, especially the last two days: his frantic call to the police, the questions, the calls to Bree's family, the calls to friends, the sudden involvement of the FBI. What was Ferroni saying? Kevin forced himself to listen.

"She's been gone long enough for us to consider her a missing person," the agent said. Fifty-three years old and nearing retirement, Ferroni realized that he'd seen the look on Carter's face far too often in the past twenty-eight years, always on the faces of those left behind. Shock. Fear. Heartsick that the person they love may not be alive.

Carter was the boyfriend, or ex-boyfriend. He'd freely admitted that he and Matthews had quarreled. Ferroni wasn't eliminating him as a suspect, but he seemed unlikely and his alibi checked out. Bridget, or Bree, as her friends called her, had been in her house on Saturday, that much they knew. They had not been able to locate anyone who saw or spoke to her on Sunday, though, and she hadn't shown up for her court appointment on Monday.

"Let's go over it again," Ferroni suggested. "You say that Miss Matthews' housekeeper was surprised to find the bed made and dishes done when she came in Monday morning?" He had already spoken with the housekeeper, but wanted to see if there were any discrepancies in Carter's story.

Kevin nodded. "I called Ica as soon as I realized Bree was missing. She has a key to Bree's place. I picked her up and she let me in. Of course Bree wasn't there. Ica told me that when she went in on Monday morning she couldn't understand why the bed was made and the dishes run through in the dishwasher. It just wasn't normal. Bree never made the bed on Monday because that was when Ica changed it. So that meant the bed had not been slept in Sunday night, and that Bree could have vanished any time between Saturday and Sunday night."

Ferroni's gut instinct told him that the misery he was seeing in Kevin Carter's face was genuine. So if he didn't do it, who did that leave? Richie Ombert, the contractor Matthews was suing, had had several complaints filed against him for using abusive language and threatening gestures toward disgruntled customers.

Certainly the renovation business caused tempers to flare. Ferroni knew that firsthand. His wife had been ready to practically murder the guy who built the addition on their house. Ombert, though, seemed worse than most. He had a nasty edge, and for the moment he was a prime suspect in Bridget Matthews' disappearance.

There was one aspect of this case Ferroni was not prepared to share with Carter. The computer of VICAP, the FBI's violent criminal apprehension program, had been tracking a particular pattern of disappearing young women. The trail started some ten years ago in California, when a young art student disappeared. Her body showed up three weeks later; she had been strangled. The weird part was that when she was found she was dressed in the same clothes as when she had disappeared, and they were freshly washed and pressed. There was no sign of molestation, no hint of violence beyond the obvious cause of death. But where had she been those three weeks?

Shortly afterwards the VICAP computer spat out a case in Arizona with striking similarities. One followed in New Mexico, then Colorado . . . North Dakota . . . Wisconsin . . . Kansas . . . Missouri . . . Indiana . . . Ohio . . . Pennsylvania. . . . Finally, six months ago, there in D.C., an art student, Tiffany Wright, had disappeared. Her body was fished out of a Washington canal three weeks later, but it had been there only a short time. Except for the effect the water had had on her clothes, they were neat. The only odd note was some faint spots of red paint, the kind artists use, still visible on her blouse.

That little clue had started them working on the art student angle, looking among her classmates. It was the first time there had been any kind of stain or mark or rip or tear on any of the women's clothes. So far, however, it had led nowhere. Odds were that the disappearance of Bridget Matthews was not tied to the death of Tiffany Wright. It would be a marked departure in the serial killer's method of operation for him to strike twice in one city, but then maybe he was changing his habits.

"By any chance is Miss Matthews interested in art?" Ferroni asked Carter. "Does she take art lessons as a hobby?"

Kevin kneaded his forehead, trying to relieve the ache that reminded him of the one time in his life he had had too much to drink.

Bree, where are you?

"She never took art lessons that I know of. Bree was more into music and the theater," he said. "We went to Kennedy Center pretty frequently. She particularly liked concerts."

Liked? he thought. Why am I using the past tense? No, God, no!

Ferroni consulted the notes in his hand. "Kevin, I want to go over this again. It's important. You were familiar with the house. There may be something you noticed when you went in with the housekeeper."

Kevin hesitated.

"What is it?" Ferroni asked quickly.

Through haggard eyes, Kevin stared at him. Then he glumly shook his head. "There *was* something different; I sensed it at the time. But I don't know what it was."

How many days have I been here? Bree asked herself. She had lost count. Three? Five? They were all blending together. Mensch had just gone upstairs with her breakfast tray. She knew he'd be back within the hour for her to begin reading to him again.

He had a routine he followed rigidly. In the morning, he came down carrying fresh clothing for her, a blouse or sweater, jeans or slacks. Obviously he had taken the time to go through her closet and dresser after he had knocked her out. It appeared that he had only brought casual clothes that were washable.

Next he would unshackle her hands, connect the leg restraints to each other at the ankles, then lead her to the bathroom, drop the clean clothes on a chair, and lock her in. A minute later she'd hear the whir of the vacuum.

She had studied him closely. He was thin but strong. No matter how she tried to think of a way to escape, she was sure she couldn't manage it. The ankle restraints forced her to shuffle a few feet at a time, so she clearly couldn't outrun him. There was nothing that she could use to stun him long enough for her to get up the stairs and out the door.

She knew where she was — the basement of his town house. The wall on the right was the one that they shared. She thought of how upset she had been about the stained wallpaper on that wall. No, not wall*paper* — wall*hanging*, Bree reminded herself, fighting back an hysterical wave of laughter.

By now the police are looking for me, she thought. Kevin will tell them how I accused Mensch of causing the leak in the roof. They'll investigate him, then they'll realize there's something weird about him. Surely they can't miss that?

Will Mom and Dad tell Gran that I'm missing? Please God, don't let them tell her. It would be too much of a shock for her.

She had to believe that somehow the police would start to investigate Mensch. It seemed so obvious that he must have kidnapped her. Surely they would figure it out? But, of course, trapped here in this cell she had no idea what anyone outside might be thinking. Someone would have missed her by now — she was certain of that — but where were they looking? She had absolutely no idea, and unless Mensch radically altered his routine, there would be no opportunity to let them know she was here. No, she would just have to wait and hope. And stay alive. To stay alive she had to keep him appeased until help came. As long as she read the children's books to him, he seemed to be satisfied.

Last night she had given him a list of books by Roald Dahl that he should get. He had been pleased. "None of my guests were as nice as you," he told her.

What had he *done* to those women? Don't think about that, Bree warned herself fiercely — it worries him when you show that you're afraid. She had realized that the one time she broke down sobbing and begged him to release her. That was when he told her that the police had rung his bell and asked when the last time was that he had seen Miss Matthews.

"I told them I was on my way back from the supermarket Saturday, around two o'clock, and I saw you go out. They asked what you were wearing. I said it was overcast and you had on a bright yellow raincoat and slacks. They thanked me and said I was very helpful," he said calmly, in his sing-song voice.

That was when she became almost hysterical.

"You're making too much noise," he told her. He put one hand on her mouth, while the other encircled her throat. For a moment she thought he was going to strangle her. But then he hesitated and said, "Promise to be quiet, and I'll let you read to me. Please, Mommy, don't cry."

Since then she had managed to hold her emotion in check.

Bree steeled herself. She could sense that he'd be back any moment. Then she heard it, the turning of the handle. Oh, God, please, she prayed, let them find me.

Mensch came in. She could see that he looked troubled. "My landlord phoned," he told her. "He said that according to the contract he has the right to show this place two weeks before the lease is up. That's Monday, and it's Friday already. And I have to take all the decorations down from here and whitewash the walls and also the walls of the bathroom and give them time to dry. That will take the whole weekend. So this has to be our last day together, Bridget. I'm sorry. I'll go out and buy some more books, but I guess you should try to read to me a little faster. . . ."

At ten o'clock on Friday morning, Kevin was once again in Lou Ferroni's office in the FBI building.

"Thanks to the publicity, we've been able to pretty much cover Miss Matthews' activities on Saturday," Agent Ferroni told him. "Several neighbors reported they saw her walking down the street at about two o'clock on Saturday. They agree that she was wearing a bright yellow raincoat and jeans and carrying a shoulder bag. We know the raincoat and bag are missing from her home. We don't know what she did on Saturday afternoon, but we do know she had dinner alone at Antonio's in Georgetown and went to the nine o'clock showing of the new Batman film at the Beacon Theater."

Bree had dinner alone on Saturday night, Kevin thought. So did I. And she genuinely likes those crazy Batman films. We've laughed about that. I can't stand them, but I had promised to see that one with her.

"No one seems to have seen Miss Matthews after that," Ferroni continued. "But we do have one piece of information that we find significant. We've learned that the contractor she was suing was in the same movie theater that night at the same showing. He claims he drove directly home, but there's no one to back up his story. He apparently separated from his wife recently."

Ferroni did not add that the contractor had mouthed off to a number of people about what he'd like to do to the dame who was hauling him into court over what he termed "some silly leak."

"We're working on the theory that Miss Matthews did not get home that night. Was she in the habit of using the Metro instead of her car?"

"The Metro or a cab if she was going directly from place to place. She said trying to park was too much of a nuisance." Kevin could see that Ferroni was starting to believe that Richie Ombert, the contractor, was responsible for Bree's disappearance. He thought of Ombert in court this past Monday. Surly. Aggravated. Noisily elated when the judge dismissed the complaint.

He wasn't acting, Kevin thought. He seemed genuinely surprised and relieved when Bree didn't show up. No, Ombert is not the answer. He shook his head, trying to clear it. He suddenly felt as though he were being smothered. He had to get out of here. "There are no other leads?" he asked Ferroni.

The FBI agent thought of the briefly considered theory that Bree Matthews had been abducted by a serial killer. "No," he said firmly, then added, "How is Miss Matthews' family? Has her father gone back to Connecticut?"

"He had to. We're in constant touch, but Bree's grandmother had a mild heart attack Tuesday evening. One of those horrible coincidences. Bree's mother is with her. You can imagine the state she's in. That's why Bree's father went back."

Ferroni shook his head. "I'm sorry. I wish I thought we'd get good news." He realized that in a way it would have been better if they thought the serial killer had Matthews. All the women he had abducted had lived for several weeks after disappearing. That would at least give them more time.

Kevin got up. "I'm going to Bree's house," he said. "I'm going to call every one of the people in her phone book."

Ferroni raised his eyebrows.

"I want to see if anyone spoke to her on Sunday," Kevin said simply.

"With all the publicity these last few days about her disappearance, any friend who spoke to her would have come forward, I'm sure of that," Ferroni told him. "How do you think we traced her movements on Saturday?"

Kevin did not answer.

"What about her answering machine? Were there any messages on it?" Kevin asked.

"Not from Sunday, or if there had been, they were erased," Ferroni replied. "At first we thought it might be significant, but then we realized that she could have called in and gotten them just by using the machine's code."

Kevin shook his head dejectedly. He had to get out of there. He had promised to phone Ica after his meeting with Ferroni but decided to wait and call her from Bree's house instead. He realized he was frantic to be there, that somehow being around her things made him feel nearer to Bree.

Her neighbor, the guy with the ponytail, was coming down the block when Kevin parked in front of the house. He was carrying a shopping bag from the bookstore. Their eyes met, but neither man spoke. Instead the neighbor nodded, then turned to go up his walk.

Wouldn't you think he'd have the decency to at least *ask* about Bree? Kevin thought bitterly. Too damn busy washing his windows or tending his lawn to give a damn about anyone else.

Or maybe he's embarrassed to ask. Afraid of what he'll hear. Kevin took out the key Ica had given him, let himself in to the house, and phoned her.

"Can you come over and help me?" he asked. "There's something about this place that's bugging me. Something's just not quite right, and I can't figure out what it is. Maybe you can help."

While he waited, he stared at the phone. Bree was one of the few women he had ever known who considered the phone an intrusion. "At home we always turned off the ringer at mealtime," she had told him. "It's so much more civilized."

So civilized that now we don't know if anyone spoke to you on Sunday, Kevin thought. He looked around; there's got to be a clue here somewhere, he told himself. Why was he so sure that the contractor wasn't the answer to Bree's disappearance?

Restlessly he began to walk around the downstairs floor. He stopped at the door of the front room. The contrast to the cheery kitchen and den was striking. Here as in the dining room, because of the water damage, the furniture and carpet were covered with plastic and pushed to the center of the room.

The wallpaper — or wall*hanging* (as Bree had insisted it be called) — a soft ivory with a faint stripe, was stained and bubbled.

Kevin remembered how happy Bree had been when all the decorating was supposedly finished three months ago. They'd even talked around the subject of marriage, in the same sentence mentioning her town house and the marvelous old farmhouse he had bought for Virginia weekends.

Too damn cautious to commit ourselves, Kevin thought bitterly. But not too cautious to have a fight over nothing. It had all been so silly.

He thought about sitting with her in that same room, the warm ivories and reds and blues of the Persian carpet repeated up in the newly reupholstered couch and chairs. Bree had pointed to the vertical metal blinds.

"I hate those damn things," she had said. "The last one doesn't even close properly, but I wanted to get everything else in before I choose draperies."

The blinds. He looked up.

The doorbell rang, interrupting his train of thought. It was Ica. The handsome Jamaican woman's face mirrored the misery he felt. "I haven't slept two hours straight this week," she said. "Looks to me as though you haven't either."

Kevin nodded. "Ica, there's something about this house that's bothering me, something I ought to be noticing. Help me."

She nodded. "It's funny you should say that, 'cause I felt that way too, but blamed it on finding the bed being made and the dishes done. But if Bree didn't get home Saturday night, then that would explain those things. She never left the place untidy."

Together they walked up the stairs to the bedroom. Ica looked around uncertainly. "The room felt different when I got here Monday, different from the way it usually feels," she said hesitantly.

"In what way?" Kevin asked quickly.

"It was . . . well, it was way too neat." Ica walked over to the bed. "Those throw pillows, Bree just tossed them around, like the way they are now."

"What are you telling me?" Kevin asked. He grabbed her arm, aware that Ica was about to tell him what he needed to know.

"This whole place felt just — too neat. I stripped the bed even though it was made because I wanted to change the sheets. I had to dig and pull the sheets and blanket loose, they were tucked in so tight. And the throw pillows on top of the quilt were all lined up against the headboard like little soldiers."

"Anything else? Please just keep talking, Ica. We may be getting somewhere," Kevin begged.

"Yes," Ica said excitedly. "Last week Bree had let a pot boil over. I scoured it as best I could and left a note for her to pick up some steel wool and scouring powder; I said I'd finish it when I came back. Monday morning that pot was sitting out on the stove, scrubbed clean as could be. I know my Bree. She never would have touched it. She told me those strong soaps made her hands break out. Come on, I'll show it to you."

Together they ran down the stairs into the kitchen. From the cupboard she pulled out a gleaming pot. "There isn't even a mark on the bottom," she said. "You'd think it was practically brand new." She looked excitedly at Kevin. "Things just weren't right here. The bed was made too neatly. This pot is too clean."

"And . . . and the blind in the front window has been fixed," Kevin shouted. "It's lined up like the ones next door."

He didn't know he had been about to say that, but suddenly he realized that was what had been bothering him all along. He had sensed the difference right away, but the effect had been so subtle, it had registered only in his subconscious. But now that he had brought it into focus, he thought of the neighbor, the quiet guy with the ponytail, the one who was always washing his windows or trimming his lawn or sweeping his walk.

What did anyone know about him? If he rang the bell, Bree might have let him in. And he had offered to fix the blind — Bree had mentioned that. Kevin pulled Ferroni's card from his pocket and handed it to Ica. "I'm going next door. Tell Ferroni to get over here fast."

"Just one more book. That's all we'll have time for. Then you'll leave me again, Mommy. Just like she did. Just like all of them did."

In the two hours she had been reading to him, Bree had watched Mensch regress from adoring to angry child. He's working up the courage to kill me, she thought.

He was sitting cross-legged beside her on the mat.

"But I want to read *all* of them to you," she said, her voice soothing, coaxing. "I know you'll love them. Then tomorrow I could help you to paint the walls. We could get it done so much faster if we work together. Then we could go away somewhere together, so I can keep reading to you."

He stood up abruptly. "You're trying to trick me. You don't want to go with me. You're just like all the others." He stared at her, his eyes shuttered and small with anger. "I saw your boyfriend go into your house a little while ago. He's too nosy. It's good that you're wearing the jeans. I have to get your raincoat and shoulder bag." He looked as if he was about to cry. "There's no time for any more books," he said sadly.

He rushed out. I'm going to die, Bree thought. Frantically she tried to pull her arms and legs free of the restraints. Her right arm swung up and she realized that he'd forgotten to refasten the shackle to the wall. He had said Kevin was next door. She had heard that you can transfer thoughts. She closed her eyes and concentrated: *Kevin, help me. Kevin, I need you.*

She had to play for time. She would have only one chance at him, one moment of surprise. She would swing at his head with the dangling shackle, try to stun him. But what good would that do? Save her for a few seconds? *Then* what? she thought despondently. How could she stop him?

Her eyes fell on the stack of books. Maybe there was a way. She grabbed the first one and began tearing the pages, scattering the pieces, forcing them to flutter hither and yon across the bright yellow mattress.

I must have known that today was the day, Mensch thought as he retrieved Bree's raincoat and shoulder bag from the bedroom closet. I laid out jeans and the red sweater she was wearing that Saturday. When they find her it will be like all the others. And again they will ask that same question: Where was she for the days she had been missing? It would be fun to read about it. Everyone wanting to know, and only he would have the answer.

As he came down the stairs, he stopped suddenly. The doorbell was ringing. The button was being held down. He laid down the pocketbook and the coat and stood frozen momentarily with uncertainty. Should he answer? Would it seem suspicious if he didn't? No. Better to get rid of her, get her out of here fast, he decided.

Mensch picked up the raincoat and rushed down the basement stairs.

I know he's in there, Kevin thought, but he's not answering. I've got to get inside.

Ica was running across the lawn. "Mr. Ferroni is on his way. He said to absolutely wait for him. Not to ring the bell anymore. He got all excited when I talked about everything being so neat. He said if it's what he thinks it is, Bree will still be alive."

It seemed to Kevin that he could hear Bree crying out to him. He was overwhelmed by a sense of running out of time, by an awareness that he had to get into Mensch's house immediately. He ran to the front window and strained to look in. Through the slats he could see the rigidly neat living room. Craning his head, he could see the stairway in the foyer. Then his blood froze. A woman's leather shoulder bag was on the last step. Bree's shoulder bag! He recognized it; he had given it to her for her birthday.

Frantically he ran to the sidewalk where a refuse can stood waiting to be emptied. He dumped the contents onto the street, ran back with the can, and overturned it under the window. As Ica steadied it for him, he climbed up, then kicked in the window. As the glass shattered, he kicked away the knifelike edges and jumped into the room. He raced up the stairs, shouting Bree's name.

Finding no one there, he clattered down the stairs again, pausing only long enough to open the front door. "Tell the FBI I'm inside, Ica."

He raced through the rooms on the ground floor and still found no one.

There was only one place left to search: the basement.

Finally the ringing stopped. Whoever had been at the door had gone away. Mensch knew he had to hurry. The raincoat and a plastic bag over his arm, he strode across the basement, through the boiler room, and opened the door to the secret room.

Then he froze. Bits of paper littered the yellow plastic. Matthews was tearing up the books, his baby books. "Stop it!" he shrieked.

His head hurt, his throat was closing. He had a pain in his chest. The room was a mess; he had to clean it up.

He felt dizzy, almost as if he couldn't breathe. It was as if the mess of papers was smothering him! He had to clean it up so he could breathe!

Then he would kill her. Kill her slowly. He ran into the bathroom, grabbed the wastebasket, ran back and began scooping up the shredded paper and mangled books. His frenzied hands worked quickly, efficiently. In only minutes there wasn't a single scrap left.

He looked about him. Matthews was cowering against the mattress. He stood over her. "You're a pig, just like my mommy. This is what I did to her." He knelt beside her, the plastic bag in his hands. Then her hand swung up. The shackle on her wrist slammed into his face.

He screamed, and for an instant he was stunned, then with a snarl he snapped his fingers around her throat.

The basement was empty too. Where was she? Kevin thought desperately. He was about to run into the garage, when from somewhere behind the boiler room he heard Mensch howl in pain. And then there came a scream. A woman's scream. Bree was screaming!

An instant later, as August Mensch tightened his hands on Bree Matthews' neck, he felt his head yanked back and then there was a violent punch that caused his knees to buckle. Dazed, he shook his head and then with a guttural cry sprang to his feet.

Bree reached out and grabbed his ankle, pulling him off balance as Kevin caught him in a hammer grip around the throat.

Moments later, pounding feet on the basement stairs announced the arrival of the FBI. One minute later Bree, now in the shelter of Kevin's arms, watched as Mensch was manacled with chains at his waist and hands and legs, looking dazed.

"Let's see how *you* like being tied up," she screamed at him.

Two days later, Bree and Kevin stood together at her grandmother's bedside in Connecticut. "The doctor said you'll be fine, Gran," Bree told her.

"Of course I'm fine. Forget the health talk. Let's hear about your place. I bet you made that contractor squirm in court, didn't you?"

Bree grinned at Kevin's raised eyebrows. "Oh, Gran, I decided to accept his settlement offer after all. I've finally realized that I really hate getting into fights."

MERRILL JOAN GERBER

This Is a Voice from Your Past

FROM *Chattahoochee Review*

EVERY WOMAN gets a call like this sooner or later. The phone rings, a man says: "This is a voice from your past." If you're in the mood and the caller doesn't find you in a room where other people are (particularly your husband), and if you have some time to spare, you might enjoy playing the game.

"Who is this?" I said, when my call came.

"Don't you recognize my voice?"

"Not exactly."

"Alvord's class? Florida? Your senior year?"

I paused. There had been a number of young men in my life in college, in Florida, in my senior year — and most of them were in Alvord's class.

This call — the first from Ricky — came just after I had given birth to my second daughter. I was living in California. I was in the kitchen cutting a hot dog into little greasy pieces for my two-year-old's lunch and at the same time I felt my milk coming down, that sharp burning pain in both nipples, like an ooze of fire.

"Janet?" His voice was husky, or he was whispering. "This is a serious voice from your past. You know who I am. I think of you all the time. And I work at the phone company, I get free calls, so don't worry about this long-distance shit, I can talk to you all night if I want to."

"Tell me who you are," I said, just stalling for time, but suddenly I knew and was truly astounded. I had thought of Ricky often in the kind of reveries in which we all engage when we count the lives that never were meant to be for us.

"You must know. I know you know."

"Well, it must be you, Ricky, isn't it? But I don't have all night. I have two babies now, and I'm feeding them right this minute."

"Is your old man there?"

"No."

"Good, get the kids settled down and I'll hold on. And don't worry, I'm not going to complicate your life. I can't even get to you. I'm in Pennsylvania — and out of money."

"Hang on." I did some things I had to do for the children and then talked to him with my big girl eating in her high chair a foot away from the frayed green couch where I reclined on a pillow, letting the baby suck from my breast. Ricky told me then that he couldn't write a word anymore, it was killing him, he was drinking all the time, he had six kids, his wife was running around with someone else, and could I believe it, he, *he*, was working for the fucking phone company.

"I'm sorry," I said. "I'm really sorry, Ricky."

It occurred to me that anything else I said would sound trite, like: "We all have to make compromises," or "Maybe at some point we have to give up our dreams." The fact was, I hadn't given up mine but pursued it with a kind of dauntless energy. I didn't count the dream that he might have been my true love because I knew even then, all those years ago, that it was impossible. When he read his brilliant stories in class, he was married and living with his wife in a trailer on the outskirts of the campus. He'd already written his prize-winning story that had brought our writing-class to its knees, the one chosen later for an O. Henry Award.

Alvord, our professor, a famous teacher and esteemed novelist, had informed us in class, in front of Ricky, that the boy had been touched by the wand of the muse. He spoke of Ricky as if a halo gleamed over his head. He made it clear that none of us would ever reach the heights (and should not hope to) for which this golden boy was destined. "A talent like his," he told us once, "is like a comet. It appears only once every hundred years or so."

I clung to my own modest talent and I was working on it; I couldn't envy Ricky his, based as it was in Catholic guilt to which I had no access (his stories were all about sin and redemption). What I envied during that hungry, virginal senior year of college was his wife, the woman he held in his arms each night, the one whose face was caressed by the gaze of his deep-seeing, supernaturally wise, marble-blue eyes.

That day he called me as I sat nursing my baby girl, feeling the electric suck of her pulsing lips sizzle in a lightning rod strike from nipple to womb, I remembered an image of Ricky that rose up like an illumination. We were in the university library. Ricky had come in alone and had chosen to sit across from me at one of the long, mahogany tables where I was studying. He had his magic pencil in his long fingers and was bent over his lined notebook paper to create whatever piece of brilliant, remorse-filled prose he was writing. A long lock of his dirty-blond hair fell across his forehead, and his fingers scribbled, bent like crab pincers racing over the lined notebook page, wrote words that according to Alvord would turn out to be second only to James Joyce's.

Ricky had told me that his wife worked in some office, typing business documents. He explained, in his breathy east-coast accent, that she was ordinary and dull and he had too young been seduced by her beauty, her astonishing breasts, and his own fierce desire. He assured me I knew him in a way that she never could. Our discussions after Alvord's class, and in the cafeteria over coffee, and on benches in front of the library, our debates about literature and genius — who knows now if their content held anything more remarkable than youth and idealism cooked up in a predictable collegiate stew?

Still, that night in the library, he stopped his work to stare intensely at me across the table time after time — but didn't smile. We were conspirators, we shared a plan, an ingenious plot to outfox time, mortality, death. We were both going to be famous writers, and we would, by our words alone, live forever.

At some point that evening, in his frenzy of writing, Ricky's cramped fingers relaxed, his head dropped sideways onto his arm on the table-top, and he fell asleep in the library. He remained there, vulnerable and naked in my gaze, breathing as I knew he must breathe as he slept beside his wife in that trailer, his mouth slightly open, his blue-veined eyelids closed over his blue eyes, his nostrils flaring slightly with each breath.

I watched him till the library closed, watched his face and memorized every line of his fair cheek, the angle of his chin, watched fascinated as a thin thread of drool spooled from his slightly parted lips to the table-top. I looked around me to be sure no one was near or watching. Then, before he woke, I very slowly moved my hand across the table and anointed the tip of my pencil with his silver spit.

The second time Ricky called me my husband was in the room. It was thirty years later, a day in late August. I, with a slow but certain fortitude, had written and published a number of novels by then. My three daughters were grown. The baby who had been at my breast at the time of his first call was in graduate school, older than I had been when Ricky slept opposite my gaze in the library.

"Janet? This is a voice from your past."

A warning bell rang in my chest. At that moment my husband and I were deeply absorbed in a discussion about some family troubles. I felt rudely interrupted. I had no interest in the game he wanted to play.

"Which past?" I said. "I have many."

"It's Ricky, your old buddy."

"Well — Ricky! How are you?" I said his name with some enthusiasm because he expected it, but I felt my heart sink because I knew I would have to listen to his troubles and I had no patience just then. The game of "remember what we meant to each other" had lost its appeal. By this time everyone I loved filled up my life completely. I had not even a small chink of space left for a latecomer.

"Are you still living in Pennsylvania?"

"No, I'm right here!"

"Right here?" I looked down into my lap as if I might find him there.

"In sunny California. In your very city. And I'm here for good."

"How did you know where to reach me? My number isn't even listed!"

"I found one of your books back east and on the cover it said what city you lived in. So when I got here — and I want you to know I picked this city because of you — I went to the library and asked the librarian. I knew a librarian was bound to know where the city's most famous writer lived. I told her I was your old buddy and she gave me your phone number."

"I'm not famous, Ricky."

"Me neither," he said. "How about that?"

*

I told him I would call him back in a half hour — and in that time I explained to my husband, more or less, who he was. An old college friend. A used-to-be-writer. A drunk. I don't know why I dismissed Ricky so harshly. Something in his voice had put me on guard. I could see that this game of playing tag with time made no sense. By now I had settled into my ordained life like concrete setting in a mold, and I no longer trifled with the idea that I might want to change it, especially not by mooning after long-expired romantic visions. With a sense of duty, though, I phoned him back . . . and braced myself.

"You won't believe the stuff that's happened to me," he said. He laughed — he almost cackled — and I shivered. "Can we get together?"

When I hesitated, he said, "I've been through AA, I'm a new person. I'm going to join up here, too, of course. The pity is that before I turned myself around I lost every friend I ever had."

"How come?"

"How come? Because an alcoholic will steal from his best friend if he has to, he'll lie with an innocent face like a newborn baby. There's nothing I haven't stooped to, Janet. I've been to the bottom, that's where you have to be before you can come back. I've rented a little room in town here, and I'm hoping . . . well, I'm hoping that we can be friends again."

"Well, why not," I said. I felt my vision darken as if I were entering a tunnel.

"But mainly — I'm hoping you'll let me come to your class. I want to get started writing again."

"How did you know I teach a class?"

"It says on your book, Janet. That you teach writing at some university or other."

"Well, you certainly are a detective, aren't you?"

"I'm sly as a fox."

"I guess you could visit my class when it begins after Labor Day. I'll tell my students that you studied with me in Alvord's class. Since most of my old students will be coming back to take the advanced class, they already know about Alvord. In fact, I quote him all the time. We use all his old terms — 'action proper, enveloping action.' We talk about his dedication to point of view. Maybe we can even get a copy of your old prize story and discuss it."

"Great. So when can we get this friendship on the road again?"

"Look — I'm having a Labor Day barbecue for my family and some friends on Sunday — why don't you come? Do you have a car?"

"I can borrow one."

"Do you need directions? I'll have my husband give them to you." I called Danny to the phone and handed him the receiver. "Tell my friend Ricky the best way to get here." I wanted Ricky to hear Danny's voice, to know unequivocally that I was taken, connected, committed . . . that I wasn't under any circumstances available.

A stranger rang the doorbell, a man eighty years old, skin jaundiced, skeletal bones shaping his face. The golden hair was gray and thin. Only his voice, with an accent on his tongue like the young Frank Sinatra, convinced me he was the same Ricky. When I shook his hand, I felt his skin to be leathery, dry. When I looked down, I saw that the nails were bitten to the quick.

He came inside. I felt him take in the living room in one practiced glance — the art work, the antiques, the furniture — and then we passed out the screen door to the backyard where the party had begun.

Danny was on the patio, grilling hamburgers and hot dogs over the coals. My three daughters, one already married, and two home from their respective graduate schools, looked beautiful in their summer blouses and white shorts. I saw the backyard as Ricky must have seen it — alive with summer beauty, the plum tree heavy with purple fruit, the jasmine in bloom, the huge cactus plants in Mexican painted bowls growing new little shoots, fierce with baby spines.

My other guests included my sister and her sons, my eldest daughter's husband, a few of my students, several women with whom I had been in a book club for the last fifteen years. Ricky looked around; I could feel him adding up my life and registering it in his bloodshot eyes.

I took him over to meet Danny and then said: "Let's go sit on the swings and talk." We crossed the brilliant green of the grass to the swingset where my daughters used to play. Ricky was wearing a gray wool business suit, his bony frame almost lost inside its wide shoulders. He swung slowly back and forth, sitting on the splintery wood seat, his hands clutching the rusty chains. He talked, looking forward, into air.

"My son Bobby is the one who invited me out to California. He made it big-time," Ricky said, and laughed.

"Is he in movies?" I asked.

"Not exactly. He dove into a city pool in Philly and broke his spine. Now he's in a wheelchair for life. I got him a sharp lawyer who brought a deep pockets lawsuit against the city. Bobby was awarded a million and a half bucks, enough to take care of him the rest of his life and, if I play it right, take care of me, too. My other kids don't talk to me, so Bobby is my salvation."

"But why is he in California?"

"He's in a fantastic halfway house out here — the best in the world for paraplegics. Bobby gets all kinds of services, I even bring my laundry over there and he'll get it done for me free. And he's got enough extra pocket money to pay my rent till I get a job."

"What a terrible thing to happen to him."

"No, just the opposite. He was a beach bum, a loser. Now he's got it all together, the whole future taken care of. I think he's relieved. He can use his arms — he plays wheelchair basketball. He lifts weights. He gets counseling, he gets his meals served. Sometimes I wish I could change places with him. But no, I'm back at square one, looking for a job again."

"No more phone company?"

Ricky made a strangling noise in his throat. "I'm going to write my novel, Janet. Finally. I'm going to get it together before I die. If I can sit in on your class, I figure it will start my motor again. You probably teach something like the way Alvord taught us. That old magic. Maybe I can feel that excitement again. I'm counting on it, it's my last hope."

"Do you ever hear from Alvord? Did you stay in touch?"

"In touch! I lived with him for a year in Florida when I was really down and out. He took me in, told me he loved me like a son. The trouble was he didn't feed me, Janet. He offered me a place to stay on that farm of his, and then all I could find to eat in the house was Campbell's soup. One day he actually hid the bacon from me. So I took his truck into town with some money of his to get some food, but I'd been drinking again and I totaled it. He told me I had to leave, gave me fifty bucks and a train ticket back to Philly. But he was a pain, anyway, preaching to me all the time about being a man, taking responsibility for my kids. I swear, the man was a genius but he's losing it, Janet. He's in his eighties now. He used to think I walked on water."

"We all did."

"That's why I came to live near you. You're the only one on earth who really knows my genius."

I didn't actually count, but I had the sense Ricky ate at least five hamburgers, and as many hot dogs. He hung around the food table, his mouth going, not talking to anyone, but looking at my women friends, their faces, their forms. He looked my daughters up and down — there was no way to stop him. At one point he came to me and said, "Your daughters are really beautiful. All three of them. They have your soul in their eyes." I wanted to distract him. I asked him how often he saw his son. He said, "As often as I can; he gives me CARE packages. I don't have much food in the new place."

After our guests left, I packed up all the leftovers for Ricky: potato chips, lukewarm baked beans, the remaining coleslaw, a package of raw hot dogs and buns to go with them, a quarter of a watermelon, lettuce, and sliced tomatoes, even pickles, even mustard and ketchup.

"Listen, thanks," he said. "You're a lifesaver. You don't know how lucky I feel to have found you again. Could I ask you one more favor, though? Would you mind if I came back tomorrow and used your typewriter? I need to write a letter to apply for a job. Someone gave me a tip about a job being night watchman in a truck yard. All I would have to do is sit in a little shed and watch for thieves. I figure I could write all night if I get it."

My reaction was instinctive. I knew I didn't want him back in my house again. "Why don't you let me lend you my electric typewriter? I use a computer now, so I won't need it for a while. I do love it, though — it's the typewriter I wrote my first novel on."

"Then maybe it will be lucky for me. I'll guard it with my life."

"Okay, give me a minute, I'll go put it in its case." I left him standing in the living room with my husband, but I heard no conversation at all — not even ordinary chatter. I could see why Danny was unable to think of a single thing to say to him.

Ricky finally left, laden like an immigrant — bags of food, paper, carbon paper, envelopes, stamps, my typewriter. He stuffed it all into the trunk of an old red car.

Danny and I watched him drive away. He didn't wave — he tore from the curb like one possessed.

"Funny guy," Danny said.

"I don't think we know the half of it," I told him.

I found Ricky's O. Henry prize story and had thirty photocopies made for my students. At the start of class I distributed the copies and told my students that at 7:30 a guest was arriving, a writer of unique skill and vision, a man we were honored to have visit our class. I warned them about the pitfalls of the writer's life, how one could not count on it to earn a living, how so many talented writers fell by the wayside because of the pressures of ordinary life. This visitor, I said, a very close friend of mine from the past who had missed what you might call "his window of opportunity," hoped to join our class and work as hard as anyone in it. "He had a whole life in between, doing something else he had to do. All of you are young, at the start of your first life, and if you really want this, this is the time to do it."

When Ricky arrived at my classroom, it was almost nine o'clock. He apologized, saying the bus had been late. He was wearing a red V-necked sweater, and looked less cadaverous than at the barbecue, but still much older than his years. He seemed elated to find that a copy of his story was on every desk, and when one of the students asked him how he got the idea for it, he said, simply, "I had thought many times of murdering my brother."

By then, we were already in the midst of having another student read his story; I told the class that next week we would discuss Ricky's story.

I nodded for Harold to go on reading; his story was about a day in the cotton fields of Arkansas, and how the men, women, and children picking cotton on a burning hot day reacted when the truck that delivered them failed to leave off drinking water. When the last line had been read, Ricky spoke out in the exact tones of our teacher, Alvord.

"It comes alive on the last page, finally, you see, because it uses all the senses. Since a crying baby can seduce a reader from the very death of Hamlet himself, the writer must bring everything to life. And you do, young man! You do!"

The class was silent, and then a few students applauded Harold and then everyone did — till his embarrassed smile lit up the room. I announced that we would take our usual ten minute break. When the class had filed out, I thought I would find Ricky waiting to talk to me about my students, to tell me how the class had seemed to him, if it would suit his purposes. But he left the room without a glance in my direction, and when I looked out into the hall, I saw him in deep conversation with one of my students, a young woman. When the class reconvened, neither of them returned for the second half.

At seven the next morning, my student phoned me. "This is Alice Miller. I'm so sorry to disturb you," she said, "but your friend, the famous writer, borrowed my car last night. We went out for coffee and afterward he said he had an urgent errand to go on, he practically got on his knees to beg to borrow the car. He said that although he knew I didn't know him very well, you could vouch for him, and he promised he would have my car back in my carport by midnight. He borrowed ten dollars, too. He never came back. And I can't get to work without it!"

"I'll see if I can reach him," I told her. "I'm so sorry. I'll call you right back."

But his landlady did not find him in his room. I called Alice back and told her I could only imagine that there was some emergency with his son who was a paraplegic. I reassured her that he would surely have the car back to her very shortly but in the meantime to take a taxi to work, that I would pay for it.

I learned later that when finally Ricky did return the car to Alice, he never even rang her bell. He left the car at the curb. She found the inside of it littered with cigarette butts, racing forms, empty paper cups, and the greasy wrappers from McDonald's hamburgers. There was not enough gas left in the tank for Alice to get to a gas station.

Toward the end of September, I was applying for a fellowship and realized that I needed my typewriter to fill out the application form. My anger overcame my revulsion, and I dialed the number Ricky had originally given me. His landlady answered, informing me that he'd moved out bag and baggage — that "he shipped out to sea."

"To sea!" I imagined him on a whaling ship, thinking he was

Melville, or more likely that he was one of the sailors in Stephen Crane's story about men doomed at sea, "The Open Boat," a piece of work whose first line Alvord had often quoted: "None of them knew the color of the sky."

But my typewriter! I wanted it, it was mine. I felt as if Ricky had kidnapped one of my children.

"Let it go," my husband said. "It's an old typewriter, I'll get you a new one; it doesn't matter. Write it off as a business loss. Write him off — your old friend — if you can as one of those mistakes we all make in life."

In the days following, I had trouble sleeping. I held imaginary conversations with Ricky, by turns furious, accusatory, damning, murderous. "I trusted you!" I cried out, and in return I heard his laugh . . . his cackle. Alvord had often talked about evil in his class; the reality of it, how it existed, how it was as real as the spinning globe to which we clung.

Days later, in a frenzy, I began calling hospitals, halfway houses, rehab clinics, trying to find the place where Ricky's son lived — if indeed he had a son.

"Don't do this to yourself," Danny said. He saw me on the phone, sweating, asking questions, shaking with anger, trembling with outrage.

But one day I actually located the boy. He was in a hospital in a city only a half hour's drive from my house. I named his name, Bobby, with Ricky's last name, and someone asked me to wait, they would call him to the phone. And a man picked up the phone and said "Yes? This is Bobby."

I told him I was a friend of his father, that his father had my typewriter.

"Oh sure, I know about that. You're his old friend. He left the typewriter here with me. You can come and get it." His voice had the same tones as Ricky's voice. The same seductive sound — the "Oh sure" a kind of promise, the "come and get it" the serpent's invitation.

"His landlady said he went to sea. . . ." I felt I must have another piece of the puzzle, at least one more piece.

"Yeah — he got a job teaching English on a Navy ship. I told him he better take it, he wasn't going to freeload off me the rest of his life."

"I'm sorry," I said to the boy. "I'm sorry about your accident . . . and about your troubles with your father."

"Hey, don't worry about it. It's nothing new. But if you want his address on the ship I could give it to you."

"No — thank you," I said. "I don't want it. I think your father and I have come to a parting of the ways. Good-bye, Bobby, I wish you good luck."

"You, too," Bobby said. "Anyone who knows my father needs it."

Then, two years after I talked to his son, I got the third phone call. "This is a voice out of your fucking past."

"Hello, Ricky." My heart was banging so hard I had to sit down.

"I heard from my son you want your goddamned typewriter back."

"No, no —"

"You'll have it back. It's in little pieces. I'll be on your doorstep with it in twenty minutes."

"I don't want it, Ricky. Don't come here! Keep it."

"I said you'll have it back. I always keep my word, you fucking . . ."

"Please, keep it. I don't need it! Keep it and write your book on it!"

"Just expect me," Ricky said. "I'll be there, you count on it. Watch out your window for me."

I did. For a week. For a month. I keep watching and sometimes, when the phone rings, I let it ring and don't answer it.

EDWARD D. HOCH

The Old Spies Club

FROM *Ellery Queen's Mystery Magazine*

RAND HAD BEEN retired from British Intelligence for a good
many years, but it was not until he turned sixty that he was invited to
join the Old Spies Club. That was not its official name, of course,
but around London's clubland it was often called that, especially by
nonmembers who may have been a bit jealous of its exclusive status
and impressive membership.

The club itself occupied three floors of a late-Victorian building
on St. James's Street, just a short walk from Piccadilly. The main
floor was given over to the gentlemen's lounge and the dining
room, with a billiard room, card room, smoking lounge, library,
and the other amenities one might expect. On the second floor
were rooms for meetings or private dinners, along with the club's
offices. The third floor contained three dozen residential rooms
where members might stay for a day or a year. These were often
occupied by members in the city on a visit, although some members
also found them useful when death or divorce suddenly changed
their marital status.

Rand had taken a good deal of kidding from his wife Leila about
being elderly enough for the Old Spies Club, and in truth he had
never been much of a joiner. He was a bit dismayed the first time he
took the train up from Reading and stopped in the place one warm
July afternoon. The first person he met, just inside the door, was
Colonel Cheever, a blustering old man who could have starred in
any number of film comedies about the army. It was hard to imagine he'd ever been engaged in any sort of intelligence work.

"Rand! How are you, old chap? I saw your name come up on the
new member postings. Good to have you aboard." His gray mous-

tache drooped around his thick lips and he had a habit of spitting when he spoke quickly, but Rand had to admit he seemed trim and in good health for his age. Cheever had been in army intelligence, far from Rand's own sphere of activity. Their paths had only crossed a few times at government functions Rand couldn't avoid.

Now, in trying to be politely friendly, he asked Cheever, "Do you come here often, Colonel?"

"I'm here for the meeting at two o'clock. I expect you are too."

"No," Rand admitted. "I was just in the city for the day and thought I'd acquaint myself with the place."

Colonel Cheever smiled. "Let me give you the tour."

Rand admired the comfortable leather armchairs in the lounge, wondering if he'd ever be elderly enough to pass his afternoons in such a place. "The air in here used to be blue with cigar smoke," the colonel explained, "but now the smokers have been relegated to a smaller lounge down the hall. Times do change."

He led the way through the spacious billiard room and the card room, where green-shaded lights hung down over felt-covered tables.

"I imagine there are some wicked card games in here," Rand commented.

"Wicked, indeed! I prefer bridge, but most players like faster methods of losing their money."

The dining room, with its rows of neatly arranged tables, was quite inviting and Rand made a mental note to dine there sometime with Leila. When they'd reached the second-floor meeting rooms it was two o'clock, time for the colonel's meeting. Rand started to excuse himself but saw another familiar face among those entering the meeting room. "Harry! Harry Vestry!"

The slender smiling man turned at the sound of his name. "Well, if it isn't Rand! Good to see you, old chap. How long have you been gone from Concealed Communications now?"

"Too long, Harry. I'm old enough to qualify for this club, after all. And Double-C doesn't even exist anymore under that name."

Vestry chuckled. Rand had been a close friend of Vestry's when they were recruited together for intelligence work, but the vagaries of overseas assignments had separated them after a few years. "Look, why don't you sit in on our meeting, Rand? It's nothing really secret, and you may have some good suggestions to toss in."

"I don't even know what it's about," Rand protested mildly.

Vestry smoothed back his thinning gray hair. "Finding the truth, old chap. That's what it's about." Then, acknowledging Cheever for the first time, he urged, "Bring him along, Colonel. It's an open meeting."

Cheever placed a hand on Rand's shoulder. "You heard the man. Come along and join us."

There were a dozen of them around the long oval table, though seats had been provided for twice that number. Rand had already observed that, like most London clubs, this one had not yet progressed to admitting women. Harry Vestry took his place at the head of the table, ready to conduct the meeting, and it was obvious he'd been within his rights when he invited Rand to sit in. Looking around the table at the other men, all about his age or slightly older, Rand was surprised that he knew so few. Cheever and Vestry were the only two he could have named, though a tall man with a red face and a bald head like a bullet seemed familiar.

"I think we all know the purpose of this meeting," Vestry began when the others had quieted their conversations.

Rand raised his hand. "I'm afraid I don't."

"Of course, Jeffrey. I forgot. Well, you probably read in the papers last winter about the death of Cedric Barnes during heart surgery. He was the author of all those books on famous British spies, double agents, MI5, MI6, and Air Intelligence. I believe he even did a volume on Concealed Communications, your old department."

Rand remembered. He'd read it when it came out, feeling a perverted sense of pride when he found sixteen references to himself in the index. Even in a top-secret organization it was nice to achieve some level of recognition. Oddly enough, he'd thought of Cedric Barnes just a few days earlier, after reading a news account from America that stated that the CIA had agreed to stop employing journalists in the gathering of intelligence data. "I had lunch with the man once," Rand said. "He wanted an interview but it was forbidden by the Official Secrets Act. I don't know where he obtained all his information."

"It hardly matters now," Vestry said. "What matters is that his daughter Magda intends to auction off the furnishings from his country house. Barnes's wife has been dead about ten years, so everything went to the daughter. The auction is scheduled here in

London next week, at Sotheby's. Many of us believe grave danger can be done to the country if that auction is allowed to go forward."

Rand was a bit surprised when he allowed his gaze to circle the table and saw that the others were taking this seriously. "Do you really think he had some top-secret papers hidden in a piano leg?"

"Such things are possible," the tall red-faced man said. "He worked at home with his daughter's help, and we already know certain well-placed journalists will be bidding on select pieces. A diary or journal could be invaluable."

Harry Vestry continued. "My proposal, gentlemen, is that we stop this auction by placing a preemptive bid for the entire offering. I have already spoken to Magda Barnes about the possibility and she is agreeable."

"How much does she want?" Colonel Cheever asked.

"One million pounds."

There were sighs and groans from around the table. "The club doesn't have that sort of money," someone said.

"We may be able to negotiate a lower figure," Vestry tried to reassure them. "But we must all realize the importance of this matter."

Rand spoke again. "If it's so important, why doesn't the government step in and take action?"

"We understand they have done all they can on an official basis," Vestry answered vaguely. Rand wondered if he was implying that the government had appealed to the Old Spies Club for financial backing in the matter.

It was Colonel Cheever who seemed most vocal in opposing Vestry. "Are you saying you expect the members in this room to come up with the million pounds necessary to cancel the auction? Such a suggestion borders on the ridiculous!"

Vestry tried to remain calm against this attack, but the members around the table quickly chose sides. After most of them had spoken, it seemed obvious he was in the minority. "The money just isn't there," the red-faced man said.

"Do you have any other suggestions, Shirley?" Vestry asked.

At first the use of the feminine name jarred Rand, but then something clicked in his memory. Shirley Watkins, the man with a woman's name. During his years of covert government service Shirley's job had always been assassination. Few knew his name and fewer still had seen his face. Rand had met him just once in Berlin, twenty years ago, but supposed him long dead. Could this possibly be the same man?

"Let me talk to the daughter," Shirley suggested. "Maybe I can make her see reason."

It might have been an innocent remark, but coming from this man it could also have been a death threat. Rand knew his imagination was running away with him but still he raised his hand and spoke. "If you'll excuse me, I wonder if I might be of service, gentlemen. As I said, I had lunch with Cedric Barnes a few years back when he wanted an interview for the Double-C book. His daughter might remember my name if she helped him with the book."

"That's very good of you, Rand," Colonel Cheever said at once. "What say you all? Shall we take Jeffrey up on his offer?"

There were assents from around the table, and perhaps a sense of relief. Rand wondered what he was getting himself into.

Sotheby's London auction rooms were located on New Bond Street, in a remodeled four-story building that probably dated from Georgian times. The building ran through the block to St. George Street, and the main entrance was around the back. It was here that Rand entered, stopping to purchase a pricey full-color catalogue of that week's lots to be auctioned. The one that interested him was titled simply *Items from the Country House of an Author and Journalist.*

He went upstairs to the second-floor exhibition hall and spent the better part of the next hour inspecting an array of furniture including antique desks, chairs, tables, lamps, even a four-poster bed with a canopy. Barnes's old manual typewriter was there with a shiny new plastic ribbon in place. A pile of books, neatly tied in manageable bundles of twenty or so, was being sold as a separate lot. Glancing over the titles, Rand recognized some of the Cold War classics, plus a few books on espionage in general and World War II in particular. David Kahn's thick volume *The Code Breakers* was there, along with *Hitler's Spies,* and Robert Harris's recent novel *Enigma.* There was also a complete set of Cedric Barnes's own books, many in foreign-language editions, leaving little doubt as to the identity of the "author and journalist." An array of office supplies, a camera, and a tape recorder completed the lot.

Rand spent the rest of his time studying the others who roamed through the exhibition hall. One that he recognized at once was Simon Spalding, a columnist for the *Speculator.* He was an expert at digging up dirt on the Royal Family, and perhaps now he was widening his horizons.

On his way out Rand stopped in the office and requested a ticket to the auction itself. The young woman behind the desk informed him that no tickets were necessary. "Anyone may attend our regularly scheduled auctions," she said. "However, if you think you might be bidding you should register at the door and receive a numbered paddle which you hold up to signify a bid."

"I wonder if you could help me with one other matter. Could you put me in touch with a family member regarding this auction?"

Apparently she was accustomed to such requests. "You may place an early bid with us for any item you wish."

"This is more of a family matter," he said, purposely vague.

She glanced toward the closed door to an inner office. "Just a minute, please." She tapped lightly on the closed door and then entered.

After a moment she emerged with a dark-haired woman, perhaps in her middle thirties, wearing a bright summer dress that looked expensive to Rand's untrained eye. She smiled and extended her hand. "I'm Magda Barnes. The items to be auctioned are from my father's house. I came by today to see how they were being displayed. May I be of service?"

He accepted the hand, which was surprisingly soft. "Is there somewhere we could talk in private, Miss Barnes?"

"I was using their conference room to review the catalogue. Perhaps we could talk in there." She glanced at the secretary, who nodded permission.

Inside the small room Rand introduced himself and came right to the point. "Your father was a respected journalist. I met him once and you may recall I was mentioned several times in his book on the Department of Concealed Communications. Some of us, now retired from the Service, are concerned that your father's possessions might contain some hidden notes that could fall into the wrong hands."

She smiled at the thought. "No, no — I've been over everything being offered at auction. I examined and searched each item at least twice. There are no hidden notes or journals. All his personal papers and manuscripts will be given to Cambridge University."

"Miss Barnes, the feeling is that he might have come into possession of material he could not publish under the Official Secrets Act. Do you know what he was working on at the time of his death?"

The smile faded as she began to comprehend the people he represented. "Did that man Vestry send you?"

"I have spoken with Harry Vestry. He did not send me."

"He knows my price."

"One million pounds is beyond our resources."

"Then the auction will go on as planned, even though I realize I won't come close to that figure. Men like Vestry fought my father all his life. I owe him nothing."

"When I was looking over the items just now I spotted a familiar face. Simon Spalding. You certainly don't owe him anything."

The news didn't seem to bother her. "He knew my father years ago. I remember him visiting the house once around the time of Sadat's assassination. It's not surprising he'd be interested in the exhibition. Perhaps he might even bid on something."

"Has he approached you about any particular piece?"

"No." She stood up from the table and said, "I really must be going, Mr. Rand. We have nothing further to discuss. Tell Harry Vestry the auction will go on as planned."

He sighed and left the room after a few polite words. Then he went downstairs into the warm July afternoon. He'd walked about a block when someone fell into step beside him. It was the bullet-headed former assassin, Shirley Watkins. "Didn't do so well, did you, Mr. Rand? I could have told you that. She's the sort of woman needs a little fright before she sees reason."

The following morning, as she was leaving to deliver one of her summer lectures on Egyptian archaeology at Reading University, Rand told Leila he'd be going into London again. "Two days in a row?" she asked, somewhat surprised.

"Maybe three. There's an auction at Sotheby's tomorrow that I should attend. It's part of Cedric Barnes's estate, the fellow who wrote those insider books about British Intelligence."

"I hope you're not going to buy anything."

"I'll try not to," he said with a grin.

This time only three of them were in the meeting room on the second floor of the Old Spies Club. Vestry and Colonel Cheever listened intently as Rand told them what had transpired the previous afternoon. "When I suggested contacting Magda Barnes I had no idea that Shirley would be dogging my steps. Did one of you send him after me?"

"Hardly, old boy," Cheever answered. "You know Shirley. He has a mind of his own."

"Look, the auction is taking place tomorrow morning. Shirley can't stop it. You can't allow him to threaten that woman in any manner."

"Nothing could be further from our minds," Vestry assured him.

"We're out of the game now, retired. I don't break codes anymore and Shirley Watkins doesn't kill people. Is that understood?"

Colonel Cheever snorted. "I doubt that he ever did kill people. It was probably all a scare campaign to intimidate the other side."

"Maybe he started believing the campaign himself. He spoke of Barnes's daughter needing a little fright to see reason. I told him to leave her alone."

"Did you look over the auction items?" Vestry asked. "Any likely hiding places for notes or a journal?"

"A desk or coffee table could have a hidden drawer or a false bottom. If it's on microfilm or a microdot the possibilities are endless." Rand decided it was time to bring things out in the open. "Look here, there's something about this whole business you're not telling me. You talk of spending upwards of a million pounds, of threatening Barnes's daughter, of keeping the press away. From what? What's in this journal that makes it so valuable?"

Vestry maintained an uneasy silence until Colonel Cheever started to speak. Then he interrupted to say, "You might as well know, Rand. Rumor has it that Cedric Barnes once interviewed a double agent, someone working for us who was on the verge of defecting to Moscow. This was to be the man's swan song, his public rationale for his actions, not to be published until he was safely out of the country."

"And — ?"

"And at the last moment something changed. The double agent never defected, and Cedric Barnes kept his word. He never published the interview."

"How long ago is this supposed to have happened?" Rand asked.

Harry Vestry shrugged. "In some versions it was 1985. Other

versions have it way back in the seventies when Barnes was still a relatively young man. Your guess is as good as mine."

"And yet the dozen men around this table yesterday all believe it happened. Not only that, they believe the interview still exists somewhere. Why would Barnes keep it all these years? Why not simply destroy it?"

"Unfortunately, he was a newspaperman," the slender man answered. "I imagine he kept it all these years on the off chance that the man might defect after all. The Cold War ended, the Berlin Wall came down, and still he kept it."

"You have no way of knowing that with any certainty," Rand pointed out.

"Simon Spalding knows it, and he's after the journal."

Someone else knew it too, Rand suddenly realized. The man who had given the interview. Naturally he would have begged Barnes to destroy it after he decided to remain in England. Naturally he would suspect it was still in existence. He would have been most anxious to keep it out of Spalding's hands.

Rand found himself asking the obvious question. "Which of the club members first brought up this matter? Who was it that wanted the auction stopped?"

Colonel Cheever answered. "We'd all heard the rumors, of course. They say Barnes dropped hints himself on nights when he'd had a few too many brandies. When the auction was announced, several of us were concerned. I suppose Harry and I took the lead in it, but it was Shirley who talked it up and arranged for the meeting. He claimed to have two dozen of the old boys, but as you saw, only half that number really appeared when the time came."

"Eleven of us, really," Vestry corrected. "Rand was an addition, you'll remember. I'd say you and I and Shirley were the organizers. The other eight were lukewarm to the idea."

"Could you give me a list of their names?"

"What in heaven's name for?" Vestry still possessed the field agent's reluctance to commit anything to paper.

"If there's any truth to the rumors, the mysterious double agent could be retired now. He could even be a member of this club. If so, he would have been especially interested in attending your meeting yesterday."

"Nonsense!" Cheever blustered. "I've known these people for most of my life. I'd vouch for any of them."

Rand ignored him and asked Vestry, "Where can I find Shirley Watkins?"

The slim man considered his question. "If he's not here he's most likely at the Moon and Stars. It's a pub down by the river, near Canary Wharf."

The two worlds of Shirley Watkins were vastly different from one another. The quiet luxury of the Old Spies Club was only some eight kilometers from the Moon and Stars Pub at Canary Wharf, but they were separated by more than distance. Once a haven for seamen off the nearby docks, now it was a meeting place for office workers from the tallest building in England. Even a recent IRA bombing had done little to frighten people out of the area. On this summer Wednesday the place was crowded and the aroma of beer mixed with a haze of cigarette smoke.

Rand spotted Shirley Watkins at once, seated in a booth with a middle-aged woman wearing too much makeup. He had on a suit and tie, and his bald bullet head seemed to reflect the overhead lights as he drank from a pint of stout. A decade or so older than the other male customers, he could still have been an executive from one of the Canary Wharf firms. When he saw Rand heading for him he told the woman, "Here's business. I'll talk to you later." She gave Rand a sour look and exited the booth.

Rand slipped in to take her place. "I want to speak with you about the auction," he began.

Shirley eyed him, sizing him up. "How'd you find me?"

"Harry Vestry said you might be here."

"Yeah, Harry. I think he still spies on all of us, just to keep his hand in."

"Did you take my advice about Magda Barnes and stay away from her?"

He held up his hands in a gesture of surrender. "Whatever you say is fine with me. I was always one for obeying orders."

Rand deliberately avoided making eye contact, fearing he might detect a touch of irony in the words. "I was talking with Vestry and the colonel this afternoon. They told me about the rumors."

"What rumors?"

"The interview that Barnes is supposed to have done with a double agent before he defected."

"Yeah, that." Shirley Watkins downed the rest of his pint. "Do you believe any of it?"

"I don't know. I heard it for the first time about an hour ago."

"Well, I've got my doubts, but I'll do whatever they want."

Rand frowned at the words. "What do you mean by that?" he started to ask, then cut himself short. Another familiar face had just entered the Moon and Stars.

"What's the matter, Rand?"

"That reporter Spalding just came in. He must have followed me."

"Say the word and he'll be feeding the fishes."

Rand gave a dry chuckle. "Did you ever in your life really kill anyone, Shirley, or has it all been an act?"

"I've done my part."

"Haven't we all?" He slid out of the booth. "I'd better go talk to Spalding."

The columnist was nursing a half-pint, trying to avoid looking in the direction of the booth, when Rand joined him. "You're Simon Spalding, aren't you? I don't think we've ever been formally introduced. I'm Jeffrey Rand."

Spalding was a slender man in his early fifties with thinning brown hair and a crooked nose that might have been broken in his youth. "Oh yes. One of the retired spies. There are a great many of you around these days, aren't there? You must have hated to see the Cold War end."

Rand already knew from Spalding's columns that he didn't particularly like the man. "I retired from the Service long before the end of the Cold War," he said, and then asked, "Were you a friend of Cedric Barnes? I saw you at Sotheby's yesterday."

Spalding shrugged. "A fellow journalist. I was interested in what was being offered. I only met him once, at some awards dinner."

"I suppose his daughter has already removed anything of special value."

He shot Rand a glance that seemed an unspoken question. "We don't know that. Sometimes people have clever hiding places for their valuables. They even sell fake beer cans now so you can hide your money and jewelry in the fridge."

"Good idea, so long as the thief doesn't have a thirst. I gather you'll be at the auction tomorrow morning?"

"Sure. I'd like to pick up a souvenir of the old guy."

"There are legends about him, about the stories he didn't publish."

Simon Spalding laughed. He was warming a little toward Rand. "We all have stories that don't get published for one reason or another, same as you blokes. I remember back in nineteen eighty-one when the *Speculator* took me off the European desk and gave me the column to write, I passed along some great story leads to my successor but nothing ever happened."

"Tell me something, just between us," Rand said with a smile. "Who are you following this evening — me or Shirley?"

"They say that man is a government-authorized assassin."

"Does he look like one?"

"Damn right he does!"

"Then he's probably not. Not anymore, certainly. He's retired, same as the rest of us."

A sly look came over the columnist's face. "Member of the Old Spies Club, is he?"

"What's that?"

"The place on St. James's Street where you all go. That's what they call it, don't they? I'd do a column about it if I wasn't afraid of getting sued."

"Stick to the Royal Family," Rand advised. "It's safer."

He moved away from the bar and headed for the door, waving goodbye to Shirley Watkins.

Rand had to catch the early train into London for the auction the following morning. He was up before Leila because he wanted to clean and oil the little Beretta pistol he hadn't fired in years. Just seeing him with it would have upset her, he knew. But catching sight of himself in a mirror, he realized how foolish he looked. He was too old for these things. Deadly weapons were not for Sotheby's, and certainly not for the Old Spies Club.

The first familiar face he saw as he entered the auction house and registered for his plastic paddle was Harry Vestry, standing near the door and glancing at his watch. "I was hoping you'd be here, Rand." He glanced at Rand's paddle. "Number Seventy-seven! Sure to be lucky if you care to bid. If Cheever and Watkins get here too, I'd like to position us in different parts of the hall where we can keep track of the bidding. I know it's often impossible to identify the high bidder, especially if it's made by phone, but we can try."

Still playing the old spy, Rand thought. "Simon Spalding is sure to be here, bidding on something. I'll keep an eye on him."

"Good! I saw him go in a few minutes ago. He took a paddle, so he plans to bid."

But when Rand entered the large high-ceilinged auction room with its twin chandeliers and rows of folding chairs, the first person he saw was Magda Barnes, immaculate in a white summer suit. "We meet again, Mr. Rand."

"So it seems."

"Will you be bidding on any of my father's items?"

"I may." He lifted number seventy-seven and gave it a little twirl. "Good luck! You have a nice crowd." Then he went off to find a seat.

The auction had already started and they were on the fifth item. Rand estimated there were about a hundred and fifty people in the room. Some, apparently the high bidders, were in glass booths above floor level. They seemed to be connected by telephone to their agents on the floor. Above the stage where the auctioneer stood, a large electronic sign gave the latest bids in pounds sterling, dollars, francs, yen, and other currencies. As each item was announced for bidding it was shown on a turntable next to the auctioneer. Spotters along each side of the room watched for bids that the auctioneer might miss.

Rand could see that the prices were running fairly high for the antique items. Personal items and office supplies brought less, although Simon Spalding, seated a few rows ahead of Rand, paid two hundred pounds for Barnes's old manual typewriter. Rand was surprised when Colonel Cheever suddenly appeared, raising his paddle from a back row to bid on the collection of books. The bidding was lively but Cheever finally lost out.

The canopied four-poster bed, too large for the turntable, was wheeled onto the stage. It went to a dark-complexioned man who may have been an Arab. Barnes's writing desk fetched a good sum from a neatly dressed young couple.

Finally Rand spotted Shirley seated on the aisle near the rear. He held a plastic paddle with the number sixty-eight on it. That probably meant he'd come in before Rand, yet Harry Vestry at the door hadn't noticed him. It signified nothing, of course. Vestry might have stopped in the men's room for a moment.

The collection of Cedric Barnes's own books, in various languages, was the last item to be auctioned. This time Colonel Cheever tried again, with better results. He took the lot for eleven hundred pounds.

Several of the winning bidders went to the office to settle up and claim the items if they were small enough to carry. Rand was on his way out when he ran into Simon Spalding at the St. George Street entrance. "Did you bid on anything?" the columnist asked.

"Not a thing. But I see you picked up that old typewriter."

Spalding hefted it in its leather carrying case. "It's worth about a tenth of what I paid, but I wanted a remembrance of the old guy. He was one of the tops in the business."

Rand smiled in agreement. "He certainly was that." He glanced at his watch. "Look here, Spalding, it's nearly one o'clock. We both could stand a spot of lunch. The Old Spies Club, as you referred to it, is only a few blocks away, just across Piccadilly. Come along with me and I'll treat you."

Spalding quickly accepted. "That's very generous of you, Rand. I'll admit to being curious about the place."

As they entered the club, he suggested that Spalding might want to leave the typewriter in the checkroom, but the columnist clutched it firmly. "Oh no! This cost me two hundred pounds and I'm hanging onto it."

Rand chuckled and led the way into the dining room. After a luncheon of roast beef and blood pudding, topped with red wine and finished off with trifle for dessert, Spalding took out a cigar and they adjourned to the gentlemen's smoking lounge. It was deserted at this hour of the afternoon except for one man sleeping in an armchair, his bald head visible over its top. The columnist lit his cigar, offering one to Rand, who declined. Then they settled back in the comfort of the overstuffed leather armchairs.

"I can see why you chaps like this place," Spalding said. "It's a perfect setting to wile away one's retirement."

Rand smiled slightly. "Now that we're comfortable, suppose you show me the typewriter."

"What? This thing?"

"The very same."

"What for?"

"So I can confirm my suspicion as to the identity of the fabled double agent."

Simon Spalding laughed. "You think this old manual typewriter of Barnes's will tell you that?"

"I know it will, and so do you. Who ever saw a shiny plastic ribbon on a manual typewriter? They all used fabric ribbons." He reached down and unzipped the leather carrying case. The columnist made no attempt to stop him. "It's a bit narrower than the quarter-inch plastic ribbons that electric typewriters use. There was all this talk of a journal, but Cedric Barnes used a tape recorder for interviews, didn't he? They even auctioned one off today." Rand removed the ribbon from the machine. "It's a tape, masquerading as a typewriter ribbon. The tape of Barnes's infamous last interview with the double agent."

"It's going to make me a rich man," Simon Spalding said.

"Or a dead one. Suppose I get a machine and we play this tape right now."

"Here?"

"We're alone except for that fellow sleeping in his chair. We won't disturb him. Don't you want to know the size of the fish you've landed?"

"I'd rather find out back in the office."

"Funny thing," Rand said, keeping his voice light. "You told me yesterday you only met Cedric Barnes once, at an awards dinner. But his daughter said you were at their house back around the time of Sadat's assassination. That would have been nineteen eighty-one, wouldn't it?"

"You have a better memory for dates than I do."

"There were rumors about Barnes's unpublished interview with a double agent, a defector who changed his mind at the last minute. Rumors of a journal Barnes kept of the interview. Only Barnes didn't keep journals, he used a tape recorder. One person would have known that for sure, would have known exactly what to look for among the items to be auctioned, would have spotted that recording tape disguised as a typewriter ribbon. The man Barnes interviewed, the double agent himself."

"Damn you, Rand!"

"If I'm wrong, play the tape for me."

Spalding's hand came out of his pocket holding a small automatic pistol. Rand remembered his own gun and wished now that he'd brought it.

"I'm a journalist, remember, not one of you spy boys!"

"You don't look much like a journalist with that gun. I suppose the British and Russians used journalists occasionally, just as the CIA is sometimes accused of doing. Your job on the European desk was the perfect place to gather information. As for that interview, a journalist would be the most aware of a good news story, and the most likely to tell Barnes his side of the story before he defected."

Simon Spalding held the gun very steady. Behind him, Rand thought he could hear the sound of the bald man snoring. "If what you say is true, why would I change my mind after giving Barnes the interview?"

"Because the *Speculator* gave you a column."

His face had become a frozen mask. "How could you know that?"

"Magda Barnes remembers you at the house in nineteen eighty-one, around the time of Sadat's assassination. You told me last evening they took you off the European desk and gave you the column in eighty-one. Did you desert Communism for a newspaper column, Simon?"

"That's what Barnes asked me! I should have killed him before his tongue got loose and he started those rumors. I thought I'd put it all behind me, especially after the collapse of the Soviet Union."

Rand reached out his hand. "Give me the gun. It's much too late in the game to be shooting people."

Spalding raised the pistol, to fire or to surrender it. Rand would never know which. There was a low cough from behind the man's chair and a flower of blood burst from his chest. His head went back and he lay there dead.

The bald man was Shirley Watkins, and the silenced pistol was out of sight before Rand ever saw it. "Thought you might need help," he said. "Hated to put a hole through the chair, though."

"You were already here when we entered," Rand protested.

"Saw him waving his cigar around the dining room. Knew you'd head this way."

Rand stared at the body, and then at Shirley. "You really are an assassin."

"I was once, in my younger days."

"What do we do now?"

"Forget it ever happened. I'll handle everything. If that tape is what you say, the whole thing will be hushed up. This is the Old Spies Club, remember?"

Rand caught the evening train home.

PAT JORDAN

Beyond Dog

FROM *Playboy*

THE TWO WAITRESSES stood in the shade of the service bar waiting for their drink orders. The brunette sneaked a drag of her cigarette and put it back in the ashtray on the bar.

The blonde said, "You gonna tell 'em, or me?"

The brunette glanced over her shoulder. The outdoor tables on the deck of the Mark Hotel's Chickee Bar were filled mostly with tourists drinking margaritas and rumrunners in the hot Fort Lauderdale sun. Some wore baggy shorts and T-shirts with PARTY NAKED on the front. Others wore cruisewear bathing suits from Bloomingdale's. They didn't talk much, except now and then to whisper to one another and point down below at the male and female strippers lying on the sand, wearing only G-string bikinis, their perfectly tanned bodies glistening with coconut oil.

"You mean the mutt?" said the brunette. "With Spike and the hunk?"

"Who else?"

A man and a woman were seated off by themselves at the far corner of the deck. Only their backs were visible to the waitresses. The man looked like a bodybuilder, hugely muscular and tanned, with a bleached-blond ponytail and narrow, dark eyes. The woman was older, muscled, tanned and bleached blonde, too, with close-cropped hair that stood up like spring grass. She wore a G-string bikini and smoked a cigarette, very lady-like, limp-wristed, while with her other hand she stroked the fur of the dog sitting at her feet. The dog had reddish-orange-and-white fur and looked like a cross between a wolf and a fox.

The blonde waitress set down their drinks. Jim Beam, rocks, for him. Vodka, rocks, for her. The man handed her a twenty and told her to keep the change.

"Thank you, sir," the waitress said. She stood there, hesitating.

The woman ignored her. She sipped her vodka and said to the man, "What time is he supposed to get here?"

"Twenty minutes ago," said the man.

The waitress hovered. Finally, she said, "Excuse me." The woman glanced up, still stroking her dog. "I'm terribly sorry," the waitress said, "but it's against the rules." She pointed at the dog. The dog looked up at her with an eerily human expression. "No dogs, I'm afraid."

The woman took a drag from her cigarette and exhaled. "Really?" she said. She was older than she looked from behind, maybe 45, but attractive. The woman smiled down at the dog. "Did you hear that, Hosh? You're not welcome." She poured her glass of water into a tin bowl and put it down for the dog.

The waitress shrugged and returned to the service bar as a bald man with a big belly and a goatee walked toward the table. Sunlight glinted off his gold-framed sunglasses, his gold necklaces, his gold bracelets, his gold Rolex. His buttondown shirt was open to the navel, exposing his chest hair. Three beepers were hooked to his white tennis shorts.

"Hello, Sheila," he said, leaning down to kiss the woman on the cheek. He sat down across from Bobby.

"Hello, Solly," she said.

"A day late, Solly," said Bobby.

"I had things to do."

The dog raised up on his hind legs and put his paws on Sol's arm. "The Hosh!" Sol said. "How's my man?" The dog wagged his tail. When the waitress appeared at Sol's side, the dog sat down quickly, as if to be unobtrusive.

"I'll have a rumrunner, honey," Sol said. "And a hamburger."

"What are you, a fucking tourist?" Bobby said when the waitress had gone.

"Right," Sheila said. "With three beepers on his hip."

Bobby leaned across the table and said, "So, what's the big hurry, Sol, that you bring us out with all the tourists?"

"I thought I'd toss this one to you, Bobby. Some sandblasted types in Miami. I don't feature dealing with them." He grinned. "I

figure you and the spics have something in common, you know.
Men of color and all."

Bobby smiled. "What's the product?"

The bald man looked around at the tourists, studying them.

"Oh, Solly," Sheila said, "you're so fucking dramatic."

The waitress came back with the rumrunner and burger and Sol
raised his eyebrows for silence. After she left, he said, "Do you
mind if we get back to business?" Bobby nodded. Sol leaned toward
him. "The spic needs a few pieces, Bobby, maybe a couple hundred. Small stuff, mostly. CZs. AKs. Uzis. They like that foreign shit.
He says that he already got his big stuff — SAMs, Stingers — from
some raghead in Boca."

"So why does he need us?" Bobby said.

"Because, fuckhead, he can't buy the stuff in Miami. He's a big-
fucking-deal exile, on TV all the time, screaming how him and his
compatriots are gonna take back their fucking island paradise by
force. Building an army, he says, a lot of fat old spics in camouflage
out in the Everglades, huffin' and puffin' through the fuckin'
swamp, blasting gators with grenade launchers."

"So why doesn't he just come up here to get his product?"

"You know how spics are, Bobby. Like guineas in the Bronx. Hate
to leave their stoop. Besides, a sandblasted nigger like him in Lauderdale, sniffing around for product, would draw flies. He needs a
buyer. Someone knows his way up here, got contacts. Preferably a
white man, he says." Sol grinned evilly and winked at Sheila. "What
they call that, honey?"

Sheila looked startled, then smiled. "I think you mean irony."

"Irony, Bobby! You and him become asshole buddies, talk politics, maybe he can loan you some Stingers so's you can recapture
the fucking Indian reservation. Dinner at his hacienda. Him and
his wife, you and Sheila." Sol took a bite of his hamburger. "Know
any Spanish?"

Sheila stubbed out her cigarette and looked for the waitress, to
order another drink. When she turned back, Sol was sneaking a
piece of hamburger to Hoshi.

"Solly! I told you not to feed him that shit."

"He's a dog, for Christ's sake. He eats meat."

"Yeah, well, not that stuff. It fucks up his stomach, so please, Sol?
And another thing: Don't call him a dog."

"Jesus. He is a dog."

"No he's not. He's beyond dog."

"All right, all right." But the hamburger had already disappeared and Sol turned back to Bobby. "The spic expects you at his house tonight for dinner. Midnight. Them spics eat late. It's in the Gables." Sol slid a folded piece of paper across the table. Bobby unfolded it and looked at it.

The waitress appeared. "Another round," Sheila said. Then, smiling at Sol, she added, "And don't forget to put the little umbrella in his rumrunner. OK, honey?"

Sol ignored her and went on. "There's no number on the front gate. But you can't miss it. Big fucking concrete wall, razor wire on top. You know how they are. Makes 'em feel important. I told him to expect a Mr. Bobby Squared. Just announce yourself at the gate. They got this little box you talk into, they let you in."

Sol lowered his voice and leaned closer to Bobby. "One other thing. Don't pack. He's fuckin' paranoid." He smiled at Sheila.

"Very good, Sol."

"Par-a-noid, Bobby. Drives one of them ten-ton Bentleys that fucking bazookas bounce off. Guats patrolling the grounds with Mac-10s and guard dogs, big fucking mutts like in the movies."

"Rottweilers," Sheila said.

"Whatever. Dog shit everywhere. Wear your cowboy boots, Bobby. And don't pack. They'll pat you down at the front door, and you don't want to piss these guys off."

Bobby nodded. "What's my end?"

"All of it. It's a present. You always stood up for me." Sol's tone changed for an instant, not the wise guy now, but genuine. Then he went on talking, all business again. "The product will cost ya, maybe 75 large. The spic will give you a hundred. You keep the change." He leaned closer to Bobby and said softly, "Bobby, you know there's only one guy deals in so much product."

"I know."

"You ever met him?"

Bobby shook his head.

"He's fucking wacko. Old bastard thinks he's God. From the Old Testament — you know what I mean. Watch yourself." Absentmindedly, Sol broke off another piece of his hamburger and handed it to Hoshi. The dog wolfed it down.

"Jesus, Sol. What did I tell you? You're a fucking mule!" Sheila stood up. "Come on, Hosh." She walked off the deck onto the sand and headed toward the ocean.

"What'd I do?" Sol said.

"You pissed her off," Bobby said. He followed Sheila with his eyes as she walked in the sand in that distinctive way of hers that always turned him on. She twisted the balls of her feet so that her small, high ass swiveled left and right. Bobby watched as she turned at the water's edge and began walking away. Hoshi trotted beside her, well away from the water. The only time he ever pissed and moaned was when they gave him a bath.

Sheila stared silently through the blacked-out windows of Bobby's black SHO as they drove south on I-95. Finally, Bobby said, "What's the matter?"

"Nothing!" she snapped, not looking at him. Then, turning to him, she said, "I'm sorry, baby. It's not your fault." She looked down at herself dressed in a beige silk pleated jumpsuit. She was wearing a matronly wig, brown flecked with gray, twisted into a bun at her nape. "It's this fucking girdle. Reminds me of my age."

Bobby reached a hand across the seat and placed it on her thigh. "I'm sorry, baby."

"That's all right, Bobby." She smiled at him as they passed the Miami skyline, the glass skyscrapers illuminated eerily by pastel lights, pink and green and blue. "I'm curious, though. Why do I have to wear a girdle?"

"You got your Seecamp?"

Sheila rummaged through her handbag and pulled out her chrome-plated Seecamp .32, six shots, double action only. He'd given it to her two years ago. "It's so pretty," she'd said when he handed it to her. "So tiny. It doesn't seem real."

"Now, stick the gun inside your girdle. The spic isn't going to pat you down . . . I hope."

She unbuttoned the jumpsuit to her navel and stuck the little gun into the front of it. "It's cold," she said. She moved her hips seductively. "Feels good, though."

When they reached Coral Gables they turned left, toward the ocean. Bobby slowed the car, pulled out Sol's piece of paper and squinted at the numbers on it, then glanced at the numbers on the houses. Mansions. Spanish Mediterranean, most of them. Some looked like English Tudors. The Anglos, Sheila thought. She looked up. An insistent breeze from the ocean rustled the leaves of the big royal palms lining the street, reflecting the white moonlight.

"We're getting close," Bobby said. Sheila appreciated the tall, wrought-iron gates and fences, the big circular driveways, the Rolls Royces, Benzes, Ferraris and BMWs, all illuminated by landscape lights. Another world, she thought.

"At dinner, baby," Bobby was saying, "you make sure to sit by me. Things start to go bad, you'll know. You get up, go to the ladies' room to powder your nose. Take the Seecamp out, put it in your purse, come back, put the purse under the table, at your feet. A few minutes later, you drop your napkin, something, reach under the table, drop the Seecamp into my boot."

She smiled at him.

A few minutes later, Bobby muttered "Jesus" and stopped in front of a 12-foot-high concrete wall topped with razor wire. "You think this is it?"

Bobby announced himself at the call box and the big wrought-iron gate opened electronically. They drove slowly up the long driveway, past the palms and hibiscuses and frangipani. Two men, cradling Uzis, stood guard at the front, one of them leashed to an enormous rottweiler. The one with the dog hurried to Sheila's door and opened it, but when she reached out her hand he ignored it and reached for her handbag. On his opposite side, the dog strained at its collar. Sheila stepped out of the car and stared directly into the dog's eyes with her own cool blue eyes. It looked away and whimpered. Sheila reached down to stroke the fur behind its ears. "Nice boy," she said. The dog pulled away from her touch.

The other man gestured with his Uzi and Bobby got out and raised his hands over his head. The man patted him down as the big, hand-carved door opened. A pudgy little man in a white linen suit stood outlined in the light of the doorway. His tiny feet were in black patent leather Guccis and his long, black hair, flecked with silver, was greased and combed straight back from a soft, pouty face. His eyes were big and dark, like a child's.

"Señor Esquared," the man said, smiling. "Señor Rogers has told me much about you."

"Señor Rogers?" Bobby asked.

The man looked confused. "Señor Esol Rogers, your associate."

"Oh, yes. Señor Rogers. He has told me great things about you, too, Señor Medina."

The man grinned and nodded with satisfaction.

Smugglers, Bobby thought. They crave recognition.

The man who had searched Sheila's bag was now patting her down, running his hands down her back. Señor Medina frowned and snapped something in Spanish. The man yanked his hand away.

"Please excuse the precautions, señorita," Medina said to Sheila. "A man in my position. . . ." He shrugged.

"You're too kind, señor. But, of course, it's señora. Señora Sheila Doyle." She reached out a hand.

He shook the tips of her fingers. Then he stared at her for a moment, this tall Anglo woman. He said something in Spanish to his two men and barely perceptible smiles crossed their lips.

"*Gracias*, Señor Medina," Sheila said. "*Por los complimientos.*"

Medina looked startled. Then he smiled. "You speak my tongue, señora?"

"*Un poquito.*" Sheila wiggled her fingers a bit.

"Come in, come in," the man said. "Welcome to my humble *campesino* house." He turned and walked inside.

Right, Bobby thought. A poor man's shack. Maybe five, six mil, not counting the half mil in electronic security.

Bobby followed Sheila through the door. She glanced back and whispered, "That's the only Spanish sentence I know."

Yeah, Bobby thought, but now the little bastard thinks we understand Spanish. Which couldn't hurt.

Medina led them into the living room, his tiny Gucci heels clicking against the white tile floor. The living room looked like the set for one of those born-again-Christian TV programs. Overstuffed lavender sofa. Two pink armchairs shaded with gilt. China figurines. Hummels. Expensive kitsch bought by people with no taste. Bobby looked for the big cross, but saw only a huge color photo over the marble fireplace.

"Ah, you noticed," said Medina, gesturing toward the photograph. "My wife, Lucinda."

"Beautiful," said Bobby. The woman looked about 35, heavily made-up, a puff of pinkish blonde hair like a halo surrounding her pretty, small-featured face, which wouldn't age well. She'd get fat, Bobby thought, and look like a plump pigeon.

Medina stepped through sliding glass doors to an outdoor bar alongside a heart-shaped swimming pool. His wife, sitting at the bar nursing a drink, looked up with a small jerk, as if frightened. She was maybe 20 years older than her picture, 20 pounds heavier. Just like a pigeon, Bobby thought, a plump pigeon in a flowing pink caftan.

Medina introduced them. Sheila flashed Lucinda her patented 8 × 10-glossy smile. Lucinda returned a quick, nervous little smile. A Nicaraguan bartender in white served drinks. Another servant appeared with a tray of caviar and toast. Medina snapped something in Spanish and one of the white-clad servants hovering in the darkness hustled inside. He returned with a long box, which Medina opened, showing it to Bobby and Sheila. Nestled on tissue paper was a replica of an Uzi machine gun, except that it was carved out of ivory.

"My good friends from the estate of Israel gave me this," he said. "In gratitude for my assistance. A little matter of a Hamas terrorist. He turned up in Miami trying to buy Cemtex. He was very foolish. Made the wrong connections. Poof!" Medina wiped the palms of his hands as if to clean them of blood. "It is lovely, no?"

"Lovely!" said Sheila.

"But at times, a patriot needs more than artifacts, eh, señora?"

Sheila smiled and nodded.

"Come, Señor Esquared. Let the women talk while I show you the grounds."

Bobby and Medina walked into the warm, humid darkness, leaving the two women at the bar. Bobby glanced back to see Sheila, smiling, trying to make conversation. The plump woman nodded nervously, like a toy bird dipping its head for water.

"I have lived in your country 30 years," said Medina as they walked across the huge expanse of lawn toward what looked like a garage. "But I am still a Cuban. My wife is a Cuban. My children. We will die only Cubans. Do you understand?" Bobby nodded. Medina went on. "Even here in exile I go to Mass every morning as I did in Havana, years ago, before that bandit destroyed my country."

He stepped into a dark mound in the grass and screamed, "Aiee! Fucking dogs!" He danced aside and wiped his shoe furiously on the grass.

When they came to the garage, Medina pushed a button to open the doors. The doors rolled up, a light went on and Bobby was staring at a beautifully restored, lipstick red 1957 Cadillac Coupe de Ville convertible with white leather upholstery.

"Is beautiful, no?" Medina said, smiling at the car.

"Very beautiful," Bobby said.

The little man went over to the gleaming car, ran his hands lovingly along its fender. "It is the same model I used to ride through the streets of Havana," he said. "I found this one and restored it myself. A hobby of mine, mechanical things. It took me five years but that did not matter." He looked at Bobby. "Do you know what sustained me, Señor Esquared?" Bobby shook his head no. Medina said, "The knowledge that one day Lucinda and I will drive this car again through the streets of Havana, past cheering crowds welcoming me home from exile. I come here at night to stare at this beautiful thing. I see myself in it back in Cuba." He looked at Bobby. "I'd give it all up, you know. This house, the life, to return."

Sure you would, Bobby thought. A humble patriot. Not a fucking ruthless butcher. Not a guy who once, Sol claimed, blew a Cuban airliner out of the sky. Two hundred eighty-eight innocent people, some of them exiles from Miami, because he wanted to make a point. "You know what they call him?" Sol had said. "*El Loco*. The Crazy One."

"Don't misunderstand me, Señor Esquared," Medina was saying. "I am grateful to America. It's been very good to me. And it's made me rich. But a patriot needs something more. His roots. My roots are in Havana. My father is buried there. He was a great patriot. He fought that butcher, Castro, until my father was captured. I was only a boy. My mother and I were called to the prison to watch. We had to stand in the hot sun while they brought my father out in front of Castro. Castro made him kneel at his feet. He told him to bow his head, but my father refused. He looked up into that butcher's eyes and defied him to kill him man-to-man. And that coward, that bastard. . . ." Medina's fingers jabbed the night air, saliva forming in his cheeks, spittle on his lips, as he raged on. "That pig bastard didn't have the courage. He turned to one of his henchmen, an American, a hired assassin, this big fucking gringo, and he handed him his *pistola*, a P-38, a Nazi gun, of course, and said, 'Here, gringo, you do it. He is not worth my time.' And the gringo shot my father between the eyes."

Medina stopped talking. Finally, he said, "Excuse me, Señor
Esquared. I am a man of passion. You understand. For my people,
passion is everything. Passion is the food that keeps me alive. Makes
me remember my enemies." He smiled. "And my friends. Will you
be my friend, Señor Esquared?"

Bobby dipped his head slightly, as if to bow, and stretched out his
hand. "It would be an honor to be your friend, Señor Medina."

The little man nodded, took the tips of Bobby's fingers in his and
held them a moment. In the moonlight, Bobby could see that his
face was still dark from his outburst.

"Good, señor. That is good. I know I can trust you."

Yeah, Bobby thought. But can I trust you?

During dinner Medina hardly spoke, except to snap at his servants
and once to whisper a few words to one of his bodyguards. The man
backed off slowly, bowing slightly, turned and disappeared through
the sliding glass doors.

Sheila looked quizzically at Bobby, but he shook his head and put
a firm hand on her arm to prevent her from going to the bathroom. No sense taking chances. Señor Medina's mood had soured.
The little bastard's mind was still back in Havana and he seemed to
be tasting revenge with every morsel of food he jabbed into his
mouth. His wife ate with her head down, the good Cuban wife. She
must be terrified out of her wits, Bobby thought, the things she
knows. Jesus, the poor old broad!

Bobby tried to make small talk with Señora Medina, but the
woman just flashed her tiny, terrified smile and looked down again
at her food.

When the silent dinner was over, Medina snapped his fingers
and a servant appeared with a leather briefcase. Medina handed it
to Bobby. "My grocery list, Señor Esquared. Do you think you can
fill it?"

"No problem," said Bobby.

"It is a very extensive list, Señor Esquared."

"I can fill it."

"I have heard of only one man in your city who can supply such
items. Difficult to contact."

"I have my sources."

"Yes, that's what I am told." The man was silent for a moment.

Then he said, "You know, of course, this man, this man with the guns, is not sympathetic to my cause."

"No?"

"I have heard this." He smiled. "I, too, have my sources. They tell me it is necessary you exercise, how do you say, discretion as to your buyer with this man."

"It is understood, Señor Medina."

"Good. Then how long will it take you?"

"Maybe a few weeks."

"A few weeks is no problem. More than that . . ." Medina shrugged. "So let us agree, two weeks it is."

Bobby reached his hand toward Medina. The little man took his fingertips. His fingers were cold.

"Agreed," Bobby said.

"A telephone number and a name are on the list. My associate Raoul. You will contact only him from now on. He will explain the details of the transfer of the groceries."

Bobby nodded.

"The dollars, of course, are there too."

"Of course."

"Would you like to count them?"

"It's not necessary."

"Good."

Later, as they drove back to Fort Lauderdale, Bobby told Sheila what had happened in the *campesino* hut, and, for the first time, he told her about Sol's warnings.

Sheila shuddered. "What a scary little man!"

Two weeks later, during spring break, a college student — a wrestler from the University of Pennsylvania — was strolling on Fort Lauderdale beach, taking in all the girls glistening in the sun a few yards from the Mark Hotel's Chickee Bar. His eye fell on a gorgeous one lying close to the water, on her stomach. A small red-and-white dog lay on the blanket beside her, sunning itself too. She had a perfect tan, a beautiful ass and short blonde hair like a crew cut. He paused a moment, looked down at his own winter-white body, then made up his mind.

"Excuse me," he said. The dog sat up, alert. "Excuse me!" he said more loudly. She rolled over onto her back, shading her eyes with

the flat of her hand. He felt foolish. This woman was in her late
thirties. "I'm sorry," he said. "I was just wondering what kind of dog
you have." He smiled.

She looked at him with cold blue eyes and rolled back onto her
stomach. The boy hesitated uncertainly, and then retreated.

It had been funny at first, Sheila thought. College boys hitting on
her. Now it was a pain. She shaded her eyes again and looked up at
the Chickee Bar, where Bobby was conducting business with a character called Machine Gun Bob. They sat at a table close to the sand.
Bobby was in his bikini, all tan and muscles, and Machine Gun was
in his camouflage cutoffs and SS thunderbolt necklace, with swas-
tika tattoos on his reddish-burnt skin. Fucking poster boy for Hitler
youth, Sheila thought. She did not like Machine Gun.

She saw Bobby stand up and shake Machine Gun's hand. He
came toward her now, his big body shaded by the sun at his back.
Hoshi scrambled up to greet him and Bobby bent to ruffle the fur
at the base of his neck. Sheila looked into Bobby's shadowed face,
her eyebrows raised.

"It's all settled, baby," he said. "Tomorrow at midnight."

"I can't stand that guy," she said. "Just look at him."

Bobby laughed. "Yeah, they're all into that shit, those gun freaks.
You should see his van. Nazi helmets, uniforms, medals."

"Yeah, well, it's spooky."

"Don't worry, baby. Machine Gun's OK. Just your average stoned
Nazi surfer dude who deals in guns."

"He's a pig."

Bobby was losing patience. "Listen, baby. I need him. Nobody
gets to the man with the guns without Machine Gun. And Machine
Gun is coming through for us. For $25,000, what's not to like?"

The next evening as they drove west on State Road 84, Hoshi sat on
the briefcase beside Bobby. Sheila sat by the passenger window,
staring out at the gas stations, the ramshackle barbecue joints, the
seedy country-and-western bars, their parking lots filled with trucks
owned by rednecks who fancied themselves to be cowboys.

"Keep your eyes peeled for the diner, baby," Bobby said. "It looks
like one of those old-fashioned Airstream trailers. That's where
Medina's man will be with the van." He had already told her the
plan. They would park at the diner, drive the van out to the ranch
where the guns were, load them, return the van to Medina's man

at the diner and drive back home with their cut. Twenty-five thousand.

Sheila absentmindedly began stroking the fur behind Hoshi's left ear. "Bobby," she said. "I still don't know why we had to bring Hosh. It could be dangerous."

"Hoshi's the burglar alarm." He glanced at her. "He's gotta earn his keep, too. Ain't that right, Hosh?" The dog looked at him and then out the front window. No dog's as smart as a Shibu Inu, Bobby thought.

Sheila reached into her leather satchel, felt the cool, chrome-plated Seecamp, found her cigarettes. She lit one and inhaled.

"Here, baby. Take the wheel."

She held the steering wheel while Bobby reached behind his back. He withdrew a black CZ-75, racked the slide to put a round in the chamber and stuck the gun in his belt.

"I thought you trusted that Nazi surfer," Sheila said.

He glanced at her. "The only person I trust, baby, is you."

They drove awhile in the darkness, then Bobby said, "The gun guy's some kind of Aryan Nation guy, you know, those racists. Lives out in the woods with his pit bull and enough guns to start his own revolution. The Reverend Tom of the Aryan Mountain Kirk, whatever the fuck that means. Has all these skinheads and Nazis out to his ranch for midnight cross burnings, then a nice church supper prepared by the ladies." Bobby laughed. "The reverend hates niggers but hates spics even more."

"There it is." Sheila pointed ahead to a shiny aluminum diner set back off the road. Bobby turned into the deserted parking lot and reminded himself that the lot would probably be full of trucks when they returned with the guns. He drove around the brightly lit diner to the dark back parking lot and pulled in next to a white van.

"You wait here," he said, and got out.

Hoshi leaped up and followed Bobby with his eyes. "Good boy, Hosh," Sheila said, stroking his neck. A man got out of the van. She couldn't make out his face in the darkened lot, but he seemed tiny next to Bobby's bulk. He handed Bobby something and walked around to the front of the diner. Bobby waved for Sheila.

Sheila took the briefcase and her bag and got out. Hoshi jumped out after her. When she slid into the van's passenger seat, Hoshi stood outside. He began to bark and back up nervously.

"Come on, Hosh," Sheila said. But the dog kept barking and

backing up, then lunging at Sheila. He took her jeans cuff in his teeth.

"What the hell's the matter with him?" Bobby snapped. "Get him into the fucking van."

Sheila grabbed Hoshi's collar and pulled him onto her lap. He squirmed. "What's the matter, baby?" she said.

"Hoshi, cut it out for Christ's sake!" Bobby snapped again. The dog stopped squirming but began to whimper, staring at Bobby. Bobby ignored him and held up the keys the man had given him. "One's to arm the engine burglar alarm," Bobby said. "The other's to arm the rear doors so they can't be opened." Bobby found the remote transmitter with a strip of white tape on it. He pressed the button and all the doors locked with a click, the front lights blinked and the alarm armed itself with a chirp. Bobby started the engine.

"What about the rear doors?" Sheila asked.

Bobby showed her the remote with the red tape on it. "Red for the rear. The back-door remote operates only with a full load in back. The little spic was very specific. *Muy importante* we arm the rear doors the minute the van is loaded with the guns. No sooner, no later. Fucking paranoid Medina." Bobby backed the van out of the space and drove around the diner. Through the diner's windows, he saw the little man seated alone at the counter, sipping coffee. "We come back with the guns," Bobby said, "we just hand the little spic the keys and we're home free."

Fifteen minutes later, they were bouncing over a rutted dirt road so narrow that scrub bushes and small pines brushed against their windows. Off to the left, tiny green lights flickered and disappeared.

"Deer," Bobby said.

Soon they arrived at a clearing, then a small rise, more like a bump in the road, and then a hand-painted sign that said ARYAN MOUNTAIN KIRK. PASTOR TOM MILLER. A small, dilapidated, wood-frame cracker house was up ahead and beside it sat a Quonset hut–like barn of corrugated aluminum painted in green and brown camouflage patches.

Bobby parked the van a few yards from the front door and waited. A light came on over the door, and a huge, older man filled the doorway. He must have been 6'6", 300 pounds. "Jesus H.

Christ," Bobby said. The man was mythic-looking, with a John Brown spade beard and combat boots and bib overalls that strained against his belly and chest.

"Wait here," Bobby said. "I don't come out in ten minutes, you start the engine and drive the fuck out of here."

She showed him her Seecamp. "You don't come out, I'm going in after you."

"Christ, Sheila. That little thing will only piss him off. A couple of shots from that would be like mosquito bites."

Sheila shrugged. "Whatever, Bobby. Sure."

Bobby got out of the van and the huge man approached, followed by a muscular white pit bull, about Hoshi's size. Hoshi flattened his ears and began to growl low in his throat.

A few words were exchanged, the men shook hands and then the huge man seemed to embrace Bobby. He picked the pistol out of Bobby's belt with thumb and forefinger, as if it were something rancid, and tossed it into the bushes. Then he put one of his massive arms around Bobby's shoulders and walked him toward the Quonset hut. It was the first time Bobby had ever looked small to Sheila.

The fur on Hoshi's back bristled, and he growled again. Sheila scratched his ears, but he paid no attention. "Everything's going to be all right, Hosh," she said as the two men and the pit bull disappeared into the hut.

Inside the hut, the Reverend Miller introduced his dog. "I call him Dog-Dog," he said, and reached down to pat his head. "He's a loyal guy. An Aryan, too." He winked at Bobby and smiled. "White race got to stick together, Bobby." He laughed. "You can go ahead and pet him. He won't bite. Not unless I tell him to."

Bobby stroked the pit bull's back, which was covered with scars. His ears were clipped for fighting and his eyes were mean and yellow.

"Bobby Squared, huh?" the reverend said. "What kind of a name is that?"

Bobby thought for a moment, decided to chance it, looked up into the huge man's eyes and said, "It used to be Robert Redfeather, when I was on the reservation."

"It did, huh? You should have kept it. Indians are a noble

race. They should never have let us in. Ruined the whole damn
neighborhood." He threw his head back and roared with laughter.
"Come on. Let's see what I got for you."

The Quonset hut was hot and smelled of mildew and hay and
horseshit and, strangely, gun oil. A card table was stacked high with
pamphlets and books: *Letters from the Mountain Kirk. The Turner
Diaries. The Brotherhood. The Order.* The reverend palmed a copy of
The Holy Book of Adolf Hitler. "What a great man, eh, Bobby?"

"If you say so, Reverend."

The man winked again and then, with a vast gesture of his meaty
arm, motioned toward the far end of the hut, where Bobby saw a
barren altar with a wooden pulpit and behind it not a cross but an
enormous Nazi flag pinned to the wall.

"The faithful love that shit," said the reverend. "Hitler, swastikas,
burning crosses. Keeps 'em happy." He shook his head mournfully.
"But so what? If that's what they want, fine, I'll give it to 'em."

"Where were you ordained, Reverend?" Bobby said.

"Where?" The man glared. "Where? Right fucking here. I came
out here one night and ordained myself." He crossed the room and
unlocked a door to the right of his pulpit. "I'm my own fucking god,
Bobby. After you."

Bobby stepped into a smaller room filled floor to ceiling with
cardboard boxes. They were stamped in black letters: BRNO.
PRODUCT OF CZECHOSLOVAKIA; ISRAELI MILITARY INDUS-
TRIES; LLAMA GABILANDO. PRODUCT OF SPAIN; NORINCO.
PRODUCT OF THE PEOPLE'S REPUBLIC OF CHINA; BERETTA.
PRODUCT OF ITALY. The reverend opened a box stamped NOR-
INCO and held up an AK-17. "I believe this is what you're looking
for?" He racked the side, aimed the AK at Bobby's forehead and
pulled the trigger. *Click.* He threw back his head and roared again,
his booming laughter echoing off the aluminum walls. He tossed
the AK to Bobby and began to open other boxes, producing CZ-75
pistols, Uzis, a Llama 45.

Bobby handed back the AK. "Everything but the Llama," he said.
"My man doesn't like those spic guns."

"A man after my own heart. Here, let me show you something."
He went over to a closet and opened the door. Ten big tins labeled
SURVIVAL CRACKERS were stacked on the floor. The clothes rack
was lined with satin Ku Klux Klan robes in several colors. "I got red,

I got green, I got yellow." The reverend touched them. "Robes for every occasion. Formal, casual, beachwear. They love it. But this" — he pulled a box from one of the upper shelves and held it out to Bobby — "is what I wanted to show you." He opened the lid and gently parted the layers of tissue paper.

It was a Cuban flag. Three blue stripes, two white stripes, a white star in a red triangle. The flag was soiled and ripped in places, blackened with gunpowder, stained with dried blood. The reverend watched Bobby as he looked at the flag, then he, too, looked at it.

"I fought for this flag," he said, tapping Bobby's arm for emphasis. "I believed in it. It was the only thing I ever believed in. I carried it into battle in the Sierra Maestra, and into Havana after we routed Batista. I was mobbed, like a god. The people shouted, "Gringo! Gringo!" I could have had anything I wanted. Anything! But I only wanted the revolution to work. They were good people. I became an outlaw in my own country for them."

He spat on the floor. "And how did that bastard Castro repay me? He waited until we cleaned the Batista forces out, then he came in two days later, the conquering hero. He pinned a medal on my chest in the middle of Havana, with a couple hundred thousand people screaming, "Gringo! Gringo!" Fidel bent over and whispered in my ear, 'You think you're bigger than me, gringo?' So he put me in charge of the execution squads. The dirtiest fucking job, to humiliate me. I told him the Batistas had fought bravely, that we should let them into the revolution now. But he wouldn't listen. I went around the countryside with a firing squad. A shit detail."

The reverend shook his head. "But I only once pulled the trigger myself. Fidel was going to shoot this poor little bastard himself, with the guy's wife and little kid watching, the worst thing you can think of. They made the guy kneel in front of Fidel, but the bastard had heart. He looked right into Fidel's eyes and told him to pull the trigger. Fucking Fidel tossed me his gun and told me to do it. I'll never forget it. A chromed P-38, a Nazi gun. Fidel was never a Communist. He was a Nazi." The reverend's eyes went blank. "So I shot him, poor guy. Two weeks later, Fidel put out a warrant for my arrest. Treason." He slammed the lid on the box and shoved it back into the closet. "I took a slow boat to Miami."

When he turned back, Bobby saw with surprise that there were tears in his eyes. "After that, I didn't give a shit. Fuck 'em all. I'll arm everyone. The Jews, Hamas, the IRA, the Ulster Defense Force, both sides. Let 'em kill each other off. God can sort 'em out." He smiled. "So you see, Bobby. I don't give a shit who these guns are for, as long as they're not for spics. Spics like to kill their own. They enjoy it."

When Bobby and the huge man came out of the Quonset hut, pushing a dolly loaded with boxes, Sheila sighed with relief. Bobby signaled for her to back the van up to the hut. She did, and heard the van's back doors open and the thud of boxes dropping. As she lit a cigarette, she saw the pit bull sitting outside her door, staring up. Hoshi climbed onto her lap, put his paws against the window and growled. "It's all right, Hosh," she said. "It's all right."

When the van was loaded with the boxes, the doors slammed and Sheila opened the window to hand Bobby the briefcase. Bobby counted out a wad of bills and handed it back to Sheila. He shook the man's hand.

"Good to do business with you, Reverend."

The reverend nodded. "You, too, Robert Redfeather."

Bobby opened the driver's side door and Hoshi leaped out. "Get back here," Bobby yelled, but the dogs had already squared off. Before he could reach them, they sprang, snapping and snarling, their teeth flashing. The pit bull, less agile, lunged at Hoshi like a clumsy boxer, but Hoshi pranced sideways, avoiding the lunge and snapping at the pit bull's rear haunch, drawing blood. The pit bull reared back, faked to the left and caught Hoshi by the scruff of his neck, also drawing blood. Three quick shots rang out, kicking up dirt at the dogs' feet, and they separated, startled and whimpering. Both eyed Sheila, who now held her Seecamp steady at the pit bull. Bobby scooped Hoshi into his arms, while the reverend fell to his knees and hugged his scarred warrior, crying, "Dog-Dog, Dog-Dog, are you all right?"

Dog-Dog writhed in his grip, straining to get at Hoshi, but Bobby already had him in the van with the door closed, snarling at the open window. Sheila pulled Hoshi onto her lap and hugged him while Bobby started the engine and drove off.

"Is he all right?" Bobby said.

Sheila pressed a handkerchief against his neck. "I think so. It's just the skin."

Bobby glanced in his sideview mirror at the reverend, still on his knees and hugging his dog. "That poor old bastard."

They drove in silence for a few minutes until they were back on State Road 84, heading east. Sheila inspected the bites on Hoshi's neck. "The bleeding's stopped. You're OK, aren't you, Hosh?" The dog licked her face.

"Tough guy, eh, Hosh?" Bobby smiled. "Bit off more than you could chew this time. Why didn't you kill him, Sheila? The dog, I mean."

"He's a dog, Bobby. Only people deserve their own executions."

"Yeah, well, a couple more minutes, maybe Hoshi would have had his own execution."

"Then I would have killed the dog."

At two A.M., they pulled into the diner parking lot, now crowded with cars. Cowboys filled the tables at the windows, having breakfast. Bobby drove around to the back and parked the van next to his SHO.

"The spic's inside, Raoul," he said. "I'll be right back."

"I'm going in, too. I want to clean Hoshi in the ladies' room." Sheila looked down at her own shirt, soaked with blood. "And myself."

Bobby grabbed the briefcase and Sheila hoisted Hoshi into her arms.

Inside the noisy diner, she brushed through the crowd back toward the ladies' room. A waitress stopped her. "You can't bring a dog in here, honey," the waitress said.

"Watch me."

Meanwhile, Bobby looked for the spic. I'll never find that bastard with all these rednecks, he thought. They were all dressed up like cowboys, talking loud, letting out rebel yells and eating with their hats on. Some of the rednecks glanced at him, a big muscular guy with a briefcase and a ponytail. "Faggot," one of them muttered.

"Honey," Bobby said to one of the waitresses. She balanced a tray of eggs and grits on her arm. "Did you see a little Latin guy in here?"

The waitress blew a wisp of hair off her eyes. "I got time to look for spics?" She brushed past him.

Another waitress told him, "Baby, I ain't seen or heard nothing since 1967. I thought I was deaf and blind till I seen you standing there."

The third waitress remembered him. "A couple hours ago. Nervous little guy. Had a quick coffee, made a phone call and split."

Bobby wondered if maybe the rednecks had scared him off. He decided to check for messages. "Where's the phone, hon?" he said to the waitress.

She pointed to the end of the diner. "By the little boys' room."

The telephone was next to an open window that faced the back parking lot. He dialed his own number, and it began to ring. Through the window, Bobby saw his SHO, then the white van, the white van with all those guns in it, the white van with nobody watching it, no alarm turned on. "Shit," he muttered. He dug the keys from his pocket while the phone still rang, found the remote with the red tape on it, held it out the window and pressed the button.

The van's rear lights blinked twice, the alarm chirped and then the whole thing exploded. The rear doors blew off, the side panels blew off, the guns blew out of the van in pieces, engulfed by flames and black smoke, and scattered all over the lot. The van was in flames, twisted grotesquely out of shape, and the whole left side of his SHO was caved in. Glass was everywhere, metal gun parts, van doors and the bumper.

"Jesus fucking Christ," said Bobby.

He dropped the phone, rushed out and almost bumped into Sheila, wide-eyed and scared, still holding Hoshi. "Bobby! What happened? Are you all right?"

He grabbed her hard by the arm and half-dragged her out of the diner. The cowboys and waitresses were already outside. Bobby led Sheila through the crowd toward the highway and started walking very fast along the side of the road. In the distance, he could already hear the sirens of police cars and fire engines. They walked in the darkness until Sheila jerked him to a stop. "Enough! What happened?" She put Hoshi down.

Bobby looked back at the smoke billowing above the diner. "It was a setup." he said. He told her about the reverend's story. "I should have figured it out. Medina knew who I was getting the guns from. He set us up. Medina didn't give a shit about the guns. It was revenge he wanted. 'Be my friend, Señor Esquared,' yeah. Friends or enemies, it made no difference to him. The reverend was right. They kill their own."

They started walking again, with Hoshi trotting at their feet. When they came to a pay phone, Bobby called a taxi. They waited, Bobby, Sheila and the dog. Bobby reached down and stroked the fur behind Hoshi's ears. "I should have listened to you, Hosh," he said. The dog's tail wagged.

When the taxi arrived, Sheila got in first and Hoshi jumped in beside her. When Bobby got in and shut the door, the cabbie, a Pakistani, turned and said, "No dogs."

Bobby looked at Sheila. "You see a dog in here, baby?" he said.

"Nope." She smiled and shook her head.

Bobby smiled at the cabbie in the rearview mirror. "We don't see any dog, Mr. 7-Eleven. Just drive."

STUART M. KAMINSKY

Find Miriam

FROM *New Mystery*

"HOW OLD would you say I am?"

I looked at the dark handsome man standing next to the railing of his penthouse balcony overlooking Sarasota Bay. He was just a bit bigger than I am, about six feet and somewhere in the range of one hundred and ninety pounds. His open blue shirt, which may have been silk, showed a well-muscled body with a chest of gray-brown hair. The hair on his head was the same color, plentiful, neat. And he was carefully and gently tanned. He had a glass of V-8 in his hand. He had offered me the same. I had settled for water. There was a slight accent, very slight when he spoke and I realized he reminded me of Ricardo Montalban.

I'm forty-four, on the thin side, losing my hair and usually broke or close to it. I'd come to Sarasota two years earlier, just drove till my car gave out and I felt safely in the sunshine after spending my life in the gray of Chicago. I had driven away from a wife who had dumped me and a dead-end investigator's job with the State's Attorney's Office.

Now, I made my living finding people, asking questions, answering to nobody. I had a growing number of Sarasota lawyers using me to deliver a summons or find a local resident who hadn't turned up for a court or divorce hearing. Occasionally, I would turn up some street trade, a referral from a bartender or Dave the owner of the Dairy Queen next door to the run-down two-story office building where I had my office and where I lived. I had a deal with the building manager. The landlord lived in Seattle. By giving the manager a few extra dollars a month beyond the reasonable rent for a seedy two-room suite, he ignored the fact that I was living in the second room of a two-room office. The outer room was designed as a reception room. I had turned it into an office. The room behind it was a small windowed office which I had turned into a living space. I had fixed it up to my satisfaction and the clothes I had brought with me from Chicago would hold out for another year or two. I had a bed, an old dresser, a sink in the corner, a television set and an aging green sofa and matching armchair. The only real inconvenience was that the office, like all the others, opened onto a balcony with a rusting railing facing a parking lot shared with the Dairy Queen and, beyond it, the heavy traffic of Route 301. To get to the bathroom, which had no bath, I had to walk past five offices and take whatever the weather had to offer. I showered every morning after I worked out at the downtown YMCA.

There was nothing but my name printed on the white-on-black plastic plate that slid into the slot on my door. I wasn't a private detective, didn't want to be. I did what I know how to do, ask questions, find people.

"Just a guess," Raymond Sebastian asked again, looking away from the beautiful sight of the boats bobbing in the bay and the busy bridge going over to Bird Key.

Answering a question like that could lose me a job, but I hadn't come to this town to go back to saying "yes, boss" to people I liked and didn't like.

"Sixty," I guessed, standing a few feet away from him and looking him in the eyes.

"Closer to seventy," he said with some satisfaction. "I was blessed by the Lord in many ways. My genes are excellent. My mother is ninety-two and still lives in good health. My father died when he was ninety-four. I have uncles, aunts . . . you wouldn't believe."

"Not without seeing them," I said.

Sebastian laughed. There wasn't much joy in his laugh. He looked at his now-empty V-8 glass and set it on a glass-top table on the balcony.

"Lawrence told you my problem?" he asked facing me, his gray-blue eyes unblinking, sincere.

"Your wife left. You want to find her. That's all."

Lawrence Werring was a lawyer, civil cases, injury law suits primarily, an ambulance chaser and proud of it. It had bought him a beautiful wife, a leather-appointed office and a four bedroom house on the water on Longboat Key. If I knew which one it was, I could probably see it from where Sebastian and I were standing.

"My wife's name is Miriam," Sebastian said handing me a folder that lay next to the now-empty V-8 glass. "She is considerably younger than I, thirty-six, but I believed she loved me. I was vain enough to think it was true and for some time it seemed true. And then one afternoon . . ."

He looked around as if she might suddenly rematerialize.

". . . She was gone. I came home and her clothes, jewelry, gone. No note, nothing. That was, let me see, last Thursday. I kept expecting to hear from her or a kidnapper or something, but . . ."

I opened the folder. There were a few neatly typed pages of biography. I skimmed them. Miriam Latham Sebastian was born in Utah, earned an undergraduate degree in social science at the University of Florida and moved with her parents, now both dead, to Sarasota where she worked for a Catholic services agency as a case worker till she married Sebastian four years earlier. There was also a photograph of Miriam Sebastian. She was wearing red shorts, a white blouse and a great smile. Her dark hair was long and blowing in the breeze. She had her arm lovingly around her husband who stood tall, tan and shirtless in a pair of white trunks looking at the camera. They were standing on the wide sands of a Florida Gulf Coast beach, a few apartments or condos behind them.

"Pretty," I said closing the folder.

"Beautiful," he corrected. "Exquisite. Charming."

"Any guesses?" I said. "About what happened?"

He shrugged and moved from the balcony back into the penthouse apartment. I followed as he talked. We stopped in front of a painting of his wife on the wall over a big white sofa. The whole room was white, but not a modern white. There was a look of tasteful antique about the place. Not my kind of home, but I could appreciate it.

"Another man perhaps, but I doubt it," he said. "We have had no major quarrels. I denied her nothing, nothing. I am far from a poor man, Mr. Fonesca and . . ."

He paused and sighed deeply.

"And," he continued composing himself, "I have checked our

joint checking and savings accounts. Most of the money has been removed. A little is left. I have my corporate attorney checking other holdings which Miriam might have had access to. I find it impossible to believe she would simply take as much money as she could and just walk out on me."

"You had a little hitch in your voice when you mentioned another man," I said having decided the chairs in the room were too white for me to sit on.

"She has had a good friend," he said gently. "This is very difficult for me. I am a proud man from a proud family."

"A good friend?" I repeated.

"For about the last year," he said, "Miriam has been seeing a psychiatrist, nothing major, problems to be worked out about her childhood, her relationship to her parents. The psychiatrist's name is Gerald Bermeister. He's got a practice over one of those antique stores on Palm Avenue. I'm not a young man. I am not immune to jealousy. Gerald Bermeister is both young and good looking. There were times when I could not determine whether my suspicions were simply that of an older man afraid of losing his beautiful young wife or were valid concerns."

"I'll check it out," I said.

"Miriam was a bit of a loner," he went on. "But because of business connections we belong to a wide variety of organizations, Selby Gardens, Asolo Angels, charity groups, and we're seen at balls and dances. Miriam said that in three years we had been on the *Herald-Tribune*'s society page eleven times. In spite of this, Miriam had no really close friends with one possible exception, Caroline Wilkerson, the widow of my late partner."

"And what do you want me to do?" I asked.

"Find her, of course," Sebastian said turning from the painting to look at me.

"Has she committed a crime?" I asked.

"I don't know. I don't think so," he said.

"So, she's free to go where she wants to go, even to leave her husband, take money out of your joint accounts and wander away. It may be a boyfriend. It may be a lot of things."

"I just want you to find her," he said. "I just want to talk to her. I just want to find out what happened and if there is anything I can do to get her back."

"She could be half way to Singapore by now," I said.

"Your expense account is unlimited," he answered. "I will want you to keep me informed if you leave town in search of Miriam and I would expect you would, as a professional, keep expenses to a minimum and give me a full accounting of all such expenses when you find her."

"If I find her," I said. "I'll do my best to find out why she left. I'll have to ask her if she's willing to talk to you. I'll tell you where she is if she gives me permission to tell you."

"I understand," he said.

He moved again. I followed into an office where he moved to a desk and picked something up next to a computer.

"Here's a check in advance," he said. "Larry said your fee was negotiable. Consider this expenses and, if anything is left, part of your payment. I propose one hundred and twenty dollars a day plus expenses."

I nodded to show it was fair and took the check. It was made out to me for five hundred dollars. He had been ready and expecting that I'd take the job.

"How long?" I asked.

"How long?"

"Do I keep looking before I give up? I expect to find her, but it may be hard or easy. It may, if she's really smart, be impossible."

"Let's say we re-evaluate after two weeks if it goes that long," he said. "But I want her back if it's at all possible. I'm too old to start again and I love Miriam. Do you understand?"

I nodded, tucked the folder under my arm after dropping the check into it and asked him for the numbers of any credit cards they shared, the tag number and make of her car and various other things that would make my job easier.

While he found what I asked for he admitted, "I tried going to the police first, but they said they really had no reason to look for Miriam unless I thought she might be dangerous to herself or had been taken against her will. They also said I could file a missing persons report but there was little they could do even if they found her other than inform me that she was alive and well, unless she had committed a crime, which she hadn't. I'm talking too much."

"It's understandable," I said as he ushered me to the door and handed me an embossed business card, tasteful, easily readable black script: Raymond Sebastian, Investments, Real Estate. There was an office address and phone number in the lower left-hand corner. He had written his home phone number on the back of the card but I already had that.

"Keep me informed," he said taking my hand. "Call any time. As often as you like."

He waited with me at the elevator. His was the only apartment on the floor, but he was on the twelfth floor and the elevator took a few minutes.

"Anything else I can tell you?" he asked.

"She have any living relatives?"

"No, it's all in the material I've given you," he said. "Just me. I don't think she's gone far. We've traveled all around the world, but she considers the Gulf Coast her home. I could be wrong."

"I'm going to start with her friend Mrs. Wilkerson," I said.

"Good idea though I don't know what Caroline can tell you that I haven't. Yet, maybe there was something said, some . . . I don't know."

The elevator bell rang and the doors opened. I stepped in and smiled confidently at Raymond Sebastian who now looked a little older than he had on his balcony.

When I'm not working, I bike. Not a motorcycle. A bike. Sarasota isn't that big and it has a good cheap bus system that not enough people use. When I'm on a case, I rent a car and charge it to my client. I had left my bike, an old one-speed, chained to a tree. No one had taken my battered bike pack. It wasn't worth the effort and besides, we were a little off the regular haunts of Sarasota's downtown homeless. I put the folder in the bike pack, took off the chain and dropped it into the second pouch of the pack. I biked. It was summer, the day was hot. I pedaled to my place behind the Dairy Queen on 301. I pedaled slowly. I was wearing my best clothes — sport jacket, pressed pants, white shirt — and I didn't want to get them sweat drenched if I could help it.

When I got back to my office, I made three calls. First, I called the little independent car rental company I used and we agreed on our usual deal. I said I'd be over to pick up a Toyota Tercel within the hour. Then I called Caroline Wilkerson, who was in the phone book, and made an appointment with her that afternoon. She said she was worried about Miriam and Raymond and would be happy to talk to me. I called Dr. Gerald Bermeister, got a typical he'll-call-you-back. I told her it was urgent, about Miriam Sebastian. The woman put me on hold for a minute so I could listen to the Beach Boys and then came back on to say Dr. Bermeister could see me for fifteen minutes at four-forty-five. I said I'd be there.

I put on my jeans and a black pull-over tee shirt, washed my face and went down to the DQ where I had a burger and a Blizzard and talked to Dave who owned the place. Dave was probably about my age but years of working in the sun on his boat had turned his skin to dark leather. I'm a sucker for junk food and I've got no one to tell me to eat well. Dave doesn't eat his own food, but I knew he kept the place clean. I worked out every day at the YMCA where I biked every day and told myself that covered the burgers, fried chicken, ribs and hot dogs. I could tell myself lies. Who was there to contradict me?

I walked to the car rental office about a mile and a half north on 301, past antique shops, a girlie bar, a pawn shop, some offices and restaurants, a rebuilt and new tire garage and a Popeye's chicken. I had worked up a sweat when I got the car. I turned on the air conditioning and headed for Sebastian's bank where I cashed the check for five hundred. Then I drove back to my office and my room to wash and change into my good clothes.

Caroline Wilkerson met me at the Cafe Kaldi on Main Street. I had no trouble finding her even though the coffee house tables were almost full in spite of the absence of the winter tourists. She sat alone, an open notebook in front of her, reading glasses perched on the end of her nose. She was writing. A cup of coffee rested nearby. I recognized her from the society pages of the *Herald-Tribune*. When I sat across from her, she looked at me over her glasses, took them off, folded her hands on the table and gave me her attention.

The widow Caroline was a beauty, better in person than in the papers. She was probably in her late forties, short, straight silver hair, a seemingly wrinkle-free face with full red lips that reminded me of Joan Fontaine. She wore a pink silky blouse with a pearl necklace and pearl earrings and a light-weight white jacket.

"Would you like to order a coffee?" she asked.

"No, thanks," I said. "I've had my quota for the day."

She nodded, understandingly, and took a sip of her coffee.

"Miriam Sebastian," I said. "You know she's apparently left her husband?"

"Raymond told me," she said. "Called. Frantic. Almost in tears. I couldn't help him. She hasn't contacted me. I would have thought, as Raymond did, that if Miriam did something like this, she'd get in touch with me, but . . ."

Caroline Wilkerson shrugged.

"Did they have a fight?"

A trio of young women suddenly laughed loudly a few tables behind me. When they stopped, Caroline Wilkerson closed her notebook.

"I don't think so," she said. "I can't be certain. But Raymond said nothing about a fight and I don't recall ever seeing them fight or hearing from Miriam that they had fought. Frankly, I'm worried about her."

"Any idea of where she might have gone?" I asked.

The pause was long. She bit her lower lip, made up her mind, sighed. "Gerry Bermeister," she said softly meeting my eyes. "He's her analyst and . . . I think that's all I can say."

"Mr. Sebastian thinks his wife and Dr. Bermeister might have had an affair, that she may have left to be with him."

She shrugged again. I handed her one of my cards, asked her to get in touch with me if she heard from Miriam Sebastian, and said that she should tell her friend that her husband simply wanted to know what happened and if he could talk to her.

She took the card and I stood up.

"I hope you find her," she said. "Miriam has had problems recently, depression. One of her relatives, her only close relative, a cousin I think, recently died. That's hardly a reason for what she's done, but . . . I frankly don't know what to make of it."

At the moment, that made two of us.

"Are you permitted to let me know if you find out anything about where Miriam is and why she's . . ."

I must have been shaking my head "no" because she stopped.

"I'm sorry," I said. "You'll have to get that from her or from Mr. Sebastian. Whatever I find is between me and my client."

"I understand," she said with a sad smile showing perfect white teeth. "That's what I would expect if you were working for me."

When I got to the coffee house door, I looked back at Caroline

Wilkerson. Her half glasses were back on and her notebook was open.

One of the criminal attorneys I did some work for had access to computer networks, very sophisticated access. An individual in his office did the computer work and was well paid. Since some of what he did on the network was on the borderline of illegal, the attorney never acknowledged his access to information the police, credit agencies, banks and almost every major corporation had. I had some time before I saw Bermeister so I dropped by the attorney's office. He was with a client but he gave me permission through his secretary to talk to Harvey, the computer whiz. I found Harvey in his small windowless office in front of his computer. Harvey looked more like an ex–movie star than a computer hacker. He was tall, dark, wearing a suit and sporting shot hair of gold. Harvey was MIT. Harvey was also a convicted cocaine user and former alcoholic.

It took Harvey ten minutes to determine that Miriam Sebastian had not used any of her credit cards during the past four days. Nor had she, at least under her own name, rented a car or taken a plane out of Sarasota, Clearwater, St. Petersburg, Tampa or Fort Meyers.

"You want me to keep checking every day to see if I can find her?" he said.

"I'll bill my client," I said.

"Suit yourself," said Harvey showing capped teeth. "I like a challenge like this, pay or no pay. Me against her. She hides. I find her."

"You want her Social Security number?" I asked.

Harvey smiled.

"That I can get and access to bank accounts and credit cards. You want that?"

"Sure. I'll call you later."

I made it to Dr. Bermeister's office with ten minutes to spare. The matronly receptionist took my name and asked me to have a seat. The only other person in the waiting area was a nervous young woman, about twenty, who hadn't done much to look her best. Her hair was short and dark. Her brown skirt didn't really go with her gray blouse. She ruffled through a magazine.

I was reading an article about Clint Eastwood in *People* magazine when Bermeister's door opened. He was in his thirties, dark suit, dark hair and ruggedly good looking.

"I'll be with you in a few minutes, Audrey," he said to the nervous Audrey who nodded frowning.

"Mr. Fonesca?" he said looking at me. "Please come in."

I followed him into his office. He opened his drapes and let in the sun and a view of Ringling Boulevard. The office wasn't overly large, room for a desk and chair, a small sofa and two armchairs. The colors were all subdued blues. A painting on the wall showed a woman standing on a hill looking into a valley beyond at the ruins of a castle. Her face wasn't visible.

"Like it?" Bermeister said sitting behind his desk and offering me the couch or one of the chairs. I took a chair so I could face him.

"The painting? Yes," I said.

"One of my patients did it," he said. "An artist. A man. We spent a lot of time talking about that painting."

"Haunting," I said.

"Gothic," he said. "I'm sorry, Mr. Fonesca, but I'm going to have to get right to your questions."

"I understand. Miriam Latham Sebastian," I said.

"I can't give you any information about why she was seeing me, what was said."

"I know," I said feeling comfortable in the chair. "Do you know where Mrs. Sebastian is?"

"No," he said.

The answer had come slowly.

"Any ideas?"

"Maybe," he said.

"Want to share them?" I asked.

He didn't answer.

"This one will probably get me kicked out, but you're in a hurry. Mr. Sebastian, and he's not the only one, thinks you and Miriam Sebastian were having an affair."

Bermeister cocked his head and looked interested.

"And if we were?"

"Or are," I amended. "Well, it might suggest that she would come to you. Her husband just wants to talk to her."

"And you just want to find her for him?" he asked.

"That's it," I said.

"First," he said getting up from his desk chair. "I am not and have not been having an affair with Miriam Sebastian. In fact, Mr. Fonesca, I can offer more than ample proof that I am gay. It is a relatively open secret which, in fact, hasn't hurt my practice at all. I get the gay clients, men and women, and I get women who feel more comfortable talking to me. What I don't get are many straight men."

"Mrs. Sebastian," I said.

"She doesn't want to see her husband," he said sitting on the sofa and crossing his legs. "She doesn't want him to know where she is."

"I told Sebastian that I planned to talk to her if I found her and that I wouldn't tell her husband where she was if she told me she wouldn't talk to him under any circumstances."

"Which," said Bermeister, "is what she would say."

"I want to hear it from her," I said. "Until I do, she can't use a credit card, can't cash a check in her own name, can't use her Social Security number without my finding her. My job is finding people, doctor. I do a good job. If you want references. . . ."

His right hand was up indicating that I should stop. He looked up at the painting of the woman looking down at the ruins.

"I made some calls about you after I scheduled this appointment," he said. "Actually, Doreen, my secretary, made the calls. You haven't been here long, but your reputation is very good."

"Small city," I said.

"Big enough," he said taking a pad out of his pocket and writing something. He tore the page out and looked at it.

"I have your word," he said.

"I talk to her. Try to talk her into at least a phone call and then I drop it if she wants to be left alone."

He handed me the sheet of paper. It had two words on it: Harrington House. I folded the sheet and put it in my jacket pocket.

"I don't want people hounding Miriam," he said. "She . . . she can tell you why if she wants to. By the way, I plan to call her the instant you leave. She may choose to pack and leave before you get there."

"I think it would be a good idea if she just talked to me."

"I think you may be right," he said. "I'll suggest that she do so."

He ushered me to the door and shook my hand.

"I'm trusting you," he said.

I nodded and he turned to the nervous young woman.

"I have to make one quick call, Audrey," he said smiling at her.

She had no response and he disappeared back into his office.

I was parked in front of the hardware store on Main. I stopped at an outdoor phone booth where there was a complete phone book and had no trouble finding Harrington House. It was in Holmes

Beach, a Bed and Breakfast. That was on Anna Maria Island. I'd been there to try to find the house where Georges Simenon had lived for a while. The house was gone. I called Harvey the computer whiz.

"Miriam Latham Sebastian has been turning her investments into cash and emptying her joint bank accounts," he said happily. "I've got a feeling there's more."

"Keep at it," I said.

I hung up and wondered why Dr. Gerald Bermeister had been so cooperative. I considered calling Harvey back and asking him to check on the good doctor, but decided that could wait.

I got into my rented car, flipped on the air conditioner and eased back through a break in traffic. I made a left and then another left and then another which brought me right back to Bermeister's office building. I got out fast, ran into the office building, rode the elevator up to Bermeister's floor and then rode back down again and got into my car.

The blue Buick was idling half way down the block near the curb. He had followed me around the block and was waiting for me now. I hoped I had given the impression of someone who had left something in the doctor's office.

I had noticed the blue Buick when I picked up my rental car, but it hadn't really registered. I hadn't been looking for someone who might be following me. But I had spotted what I thought was the same car when I came out of the Cafe Kaldi. Now I was sure. I eased past the Buick, looking both ways at the intersection and catching a glimpse of the man behind the wheel. This guy was short, wore a blue short-sleeve shirt and looked, from the color of his hair and sag of his tough face, about fifty.

There must have been lots of reasons for someone to follow me, but I couldn't think of any good ones other than that the guy in the Buick was hoping I would lead him to Miriam Sebastian. I could have been dead wrong, but I didn't take chances.

He was a good driver, a very good driver, and he kept up with me as I headed for Tamiami Trail. I pulled into the carry-out lane at the McDonald's across from the airport hoping he would follow me in line. I even timed it so a car would be behind me other than the Buick which was the way the guy who was following me would want it, too. My plan was to order a sandwich and pull away while the

Buick was stuck behind the car behind me. If I was lucky, there would also be a car behind him so he couldn't back up.

He was too smart. He simply drove around and parked between a van and a pick-up truck in the parking lot.

Hell. I decided it was all-out now. He had almost certainly figured I had spotted him by now, and I didn't have time to keep playing tag. Miriam Sebastian might be gone by the time I got to Harrington House which was still at least forty minutes from where I took my cheeseburger, put it on the seat next to me and peeled off fast to the right, away from the direction I wanted to go. In the rear-view, I watched the Buick back out as I sailed at sixty down Route 41. He was good, but there's a definite advantage in being the one who is followed. It took me ten minutes to lose him. By then I guessed he knew I wasn't going to lead him to Miriam Sebastian. I ate the burger while I drove.

I took the bridge across to St. Armand's, the same bridge you could see from Raymond Sebastian's apartment, and then drove straight up Longboat Key through the canyon of high-rise resorts and past streets that held some of the most expensive houses, mansions and estates in the county.

I went over the short bridge at the end of the Key and drove through the far less up-scale and often ramshackle hotels and rental houses along the water in Bradenton Beach. Ten minutes later, I spotted the sign for Harrington House and pulled into the shaded driveway. I parked on the white crushed shell and white pebble lot which held only two other cars.

Harrington House was a white three-floor 1920s stucco over cement block with green wooden shutters. There were flowers behind a low picket fence and a sign to the right of the house pointing toward the entrance. I walked up the brick path for about a dozen steps and came to a door. I found myself inside a very large lodge-style living room with a carpeted dark wooden stairway leading up to a small landing and, I assumed, rooms. There were book cases whose shelves were filled and a chess table with checkers lined up and ready to go. The big fireplace was probably original and used no more than a few days during the Central Florida winter.

I hit the bell on a desk by the corner next to a basket of wrapped bars of soap with a sketch of the house on the wrapper. I smelled a bar and was doing so when a blonde woman came bouncing in with a smile. She was about fifty and seemed to be full of an energy I didn't feel. I put down the soap.

"Yes sir?" she said. "You have a reservation."

"No," I said. "I'm looking for Miriam Sebastian, a guest here."

Some of the bounce left the woman but there was still a smile when she said, "No guest by that name registered."

I pulled out the photograph Raymond Sebastian had given me and showed it to her. She took it and looked long and hard.

"Are you a friend of hers?"

"I'm not an enemy."

She looked hard at the photograph again.

"I suppose you'll hang around even if I tell you I don't know these people."

"Beach is public," I said. "And I like to look at birds and waves."

"That picture was taken three or four years ago, right out on the beach behind the house," she said. "You'll recognize some of the houses in the background if you go out there."

I went out there. There was a small, clear-blue swimming pool behind the house and a chest-high picket fence just beyond it. The waves were coming in low on the beach about thirty yards away, but still moaned as they hit the white sand and brought in a new crop of broken shells and an occasional fossilized shark's tooth or dead fish.

I went through the gate to the beach and looked around. A toddler was chasing gulls and not even coming close, which was in the kid's best interest. A couple, probably the kid's parents, sat on a brightly painted beach cloth watching the child and talking. Individuals, duos, trios and quartets of all ages walked along the shoreline in bare feet or floppy sandals. Miriam Sebastian was easy to find. There were five aluminum beach loungers covered in strips of white vinyl. Miriam Sebastian sat in the middle lounger. The others were empty.

She wore a wide-brimmed straw hat, dark sunglasses and a two-piece solid white bathing suit. She glistened from the bottle of lotion that sat on the lounger next to her along with a fluffy towel. She was reading a book or acting as if she was knowing I was on the way. I stood in front of her.

"*War and Peace,*" she said holding up the heavy book. "Always wanted to read it, never did. I plan to read as many of the so-called

classics as I can. It's my impression that few people have really read
them though they claim to have. Please have a seat, Mr. Fonesca."

I sat on the lounger to her right, the one that didn't have lotion
and a towel, and she moved a book mark and laid the book on her
lap. She took off her sunglasses. She was definitely the woman in
the picture, still beautiful, naturally beautiful though the woman
looking at me seemed older than the one in the picture. I showed
her the picture.

"Mr. Sebastian would like to talk to you," I said.

She looked at the photograph and shook her head before handing it back.

"We spent two nights here after our honeymoon in Spain," she
said. "You would think Raymond might remember and at least call
on the chance that I might return. But . . ."

"Will you talk to him?" I asked.

She sat for about thirty seconds and simply looked at me. I was
decidedly uncomfortable and wished I had sunglasses. I looked at
the kid still chasing gulls. He was getting no closer.

"You're not here to kill me," she said conversationally.

"Kill you?"

"I think Raymond is planning to have me killed," she said turning
slightly toward me. "But I think you're not the one."

"Why does your husband want to kill you?" I asked.

"Money," she said and then she smiled. "People thought I married Raymond for his money. I didn't, Mr. Fonesca. I loved him. I
would have gone on loving him. He was worth about one hundred
thousand when we married, give or take a percentage or two in
either direction. I, however, was worth close to eleven million dollars from an annuity, the sale of my father's business when he died,
and a very high yield insurance policy on both my parents."

"It doesn't make sense, Mrs. Sebastian," I said.

"Miriam," she said. "Call me Miriam. Your first name?"

"Lewis," I said. "Lew."

"It makes perfect sense to me," she said. "I know that Raymond
has been telling people that I am having an affair with Dr. Bermeister. Lew, I've been faithful to my husband from the day we met.
Unfortunately, I can't say the same about him. I have ample evidence, including almost interrupting a session between Raymond
and Caroline Wilkerson in the buff in our bed about five weeks ago.

It seems the man almost old enough to be my grandfather married me for my money. After I carefully closed the door without Raymond or Caroline seeing me, I went out, stayed in a hotel and returned the day I was supposed to."

"Reason for divorce," I said.

"My word against theirs," she said. "He'd drag it on, hold up my assets. I haven't the time, Lew."

"So . . . ?"

"So," she said, "I did a little digging and discovered that Caroline was far from the first. I don't know if he is just an old man afraid of accepting his age or if he simply craves the chase and the sex. I know he had no great interest in me in that department for the past year."

"You waited five weeks after you knew all this and then suddenly walked out?" I asked.

"It took me five weeks to convert all my stocks and my life insurance policy to cash and to withdraw every penny I have in bank accounts. I didn't want a scene and I didn't want Raymond to know what I was doing, but by now he knows."

"And you think he wants to kill you?"

"Yes. I don't think he knows the extent of what I've done, nor that I've cashed in the insurance policy," she said. "Raymond claims to be a real estate dealer. He has averaged a little over twenty-thousand dollars on his real estate deals each of the years we've been married. As for his investments, he has consistently lost money. I'd say that at the moment my husband, who is nearing seventy, thinks he'll have millions when, in fact, he has what's left on his credit cards, ten thousand dollars in his own bank account and a 1995 paid-for Lincoln Town Car."

"And he's trying to kill you before you get rid of your money?"

"Yes. But it's too late. I've put all the money, but the thirty thousand I've kept with me in cash, into boxes and sent the boxes anonymously to various charities including the National Negro College Fund, the Salvation Army and many others."

"Why don't you just tell him?" I asked. "Or I can tell him."

The toddler's mother screamed at the boy who had wandered too far in pursuit of the gulls. The kid's name was Harry.

"Then he wouldn't try to have me killed," she said.

"That's the picture," I said. "You know a short bulldog of a man, drives a blue Buick? He's probably about ten years younger than your husband."

"Zito," she said. "Irving Zito."

"He was following me today. I lost him."

She shrugged.

"Irving is Raymond's 'personal' assistant," she said. "He has a record including a conviction for Murder Two. Don't ask me how he and Raymond came together. The story I was told didn't make much sense. So Irving Zito is the designated killer."

"If you don't tell your husband your money is gone and you just stay here, he'll find you even if I don't tell him."

"And you don't plan to tell him?" she asked.

"Not if you say 'no,'" I said.

"Good. I say 'no.' Did he pay you by check?"

"Yes."

"Cash it fast."

"I did," I said, "I thought it was too easy."

"Too easy?"

"Finding you. Talk to Caroline Wilkerson at your husband's suggestion. She sends me to Dr. Bermeister. He sends me to you and you wait for me. You wanted me to find you."

"I wanted whoever was going to kill me to find me," she said. "I'll just have to wait till Zito and Raymond figure it out. If they don't, Raymond will probably find another private detective with fewer scruples than you who will find me right here. I hope I have time to finish Tolstoy before he does."

"You want to die?"

"I've left a letter with my lawyer, with documents, proving my husband's infidelity, misuse of my money which I knew about but chose to ignore, and the statement that if I am found dead under suspicious circumstances, a full investigation of the likelihood of my husband's being responsible is almost a certainty. Now that I know Irving Zito is involved, I'll drive into Sarasota with a new letter including Zito's name and add it to the statement I've given my lawyer."

"You want to die," I repeated though this time it wasn't a question.

"No," she said. "I don't. But I'm going to within a few months even if Raymond doesn't get the job done. I'm dying, Lew. Dr.

Bermeister knows it. I started seeing him as a therapist when I first learned about the tumor more than a year ago. I didn't want my husband to know. I arranged for treatment and surgery in New York and told my husband I simply wanted six weeks or so with old school friends, one of whom was getting married. He had no objections. I caught him and Caroline in bed the day I returned. I had hurried home a day early. Obviously, I wasn't expected. Treatment and surgery proved relatively ineffective. The tumor is in a vital part of my brain and getting bigger. Raymond has never even noticed that I was ill. I don't wish to die slowly in the hospital."

"So you set your husband up," I said.

Harry the toddler was back with his mother who was standing and brushing sand from the boy who was trying to pull away. There were gulls to chase and water to wade in.

"Yes," she said. "You disapprove?"

"I don't know," I answered. "It's your life."

JANICE LAW

Secrets

FROM *Alfred Hitchcock Mystery Magazine*

MY FIRST AND only failing grade in school came in sixth grade, when Miss Solway asked us to write a paragraph about a secret. Patty Tolliver set to work about a surprise birthday party for her dad. I could see "birthday party" and "hiding presents" and the rest of the story emerging in her big curling script. Eric Rodriguez printed something about fireworks in steeply angled lines. His letters grew smaller and messier as they approached the right edge of his paper, then swelled again into big, assertive words with each new line. Even Jon Hansem, the slowest kid in the class, was hard at work, but my mind refused to function. I sat sweating at my desk and turned in a blank page. At the end of the period Miss Solway called me up to her desk. She looked disappointed and asked if I was feeling all right. I said I was fine; I just didn't have any secrets worth writing about. Miss Solway was unconvinced: I was considered a good, even an imaginative, student.

"I just couldn't think of anything," I wailed, and though Miss Solway was one of my favorite teachers, I added, "It was a dumb topic anyway." I was almost twelve years old, and I already knew that there are some secrets too big to tell, like the one about my mother and Mr. Conklin and what happened the July that I was ten years old.

That summer was hot, dreadfully, dreadfully hot. We should have been used to it after three years in Hartford, but we weren't. Days when the thermometer crept up into the eighties and then the nineties, my mother would wipe her face and say, "What I wouldn't give to be back in Ireland now. It was never imagined to be this hot in Ireland."

Of course other days Mother "wouldn't have had Ireland as a gift," as she'd say, not with my dad dead. "Not an honest day's work to be had. Nothing but pride, poetry, and ignorance. It's bad times here, but worse there. You remember that and work hard in school, my girl." I would promise, of course. I liked school and did well, even though I was in the public school and not with the sisters, who provided a really good education. But Catholic school was out of the question, an unimaginable luxury. Although Mother worked hard, cleaning at the motel and the restaurants, we still lived from week to week. Her pay was usually owed from the moment she got it, and we ate cereal or beans for supper most Wednesdays and Thursdays.

I don't suppose we'd have managed at all if it weren't for Mr. Conklin, our tyrant and savior, who was a distant relative of my late father. Mr. Conklin owned a triple-decker house near his "Irish pub." He also owned a motel and a snack shop at the shabby end of Park Street where the Puerto Rican section stopped and the Portuguese, new immigrants like ourselves, were moving in. Their children went to the big, frightening city schools — rough and full of black people, Mr. Conklin said — while we had the top apartment of his triple-decker just over the city line in an old Irish-Italian neighborhood. The schools in the suburb were much, much better Mr. Conklin said, as "they damn well should be, considering the taxes." Both the apartment and my admission to the local elementary school were the direct result of Mr. Conklin's intercession. It was understood that either could be withdrawn at a moment's notice.

Stout and redfaced with a pug nose and a loud, jovial voice, Joseph P. Conklin was a sentimental bully with unsettling moments of gaiety and kindness. He brought me a doll once — and occasionally chocolates for Mother — and he sang "Danny Boy" every St. Patrick's Day as the restaurant was closing. But even in his best moments I was leery of him. I hated it when he wanted me to sit on his knee and tell him how I was doing in school. Fortunately his interest was usually focused on his property: the restaurants, his triple-decker, and his motel. He hiked his profits and kept his costs down by employing illegal immigrants like Mother, for whom he had originally gotten a visitor's visa.

As relatives, Mother and I occupied a privileged position; we were given the apartment and protected from the school authori-

ties. In exchange, Mr. Conklin paid Mother less than the minimum
wage and visited every Saturday around five o'clock on his way to
the restaurant. If it was nice weather, Mother would send me out on
the big front porch of the triple-decker, where I would watch the
traffic and try to spit on the drooping heads of the hydrangeas that
flanked the front steps far below. If it was bad weather, Mother
would tell me to go down and see Annie on the first floor. Annie
was a stooped, arthritic old lady with a close and cluttered apartment and a fat gray neutered cat. She was lonely for company and
never minded my visits. We would sit companionably, watching her
old black and white TV or crocheting, until I heard Mr. Conklin's
smart patent leather loafers descending the stairs. Then I would tell
Annie I had to go to dinner.

Upstairs, Mother would set the table and lay out dishes without
saying much. When we first came, she'd cried and talked to her
saint and said Aileen — this was Mr. Conklin's wife, who'd had
polio and was in a wheelchair — would put a stop to it; later on, she
was flustered and ashamed; finally she was bitter. That was when she
realized we were trapped. Mr. Conklin relied on that. "You're nobody," I heard him say to her once. "Nobody knows you're here.
You're invisible and be damn glad you are or Immigration'll have
you back on the blessed Old Sod before you can pack your bags."

Working in the restaurant and the motel and being visited by Mr.
Conklin changed my mother. She lost the prettiness I can see in her
old photographs, and she lost the playfulness and sweetness that
she had when my dad was alive. She grew tired and silent and
tough. I was not tough — not then and not for many years. That
July I was still afraid of the dark people at the far end of the street
and of the sirens and night noises and of Mr. Conklin, who held our
lives in his clean, meaty hands.

Since Mother was out working during the day, I spent afternoons
in the local park, where there was a pool, picnic tables, a playground, and an organized recreation program. Whenever the swim
team or adults had the pool, the rec department supervisors en-
couraged us in messy arts and crafts and group singing. Eventually,
some of us formed a chorus, and the plan was that we would sing
for our parents and for the local convalescent home at the end of
the summer.

Everything about the chorus was wonderful: the rehearsals under the maple trees during the hot afternoons, the schmaltzy songs like "It's a Small World" and "Frere Jacques," the giggling groups of gossipy, self-important little girls. The only difficulty came when the chorus voted to wear dresses for our concerts. I had a skirt for Mass, of course, but for the concerts a dress, preferably a pretty sundress, was essential, and for weeks I teased Mother and scoured the newspaper ads for sales. Finally she announced that she'd gotten some material. Secretly I would have preferred something from Caldor's or Ames, but the material she pulled out of the bag — light blue with small pink and yellow flowers — was soft and pretty.

"With a ruffle," I asked. "Can we have it with a ruffle?"

Mother smiled. I look at her pictures now and think how pretty she was, how very pretty before she grew tired and overworked and tough. Once she had liked nice clothes, been flirtatious, carefree, popular; she understood the importance of a ruffle. Mother started the dress early the next morning, before she went off on the bus to clean at the motel, and she finished it late the same week, after she came in from mopping up the snack bar. On Saturday morning, I found the dress waiting for me, a pinafore style with ruffles around the arm holes and two pockets on the skirt.

I put it on. It was not just a perfect fit but a perfect, transforming dress. I was undersized, bony and plain. In the dress, I seemed dainty; the effect was charming; I was enchanted.

"Take it off and hang it up," said Mother. "You'll have it dirty before the day's out. It has to be kept for good."

I hung the sundress up in our closet, but as soon as I came back from the park, I ran to look at it, to stroke the ruffles and spread out the skirt. And when, just around four, the phone rang and Mother had to go out on an errand, I could not resist trying on my dress again.

I dragged a kitchen chair into the bathroom and climbed up to look in the mirror of the medicine cabinet. I was standing there admiring myself when I heard the knock on the door followed by the sound of a key turning in the lock.

"Are you home, Patsy?" Mr. Conklin was the only one who ever called my mother Patsy.

"Patsy?" I heard him walking softly through the living room and down the hall. For a fattish man he had a light tread.

I didn't want to see him, and if I hadn't been afraid of dirtying my

dress, I'd have slipped under the bed. In my moment of hesitation
he appeared in the doorway.

"Where's your mother?"

"She had to go to the store," I said.

"Don't you answer the door when someone knocks?"

I shook my head.

"Where are your manners?" he asked. "Who else visits you every
Saturday?" Then he laughed. "But there'll be boys around soon
enough," he said, looking at me more closely. "Very pretty." He
reached out and touched the ruffle. "I must be paying Patsy more
than I thought."

I flinched away from him. "Mother made this for me," I said,
almost in tears. His remark spoiled my happiness. I wished I'd
never put on the dress; I wished Mother would come home; I
wished he was dead.

"There there now," he said, hitching up his light summer pants
and sitting down on the edge of the bed. "Who's your pal, eh? Who
brought you that Barbie doll?"

I bit my lip and didn't answer.

He ran his finger along the ruffle again, then smoothed the front
of my dress. "I don't have a little girl of my own, you know," he said.
"Wouldn't have been as pretty as you anyway. Your mother now,
there's a pretty woman. I met her on a visit to the Old Country. She
wasn't much older than you, and she was one of the prettiest girls in
Belfast; that's the truth."

He took my arm although I tried to ease away. "Come sit here for
a minute," he said. His voice sounded different, soft and sort of
sticky, like something Mother would say was "too sweet to be whole-
some." "Since your mother is out."

"You called her," I said, frightened by sudden knowledge. "You
asked her to get something for the snack shop."

"Did I now? And me with a car and going out anyway as I always
do on a Saturday evening? Would I do such a thing?"

"You called her," I said, stubborn despite my fear.

"You're a clever girl," he said, settling me on his lap. "Maybe we
should send you to the sisters at St. Bridget's. Would you like that?
Wear a nice little uniform, they do. Gray blazer," he said, running
his hand down my dress again, "little maroon tie, little maroon and
gray kilt, little gray kneesocks. Just to here. Wouldn't you like that?
Lots of nice Irish boys and girls at St. Bridget's."

I stopped trying to squirm away from him. "I like my school," I said, "but I'd like St. Bridget's better."

He laughed. "I just bet you would. I just bet you would. Well, it depends if you're good." He was stroking my knee, and I both did and did not know what he meant. I'd heard a fair bit out on the porch on those warm evenings.

"We'd have to ask my mother," I said.

"Oh, your mother can't afford St. Bridget's. Never in this life! Don't imagine your mother can afford to send you to the sisters."

"My mother decides," I said.

He laughed. "Does she now?" I could see the veins in the whites of his eyes; I could smell his aftershave, and something else, a raw, dangerous smell.

"I want to get down now," I said.

"Not yet," he said, sliding his meaty red fingers under my dress. "Not if you want to get to St. Bridget's."

A minute later I started to scream.

"Shhh," said Mr. Conklin, and when I didn't stop, he yelled, "Shut up, shut up, you little bitch!"

I wasn't tough like my mother. The scream wasn't under my control, it went echoing around my head and burned between my legs and poured out like blood from a wound. I couldn't stop, not even when he slapped me. The scream was so independent, so beyond my control, that at last it even frightened Mr. Conklin, who did up his pants and hurried down the hall and out the door.

Mother came home just minutes later. I was sitting on the bed. My dress was torn, and there was blood on my legs. Mother took one look at me, and her face went white. She wrapped her arms around me, cursing and sobbing at the same time. When she stopped, she said, "I'll fix that bastard. He'll never hurt you again." Taut with anger and pain, her face was almost unrecognizable, and I was nearly as frightened of her as of Mr. Conklin. "I promise," she said. "As God is my witness."

"No," I said, "no!" I had an intimation of disaster, loss, some terrible punishment. Good or bad, Mr. Conklin was the chief power in our small universe.

"You'll see," Mother said. "I won't bear this." Then she sat back on her heels and looked at me. "It's got to be a secret. God forgive me, you've got to keep this a secret. The police would tell Immigra-

tion. Do you understand that? We can't tell anyone what that bastard did."

I nodded my head. I didn't want to tell anyone. I had no words
for what had happened. "A secret," I said.

"A deep, dark secret," Mother said grimly.

Sometime after ten P.M. the next Friday Mr. Conklin died behind
his fast food restaurant. A stab wound stopped his heart so suddenly
that he was dead before he hit the pavement. The papers made
much of the speed of his passing, and for years I carried an image
of Mr. Conklin tumbled like a large, ungainly bird from the sky and
dying in mid-fall.

That night my mother was late coming home from work. The city
sounds made me nervous — the sudden shrieks and eerie lights of
police cars, fire trucks, and ambulances, the accelerating hot rods
with their booming radios, the hoarse, quarrelsome voices of men
drifting back from the bars — and I was still awake at eleven o'clock
when I heard her footsteps. I ran to unlock the door.

Mother's weary face was bloodless. "I'm sorry I'm so late, dar-
ling," she said. "I had to wait and lock up. Mr. Conklin didn't come
back from making the night deposit."

"I hope he never comes back," I said.

Mother gave me a sharp look. "Be careful what you wish for," she
said, then she went into the bedroom and began to pack our cases.

Mr. Conklin looked out at us from the morning paper. His picture made him seem younger and more benevolent than he ever
looked in life. The accompanying story told us about his violent
end. I was thrilled and horrified by his death, by the unlooked-
for fame of one of our acquaintances. These were sensational and
superficial emotions, but I was genuinely sorry and frightened
about leaving our apartment.

"My job's gone," Mother explained. "We don't exist. There never
were any papers, agreements."

I asked about school, about the park chorus, our concerts;
Mother looked me in the face and shook her head. I felt suspicion
dawn in a shiver of anxiety that grew stronger when we caught the
morning bus to Boston without saying goodbye to anyone, not even
to Annie. Once in Boston, the MTA took us to the South End,
where we started calling ourselves Malloy instead of O'Brien and
quietly disappeared into the Irish community. We put down a secu-

rity deposit on a shabby apartment, and a very distant relative of Mother's found her a job in a sweatshop sewing curtains.

That fall I attended a real urban school, where I learned to smoke and swear and became outwardly tough. Inside I was frightened of a lot of things, all related to secrets and to July: men, sex, sudden death, Immigration. Underneath were even deeper fears, more terrible because unacknowledged: the fear of guilt, police, and discovery; the fear, worst of all, of being separated from Mother, whose protection, I sensed, was both sure and terrible.

It was several years before I learned that my particular horrors were not unique. Fear and loss were the common experiences of my classmates, and the art of keeping secrets was so essential to our survival that, though we could not forget old fears, we could push them down relentlessly. I put away my suspicions and learned to live with ambiguity. When I graduated from high school, I joined the army, where I became a citizen and trained as a nurse. Amid the suffering of others I at last grew really tough, tough enough to ask Mother the question that had haunted my youth.

It was on another summer day, and tough or not, I would probably not have dared ask if we hadn't gone to Hartford. I had to attend a lecture at the medical center, and Mother said she'd ride along and visit a friend who lived nearby in Farmington. When I picked her up after the program, she suggested driving down to Park Street to see the old triple-decker. At once my childish fears returned. I stopped in the parking lot and looked at her.

"If it's not out of the way," said Mother, handsome in her dark navy dress. For years she had worn only dark colors, black, navy, deep purple, somber shades that gave her a vaguely European air. The rich ladies who patronized the bridal salon where Mother worked thought her taste distinguished and sophisticated.

I shook my head. "Is it wise?" I asked.

Mother gave nothing away. "Who do you think will notice us?" she answered.

Of course she was right. I parked near the house, and Mother got out on the sidewalk and looked up at the big solid building with the flaring eaves and the prowlike porches. Blue-gray vinyl siding covered the dark wood shingles, and Mother approved. "Saves the painting," she said. "Clean-looking. Young Joe must be up on all the latest."

"Young Joe?"

"Mr. Conklin's son. He must be just a few years older than you are. Aileen's probably turned everything over to him by now. It was her money, part of it anyway. Her people owned some grocery stores, you know."

I did not know, and I thought Mother might say more about the Conklins, but she took a last look up at the apartment and got back into the car. "I've never been so hot as in that third floor flat," she said. "Remember how hot it used to get?"

"Yes," I said.

"Go on down Park," Mother said. "We might as well stop by the snack shop, too."

She spoke so casually that I felt guilty for all the years of suspicion and apprehension. Nonetheless, I drove downtown carefully, nervously alert for stop signs, traffic lights, and squad cars. Next to me, Mother looked out the windows and remarked on changes in the neighborhood. The Portuguese shops had mostly gone, leaving a mix of Indian and Southeast Asian businesses: Bombay Foods, a Vietnamese market, shops that promised to speak Khmer, Vietnamese, Hindi, or Laotian. The old snack shop had been transformed into the New Thai Palace Restaurant, and Mother said, "Turn in. There's room for you to park."

I pulled next to a van labeled NEW THAI PALACE — RESTAURANT, CATERING, TAKEOUT and shut off the motor. The late spring evening was mild and pleasant. The sun turned the bricks of the restaurant to gold, and the sky was a peachy shade of pink. Mother stepped out of the car and walked around behind the restaurant where a big exhaust fan whirred out the smell of hot oil and spices. Beyond a brown board fence, children were shouting and playing, and on the sidewalk two women in saris and dark sweaters pushed their children in strollers. Mother studied the restaurant, the garbage cans, the little open porch that led into the kitchen. Long ago Mr. Conklin had been seized by some swift and terrible force right at the foot of those steps.

For years I had wondered about the precise agent. Now that I was on the verge of discovery, I found I'd rather not know. "Please let's go," I said.

Mother seemed surprised that I was nervous. She herself was perfectly composed, a fine looking woman somewhere in middle age, her hair still dark, her face only faintly lined, old hardships and weariness visible only in her eyes. The days of sweatshops and exploitation had eventually ended in Boston, where she had turned her toughness into such elegance that men admired her and were afraid of her. Six years ago she had married a brave one who owned a fancy funeral home and had become comfortable and happy.

"There is no danger," she said as she walked back to the car. "I told you that years ago."

I remembered the hot apartment, panic, fear, and pain — and Mother's contorted mask-like face. "You said you'd fix Mr. Conklin."

"I wanted to comfort you," my mother said, looking at me calmly. "But people are different. You would have been happier not knowing. You lack the taste for vengeance. It is a shame you never went to the sisters. They would have approved."

"I would have suspected anyway," I said. "We packed right up and left."

Mother gave a slight shrug. "We'd have gone immediately in any case. Aileen hated me; she'd have had us out of the apartment before his funeral."

"I was terrified you'd be questioned," I said. "For years I worried that someone would come, that you'd be taken away, that somehow . . ."

"We didn't exist," said Mother. "If he told me that once, he told me a hundred times."

"But the knife, the fingerprints, the other workers? There must have been evidence. Look at this place — where was there to hide anything?"

Mother got back in the car and fastened her seatbelt before answering. "I didn't have a plan," she said. "I've been told that makes a difference, not planning I mean. I don't even know all that was in my mind when I went out the door after him. It was around ten fifteen. He was going to the night deposit, but first he stepped out for a smoke — one of those vile cigars. There was a boning knife on the counter, sharp as a razor. I picked it up because I wanted him to know I was serious. I was desperate and hot and sick, and my heart was breaking. He'd gone too far. I wanted to tell him that he was never, ever to touch either of us again."

"What did he say?"

Mother's face grew dark and reflective. "He laughed," she said. "He had trampled my heart; he had hurt the one person I had left, my only treasure, and still he laughed — you see what it is to be rich and powerful. Then he said that I was looking older, and I understood everything. We were nothing to him, nothing at all, and he was thinking of you for a replacement."

"I was ten years old," I said in a small voice.

"There was really nothing else to do," Mother said. "I was surprised he took such a long time to fall."

I imagined the night parking lot with the moths swirling around the security lights, the long shadows, the urban smells of hot asphalt, exhaust, and garbage cans, and my mother, young then and frightened, standing by the stair with a knife in her hand.

"Everyone thought it was a robbery," I said.

"So it was: the day's taking from two restaurants," Mother said with a slight smile. "The police blamed the gangs, the Puerto Ricans, wild kids from the project. What else could they do? He'd managed very carefully, and very few people knew me."

"But the knife?" I asked. "What about the knife?"

"You don't know restaurants," she said. "Restaurants are full of knives. I rinsed off the boning knife in the sink and threw it in the dishwasher. As far as I was thinking at all, I figured the staff would unload it the next morning and put it back in the rack as usual."

"Of course," I said. I realized that my brave and decisive mother was untouched by fantasy. While I had been tormented for years by fears of discovery and loss and guilt, failure had never crossed her mind. She was a woman without imagination. "But didn't he have a wallet? Didn't he used to carry something for the money?"

Mother opened her pocketbook and pulled out a battered green leather zippered purse that I'd seen a thousand times without recognition. "No matter where you discard things, they're apt to be found," she said calmly.

I was dazzled by the simplicity of her strategy, which had required only nerve and silence. Until now. I could not decide whether her guilty secret had finally and irresistibly resurfaced — as guilty secrets are supposed to do — or whether she felt a satisfaction that demanded recognition. I realized uneasily that the parish gentlemen who admired and feared my mother were right. Life had made her desperate, and then it had made her remarkable. Mr. Conklin had been hit by a force quite out of his reckoning.

JOHN H. WATSON, M.D.

EDITED BY JOHN T. LESCROART

The Adventure of the Giant Rat of Sumatra

FROM *Mary Higgins Clark Mystery Magazine*

WE WERE SEATED over breakfast, my friend Mr. Sherlock Holmes deeply engrossed in his morning paper, when I heard him mutter something. "I beg your pardon, Holmes?" I asked.

"Sumatra," he repeated, all but to himself. "My God, even for Moriarty this is appalling!"

"Holmes," I exclaimed, "what is it?"

He put down the paper and looked in my direction, but he appeared not to see me. That in itself was so singular that I was immediately on my guard. When Sherlock Holmes looked, he saw — it was one of his dicta. But on that cold December morning in 1888, he stared as if through me out to the drizzly fog that enshrouded London.

I tried again to speak to him, but he waved me off impatiently. "Watson, please, don't interrupt me. It may already be too late."

Accustomed as I was to his outbursts, his tone still smarted. I started to remonstrate, but he had already risen and gone to the corner by the coal scuttle in our rooms at 221B Baker Street. There he kept his stack of past editions of London's newspapers. As I watched in growing concern, he attacked the pile, throwing whole sections out behind him when they didn't contain that for which he was searching.

Then, with an armload of papers, he half fell into his chair, grabbing his pipe on the way down. For the next quarter hour he sat engulfed in tobacco smoke, muttering or cursing one moment, and the next falling into a quiet and desperate depression. After watching him for a time, I ventured another syllable.

"Holmes?"

He flung some of the papers at me. "Read it for yourself, Watson. It may be the end of us all."

I picked the papers from the floor and began perusing them. Some were up to two years old, and I must confess I saw nothing in them but yesterday's news. Nevertheless, I slogged through the sections, pausing from time to time at a familiar name or at the mention of a case in which Holmes and I had been involved. While I read, Holmes evidently finished his work and rang for Mrs. Hudson. When our landlady appeared, he sent her to fetch Billy the page, saying it was a matter of the utmost urgency.

Quickly, he scratched a note on a pad and then, filling another pipe, turned to me as he lit it. "Well, Watson, I must say that as a doctor you are calm enough about it."

I must have looked at him blankly.

"The plague, Watson! The plague! Can it be you don't see it?"

Before I could respond, he had rushed to the table and snatched several of the papers away from me. "Look here!" he exclaimed. "And here! And here! You see nothing? Nothing?" He was grabbing and pulling the sections every which way. I had never seen him so agitated.

"Holmes! There's no need to be rude."

That brought him up short. He visibly summoned that control upon which he prides himself, straightening himself to his full height, taking a deep breath. "My dear man, please forgive me."

"It's nothing, Holmes, it's forgotten. But what is it? Please tell me."

Looking at the door, he came to some decision. "Well, I guess there is time before Billy comes." And he sat down, pulling that day's *Times* in front of him.

"Here, Watson, on page five — the article on our old friend Colonel Sebastian Moran."

I had read it, of course. The travels of the famous hunter were always of interest to me, both because they were often fascinating in themselves, but also and not least because of his position as Professor Moriarty's chief lieutenant. The article was an account of a Boer pirate attack on Moran's ship as it had been rounding the Horn on its return from Sumatra, loaded with hunting trophies. Moran and his crew had fought off the belligerents, hauled the injured ship back to Johannesburg and delivered it and its dead crew to the British authorities. A particular point of interest was that they had neither docked nor resupplied at port and had allowed no one to board their vessel.

"It seems like a typical Moran adventure," I said upon rereading it.

"By itself, you may be right, Watson. But what of this?"

He placed before me the oldest of the newspapers and pointed to a piece on the outbreak of bubonic plague that had occurred two years before on Siberut, a tiny island off the west coast of Sumatra.

"And these . . ."

The other articles related to a Dr. Culverton-Smith, who had announced and then retracted the news that he had developed and hoped shortly to perfect a serum that would prevent and cure bubonic plague.

I had just finished the last of these when there was a sharp rap at our door, followed immediately by the entrance into our quarters of Billy. One of the street urchins who frequented the alleys hereabouts, Billy had more than once proved a useful ally to my friend and me.

Holmes wasted no time on greeting him but handed him the note he'd scribbled earlier. "Ah, Billy, here. Deliver this at once to the address listed, and wait there for a reply."

Without a word, the boy was off, and I was again left alone with Holmes, pondering the obscure links in this bizarre chain. "What is this about, Holmes? What was that note?"

Now that he had taken some action, he reverted to that languid pose I knew so well. His eyes had become so black they appeared nearly hooded. But this time there was none of the sparkle in them that always appeared after the "view halloo" had been sounded, when the game was afoot. This time it was no game.

"The note was to Dr. Culverton-Smith, Watson — one of the most evil and brilliant men to ever grace your profession." He took a long pull at his pipe. "I wondered how long it would be before Professor Moriarty and he made each other's acquaintance." Then he sighed with an ineffable sadness. "I only wish I had acted to prevent it. I only hope now I'm not too late." He sighed again, wearily.

"What did the note say?"

He waved his pipe. "Oh, it was prosaic enough. It said, 'England will pay you more than Moriarty.'"

"For what?"

"For the serum, of course. The cure for bubonic plague."

"My God, Holmes, could it be . . . ?"

"I don't know yet. I won't know for sure until Billy comes back. Halloa? That would be him now."

He jumped up and ran to the door, opening it before the panting boy could even knock. Breathlessly, Billy handed a missive to Holmes, who ripped open the engraved envelope. As he read, his shoulders sagged.

Absently, he forced some coins on Billy and rather unceremoniously shooed him out. I thought he was a little too brusque with the boy and told him so.

"Watson, it's as I suspected. Moriarty, Moran and Culverton-Smith are in it together, and no one must know. There would be panic."

"What does the reply say?"

Holmes smiled but with no humor. "'My dear Mr. Holmes,'" he read, "'Your offer is interesting. Unfortunately, what England can pay me is rather off the point, since within a year, my associates and I will *be* England.'"

"Holmes!" I exclaimed.

"Exactly. Moriarty plans to inoculate himself and his henchmen against the plague, then introduce the disease into England."

"How would he do that?"

"Probably through an animal that Moran has captured and smuggled onto his ship."

The pieces were beginning to fit, though my own enlightenment had none of the epiphanic quality of Holmes's. "But if they merely patented the serum," I argued, "they would be millionaires many times over."

Again that frigid grin. "Power, Watson. Power is more seductive than money, and for Moriarty it is everything. His mind envisions an England desolate and depopulated but one where he is absolute ruler, a medieval king. The population not under his power —

including you and me, my friend — would die in swollen, boil-in-fested agony."

"You shock me!"

"Depend on it, Watson. I know my man."

"What can we do?"

The grin softened to a smile. "Good old Watson," he said. "Where there is danger, you have no fear. Where courage is needed, you have no peer. It would be a good epitaph."

The warmth I felt at the compliment quickly chilled at the vision of my own tomb. "Still," I said, "what can be done?"

Within moments, I had my answer. I had been reading again, trying to piece together the disparate elements of this diabolical plot, when Holmes tapped my shoulder. I must have been deeply engrossed in my researches not to have noticed Holmes leave the room. But now he was back, dressed and bundled for an excursion.

"Get your coat, Watson. I think we should pay a visit to the Diogenes Club."

The Diogenes was perhaps the strangest club in a city of strange clubs. Its members were the most private men in the City, and the charter and by-laws of the club colluded to keep them that way, since no one was allowed to speak within the club's walls, the sole exception being in the Visitor's Room. But even there, only whispering was permitted.

After a bitterly cold ride in a hansom, we found ourselves before the forbidding double doors of the building. Inside, Holmes passed his card to the doorman and we were ushered into the Visitor's Room to await the arrival of Holmes's brother, Mycroft.

Mycroft's dour face and huge bulk surprised me anew, though I had met him once before during our adventure with the Greek interpreter. That episode had not ended happily, and I found myself praying that his intercession here would produce more positive results. He took me in at a glance, somehow included a welcoming nod and turned to his brother, twelve years younger than himself. According to Holmes, Mycroft was the smartest and most powerful man in England. I reflected that his position, however it was defined, might be one that Moriarty would covet. But there was no more time for reflection.

"Sherlock," he whispered with affection, "what brings you to these hermit's haunts?"

In a few words Holmes outlined the situation. Hearing him retell it in his logical and orderly fashion, I was horrified again by the boldness and grandeur of Moriarty's twisted vision.

Could he actually pull it off? As I watched and listened to Mycroft and his brother formulate their own plan, I had no doubts at all that if Moriarty could be stopped, only one man living could do it, and that man was my friend Sherlock Holmes.

Eight days later, Holmes and I paced the deck of the HMS *Birmingham,* the twenty-eight-gun flagship of the Atlantic fleet. Earlier in the day we had passed the Canaries and now were beating farther south in African waters. Holmes had estimated that we would meet up with Colonel Moran's ship somewhere near the latitude of Dakar, off the coast of French West Africa, and that would be another day or two's hard sail.

The air was balmy, a far cry from the London winter. Some of the sailors had thought to bring a Christmas tree along — had tied it to the forward mast, decked it in red and green trimming and even placed a few wrapped boxes under it for the effect. I couldn't help but admire the spirit of these men, facing Her Majesty's sometimes terrible tasks with dignity, honor and even humor. This was an England worth fighting, even dying, for!

Of course, we were not alone. Twenty-six ships of the line were arrayed in a crescent pattern out to the sides and behind us. Mycroft had persuaded an outraged prime minister to assign the convoy to try to blockade the oncoming vessel. It was the largest armada to be assembled since the Franco-Prussian War, and I hope it will be a long, long time before such a force is needed again.

To get the kind of commitment needed for an expedition of this magnitude, Holmes had had to go to the limits of his imagination and persuasiveness, convincing Scotland Yard that Dr. Culverton-Smith must be arrested and questioned. Though none of the serum had been found in his possession — what a boon to mankind that would have been! — his personal notes and laboratories provided enough evidence, and the potential danger was serious enough, that the reluctant PM had finally assigned the fleet. But he had made it clear that if Holmes were wrong, both his career and that of his brother would be finished. Even criminal charges against them would not be out of the question!

But these concerns were the last things on Holmes's mind as we restlessly paced the deck, checking and rechecking the horizon for any sign of the hostile ship.

"It is too easy," he said. "Even now, as we stalk the prey, I am filled with misgivings."

"Whatever for, Holmes? Surely Colonel Moran is no match for Her Majesty's Navy?"

"Moran, though formidable, is not the opponent I fear. No, Watson, I speak of Moriarty, the Napoleon of Crime. His net is world-wide, his contacts rival those of any government. Just when you think you have set your trap is when you must be on your closest guard."

"But . . ."

"Mark my words! It has happened before. His brain is like a spider's web — spirals within spirals. Moriarty lives to spin that web, and he feels the slightest tremor at its periphery. You may rest assured he knows we are on the seas, and that he is somehow . . ." Holmes paused, taking in a lungful of tobacco smoke and letting it out slowly. "Somehow, he is stalking us."

"Come now, Holmes — stalking the Royal Navy?"

"You may laugh, Watson, but it is difficult to overestimate Moriarty's determination."

One of the crewmen appeared with a couple of cups of tea spiked with a tot of rum, saying that the bridge thought we might appreciate a little refreshment. We thanked him and continued pacing. The tin cups were hot to the touch, so we rested them against a coil of rope.

I looked out again at the calm sea, thinking that the tension of our voyage had affected Holmes's judgment. His respect for his arch rival seemed exaggerated, bordering on the ludicrous. It occurred to me that, expecting a long ocean voyage with little outside stimulation, he might have brought along some of his cocaine, which he occasionally injects when his overactive mind needs surcease from boredom. The drug could have produced such paranoia. Lost in these thoughts, I absently took the cup of tea into my hand, blew on it and sipped.

"Spit it out, Watson! Spit it out!" Holmes was slapping me on the back, having dashed the cup to the deck. "Poison!" he said. "The tea has been poisoned! Are you all right?"

Shaking, my mouth already feeling a kind of dry numbness though I had obeyed Holmes's command instantly, I turned to my friend. "Where is that mate?" I mumbled.

But the deck was filled with uniformed men, all indistinguishable from a distance. My legs seemed to be getting weaker, and it was becoming harder to focus, to recognize any of the men. Even Holmes appeared wavy and indistinct, as though I were looking at him from under water. Then all went dark.

I could feel strong fingers digging into my shoulder, pressing against the Jezail bullet that had lodged there when I had been wounded in Afghanistan. I opened my eyes, and an unfamiliar room swam before me.

There was a hoarse whisper. "Watson?" The fingers gripped harder. "Watson? Can you hear me?"

I tried to bring the towering figure into focus in the darkened room. "Holmes? Where am I?"

"You're alive. That's what's important. You very nearly weren't."

It began to come back to me — the mate, the tea, my last memories before losing consciousness. What a fool I had been to doubt Holmes! Once again he'd been right. Moriarty's agents, it appeared, were with us even aboard this ship.

"Where are we now?" I asked. "What day is it?" The questions kept coming. "Why us, Holmes? Why poison us? Does he think we can make a difference, when the entire Navy is out to get him?"

Holmes chuckled. "I rather fancy he thinks just that. Flattering, eh?"

Groggily I sat up. "I wish I could take some pleasure in it. Just now I'm too confused."

"Come, can you get up?"

Holmes took me by the arm and walked me about the small cabin. Outside, it appeared to be closing on dusk. After a few turns from wall to wall, I regained my sea legs and my mind cleared. "What did I take? What was it?"

"One of the cyanamids, I presume. You were extremely lucky, Watson. Even trace amounts can kill. You mustn't have swallowed any at all."

The reason for that did not for a moment escape me. Once again Sherlock Holmes had saved my life.

"As to how long you've been under, thirty hours is a reasonable estimate. And as you can see, night descends." He reached into his pockets and pulled forth most of a loaf of bread, some dried meat and an orange. "You must be hungry, and you'll need all your strength. I packed this food myself as a precaution against just this sort of thing."

Twenty minutes later we were again on the deck. I had naturally brought my revolver along, and now I gratefully felt its cold weight in my pocket. Shadow figures scattered here and there, swabbing, stowing, making the vessel shipshape for the night. Even armed, I was not without trepidation, knowing that one of these men had tried to kill us only the day before. It could easily happen again.

Captain John Wagner approached. Ginger-haired and bearded, he was a sturdy sailor of the old school — hale, hearty and profane. In spite of my accident, I felt I was safe within his domain. He ran the tightest of ships.

"Good evening, Mr. Holmes. Ah, Dr. Watson," he blustered, "that such a thing should happen on my ship! I swear to you we'll find the blackguard, and I'll personally keelhaul him. My best men are on it." His voice then softened. "You had us all right worried there, sir. Good to see you back up and about."

I thanked him for his good wishes and struck up a conversation about our quarry. "Tomorrow looks to be the day, doesn't it, captain?"

He laughed. "That's your friend's estimate, doctor. But it's a big ocean. Hard to pinpoint a meeting date. Could happen any time."

"Could we miss him entirely?"

His face hardened. "We won't miss him. And once we encounter the blighter, we'll bring him to. I'll stake my reputation on that."

"Who's at the wheel now, captain?" Holmes asked blandly, walking up to us. Throughout our discussion, he had stood at the ship's rail, peering into the darkness.

"That'd be my first mate, Jeffers."

"And the lookout?"

Justifiably, I thought, the captain's eyes narrowed. "What's all this about, Mr. Holmes?"

Holmes turned and pointed out over the bow. "Unless I'm very much mistaken, captain, there's a ship running dark just off to starboard."

Wagner and I ran to the railing, squinting to make out a shape where Holmes had indicated. Before I had seen anything, the captain had turned, uttering a foul oath. As he rushed back to the bridge, his voice bellowing "Battle stations!" shook the very timbers of the ship.

We were the wedge of the armada, and within minutes flares had alerted the rest of the fleet that something had been spotted. We had no way to be sure it was Colonel Moran, but the fact that the ship had its running lights covered was more than enough to convince me.

Holmes stood beside me at the bow rail, his face a study in determination. "Now remember, Watson," he said. "No one from that ship must be allowed aboard. All its crew will have been inoculated against the plague, but there's no telling if any of them are infested with the fleas or lice that carry the disease."

"Are we to kill them all, then?" The men were fiends, but it was not like Holmes to be so cold-blooded.

"No, no, we'll shepherd them and their cargo of death to Gorée, a small island in Dakar's harbor which used to hold slaves waiting for transport. Captain Wagner knows the drill."

"And then . . . ?"

"And then Moran and his men can swim for it while we blow their ship out of the water. The salt water will leach away any vermin, and the men are all sailors — they'll have no trouble finding work. . . ."

He was about to continue when we heard a shot from somewhere behind us. I reached for my revolver and raced toward the sound, Holmes at my heels.

"Here! Up here!"

It was Jeffers, the first mate, staggering to his feet on the bridge, his hands to his bleeding head. At his feet lay a prostrate Captain Wagner.

"The captain . . ." Jeffers began.

I was there beside him, but there was nothing I could do. Captain Wagner had a bullet hole in the back of his head. The gallant sailor had completed his last command.

"What happened?" I demanded.

The mate appeared to be in shock. "I don't know. I was hit from behind, and then . . ."

At that moment, the lookout shouted from above. "Enemy ship preparing to engage!"

We looked over our shoulders and there, its running lights suddenly lit, a ship was bearing down on us on a collision course. Our crew, at battle stations, waited for the orders, but Jeffers seemed incapable of movement, watching horrified as the vessel approached.

"We can't let them engage." Holmes spoke calmly to Jeffers, but his voice cut like a knife. "Think of your orders, man."

On the deck of the enemy ship, we could see the crew manning their battle stations, with small arms and grappling hooks at the ready. These were the same men who had captured the deadly Boer pirates only two weeks before. Jeffers looked about in panic, like a caged rat, and then suddenly screamed to his own waiting crew: "Fire! Fire! Fire all guns!"

"*No!*" Holmes yelled, but his voice was drowned out by the simultaneous roar of fourteen cannons. Moran must have kept a magazine below decks, for no sooner had we recovered from the shock of the first sally than the night turned into day as the enemy ship, less than fifty yards from us now, exploded in a huge fireball.

The force of the explosion knocked us off our feet, and we lay dazed for a moment in a shocking, deathly silence. And then, as though the brutality of what we'd just witnessed were not enough, a ghastly rain of burning timber and flesh began to fall and litter our deck.

The falling debris started several small fires, and Jeffers forced himself up to direct the crew. Holmes and I sat by Wagner's body and watched the floating remains of Moran's ship flare, then smoke, as they slowly sank into the ocean.

Holmes's eyes were glazed over. His elbows rested on his knees, his hands limp between them. Glancing first at me, then at the fallen captain, he sighed aloud. "Wrong," he muttered half to himself in a tone of pure anguish. "Where could it have gone so wrong?"

There was no chance of sleeping. Eight bells in the third watch came and went, and still the crew kept at its cleanup duties. Jeffers had convened an officers' tribunal and ordered that every man account for his whereabouts at the time the captain had been murdered. One by one, the men filed wearily into the captain's stateroom, resentful and edgy. Holmes stood silent at the railing, smoking. His hunched shoulders left no doubt that he carried the burden of the deaths of Moran's crewmen as though they were his own.

I went to him. "It could not be helped," I said.

He looked coldly at me.

"Holmes," I insisted. "It was not your fault."

He shook his head. "It was not supposed to be that way. No one had to die. And we never got the proof."

"But surely the fact that they intended to engage . . . ?"

"It doesn't prove . . . Halloa," he exclaimed. "What's that?"

I looked out at the black ocean. A glint of phosphorous showed above something moving in the dark water. "What could that be?" I asked.

Holmes's dark eyes glinted in the light from his pipe. A kind of smile began to play at the corners of his mouth, and I recognized that look: He was on a scent, when he thought it had eluded him. Then, at once, the half smile faded, replaced by a grimness I had never before witnessed in him. "The monster," he said under his breath. "The unspeakable monster."

"Holmes," I began, "what —"

"Follow me," he said, "and keep your gun handy." He headed toward the bridge.

"Mate Jeffers," he yelled up from the deck, "there is a boat in the water."

The first mate, more haggard than ever, was struggling with the onus of command. He glared at Holmes as another interruption in an already impossible night. "What's that you say, sir?" he yelled down.

"There's a boat in the water." Holmes pointed. "There, at forty-five degrees off port."

The small boat could just barely be seen coming into the circle of light thrown by our ship. "My God," said Jeffers. He seemed instantly rejuvenated, taking the steps down from the bridge in bounding leaps. "Could it be that someone survived?"

"It would appear so," my friend answered. I glanced then at Sherlock Holmes, and he had in his eye a look so dangerous that even I, who knew him so well, shuddered. Yet I could not for the life of me see what had so aroused him. Questions formed in my mind, but the fierceness of his countenance forced me to hold my tongue.

Jeffers called for some men and had them begin preparing for the rescue. Out in the night, I could just make out the lifeboat. On board was a single man, standing and waving. His "Ahoy," small yet haunting, carried across the water. In the boat with him appeared to be a large box of some sort — probably, I thought, some possessions he'd managed to escape with before the ship exploded.

As the boat approached, Jeffers leaned farther over the water to direct the crewmen's operations. Just at that moment, Holmes lurched forward, grabbed the mate from behind and lifted him up and over the railing. With flailing arms and an anguished cry, Jeffers hit the water with a tremendous splash.

"Holmes!" I cried.

"There's no time to explain! Quick, Watson, your weapon!"

In a flash I had drawn my revolver and leveled it at the crew members gathered around us. Holmes remained calm. "I apologize for this inconvenience, gentlemen," he said to them, "and after a moment it won't be necessary, but for now I think it better that no one try to save Mr. Jeffers."

The mate rose to the surface, spluttering. "Holmes!" he called. "What's the meaning of this? It's mutiny! Watson, I'll have you both hanged!"

"I think the pleasure will be the other way round!" Holmes countered. "If you don't drown first."

"Why should I hang?"

"First for murdering Captain Wagner, then for blowing up Moran's ship and not least for trying to poison Watson and me."

"You're mad. They were going to ram us!"

"No," Holmes replied. "But for a moment it certainly did look that way, so that your disobedience of orders seemed logical."

"What are you saying?"

"The convoy was to herd the ship to Gorée, not destroy it. And no one — no one at all, even a survivor — was to come aboard."

Jeffers treaded water awkwardly. Fully dressed as he was, the weight of his clothes would pull him down within minutes. The lifeboat, all but forgotten by us, was drifting steadily away from him.

Jeffers went under briefly and came up gagging. Looking at the lifeboat, he tried a few halfhearted breaststrokes in its direction, but the effort was too great for him. He turned back to us, breathing heavily. "Help me, Watson, and I'll see that you're pardoned!"

"If my friend hangs," I called down, "I will gladly hang beside him." Then, to Holmes, I said softly, "You're not going to let him drown, are you?"

"I rather think he'll be saved."

But as we watched, Jeffers went under again. I thought the mate was gone, but once again he broke the surface. This time the panic in his voice was not feigned. He looked up at Holmes, then across to the lifeboat and came to his fateful decision. "Moran!" he yelled. "Help me! I'm drowning!"

"You fool, Jeffers! Shut up!"

Sherlock Holmes addressed me, finally allowing himself a smile. "As I suspected, they know each other by name. It is all the proof we need." He called overboard. "You'd better see to Jeffers, Moran! The game is up."

"Who is that I'm speaking to?"

Holmes chuckled mirthlessly. "You don't recognize the voice, colonel? We've met occasionally." He leaned over the railing. "Mr. Sherlock Holmes at your service."

"Holmes? What is this?"

"You thought I'd be dead by now, eh? Poisoned?"

"What are you talking about?"

"We had better discuss it after you've saved your accomplice."

And, indeed, Moran had set to with his oars. Before long, the exhausted mate had been pulled into the lifeboat.

"Now in the name of decency, Holmes, let us aboard!" Moran cried.

"You have a great deal of gall using that word, colonel. What is that box behind you, sir?"

Moran uncovered a huge cage in which skulked something large and black, looking from our deck like a small bear. "It is nothing more than a giant Sumatran tree rat, Holmes. I was taking it to the London Zoo. It was the only thing I could save from the ship."

"Before you blew it up?"

"What are you saying?"

"I'm saying you sacrificed your entire crew so that we would naturally pluck you and your giant rat of Sumatra from the lifeboat.

You thought by now that Watson, Captain Wagner and I would all be dead and that no one would think to question your rescue."

"No!"

"That rat is infested with bubonic plague, and you yourself are host to its deadly carrier fleas. Both you and Jeffers are inoculated, but once you or the rat comes aboard this ship, the England we all love is gone."

At the word *plague,* a general murmuring arose from the men behind us. Holmes turned and addressed them. "You heard me correctly. All your officers, including Jeffers, had been briefed — no one from Moran's ship was to board a British ship of the line. Would any of you let Moran and Jeffers aboard?"

"What should we do, sir?" one of the men asked.

"Run to the stateroom and ask the ranking officer to take control here. Be off now!" Holmes turned back to the lifeboat. "Drop the cage overboard, Moran. Now!"

We could hear the vicious growls and squeals of the caged beast. It stalked back and forth, beady eyes fixed on the lights of our ship. Moran hesitated a moment, then reached behind him.

"Holmes, have pity . . ." he began.

"Fire a shot into the boat, Watson."

I did so.

Holmes continued: "Colonel, you're going to have a hard time staying afloat with a hull full of bullet holes."

"Please . . ."

"Another, Watson, if you would."

After the second shot, Moran quickly lifted the cage and dropped it into the black water. It sank like a stone, leaving no trace.

One of the officers came running up. "What's going on here, Mr. Holmes? Where's Mr. Jeffers?"

In a few dozen words the situation had been explained.

"What should we do with these two men?"

Holmes smiled. "I should think that that lifeboat, if towed at a goodly distance behind us, would make for an interesting journey back to England. Both men should be deloused by the time we arrive."

Back in our digs in Baker Street, Holmes put his feet up before the fire. We'd been back for nearly three weeks, and the trials of Moran and Jeffers were coming up, yet there were still elements unclear to me. "When did you know, exactly?" I asked.

Holmes exhaled a heady Cavendish smoke. "I believe I have mentioned before, Watson, that when all other possibilities have been exhausted, whatever remains, however implausible, must be the truth. As soon as I saw the lifeboat in the water, a conjecture occurred to me. No lifeboat could have survived that explosion. Therefore, it had been lowered before the explosion. It follows, then, that the explosion was planned. When Jeffers did not hesitate to try to bring the survivor aboard, I surmised that he was in on the plot. Of course, I had to risk mutiny to prove it, but Jeffers's involvement was the only thing that fit all the facts."

"But he was bleeding when we came upon him and Captain Wagner."

"Nothing is more convincing and easier to self-inflict than a superficial head wound."

"And our — ahem — my poisoning?"

"The crewman said that the tea was from the bridge. We both assumed he meant from the captain. But a man of Captain Wagner's personality would imprint it on his men, and if he had personally sent the drinks, the crewman would have said, 'Captain Wagner sends his compliments,' or some such thing."

"Now that you explain it, it seems so clear."

"Don't punish yourself, my friend. Neither of us saw it at the time. It was not until I saw Moran in the lifeboat that I was forced to reconsider the smallest events in the chain."

The fire burned low. "And what, finally, of Professor Moriarty?" I asked.

Holmes sighed. "Not Moran, nor Jeffers, nor Culverton-Smith will implicate him. For the present we've foiled him, but I fear Moriarty and I must await another confrontation."

"And what then?" I asked, looking into my friend's troubled face.

Sherlock Holmes gazed glassy-eyed into the fire. "And then, Watson," he said, "then one of us must surely die."

JOHN LUTZ

Night Crawlers

FROM *Ellery Queen's Mystery Magazine*

THERE'S PLANT LIFE in parts of the Everglades that's to be found nowhere else in the country, spores carried by hurricane winds from the West Indies that take root and flourish in the steamy tropical climate and are exotic and primitive and sometimes dangerous. Some say that in Mangrove City there's animal life to be found nowhere else.

Mangrove City isn't really a city unless you use the term generously. It's a stretch of ramshackle, moss-marred clapboard buildings where the road runs through the swamp along relatively dry land. The "city" is a few small shops, a restaurant, a service station with a sign warning you to fill your gas tank because the swamp's full of alligators, a barber shop with a red and white barber pole that's also green with mold. There's a police station in the same rundown frame building as the city hall, and a blackened ruin that was Muggy's Lounge until it burned down five years ago. Next to the ruin is the new and improved Muggy's, constructed of cinder block and with a corrugated steel roof. Not a city, really. Barely a town. More like something unfortunate that happened on the side of the road.

A mile before you get to Mangrove City, that is *before* if you're driving west the way Carver had, is the Glades Inn, a sixteen-unit motel. It's a low brick structure, built in a *U* to embrace a swimming pool. Carver couldn't imagine anyone ever actually swimming in the thing. The algae on its surface was green and thick. A diving board sagged toward the water and was draped with Spanish moss. From the far corner of the pool came a dull *plop* and a stirring of sluggish water as a bullfrog, tired of Carver's scrutiny, hopped for green cover. Carver set the tip of his cane on the hot gravel surface of the parking lot and limped toward the office.

As he pushed open the door, a bell tinkled. That didn't seem to mean much. The knotty-pine-paneled office was deserted. Behind the long counter, whose front was paneled to match the walls, was a half-eaten sandwich on a desk, next to an old black IBM Selectric typewriter. The only furniture on Carver's side of the desk was a red vinyl chair with a rip in its seat that revealed white cotton batting struggling to get out. On the wall near the chair was a framed color photograph of a buxom woman in a bikini and cowboy boots, riding on the back of a large alligator. She was grinning with her mouth open wide and had an arm raised as if she were waving the ten-gallon hat in her hand. Carver leaned close and studied the photograph. The woman was stuffed into the bikini. The alligator was just stuffed.

"Some sexy 'gator, don'tcha think?" a voice said.

Carver turned and saw a stooped old man with a grizzled gray beard that refused to grow over a long, curved scar on his right cheek. The right eye, near the scar, was a slightly different shade of blue from that of the left and might have been glass. The man had a wiry build beneath a ragged plaid shirt and dirty jeans. He was behind the desk, and Carver couldn't see much of the lower half of his body, but what he could see, and the way the man moved, gave the impression he was bowlegged. His complexion was like raw meat, almost as if he'd been badly burned long ago.

"I didn't see you there," Carver said, noticing now a paneled door that matched the wall paneling behind the desk.

"I was in back, heard the bell, knowed there was somebody out heah." He had an oddly clipped southern accent yet drew out the last words of his sentences: *heeah*. He leaned scrawny elbows on the desk and grinned with incredibly bad teeth, shooting a look at Carver's cane. "What can I do ya, friend?"

Carver saw now that he had a plastic nametag pinned to his shirt, but it was blank. He immediately named the man "Crusty" in his mind. It fit better than the baggy shirt and pants the man wore. And it certainly went with his faint but acrid odor of stale urine. "You can give me a room."

Crusty looked surprised. Even shocked. "You sure 'bout that?"

"Sure am. This is a motel, right?"

"Well, 'course it is. 'S'cuse my bein' put back on my heels, but this heah's the off-season."

Carver wondered when the "on" season was. And why.

Crusty got a registration card out of a desk drawer and laid it on the counter along with a plastic ballpoint pen that was lettered *Irv's Baits.* "You want smokin' or nonsmokin'?"

Carver thought he had to be kidding, but said, "Smoking. Every once in a while I enjoy a cigar."

"Be eighty-five dollars a night with tax," Crusty said.

"That's steep," Carver commented as he signed the register.

Crusty shrugged. "We're a val'able commodity, bein' the only motel for miles."

"You might be the only anything for miles that doesn't swim or fly."

"Then how come you're heah" — Crusty looked at the registration card — "Mr. Carver from Del Moray?"

"The fishing," Carver said.

Crusty's genuine-looking eye widened. "Not many folks come here for the fishin'."

"No doubt they just come to frolic in the pool," Carver said. "You take Visa?"

"Nope. Gotta be good ol' U.S. cash money."

Carver got his wallet from his pocket, held it low so Crusty couldn't see its contents, and counted out 850 dollars. The cost of doing business, he thought, and laid the bills on the desk.

Now both of Crusty's eyes bulged. The glass one — if it was glass — threatened to pop out.

"Ten nights in advance," Carver explained. "I always give myself enough time to fish until I catch something."

Crusty took the money and handed him a key with a large red plastic tag with the numeral 10 on it. "End unit, south side," he said.

Carver thanked him and moved toward the door.

"You got one of the rooms with a TV, no extra charge," Crusty said. "Ice machine's down t'other end of the buildin'. Just keep pressin' the button till the ice quits comin' out brown."

"I'll make myself at home," Carver told him and limped out into the sultry afternoon, astounded to realize it was cooler outside than in the office.

Number 10 was a small room with a dresser, a tiny corner desk, and a wall-mounted TV facing a sagging bed. The carpet was threadbare red. The drapes were sun-faded red. The bedspread matched the drapes. An old air conditioner was set in the wall beneath the single window that looked out on the unhealthy hole that was the pool, then across the road to the shadowed and menacing swamp.

Carver tossed his single scuffed-leather suitcase onto the bed, then went over and opened a door, flipped a wall switch that turned on a light, and examined the bathroom. The swimming pool should have prepared him. There was no bathtub, only a shower stall with a pebbled-glass door. The commode and sink were chipped, yellowed porcelain and so similar in design that they looked interchangeable. A fat palmetto bug, unable to bear the light, or maybe its surroundings, scurried along the base of the shower stall and disappeared in a crack in the wall behind the toilet.

I guess I've stayed in worse places, Carver thought, but in truth he couldn't remember when.

As he was unpacking and hanging his clothes in the alcove that passed for a closet, he laid his spare moccasins up on the wooden shelf and felt them hit something, scraping it over the rough wood. He reached back on the shelf and felt something hard that at first he thought was a coin, but it was a brass Aztec calendar, about two inches in diameter and with a hole drilled in it off-center, as if to make it wearable on a chain.

Carver stood for a moment wondering what to do with the brass trinket, then tossed it back up on the shelf. People might have been doing that with it for years.

He sat down on the bed and picked up the old black rotary-dial phone. Then he thought better of talking on a line that would undoubtedly be shared by Crusty the innkeeper and replaced the receiver. He decided to drive into town and make his call.

Outside Muggy's Lounge was a public phone, the kind you can park next to and use in your car, if you can park close enough and your arm is long enough. There was a dusty white van parked next to the phone, with no one in it. So Carver parked his ancient Olds convertible on the edge of the graveled lot, climbed out, and limped through the heat to the phone. If the humidity climbed another few degrees, he might be able to swim.

He used his credit card to call Ollie Frist in Del Moray. Frist was a

disabled railroad worker who'd retired to Florida ten years ago with
his wife and teenage son. The wife had died. The son, Terry, had
grown up and become a cop in the Del Moray police department.
Terry had come to Mangrove City six months ago, telling anyone
who'd asked that he was going on a fishing trip. Ollie Frist had
gotten the impression his son was working on something on his
own and wanted to learn more before he brought the matter to the
attention of his superiors. Two days later Ollie Frist was notified
that Terry had been found dead in the swamp outside Mangrove
City. At first they'd thought the death was due to natural causes
and an alligator had mauled and consumed part of the body afterward. Then the autopsy revealed that the alligator had been the
natural cause.

The Del Moray authorities had gotten in touch with the Mangrove City authorities. Accidental death, they decided. The grieving
father, Ollie Frist, didn't buy it. What he *had* bought were Carver's
services.

"Mr. Frist?" Carver asked when the phone on the other end of
the line was picked up.

"It is. That you, Carver?" Frist was hard of hearing and roared
rather than spoke.

"Me," Carver said. He knew he could keep his voice at a normal
volume; Frist had shown him the special amplifier on the phone in
his tiny Del Moray cottage. "I'm checked into the motel where
Terry stayed."

"It's a dump, right? Terry said when he phoned to let me know
where he was staying that the place wasn't four-star."

"Astronomically speaking, it's more of a black hole. Did Terry
actually tell you he was coming to this place to fish?"

"That's what he said. I didn't believe it then. Should I believe
it now?"

"No. There's some fishing here, I'm sure. But there's probably
more poaching. It's the kind of backwater place where most of
the population gets by doing this or that, this side of the law or
the other."

"You think that's what Terry was onto, some kinda alligator
poaching operation?"

"I doubt it. He wouldn't see it as that big a deal, or that unusual.
He probably would have just phoned the Mangrove City law if that
were the case." A bulky, bearded man wearing jeans and a sleeveless

black T-shirt had walked around the dusty white van and was standing and staring at Carver. Maybe waiting to use the phone. "I'll
hang around town for a while," Carver said, "see if I can pick up
on anything revealing. There's something creepy and very wrong
about this place. As of now it's just a sensation I have on the back of
my neck, but I've had it before and it's seldom been wrong." The
big man next to the van crossed his beefy arms and glared at
Carver.

"Keep me posted," Frist shouted into the phone. "Let me know if
you need anything at this end."

Carver said he'd do both those things, then hung up the phone.

He set the tip of his cane in the loose gravel and walked past the
big man, who didn't move. His muscular arms were covered with
the kind of crude, faded blue tattoos a lot of ex-cons sport from
their time in prison, and on his right cheek was tattooed a large
black spider that appeared to be crawling toward the corner of his
eye. He puffed up his chest as Carver limped past him. He probably
thought he was tough. Carver knew the type. He probably was
tough.

The striking thing about Mangrove City's main street, which was
called Cypress Avenue as it ran between the rows of struggling
business establishments, was how near the swamp was. Walls of lush
green seemed to loom close behind the buildings on each side of
the road. Towering cypress and mangrove trees leaned toward each
other over the road as if they yearned someday to embrace high
above the cracked pavement. The relentless and ratchety hum of
insects was background music, and the fetid, rotting, life-and-death
stench of the swamp was thick in the air and lay on the tongue like
a primal taste.

The humid air felt like warm velvet on his exposed skin as Carver
crossed the parking lot and entered Muggy's Lounge.

Ah! In Muggy's, it was cool.

There were early customers scattered among the booths and
tables, and a few slumped at the long bar. Carver sat on a stool near
the end of the bar and asked the bartender for a Budweiser.

The bartender brought him a can and let Carver open it. He
didn't offer a glass. He was a tall, skinny man with a pockmarked
face, intent dark eyes set too close together, and a handlebar moustache that was red despite the fact that his hair was brown.

"So whaddya think of our little town?" he asked.

It's conducive to insanity, Carver thought, but he said, "How do you know I'm not from around here?"

The bartender laughed. "There ain't that many folks from around here, and we tend to know each other even if we ain't sleeping together." Someone at the other end of the bar motioned to him and he moved away, wiping his hands on a gray towel tucked in the belt of his cut-off jeans.

Carver sipped his beer and looked around. Muggy's was a surprisingly long building with booths lining the walls beyond where the bar ended. On a shelf high above the bar was a stuffed alligator about five feet long, watching whatever went on with glass eyes that nonetheless seemed bright with evil cunning. There were box speakers mounted every ten feet or so around the edges of the ceiling, tilted downward and aimed at the customers as if they might fire bullets or dispense noxious gas. Right now they were silent. The only sound was the ticking of one of the half-dozen slowly revolving ceiling fans, stirring the air-conditioned atmosphere and moving tobacco smoke around. It occurred to Carver that the clientele in Muggy's might have stopped talking to each other when he walked inside.

The bulky man who'd been watching Carver outside entered the lounge and swaggered toward him. He was about average height but very wide, with muscle rippling under his fat like energy trapped beneath his skin and trying to escape. He smiled thinly at Carver, then sat down on the stool next to him as if using the phone in succession had formed some sort of bond between them. When he smiled, the spider tattoo near his eye crinkled. Carver had seen real spiders do that after being sprayed with insecticide.

"You Mr. Fred Carver?" the man asked in a drawl that moved about as fast as the alligator above the bar.

"How did you guess?" Carver asked, continuing to stare straight ahead at the rows of bottles near the beer taps.

"Didn't guess. I was told you checked in at the Glades Inn. I went and talked to the desk clerk, found out who you was."

"Why?"

"Curious. Stranger here's always news. Ain't much happens to amuse us 'round these parts. We take our pleasure when we can."

"You think I'm going to amuse you?"

"You got possibilities fer sure."

Carver decided to meet this cretin head-on. "Ever hear of a man named Terry Frist?"

"Sure. Got his fool self killed and damn near et up by a 'gator a while back. Terrible thing."

"Alligators usually kill their prey, then drag it back to their den at water's edge where they hide it and let it rot until they can tear it apart easier with their teeth. The way I understand it, Terry Frist's body was found on land."

"Yeah. What was left of it. He was a cop, we found out later. From over in Del Moray. Say now, ain't that where you're from?"

Maybe not such a cretin. "It is," Carver said, "but Frist and I didn't know each other. I read in the newspaper about what happened to him here."

"What is it you do for a livin' there in Del Moray?"

"I'm in research. Decided to come here for the fishing."

"Really? We ain't known for the fishin'."

"Didn't I see a bait shop when I drove into town?"

"Oh yeah. Irv's. Well, there's *some* fishin'. More likely you'll catch yourself a 'gator like that Frist fella did. Fishin' suddenly becomes huntin' when that happens, and you ain't the hunter."

The pockmarked bartender came over and asked what the big man was drinking.

"Nothin'." He slid off his stool and looked hard at Carver. "Fishin's no good this time of year at all. Not much reason for you to stay around town."

"I like a challenge."

"You're more'n likely to get one if you go fishin' in them swamp waters."

"Can I rent an airboat anywhere around here?"

"Nope. Nowheres close, neither. Fella name of Ray Orb rents 'em some miles east, but the swamp's too thick around these parts for airboats to get around in it. I think you best try someplace in an easterly direction." He winked, then turned to leave.

"You didn't mention your name," Carver said.

"I.C. is what I'm called. Last name's Unit. The I.C. stands for Intensive Care." The spider crinkled again as if dying, and I.C. threw back his head and roared out a laugh. Carver watched him swagger out through the door, noticing that all the other customers averted their gazes.

"That his real name?" Carver asked the bartender when I.C. had left.

"He says it is. Nobody much wants to differ with him."

"He as tough as he acts?"

"Oh yeah. Him and his buddies from over at Raiford."

"Raiford? The state penitentiary?"

"That's right. The three of 'em, I.C., Jake Magruder, and Luther Peevy, was in there together after they come down from Georgia and committed some heinous type crime. Some say it was murder. Luther Peevy, his folks died and left him a place nearby, so I guess that's why they all settled in here 'bout a year ago."

"I'll bet the town was happy about that," Carver said.

"This town was never happy," the bartender said and moved away and began wiping down the bar with his gray towel.

Carver finished his beer, then walked around the town for a while before going into its only restaurant, Vanilla's, for lunch, even though it was just eleven o'clock. He was hungry and he was here, and he didn't know if the Glades Inn had a restaurant and didn't want to find out. Crusty was probably the cook.

Though Vanilla's was a weathered clapboard building that leaned on its foundation, it was surprisingly neat and clean inside. Small but heavy wooden tables were grouped evenly beneath a battery of ceiling fans rotating only slightly faster than the ones in Muggy's. There was a small counter and double doors into the kitchen. Carver saw an old green Hamilton-Beach blender behind the counter and wondered if Vanilla's sold milk shakes.

There were two men in white T-shirts and bib overalls at the counter, drinking coffee and eating pie. One of them, a redheaded man wearing a ponytail, turned on his stool, glanced at Carver, then went back to work on his apple pie. They seemed to be the only other warm bodies in Vanilla's.

"'Nilla!" the redheaded man yelled. "You got yourself a customer."

The double doors opened and a heavyset, perspiring woman in her fifties emerged from the kitchen. She had a florid complexion, weary blue eyes, and wispy gray hair that stuck out above one ear as if she'd slept too long on that side. She was wearing maroon slacks and a white blouse and apron and had a faint moustache. "Sit anywhere you want," she told Carver in a hoarse voice as deep as a man's.

He was aware of her looking at his cane as he limped to a table near the wall, well away from the counter. Fly-specked menus were propped between the salt and pepper shakers. He opened one and saw that the selection was limited.

Vanilla came over with an order pad and Carver asked for a club sandwich. Then he asked her if she served milk shakes and she said she did. He said chocolate.

"Why do people call you Vanilla?" he asked when she returned with his food and a thick milk shake, half in a glass, half remaining in the cold metal container that had fit onto the mixer.

"I used to be a blonde," she said simply, then put his lunch on the table and went back into the kitchen.

Carver had eaten a few bites of the sandwich when he heard the door open and close. He looked in that direction and saw that a uniformed cop had come in, a short, obese, sixtyish man in a neatly pressed blue uniform with a gold badge on his chest.

He waddled directly to Carver's table. "I'm Mangrove City Police Chief Jerry Gordon," the cop said. He was one of those very fat men who breathe hard all the time, even when they speak.

Carver shook hands with Gordon and invited him to sit down.

"You're Fred Carver from Del Moray," Gordon said, settling his soft and wheezing bulk into the chair across the table from Carver.

"Your job to know," Carver said, unsurprised. Everyone in town apparently knew his name and where he lived.

"It is that." Gordon smiled. "You're the only guest out at the Glades Inn. Only outsider in town, matter of fact. So you're bound to be noticed. We ain't exactly Miami here, Mr. Carver."

"I guess you were told I'm here for the fishing," Carver said.

"Oh, sure. I got a yuk out of that. Most folks'd rather drop a line in water where there's more likely to be fish than something that's gonna eat their bait then have them for dessert."

"There must be some *good* fishing. Terry Frist came here a while back. He usually knew where they were biting." A different lie for Gordon. He'd told I.C. Unit he hadn't known Frist in Del Moray. Which had been the truth. Or part of the truth. The useful thing about lies was that they were so adaptable.

Chief Gordon gave Carver a dead-eyed, level look, the kind cops were so good at. "Way I recall it, Terry Frist didn't catch nothin' but a big ol' 'gator. I'd be careful walkin' in his footsteps."

"Are you warning me to be careful in and out of the swamp, Chief?"

"Cautionin' you, is the way I think of it." He put his elbows on the table and leaned toward Carver. "I gotta tell you, there's some angry people out there, in and around the swamp, all through these parts."

"Angry at what?"

"Ever'thin' from violence on TV an' in the movies to supermarket bar codes. You don't wanna do no verbal joustin' with 'em. We got folks around here, Mr. Carver, would shoot you dead over violence on TV."

"You think that's what happened to Terry Frist? An argument over politics or the price of something in produce?"

"I think somebody shoulda warned Terry Frist. I read he was a cop. Maybe he was workin' undercover, an' this was no place for him to be."

"Maybe he found out about something. Say, a drug-smuggling operation."

Chief Gordon grinned. "Why, you're fishin' already, Mr. Carver."

"Maybe. But Mangrove City's near enough to the coast that drug shipments from the sea could be brought here by airboat through the swamp, and the law would never be able to figure out the routes or the timing. A cop — as you say, maybe working undercover — was killed here recently. And I met I. C. Unit this morning in Muggy's and was told he's part of a set and recently of the Union Correctional Institution over in Raiford. And now here you are . . ."

"The local cop on the take?" Gordon didn't seem angry at the suggestion, which made Carver curious. "That's so preposterous I ain't even gonna respond to it, Mr. Carver, except to say we got creatures in the swamp more deadly than any 'gator. Maybe one of 'em killed Terry Frist."

"And you don't want to be next, is that it?"

"Nor do I want you to be, Mr. Carver. I.C. and that Peevy and Magruder, those are bad men. A 'gator grab one of 'em an' it'd spit him right out. I did feel compelled to warn you, an' now I have." Chief Gordon shoved back his chair and stood up, tucking in his blue shirt around his bulging stomach.

Carver felt sorry for him. He was past his prime and dealing with local toughs who had him and the rest of Mangrove City under their collective greasy thumb.

"Do you think Terry Frist was murdered?" Carver asked.

Again Chief Gordon was impassive. "What all I think publicly, it's all in my report, Mr. Carver. If you're really serious about doin' any fishin' while you're here, you oughta see Irv down at his bait shop. He'll tell you where they're bitin' an' you might not get bit back." He raised a pudgy forefinger and wagged it at Carver. "You remember I said might." He turned and waddled out, swinging his elbows wide to clear his holstered revolver and the clutter of gear attached to his belt.

Carver poked his straw into the thick milk shake and took a long sip. It was the best thing he'd encountered since arriving in Mangrove City.

That afternoon, Carver set out from the Glades Inn wearing loose-fitting green rubber boots, old jeans, a black pullover shirt, and half a tube of mosquito repellent. He carried a casting rod and wore a slouch cap with an array of colorful feathered lures hooked into it. He hadn't been fishing for years and didn't really know much about it, but he figured if his cover story was fishing, he'd better fish. Maybe he'd even catch something.

Irv of Irv's Baits seemed to know a lot about fishing and had recommended his night crawlers, explaining to Carver that it took the fattest, juiciest worms to catch the biggest fish. Carver thought that made an elemental kind of sense and bought two dozen of the wriggling monsters squirming around in an old takeout fried chicken bucket half full of rich black loam.

He loaded all of this into the cavernous trunk of the Olds, then drove along the road toward town until he came to a turnoff he'd noticed on his previous trip.

The narrow gravel road soon became even narrower, and the gravel became mud that threatened to bog down the big car's rear wheels. Carver braked the Olds to a stop and turned off the engine. Silence somehow made deeper by the ceaseless drone of insects closed in. Off to his right, through dense foliage shadowed by overhead tree limbs and draped Spanish moss, he saw the dull green sheen of water.

He climbed out of the Olds, got his rod and reel and bucket of worms from the trunk, then muddied the tip of his cane as he limped from what was left of the road and trudged in his boots toward the water. His motion made sensory waves in the swamp. The humming insect tone varied slightly at his passing. He heard soft and abrupt watery sounds and the quick and startled beat of wings.

When he reached a likely spot, he stopped, placed the bucket on a tree stump, and stood in the shade. He disengaged the barbed hook from the cork handle of his casting rod, used it to impale one of Irv's ill-fated night crawlers, and moved slightly to the side. Careful not to snag his line on nearby branches, he used the weight of the bait, a small lead sinker, and a red and white plastic float to cast toward a clear circle of water in the shade of an ancient cypress tree. Line whirred out, there was a faint *plop!* and Carver was ready to reel in a fish.

Irv's worm must have loafed underwater. Nothing happened for about fifteen minutes. Then the red and white float bobbed, went completely underwater, and Carver reeled in an empty hook.

So what did it matter? He was really here to establish himself as a genuine fisherman, in case anyone might be watching him. He reached into the bucket for another worm.

The fishing got better at the spot Carver had chosen. It took him only about an hour to feed the fish the rest of Irv's worms. He removed the fishing cork, cut the leader line above the hook and sinker, then selected the feathered and multiple-barbed Oh Buggie! lure and unhooked it from his cap. He attached it to the line, cast it to where he'd lost all his worms, and almost immediately a fish took it.

Carver reeled in a tiny carp. Since he didn't like to clean fish, and this one was too small to keep anyway, he worked the hook from its mouth and tossed it back. Catch and release, he thought, hoping that wouldn't happen with whoever killed Terry Frist.

He thought nothing the rest of the afternoon. That evening he drove into town and had the family meatloaf special at Vanilla's, then stopped in at Muggy's for a beer before driving back to the motel. He saw no sign of I. C. Unit or his two confederates and was pretty much ignored by the townspeople. They saw him yet they didn't, as if someone had planted in them the posthypnotic suggestion that he didn't exist, and there was a short-circuit between their eyes and their brains that made him invisible to them.

That night Carver awoke in his bed in the Glades Inn to an odd, snarling sound outside in the dark. He lay on his back in total blackness, his fingers laced behind his head, and realized he was listening to the sound of an airboat deep in the swamp. Maybe one of Ray Orb's boats. But according to I. C. Unit, Orb didn't operate in this part of the swamp because it was too dense and dangerous. And how could you not believe I.C.?

Carver fell back asleep listening to the faraway sound of the airboat and dreamed that it was a gigantic insect droning in the swamp. In the dawn and the halfway country between waking and sleep, he thought maybe his dream was possible.

It was more possible, he decided when fully awake, that the late-night droning from the swamp was indeed an airboat's engine, and the cargo was illegal narcotics.

Carver established a routine over the next five days, not doing much other than fishing with rod and reel and Oh Buggie!, going to secluded fishing spots in the evenings and staying late, tossing his infrequent catches back into the water. Carrying his fishing gear, he explored the swamp around Mangrove City. Though he came across tracks in the mud once, he never saw an alligator. And he didn't again hear the snarl of an airboat engine in the night.

Until the sixth night, when he was standing ankle-deep in water near the gnarled roots of a mangrove and heard the sudden roar of an engine, as if a boat that had been drifting nearby had abruptly started up. A light flashed, the swinging beam of a searchlight illuminating the swamp, and for an instant through the trees he saw the shimmering whir of an airboat's rear-mounted propeller spinning in its protective cage as it powered the flat-bottomed boat over the water. Judging by the size of the prop and cage, it was a large boat. Carver heard voices, then a single shouted word: "*Cuidado!*" A man yelling in Spanish to whoever was steering the boat to be careful, probably of some looming obstacle the light had revealed.

Carver stood motionless until the snarling engine had faded to silence. He could still hear water lapping in the boat's wake, even see ripples that had found their way to the moonlit patch of algae and floating debris where he was pretending to fish.

He reeled in Oh Buggie! and a tangle of weed, then returned to where the Olds was parked and drove back to the motel.

Maybe tonight he'd finally caught something.

After showering away mosquito repellent and swamp mud, he put on a fresh pair of boxer shorts, made sure the room's air conditioner was on high, then went to the alcove closet. He reached up on the shelf and found the half-dollar-size bronze Aztec calendar again and stood staring at it. No one knew for sure that the ancient circular Aztec design actually was a calendar. It was only a theory.

Carver stared at the trinket, then placed it back on the shelf. Now he had a theory, and one he believed in. Tomorrow he'd do something about it.

He sat on the edge of the sagging mattress, flicked the wall switch off with his cane, and dropped back on the bed in the warm darkness. With so much resolved, and with a clear course of action before him, he dozed off immediately and slept deeply.

He sensed it was toward morning when he dreamed again of the giant insect droning in the swamp. Only this time he was surprised to hear it buzz his name.

Abruptly he realized someone was in the room speaking to him. Without moving any other part of his body, he opened his eyes.

I. C. Unit was standing at the foot of the bed. He was holding a shotgun casually so that it was pointed at Carver.

"Carver. Carver. You best wake up. You're gonna go fishin' early this mornin'. Gonna get yourself an early start well afore sunrise. Ain't no need for you to worry about bringin' any bait."

Carver knew why. He was going to *be* bait. And not for fish.

At I.C.'s direction, he climbed out of bed and dressed in jeans and a pullover shirt, then put on his green rubber boots. His fishing outfit.

"Don't forget your rod and reel," I.C. said. "Gotta make this look realistic. Hell, maybe we'll even let you catch a fish."

When they went outside, Carver met Peevy and Magruder. There were no introductions and none were necessary. Peevy was a short man with a beer gut and a pug face. He was tattooed, like I.C., with the crude blue ink imagery of the amateur prison artist without adequate equipment. Magruder was tall and thin, with a droopy moustache and tragic dark eyes. Each man was armed with a semi-automatic twelve-gauge shotgun like I.C.'s. Their shells were probably loaded with heavy lead slugs rather than pellets, the rounds used by poachers to kill large and dangerous alligators. Awesome weapons at close range.

"He don't look like much," Magruder said in a southern drawl that sounded more like Tennessee than Georgia.

"Gonna look like less soon," Peevy said in the same flat drawl. He dug the barrel of his shotgun into the small of Carver's back, prodding him toward the parked Olds.

I.C. laughed. "Shucks, that's 'cause there's gonna *be* less of him."

Peevy drove the Olds, and I.C. sat in back with his shotgun aimed at Carver, who sat in front and wondered if he could incapacitate Peevy with a jab of his cane, then deal with I.C. and the shotgun. But he knew the answer to that one and didn't like it. Magruder followed, driving a dented black pickup truck with a camper shell mounted on its bed. As they pulled out of the Glades Inn parking lot, Carver was sure he saw a light in the office go out.

"You weren't smuggling drugs," Carver said, as they bumped over the rutted road. "You were bringing in illegal aliens from Mexico."

"From there and all over Central America," I.C. said. Now that Carver knew, he was bragging. Nothing to lose. "Boat from Mexico transfers 'em to airboats on the coast, and we know the swamp well enough to boat 'em in here. The Glades Inn is the next stop, where they pay the rest of what they owe and then are moved by car and truck on north."

"And if they can't pay?"

I.C. laughed hard and Carver felt spittle and warm breath on the back of his neck. "That's the same question that poor Terry Frist asked. Answer is, if they can't pay, they don't go no farther north."

"Nor any other direction," Peevy added, wrestling with the steering wheel as they negotiated a series of ruts.

"And Terry Frist?" Carver asked.

"'Gator got him, all right," was all I.C. said.

Peevy smiled as he drove.

They wound through the night along roads so narrow that foliage brushed the Olds's sides. Finally they reached the most desolate of Carver's fishing spots, a pool of still water glistening black in the moonlight, its edges overgrown with tall reeds and sawgrass.

As soon as they'd stopped, I.C. prodded the back of Carver's neck as an instruction to get out of the car. Carver climbed out slowly, feeling the hot, humid night envelop him, listening to the desperate screams of nocturnal insects. Magruder parked the pickup behind the Olds, then climbed out and walked forward to join them. The only illumination was from the parking lights on the Olds.

While I.C. held his shotgun to Carver's head, Magruder looped a steel chain around the ankle of Carver's right boot and fastened it in place with a padlock. Then he shoved him toward the center of the shallow pool of water. Carver noticed a thick cedar post protruding from the water.

When they reached the knee-deep center of the pool, Magruder strung the chain through a hole in the post, wrapped it tight around the thick wood, then used another padlock to secure it. He clipped his key ring back onto one of his belt loops, then stepped back. Peevy was standing nearby, his shotgun aimed at Carter.

I.C. handed Carver the casting rod. "You hold onto your prop here," he said, then snatched Carver's cane away and effortlessly snapped the hard walnut over his knee. He let both ends of the splintered cane drop into the water.

"The desk clerk at the Glades Inn knows you left with me," Carver said. "He's probably already called Chief Gordon."

"He knows ever'thin'," I.C. said. "So's Chief Gordon know, though he don't like to let on, even to his own self."

Both men backed away from Carver, leaving him standing alone and unable to move more than a foot or so in any direction.

"You wanna pass the time fishin'," I.C. said, "you go right ahead. Now us, we gotta drive back into town and do some minor mischief, establish an alibi. Magruder'll stay here an' keep you company till you don't need no company. He ain't afraid of the dark, and he likes to watch."

"Watch what?"

"This here's a special part of the swamp, Carver. It ain't at all far from where that Terry Frist fella got hisself tore all to hell by a 'gator. This here area is crawlin' with 'gators. They figured out some way in their mean little brains that there's plenty to eat here from time to time."

I.C. and Peevy sloshed through the dark water and onto damp but solid ground. "We gonna be back to pick up Magruder later,"

I.C. said without bothering to look at Carver. He and Peevy climbed into the cab of the battered black pickup and the engine kicked over.

When the old truck had rattled its way out of sight, Magruder sat himself down on a stump about fifty feet away from Carver and settled his shotgun across his knees.

"Now then," he said, "you go ahead and fish if you want. You an' me's jus' gonna wait a while an' see who catches who."

Carver stood leaning against the post driven into the earth beneath the water. He knew it was firm, driven deep or maybe even set in concrete, and the locks and chain were unbreakable. He stared into the dark swamp around him, listening to the drone of insects, the gentle deadly sounds of things stirring in the night. Though he told himself to be calm, his heart was hammering. He glanced over at Magruder, who had a lighted cigarette stuck in his mouth now, and smiled at him.

When Magruder was on his third cigarette, there was a low, guttural grunt from the dark, and off to the side water sloshed as something ponderous moved. Carver looked down and saw the water around his knees rippling. He tried swallowing his terror, tried desperately to think, but fear was like sand in the machinery of his mind.

The tall black grass stirred, and something low and long emerged. Carver knew immediately what it was.

The huge 'gator slithered out into plain view in the moonlight, sloshed around until it was at a slight angle to him, and regarded him with a bright, primitive eye.

"Sure is a big 'un!" Magruder said, obviously amused.

The 'gator switched its tail, churning the water. Carver's heart went cold. He wielded the casting rod like a weapon, as if that might help him.

And it might.

He made himself stop trembling, turned his body, and leaned hard against the post, setting his good leg tight to it.

The 'gator gave its fearsome, guttural grunt again.

"Hungry!" Magruder commented, looking from Carver to the 'gator with a sadist's keen anticipation.

Carver raised the casting rod, whipping it backward then forward. The line whirred out and fell across Magruder's shoulder. Carver reeled fast as Magruder reached for the thin but strong line.

It simply played through his fingers, cutting them. He yanked his hand away and Carver gave the rod a sharp backward tug, feeling the Oh Buggie! with its many barbed hooks set deep in the side of Magruder's neck.

Magruder yelped and jumped up in surprise, the shotgun dropping to the ground. He reached down for the shotgun but Carver yanked hard on the rod, pulling him off balance and making him yelp again in pain. He'd stumbled a few steps toward Carver, and now he couldn't get back to the gun.

Carver began reeling him in.

Magruder didn't want to come. He tried to work the lure loose from where it clung like a large insect to the side of his neck, but each time Carver would yank the rod and pain would jolt through him. The alligator was still and watching with what seemed mild interest.

Carver had Magruder stumbling steadily toward him now, led by excruciating pain. Magruder raised his right hand and tried frantically to loosen the barbed hooks, but found he couldn't withdraw the hand. It was hooked now too, held fast to the side of his neck. Blood ran in a black trickle down his wrist. With his free hand he removed the cigarette stuck to his lower lip and tried to hold the ember to the fishing line to burn through it. Carver yanked harder on the rod, and the cigarette dropped to the water. Magruder was splashing around now, falling, struggling to his feet, fighting to pull away.

And something else was splashing.

Carver looked over and saw the massive low form of the alligator gliding toward him.

Magruder was still fifty feet away.

The alligator was about the same distance away but closing fast, cutting a wake with its ugly blunt snout, its impassive gaze trained on Carver.

Carver began screaming as he worked frantically with the reel. In the back of his mind was the idea that noise might discourage the alligator. And Magruder was screaming now, thrashing panic-stricken in the shallow water.

The alligator hissed and slapped the water with its tail, sending spray high enough to drum down for a few seconds like rain.

Carver and Magruder screamed louder.

*

The dented black pickup truck approached slowly and parked in the moonlight beside the still water.

I.C. and Peevy climbed down from the cab and slammed the doors shut behind them almost in unison. They stood carrying their shotguns slung beneath their right arms.

"Been paid a visit here," Peevy said, motioning with his head toward the two lower legs and boots jutting up from the bloody water. It was obvious from the shallow depth of the water and the angle of the legs that they were attached to nothing. Other than the right leg, with the padlock and chain around its booted ankle.

"Magruder!" Peevy called.

"Will you look at that!" I.C. said. He pointed with his shotgun toward the huge alligator near the water's edge, its jaws gaping.

Neither man said anything for at least a minute, standing and staring at the alligator, their shotguns trained on it.

"Ain't movin'," Peevy said after a while.

I.C. dragged the back of his forearm across his mouth. "C'mon."

"Don't like it," Peevy said, advancing a few steps behind I.C. toward the motionless alligator.

"Nothin' here to like," I.C. said.

When they were ten feet away from the alligator they saw the black glistening holes in the side of its head, from the lead slugs Magruder used in his shotgun rounds.

Then they saw something else. The alligator's jaws were gaping because they were propped open with something — a stick or branch?

No, a cane! A broken half of a cane!

I.C. whirled and looked again at the booted legs jutting from the bloody surface of the barely stirred water.

"Them boots got laces!" he said. "Crippled man didn't have no laces in his boots! He musta somehow got Magruder's keys off'n him, then his gun!"

He and Peevy turned in the direction of a slight metallic click in the blackness near the edge of the pond, a sound not natural to the swamp. Together they raised their shotguns toward their shoulders to aim them at the source of the sound.

But Carver already had them in his sights. He squeezed the trigger over and over until the shotgun's magazine was empty.

In the vibrating silence after the explosion of gunshots, he heard only the beating of wings as startled, nested birds took flight into the black sky. They might have been the departing souls of I.C. and Peevy, only they were going in the wrong direction.

Using the empty shotgun for a cane, Carver limped out of the swamp.

MARGARET MARON

Prayer for Judgment

FROM *Shoveling Smoke*

Certain smells take you back in time as quickly as any period song. One whiff of Evening in Paris *and I am a child again, watching my mother get dressed up. The smell of woodsmoke, bacon, newly turned dirt, a damp kitten, shoe polish, Krispy Kreme doughnuts — each evokes anew its own long sequence of memories . . . like gardenias on a summer night.*

The late June evening was so hot and humid, and the air was so still, that the heavy fragrance of gardenias was held close to the earth like layers of sweet-scented chiffon. I floated on my back at the end of the pool and breathed in the rich sensuous aroma of Aunt Zell's forty-year-old bushes.

More than magnolias, gardenias are the smell of summer in central North Carolina and their scent unlocks memories and images we never think of when the weather's cool and crisp.

Blurred stars twinkled in the hazy night sky, an occasional plane passed far overhead and lightning bugs drifted lazily through the evening stillness. Drifting with them, unshackled by gravity, I seemed to float not on water but on the thick sweet air itself, half of my senses disoriented, the other half too wholly relaxed to care whether a particular point of light was insect, human or extraterrestrial.

The house is only a few blocks from the center of Dobbs, but our sidewalks roll up at nine on a week night, and there was nothing to break the small town silence except light traffic or the occasional bark of a dog. When I heard the back screen door slam, I assumed it was Aunt Zell or Uncle Ash coming out to say goodnight, but the man silhouetted against the house lights was too big and bulky. One of my brothers?

"Deb'rah?" Dwight Bryant moved cautiously down the path and along the edge of the pool, as if his eyes hadn't yet adjusted to the darkness.

"Watch out you don't fall in," I told him. "Unless you mean to."

I didn't reckon he did because my night vision was good enough to see that he had on his new sports jacket. As chief of detectives for the Colleton County Sheriff's Department, Dwight seldom wears a uniform unless he wants to look particularly official.

He followed my voice and came over to squat down on the coping and dip a hand in the water.

"Not very cool, is it?"

"Feels good though. Come on in."

"No suit," he said regretfully, "and Mr. Ash is so skinny, I couldn't get into one of his."

"Oh, you don't need a bathing suit," I teased. "Not dark as it is tonight. Besides, we're just home folks here."

Dwight snorted. Growing up, he was in and out of our farmhouse so much that he really could have been one more brother, but my brothers never went skinny-dipping if I were around. (Correction: not if they *knew* I was around. Kid sisters don't always announce their presence.)

"You're working late," I said. "What's up?"

"A young woman over in Black Creek got herself shot dead this morning. They didn't find her till nearly six this evening."

"Shot? You mean murdered?"

"Looks like it."

"Someone we know?"

"Chastity Barefoot? Everybody called her Chass."

Rang no bells with me.

"She and her husband both grew up in Harnett County. His name's Edward Barefoot."

"Now that sounds familiar for some reason." I stood up — the lap pool's only four feet deep — and Dwight reached down his big hand to haul me out beside him. I came up dripping and wrapped a towel around me as I tried to think where I'd heard that name recently. "They any kin to the Cotton Grove Barefoots?"

"Not that he said."

I finished drying off and slipped on my flip-flops and an over-sized tee-shirt and we walked back to the patio to sit and talk. Aunt Zell came out with a pitcher of iced tea and said she and Uncle Ash were going upstairs to watch the news in bed so if I'd lock up after Dwight left, she'd tell us goodnight now.

I gave her a hug and Dwight did, too, and after she'd gone inside and we were sipping the strong cold tea, I said, "This Edward Barefoot. He do the shooting?"

"Don't see how he could've," said Dwight. "Specially since you're his alibi."

"Come again?"

"He says he spent all morning in your courtroom. Says you let him off with a prayer for judgment."

"I did?"

Monday morning traffic court is such a cattle call that it's easy for the faces to blur and if Dwight had waited a week to ask me, I might not have remembered. As it was, it took me a minute to sort out which one had been Edward Barefoot.

As a district court judge, I had been presented with minor assaults, drug possession, worthless checks and a dozen other misdemeanor categories; but on the whole, traffic violations had made up the bulk of the day's calendar. Seated on the side benches had been uniformed state troopers and officers from both the town's police department and the county sheriff's department, each prepared to testify why he had ticketed and/or arrested his share of the two hundred and five individuals named on my docket today. Tracy Johnson, the prosecuting ADA, had efficiently whittled at least thirty-five names from that docket and she spent the mid-morning break period processing the rest of those who planned to plead guilty without an attorney.

At least 85 percent were male and younger than thirty. There doesn't seem to be a sexual pattern on who will come up with phony registrations, improper plates or expired inspection stickers, but most sessions have one young lead-footed female and one older female alcoholic who's blown more than the legal point-oh-eight. Yeah, and every week I get at least one middle-aged man who thinks it's his God-given right to keep driving even though his license has been so thoroughly revoked that for the rest of his life it'll barely be legal for him to get behind the steering wheel of a bumper car at the State Fair.

As I poured Dwight a second glass of tea, I remembered seeing Edward Barefoot come up to the defense table. I had wondered whether he was a first-time speeder or someone on the edge of getting his license revoked. His preppie haircut was so fresh that there was a half-inch band of white around the back edges where his hair had kept his neck from tanning, and his neat charcoal gray suit bespoke a young businessman somewhat embarrassed at finding himself in traffic court and eager to make a good impression. His pin-striped shirt and sober tie said, "I'm an upstanding taxpayer and solid citizen of the community," but his edgy good looks would have been more appropriate on one of our tight-jeaned speed jockeys.

Tracy had withdrawn the charge of driving without a valid license, but Barefoot was still left with a 78 in a 65 speed zone.

I nodded to the spit-polished highway patrolman and said, "Tell me about it."

It was the same old same old with a slight variation. Late one evening, about a week earlier, defendant got himself pulled for excessive speed on the interstate that bisects Colleton County. According to the trooper, Mr. Barefoot had been cooperative when asked to step out of the car, but there was an odor of an impairing substance about him and he didn't have his wallet or license.

"Mr. Barefoot stated that his wife was usually their designated driver, so he often left his wallet at home when they went out like that. Just put some cash in his pocket. Mrs. Barefoot was in the vehicle and she did possess a valid license, but she stated that they'd been to a party over in Raleigh and she got into the piña coladas right heavy so they felt like it'd be safer for him to drive."

"Did he blow for you?" I asked.

"Yes, ma'am. He registered a point-oh-five, three points below the legal limit. And there was nothing out of the way about his speech or appearance, other than the speeding. He stated that was because they'd promised the babysitter they'd be home before midnight and they were late. The vehicle was registered in both their names and Mr. Barefoot showed me his license before court took in this morning."

When it was his turn to speak, Barefoot freely acknowledged that he'd been driving way too fast, said he was sorry, and requested a prayer for judgment.

"Any previous violations?" I asked the trooper.

"I believe he has one speeding violation. About three years ago. Sixty-four in a fifty-five zone."

"Only one?" That surprised me because this Edward Barefoot sure looked like a racehorse.

"Just one, your honor," the trooper had said.

"Another week and his only violation would have been neutralized," I told Dwight now as I refilled my glass of iced tea, "so I let him off. Phyllis Raynor was clerking for me this morning and she or Tracy might have a better fix on the time, but I'd say he was out of there by eleven-thirty."

"That late, hmm?"

"You'd like for it to be earlier?"

"Well, we think she was killed sometime mid-morning and that would give us someplace to start. Not that we've heard of any trouble between them, but you know how it is — husbands and boyfriends, we always look hard at them first. Barefoot says he got a chicken biscuit at Bojangles on his way out of town, and then drove straight to work. If he got to his job when he says he did, he didn't have enough time to drive home first. That's almost fifty miles. And if he really was in court from nine till eleven-thirty — ?"

"Tracy could probably tell you," I said again.

According to Dwight, Chastity Barefoot had dropped her young daughter off at a day care there in Black Creek at nine-thirty that morning and then returned to the little starter home she and her husband had bought the year before in one of the many subdivisions that have sprung up since the new interstate opened and made our cheap land and low taxes attractive to people working around Raleigh. She was a part-time receptionist for a dentist in Black Creek and wasn't due in till noon; her husband worked for one of the big pharmaceuticals in the Research Triangle Park.

When she didn't turn up at work on time, the office manager had first called and then driven out to the house on her lunch hour because "And I quote," said Dwight, "'Whatever else Chass did, she never left you hanging.'"

"Whatever else?" I asked.

"Yeah, she did sort of hint that Miz Barefoot might've had hinges on her heels."

"So there *was* trouble between the Barefoots."

"Not according to the office manager." Dwight slapped at a mosquito buzzing around his ears. "She says the poor bastard didn't have a clue. Thought Chass hung the moon just for him. Anyhow, Chass's car was there, but the house was locked and no one answered the door, so she left again."

He brushed away another mosquito, drained his tea glass and stood up to go. "I'll speak to Tracy and Phyllis and we'll check every inch of Barefoot's alibi, but I have a feeling we're going to be hunting the boyfriend on this one."

That would have been the end of it as far as I was concerned except that Chastity Barefoot's grandmother was a friend of Aunt Zell's, so Aunt Zell felt she ought to attend the visitation on Wednesday evening. The only trouble was that Uncle Ash had to be out of town and she doesn't like to drive that far alone at night.

"You sure you don't mind?" she asked me that morning.

On a hot Wednesday night, I had planned nothing more exciting than reading briefs in front of the air conditioner in my sitting room.

I had originally moved in with Aunt Zell and Uncle Ash because I couldn't afford a place of my own when I first came back to Colleton County and there was no way I'd have gone back to the farm at that point. I use the self-contained efficiency apartment they fixed for Uncle Ash's mother while she was still alive, with its own separate entrance and relative privacy. We're comfortable together — too comfortable say some of my sisters-in-law who worry that I may never get married — but Uncle Ash has to be away so much, my being there gives everybody peace of mind.

No big deal to drive to the funeral home over in Harnett County, I told her.

It was still daylight, another airless, humid evening and even in a thin cotton dress and barefoot sandals, I had to keep the air conditioner on high most of the way. As we drove, Aunt Zell reminisced about her friend, Retha Minshew, and how sad it was that her little great-granddaughter would probably grow up without any memory of her mother.

"And when Edward remarries, that'll loosen the ties to the Minshews even more," she sighed.

I pricked up my ears. "You knew them? They weren't getting along?"

"No, no. I just mean that he's young and he's got a baby girl that's going to need a mother. Only natural if he took another wife after a while."

"So why did you say 'even more'?" I asked, as I passed a slow-moving pickup truck with three hounds in the back.

"Did I?" She thought about her words. "Maybe it's because the Minshews are so nice and those Barefoots —"

Trust Aunt Zell to know them root and stock.

"They say Edward's real steady and hard-working. Always putting in overtime at his office. Works nine or ten hours a day. But the rest of his family —" She hesitated, not wanting to speak badly of anybody. "I think his father spent some time in jail for beating up on his mother. Both of them were too drunk to come to the wedding, Retha says. And Retha says his two younger brothers are wild as turkeys, too. Anyhow, I get the impression the Minshews don't do much visiting back and forth with the Barefoots."

Angier is still a small town, but so many people had turned out for the wake that the line stretched across the porch, down the walk and out onto the sidewalk.

Fortunately, the lines usually move fast, and within a half-hour Aunt Zell and I were standing before the open casket. There was no sign that Chastity Minshew Barefoot had died violently. Her fair head lay lightly on the pink satin pillow, her face was smooth and unwrinkled and her pink lips hinted at secret amusement. Her small hands were clasped around a silver picture frame that held a color photograph of a suntanned little girl with curly blond hair.

A large bouquet of gardenias lay on the closed bottom half of the polished casket and the heavy sweet smell was almost overpowering.

Aunt Zell sighed, then turned to the tall gray-haired woman with red-rimmed eyes who stood next to the coffin. "Oh, Retha, honey, I'm just so sorry."

They hugged each other. Aunt Zell introduced me to Chastity's grandmother, who in turn introduced us to her son and daughter-in-law, both of whom seemed shellshocked by the murder of their daughter.

As did Edward Barefoot, who stood just beyond them. His eyes were glazed and feverish looking. Gone was the crisp young businessman of two days ago. Tonight his face was pinched, his skin was pasty, his hair disheveled. He looked five years older and if they hadn't told me who he was, I wouldn't have recognized him.

He gazed at me blankly as Aunt Zell and I paused to give our condolences. A lot of people don't recognize me without the black robe.

"I'm Judge Knott," I reminded him. "You were in my courtroom day before yesterday. I'm really sorry about your wife."

"Thank you, Judge." His eyes focussed on my face and he gave me a firm handshake. "And I want to thank you again for going so easy on me."

"Not at all," I said inanely and was then passed on to his family, a rough-looking couple who seemed uncomfortable in this formal setting, and a self-conscious youth who looked so much like Edward Barefoot that I figured he was the youngest brother. He and his parents just nodded glumly when Aunt Zell and I expressed our sympathy.

As we worked our way back through the crowd, both of us were aware of a different pitch to the usual quiet funeral home murmur. I spotted a friend out on the porch and several people stopped Aunt Zell for a word. It was nearly half an hour before we got back to my car and both of us had heard the same stories. The middle Barefoot brother had been slipping around with Chastity and he hadn't been seen since she was killed.

"Wonder if Dwight knows?" asked Aunt Zell.

"Yeah, we heard," said Dwight when I called him that evening. "George Barefoot. He's been living at home since he got out of jail and —"

"Jail?" I asked.

"Yeah. He ran a stop sign back last November and hit a Toyota. Totaled both cars and nearly killed the other driver. He blew a ten and since he already had one DWI and a string of speeding tickets, Judge Longmire gave him some jail time, too. According to his mother, he hasn't been home since Sunday night. He and the youngest brother are rough carpenters on that new subdivision over off Highway Forty-eight, but the crew chief says he hasn't seen George since quitting time Friday evening. The two brothers claim not to know where he is either."

"Are they lying?"

I could almost hear Dwight's shrug over the phone. "Who knows?"

"You put out an APB on his vehicle?"

"He doesn't have one. Longmire pulled his license. Wouldn't even give him driving privileges during work hours. That's why he's been living at home. So he could ride to work with his brother Paul."

"The husband's alibi hold up?"

"Solid as a tent pole. It's a forty-mile roundtrip to his house. Tracy says he answered the calendar call around nine-thirty — that's when his wife was dropping their kid off at the day care — and you entered his prayer for judgment between eleven-fifteen and eleven-thirty. Lucky for him, he kept his Bojangles receipt. It's the one out on the bypass, and the time on it says twelve-oh-five. It's another forty minutes to his work, and they say he was there before one o'clock and didn't leave till after five, so it looks like he's clear."

More than anybody could say for his brother George.

Poor Edward Barefoot. From what I now knew about that bunch of Barefoots, he was the only motivated member of his family. The only one to finish high school, he'd even earned an associate degree at the community college. Here was somebody who could be the poster child for bootstrapping, a man who'd worked hard and played by the rules, and what happens? Bad enough to lose the wife you adore, but then to find out she's been cheating with your sorry brother who probably shot her and took off?

Well, it wasn't for me to condemn Chass Barefoot's taste in men. I've danced with the devil enough times myself to know the attraction of no-'count charmers.

Aunt Zell went to the funeral the next day and described it for Uncle Ash and me at supper.

"That boy looked like he was strung out on the rack. And his precious little baby! Her hair's blond like her mama's, but she's been out in her wading pool so much this summer, Retha said, that she's brown as a pecan." She put a hot and fluffy biscuit on my plate. "It just broke my heart to see the way she kept her arms wrapped around her daddy's neck as if she knew her mama was gone forever. But she's only two, way too young to understand something like that."

From my experience with children who come to family court having suffered enormous loss and trauma, I knew that a two-year-old was indeed too young to understand or remember, yet something about Aunt Zell's description of the little girl kept troubling me.

For her sake, I hoped that George Barefoot would be arrested and quickly brought to trial so that her family could find closure and healing.

Unfortunately, it didn't happen quite that way.

Two days later, George Barefoot's body was found when some county workers were cleaning up an illegal trash dump on one side of the back roads just north of Dobbs. He was lying on an old sofa someone had thrown into the underbrush, and the high back had concealed him from the road.

The handgun he'd stuck in his mouth had landed on some dirt and leaves beside the sofa. It was the same gun that had killed Chastity Barefoot, a gun she'd bought to protect herself from intruders. There was a note in his pocket addressed to his brother:

> *E — God, I'm so sorry about*
> *Chass. I never meant*
> *to hurt you. You know*
> *how much you mean*
> *to me.*
> > *Love always,*
> > *George*

A rainy night and several hot humid days had mildewed the note and blurred the time of death, but the M.E. thought he could have shot himself either the day Chastity Barefoot was killed or no later than the day after.

"That road's miles from his mother's house," I told Dwight. "Wonder why he picked it? And how did he get there?"

Dwight shrugged. "It's just a few hundred feet from where Highway 70 crosses the bypass. Maybe he was hitchhiking out of the county and that's where his ride put him out. Maybe he got to feeling remorse and knew he couldn't run forever. Who knows?"

I was in Dwight's office that noonday, waiting for him to finish reading over the file so that he could send it on to our District

Attorney, official notification that the two deaths could be closed out. A copy of the suicide note lay on his desk and I'm as curious as any cat.

"Can I see that?"

"Sure."

The original was locked up of course, but this was such a clear photocopy that I could see every spot of mildew and the ragged edge of where Barefoot must have torn the page from a notepad.

"Was there a notepad on his body?" I asked idly.

"No, and no pencil either," said Dwight. "He must have written it before leaving wherever he was holed up."

I made a doubtful noise and he looked at me in exasperation.

"Don't go trying to make a mystery out of this, Deb'rah. He was bonking his sister-in-law, things got messy, so he shot her and then he shot himself. Nobody else has a motive, nobody else could've done it."

"The husband had motive."

"The husband was in your court at the time, remember?" He stuck the suicide note back in the file and stood up. "Let's go eat."

"Bonking?" I asked as we walked across the street to the Soup 'n' Sandwich Shop.

He gave a rueful smile. "Cal's starting to pick up language. I promised Jonna I'd clean up my vocabulary."

Jonna is Dwight's ex-wife and a real priss-pot.

"You don't talk dirty," I protested, but he wouldn't argue the point. When our waitress brought us our barbecue sandwiches, I noticed that her ring finger was conspicuously bare. Instead of a gaudy engagement ring, there was now only a thin circle of white skin.

"Don't tell me you and Conrad have broken up again?" I said.

Angry sparks flashed from her big blue eyes. "Good riddance to bad rubbish."

Dwight grinned at me when she was gone. "Want to bet how long before she's wearing his ring again?"

I shook my head. It would be a sucker bet.

Instead, I found myself looking at Dwight's hands as he bit into his sandwich. He had given up wearing a wedding band as soon as Jonna walked out on him, so his fingers were evenly tanned by the summer sun. Despite all the paperwork in his job, he still got out of the office a few hours every day. I reached across and pulled on the expansion band of his watch.

"What — ?"

"Just checking," I said. "Your wrist is white."

"Of course it is. I always wear my watch. Aren't you going to eat your sandwich?"

My appetite was fading, so I cut it in two and gave him half. "Hurry up and eat," I said. "I want to see that suicide note again before I have to go back to court."

Grumbling, he wolfed down his lunch; and even though his legs are much longer than mine, he had to stretch them out to keep up as I hurried back to his office.

"What?" he asked, when I was studying the note again.

"I think you ought to let the SBI's handwriting experts take a closer look at this."

"Why?"

"Well, look at it," I said, pointing to the word *about*.

"See how it juts out in the margin? And see that little mark where the *a* starts? Couldn't that be a comma? What if the original version was just *I'm sorry, Chass*? What if somebody also added the capital *E* to make you think it was a note to Edward when it was probably a love letter to Chastity?"

"Huh?" Dwight took the paper from my hand and looked at it closer.

We've known each other so long he can almost read my mind at times.

"But Edward Barefoot was in court when his wife was shot. He couldn't be two places at one time."

"Yes, he could," I said and told him how.

I cut court short that afternoon so that I'd be there when they brought Edward Barefoot in for questioning.

He denied everything and called for an attorney.

"I was in traffic court," he told Dwight when his attorney was there and questioning resumed. "Ask the judge here." He turned to me with a hopeful look. "You let me off with a prayer for judgment. You said so yourself at the funeral home."

"I was mistaken," I said gently. "It was your brother George that I let off. You three brothers look so much alike that when I saw you at the funeral home, I had no reason not to think you were the same man who'd been in court. I didn't immediately recognize you, but I thought that was because you were in shock. You're not in shock right now, though. This is your natural color."

Puzzled, his attorney said, "I beg your pardon?"

"He puts in ten or twelve hours a day at an office, so he isn't tan. The man who stood before my bench had just had a fresh haircut and he was so tanned that it left a ring of white around the hairline. When's the last time you had a haircut, Mr. Barefoot?"

He touched his hair. Clearly, it was normally short and neat. Just as clearly, he hadn't visited a barber in three or four weeks. "I've — Everything's been so —"

"Don't answer that," said his attorney.

I thought about his little daughter's nut-brown arms clasped tightly around his pale neck and I wasn't happy about where this would end for her.

"When the trooper stopped your wife's car for speeding, your brother knew he'd be facing more jail time if he gave his right name. So he gave your name instead. He could rattle off your address and birthdate glibly enough to satisfy the trooper. Then all he had to do was show up in court with your driver's license and your clean record and act respectable and contrite. Did you know he was out with Chastity that night?"

Like a stuck needle, the attorney said, "Don't answer that."

"The time and date would be on any speeding ticket he showed you," said Dwight. "Along with the license number and make of the car."

"She said she was at her friend's in Raleigh and that his girlfriend had dumped him and he was hitching a ride home," Edward burst out over the protest of his attorney. "Like I was stupid enough to believe *that* after everything else!"

"So you made George get a haircut, lent him a suit and tie, dropped him at the courthouse, with your driver's license, and then went back to your house and killed Chastity. After court, you met George here in Dobbs, killed him and dumped his body on the way out of town."

"We'll find people who were in the courtroom last Monday morning and can testify about his appearance," said Dwight. "We'll find the barber. We may even find your fingerprints on the note."

Edward Barefoot seemed to shrink down into the chair.

"You don't have to respond to any of these accusations," said his attorney. "They're just guessing."

Guessing?

Maybe.

Half of life is guesswork.

The little Barefoot girl might be only two years old, but I'm guessing that she'll never be allowed to forget that her daddy killed her mama.

Especially when gardenias are in bloom.

JAY MCINERNEY

Con Doctor

FROM *Playboy*

They've come for you at last. Outside your cell door, gathered like a storm. Each man holds a pendant sock and in the sock is a heavy steel combination lock which he has removed from the locker in his own cell. You feel them out there, every predatory one of them, and still they wait. They have found you. Finally they crowd open the cell door and pour in, flailing at you like mad drummers on amphetamines, their cats' eyes glowing yellow in the dark, hammering at the recalcitrant bones of your face and the tender regions of your prone carcass, the soft tattoo of blows interwoven with grunts of exertion. It's the old lock 'n sock. You should have known. As you wait for the end, you think that it could've been worse. It has been worse. Christ, what they do to you some nights. . . .

In the morning, over seven grain cereal and skim milk, Terri says, "The grass looks sick."

"You want the lawn doctor," McClarty says. "I'm the con doctor."

"I wish you'd go back to private practice. I can't believe you didn't report that inmate who threatened to kill you." McClarty now feels guilty that he told Terri about this little incident — a con named Lesko who made the threat after McClarty cut back his Valium — in the spirit of stoking her sexual ardor. His mention of the threat, his exploitation of it, has the unintended effect of making it seem more real.

"The association is supposed to take care of the grass," Terri says. They live in a community called Live Oakes Manor, two to four bedroom homes behind an eight-foot brick wall, with four tennis courts, a small clubhouse and a duck pond. This is the way we live now — walled in, on cul de sacs in false communities. Bradford Arms, Ridgeview Farms, Tudor Crescent, Wedgewood Heights, Oakdale Manor, Olde Towne Estates — these capricious appellations with their diminutive suggestion of the baronial, their vague Anglo-pastoral allusiveness. Terri's two-bedroom unit with sundeck and jacuzzi is described in the literature as "contemporary Georgian."

McClarty thinks about how, back in the days of pills and needles — of Percodan and Dilaudid and finally fentanyl — he didn't have these damn nightmares. In fact he didn't have dreams. Now when he's not dreaming about the prison, he dreams about the pills and also about the powders and the deliquescent Demerol mingling in the barrel of the syringe with his own brilliant blood. He dreams that he can see it glowing green beneath the skin like a radioactive isotope as it moves up the vein, warming everything in its path until it blossoms in his brain stem. Maybe, he thinks, he should go to a meeting.

"I'm going to call this morning," Terri continues. "And have them check the gutters while they're at it." She will, too. Her remarkable sense of economy and organization, which might seem comical or even obnoxious, is touching to McClarty, who sees it as a function of her recovering alcoholic's battle against chaos. He admires this. And he likes the fact that she knows how to get the oil in the cars changed or free upgrades when they fly to St. Thomas. Outside of the examining room McClarty still feels bereft of competence and will.

She kisses his widow's peak on her way out and reminds him about dinner with the Clausens, whoever they might be, God bless them and their tchatkes. Perversely, McClarty actually likes this instant new life. Just subtract narcotics & vodka and stir. He feels like a character actor who, given a cameo in a sitcom, finds himself written into the series as a regular. He moved to this southeastern city less than a year ago, after graduating from rehab in Atlanta, and lived in an apartment without furniture until he moved in with Terri.

McClarty met her at a Mexican restaurant three months ago and was charmed by her air of independence and unshakable self-assurance. She leaned across the bar and said, "Fresh jalapeños are a lot better. They have them, but you have to ask." She waved her peach-colored nails at the bartender. "Carlos, bring the gentleman some fresh peppers." Then she turned back to her conversation with a girlfriend, her mission apparently complete.

A few minutes later, sipping his Perrier, McClarty couldn't help overhearing her say to her girlfriend, "Ask *before* you go down on him, silly. Not after."

McClarty admires Terri's ruthless efficiency. Basically she has it all wired. She owns a clothing store, drives an Acura, has breasts shaped like mangoes around an implanted core of saline. *Not* silicone, she announced virtuously, the first night he touched them. If asked she can review the merits of the top plastic surgeons in town. "Dr. Milton's really lost it," she'll say. "Since he started fucking his secretary and going to Aspen his brow lifts are getting scary. He cuts way too much and makes everybody look either frightened or surprised." At forty, with his own history of psychological reconstruction, McClarty doesn't hold a few nips and tucks against a girl. Particularly when the results are so exceptionally pleasing to the eye.

"You're a *doctor?*" Instead of saying *yes, but just barely,* he nodded. Perched as she was on a stool that first night, her breasts seemed to rise on the swell of this information. Checking her out when he first sat down, Dr. Kevin McClarty thought she looked like someone who would be dating a pro athlete, or a guy with a new Ferrari who owned a chain of fitness centers. She was almost certainly a little too brassy and provocative to be the consort of a doctor, which was one of the things that excited Kevin about her; making love to her, he felt simultaneously that he was slumming and sleeping above his economic station. Best of all, she was in the program, too. When he heard her order a virgin margarita he decided to go for it. A week after the jalapeños, he moved in with her.

The uniformed guard says, "Good morning, Dr. McClarty," as he drives out the gate on his way to work. After all these years he gets a kick out of hearing the honorific attached to his own name. He grew up even more in awe of doctors than most mortals because his mother, a nurse, told him that his father was one, though she refused all further entreaties for information. Raised in the bottom half of a narrow, chilly duplex in Evanston, Illinois, he still doesn't quite believe in the reality of this new life — the sunshine, the walled and gated community, the smiling guard who calls him Doctor. Perversely, he believes in the dream, which is far more realistic than all this blue sky and imperturbable aluminum siding. He doesn't tell Terri, though. He never tells her about the dreams.

Driving to his office he thinks about Terri's breasts. They're splendid, of course. But he finds it curious that she will tell nearly anybody that they are, as we say, surgically enhanced. Last time he was in the dating pool back in the Pleistocene era, he never encountered anything but natural mammary glands. Then he got married and, suddenly, ten years later he's back in circulation and every woman he meets has gorgeous tits but whenever he reaches for them he hears: "Maybe I should mention that, they're, you know . . ." And inevitably, later: "Listen, you're a doctor, do you think, I mean, there's been a lot of negative publicity and stuff . . ." It got so he avoided saying he was a doctor, not knowing whether they were genuinely interested or just hoping to get an opinion on this weird lump under the arm, *right here, see?* Well, actually you *do* know. Despite all the years of medical school and all the sleepless hours of his internship, he never really believed he was a doctor, he felt like a pretender, although he eventually discovered that he felt like less of a pretender on 20 milligrams of Seconal.

The weather, according to the radio, is hot and hotting up. Kevin has the windows up and the climate control at 68. High between 95 to 98. Which is about as predictable as "Stairway to Heaven" on Rock 101, the station that plays all "Stairway," only "Stairway," twenty-four hours a day — a song which one of the MD junkies in rehab insisted was about dope, but to a junkie everything is about dope. Now the song makes McClarty think of Terri marching righteously on her Stairmaster.

After a lifetime in Chicago he likes the hot summers and temperate winters, and he likes the Ur-American suburban sprawl of franchises and housing developments with an affection all the greater for being self-conscious. As a bright, fatherless child he'd always felt alien and isolated; later as a doctor he felt even further removed from the general populace — it's like being a cop — which alienation was only enhanced when he also became a drug addict and *de facto* criminal. He wanted to be part of the stream, an unconscious member of the larger community, but all the morphine in the pharmacy couldn't produce the desired result. When he first came out of rehab, after years of escalating numbness, the sight of a Burger King or a familiar television show could bring him to tears, could make him feel, for the first time, like a real *American.*

He turns into the drive marked MIDSTATE CORRECTION FA-CILITY. It's no accident that you can't see the buildings from the road. With homes worth half a million within a quarter mile, construction was discreet. No hearings, since the land belonged to the State, which was happy to skip the expense of a new prison and instead board its high-security criminals with the corporation that employs Dr. Kevin McClarty. He drives along the east flank of chain-link fence and triple-coiled concertina wire.

These guards, too, greet him by name and title when he signs in. Through the bullet-proof plexi he sees the enlarged photo of an AirNike sneaker a visitor just happened to be wearing when he hit the metal detector, its sole sliced open to show a .25-caliber Beretta nesting snug as a fetus in the exposed cavity. *Hey, it musta come from the factory that way, man, like those screws and syringes and shit that got inside the Pepsi cans. I ain't never seen that piece before. What is that shit, a 25? I wouldn't be caught dead with no 25, man, you can't stop a roach with that fucking popgun.*

Dr. McClarty is buzzed through the first door, and, once it closes behind him, through the second. Inside he can sense it, the malevolent funk of the prison air, the dread ambience of the dream. The varnished concrete floor of the long white hall is as shiny as ice.

Emma, the fat nurse, buzzes him into the medical ward.

"How many signed up today?" he asks.

"Twelve so far."

McClarty retreats to his office, where Donny, the head nurse, is talking on the phone. "I surely do appreciate that. . . . Thank you kindly . . ." Donny's perennially sunny manner stands out even in this region of pandemic cheerfulness. He says good morning with the accent on the first syllable, then runs down coming attractions. "A kid beat up in D last night. He's waiting. And you know Peters from K block, the diabetic who's been bitching about the kitchen food? Saying the food's running his blood sugar up? Well, this morning they searched his cell and found three bags of cookies, a Goo Goo Cluster and two Moon Pies under the bed. I think maybe we should tell the commissary to stop selling him this junk. Yester-day his blood sugar was four hundred."

Dr. McClarty tells Donny that they can't tell the commissary any such thing, that would be a restriction of Peters's liberty — cruel and unusual punishment. He'd fill out a complaint and they'd spend four hours in court downtown, where the judge would even-tually deliver a lecture, third-hand Rousseau, on the natural Rights of Man.

Then there's Caruthers from G, who had a seizure and claims he needs to up his dose of Klonapin. Ah, yes, Mr. Caruthers, we'd *all* like to up *that* and file the edges right off our day. In McClarty's case from o mgs a day to about fifty, with a little Demerol and maybe a Dilaudid thrown into the mix just to secure the perimeter. Or, fuck it, go straight for the fentanyl. No — he mustn't think this way. Like those "impure thoughts" the priests used to warn us about, these pharmaceutical fantasies must be stamped out at all cost. He should call his sponsor, catch a meeting on the way home.

The first patient, Cribbs, a skinny little white kid, has a bloody black eye, which, on examination, proves to be an orbital fracture. That is, his eye socket has been smashed in. And while McClarty has never seen Cribbs before, the swollen face is familiar; he saw it last night in his sleep. "Lock 'n sock?" he asks.

The kid nods and then winces at the pain.

"They just come in the middle of the night, maybe five of them and started wailing on me. I was just lying there minding my own business." Obviously new, he doesn't even know the code yet — not to tell nobody nothing. He is a sniveler, a skinny chicken, an obvi-ous target. Now, away from his peers and tormentors, he seems ready to cry. But he suddenly wipes his nose and grins, shows McClarty the bloody teethmarks on his arm. "One of the sonsof-bitches bit me," he says, looking incongruously pleased.

"You enjoyed that part, did you, Mr. Cribbs?" Then, suddenly, McClarty guesses.

"That'll fix his fucking wagon," says Cribbs, smiling hideously, pink gums showing above his twisted yellow teeth. "I got something he don't want. I got the HIV."

After McClarty cleans up the eye, he writes up a hospital transfer and orders a blood test.

"They won't be messing with me no more," Cribbs says in part-

ing. In fact, in McClarty's experience there are two approaches to
AIDS cases among the inmate population. Many are indeed given a
wide berth. Or else they are killed, quickly and efficiently and
without malice, in their sleep.

Next is a surly, muscled black prisoner with a broken hand. Mr.
Brown claims to have smashed, accidentally, into the wall of the
recreation yard. "Yeah, playing handball, you know?" Amazing how
many guys hurt themselves in the yard. Brown doesn't even try to
make this story sound convincing; rather he turns up his lip and
fixes McClarty with a look that dares him to doubt it.

So far, in the year he has worked here, McClarty has been attacked only in his dreams. But he has been threatened several
times, most recently by an inmate named Lesko, who was furious
when McClarty cut off his prescription for Valium. Big pear-shaped
redneck in for aggravated assault, Lesko took a knife to a bartender
who turned him away at closing time. The bartender was stabbed
fifteen times before the bouncer hit Lesko with a bat. And while
Lesko did threaten to kill McClarty, fortunately it wasn't in front of
the other prisoners, in which case he would feel that his honor, as
well as his buzz, was at stake. Still, McClarty makes a note to check
up on Lesko; he'll ask Santiago, the guard over on D, to get a
reading on his general mood and comportment.

Dr. McClarty makes the first official phone call of the day, to
a pompous ass of a psychopharmacologist to get an opinion on
Caruthers's medication, not that McClarty doesn't have an opinion himself; he is required to consult a so-called expert. McClarty
thinks diazepam would stave off the seizures just as effectively and
more cheaply — which after all is his employers' chief concern —
whereas Caruthers's chief concern, quite apart from his seizures, is
catching that Klonapin buzz. Dr. Withers, who has already talked
with Caruthers's lawyer, keeps McClarty on hold for ten minutes
then condescendingly explains the purpose and methodology of
double-blind studies, until McClarty is finally forced to remind the
good doctor that he *did* attend medical school. In fact, he graduated second in his class at the University of Chicago. Inevitably they
assume that a prison doctor is an idiot and a quack. In the old days
McClarty would have reached through the phone and ripped this
hick doctor's eyeballs out of his skull, asked him how he liked that
for a double-blind study, but now he is happy to hide out in his
windowless office behind the three-foot-thick walls of the prison

and let some other fucker find the cure for cancer. "Thank you very much, *doctor,*" McClarty finally says, cutting the old geek off in mid sentence.

Emma announces the next patient, Peters, the Moon Pie loving diabetic, then slams the door in parting. A fat man with a jelly-like consistency, Peters is practically bouncing on the examining table. Everything about him is soft and slovenly except his eyes, which are hard and sharp, the eyes of a scavenger ever alert to the scrap beneath the feet of the predators. The eyes of a snitch.

McClarty examines his folder. "Well, Mr. Peters."

"Hey, Doc."

"Any ideas why your blood sugar's up to four hundred?"

"It's the diabetes, Doc."

"I guess it wouldn't have anything to do with that stash of candy found in your cell yesterday?"

"I was holding that stuff for a friend. Honest."

Another common refrain here in prison, this is a line McClarty remembers fondly from his drug days. It's what he told his mother the first time she found pot in the pocket of his jeans. The guys inside have employed it endlessly; the gun in the shoe or the knife or stolen television set always belongs to some other guy; they're just holding it for him. They never cease to profess amazement that the cops, the judge, the prosecutor didn't believe them, that their own court-appointed lawyers somehow sold them out at the last minute. They are *shocked.* It's all a big mistake. *Honest. Would I lie to you, Doc?* They don't belong here in prison, and they are eager to tell you why. With McClarty it's just the opposite. He *knows* he belongs in here. He dreams about it. It is more real to him than his other life, than Terri's breasts, than the ailing lawn outside these walls. But somehow, inexplicably, every day they let him walk out the door at the end of his shift. And back at Live Oakes, the guards wave him through the gate inside the walls of that residential oasis as if he really were an upstanding citizen. Of course, technically he is not a criminal. The hospital did not bring charges, in return for his agreement to resign and go into treatment. On the other hand neither the hospital administrators nor anybody else knew that it was he, McClarty, who had shot nurse Tina DeVane full of the Demerol she craved so very dearly less than an hour before she drove her car into the abutment of a bridge.

*

Terri calls just before lunch to report that the caretaker thinks the brown spots in the lawn are caused by cat urine. "I told him that's ridiculous, they're not suddenly peeing any more than they used to — oh, wait, gotta go. Kiss kiss. Don't forget about the Clausens, at seven. Don't worry, they're friends of Bill." She hangs up before McClarty can tell her he might stop off at Unity Baptist on the way home.

Toward the end of the day McClarty goes over to Block D, to check the progress of several minor complaints. He is buzzed into the block by Santiago. "Hey, Doc, what chew think about Aikman's straining his ankle? Your Cowboys, they gonna be hurtin' till he come back." Santiago labors cheerfully under the impression that McClarty is a big Dallas Cowboys fan, a notion that apparently developed after the doctor mumbled something to the effect that he really didn't pay much attention to the Oilers. McClarty has never followed sports, doesn't know Cowboys from Indians, but he is happy to play along, amused to find himself at this relatively late stage in life assigned to a team, especially after he heard the Cowboys referred to on television as "America's team." Like eating at McDonald's, it makes him feel as if he were a fully vested member of the republic.

"Hey, Doc — that sprain? That, like, a serious thing?"

"Could be," McClarty says, able at last to offer a genuine opinion on his team. "A sprain could put him out for weeks."

Santiago is jovial and relaxed, though he is the only guard on duty in a cell block of twenty-four violent criminals, most of whom are on the block this moment, lounging around the television or conspiring in small knots. If they wanted to they could overpower him in a minute; it is only the crude knowledge of greater force outside the door of the block that keeps them from doing so. McClarty himself has almost learned to suppress the fear, to dial down the crackle of active malevolence which is the permanent atmospheric of the wards, as palpable as the falling pressure and static electricity before a storm. So he is not alarmed when a cluster of inmates moves toward him, Greco and Smithfield and two others whose names he forgets. They all have their ailments and their questions and they're trotting over to him like horses crossing the field to a swinging bucket of grain.

"Hey, Doc!" they call out from all sides. And once again, he feels the rush that every doctor knows, the power of the healer, a taste of the old godlike sense of commanding the forces of life and death. This truly is the best buzz, but he could never quite believe it, or feel that he deserved it, and now he's too chastened to allow himself to really revel in the feeling. But he can still warm himself, if only briefly, in the glow of this tribal admiration, even in this harsh and straitened place. And for a moment he forgets what he has learned at such expense in so many airless smoky church basements — that he is actually powerless, that his paltry healing skills, like his sobriety, are on loan from a higher power, just as he forgets the caution he has learned from the guards and from his own experience behind these walls, and he doesn't see Lesko until it is too late, fat Lesko who is feeling even nastier than usual without his Valium, his hand striking out from the knot of inmates like the head of a cobra, projecting a deadly thin silvery tongue. McClarty feels the thud against his chest, the blunt impact which he does not immediately identify as sharp-instrument trauma. And when he sees the knife he reflects that it's a damn good thing he is not Terri, or his left breast implant would be punctured. As he falls into Lesko's arms he realizes, with a sense of recognition bordering on relief, that he is back in the dream. They've come for him at last.

Looking up from the inmate roster, Santiago is puzzled by this strange embrace — and by the expression on McClarty's face as he turns toward the guard booth. "He was smiling," Santiago would say afterwards, "like he just heard a good one and wanted to tell it to you, you know, or like he was saying, *Hey, check out my bro' Lesko here.*" Santiago told the same thing to his boss, to the board of inquiry, to the grand jury and to the prosecutor, and he would always tell the story to the new guards who trained under him. It never ceased to amaze him — that smile. And after a respectful pause and a thoughtful drag on his cigarette, Santiago would always mention that the doc was a big Cowboys fan.

WALTER MOSLEY

Black Dog

FROM *Always Outnumbered, Always Outgunned*

1

"HOW DOES your client plead, Ms. Marsh?" the pencil-faced judge
asked. He was wearing a dark sports jacket that was a size or two too
big for his bony frame.

"Not guilty, your honor," the young black lawyer said, gesturing
with her fingers pressed tightly together and using equally her lips,
tongue, and teeth.

"Fine." The judge had been distracted by something on his desk.
"Bail will be . . ."

"Your honor," spoke up the prosecutor, a chubby man who was
the color of a cup of coffee with too much milk mixed in. "Before
you decide on bail the people would like to have it pointed out that
Mr. Fortlow is a convicted felon. He was found guilty of a double
homicide in Indiana in nineteen sixty and was sentenced to life in
that state; he spent almost thirty years in prison."

"Twenty-seven years, your honor," Brenda Marsh articulated.

So much respect, so much honor, Socrates Fortlow thought. A harsh
laugh escaped his lips.

"And," Brenda Marsh continued. "He's been leading a respectable life here in Los Angeles for the past eight years. He's employed
full-time by Bounty Supermarket and he hasn't had any other negative involvement with the law."

"Still, your honor," the bulbous Negro said, "Mr. Fortlow is being
tried for a violent crime —"

"But he hasn't been convicted," said Ms. Marsh.

"Regardless," said the nameless prosecutor.

"Your honor . . ."

The Honorable Felix Fisk tore his eyes away from whatever had been distracting him. Socrates thought it was probably a picture magazine; probably about yachting, Socrates thought. He knew, from his days in prison, that many judges got rich off of the blood of felons.

"All right," Judge Fisk said. "All right. Let's see."

He fumbled around with some papers and produced a pair of glasses from the top of his head. He peered closely at whatever was written and then regarded the bulky ex-con.

"My, my," the judge muttered.

Socrates felt hair growing in his windpipe.

"The people would like to see Mr. Fortlow held without bail, your honor," chubby said.

"Your honor." Ms. Marsh's pleading didn't seem to fit with her overly precise enunciation. "Eight years and there was no serious injury."

"Intent," the prosecutor said, "informs the law."

"Twenty-five thousand dollars bail," the judge intoned.

A short brown guard next to Socrates grabbed the prisoner's beefy biceps and said, "Come on."

Socrates turned around and saw Dolly Straight at the back of the small courtroom. She had red hair and freckles, and a look of shock on her face. When her eyes caught Socrates' gaze she smiled and waved.

Then she ran out of the courtroom while still holding her hand high in greeting.

2

The night before there had been no room in the West L.A. jail so they put Socrates in a secured office for lockup. But now he was at the main courthouse. They took him to a cellblock in the basement crammed with more than a dozen prisoners. Most of them were tattooed; one had scars so violent that he could have been arrested and jailed simply because of how terrible he appeared.

Mostly young men; mostly black and Latino. There were a couple of whites by themselves in a corner at the back of the cell. Socrates wondered what those white men had done to be put in jeopardy like that.

"Hey, brother," a bearded man with an empty eye socket said to Socrates.

Socrates nodded.

"Hey, niggah," said a big, black, baby-faced man who stood next to the bearded one. "Cain't you talk?"

Socrates didn't say anything. He went past the men toward an empty spot on a bench next to a stone-faced Mexican.

"Niggah!" the baby face said again.

He laid a hand, not gently, on Socrates' shoulder. But Babyface hesitated. He felt, Socrates knew, the strength in that old shoulder. And in that brief moment Socrates shot out his left hand to grab the young man's throat. The man threw a fist but Socrates caught that with his right hand while increasing the pressure in his left.

The boy's eyes bulged and he went down on his knees as Socrates stood up. First Babyface tried to dislodge the big fist from his throat, then he tried slugging Socrates' arm and side.

While he was dying the men stood around.

Sounds like the snapping of brittle twigs came from the boy's throat.

His dying eyes flitted from one prisoner to another but no one moved to help him.

A few seconds before the boy would have lost consciousness, no more than fifteen seconds before he'd've died, Socrates let go.

The boy sucked in a breath of life so deep and so hoarse that a guard came down to see what was happening.

Some of the men were laughing.

"What's goin' on?" the guard asked.

"I was just showin' the boy a trick," the big bearded Negro with one eye said.

The guard regarded the boy.

"You okay, Peters?"

There was no voice in Peters's throat but he nodded.

"Okay," the guard said. "Now cut it out down here."

Socrates took his place on the bench. The fight was just an initiation. Now everyone in the cell knew: Socrates was not a man to be taken lightly.

"Fortlow?" the same guard called out forty-five minutes later.

"Yo."

"Socrates Fortlow?"

"That's right." It hadn't been long but the feeling of freedom had already drained from Socrates' bones and flesh.

He'd checked out every man in the holding cell; witnessed one of the white men get beaten while his buddy backed away. He'd made up his mind to go against the bearded Negro, Benny Hite, if they remained in the cell together.

Benny was a leader and naturally wanted to hold everyone else down. But Socrates wouldn't go down for anyone and so there had to be blood before there could be sleep.

"Come with me," the guard said. He had two large policemen with him.

3

"Hi, Mr. Fortlow," Dolly Straight said. Her skin was pale under thousands of orange and brown freckles. "I posted your bail."

They'd given him his street clothes back but it was too late; the body lice, crabs, from the prison garb had already begun to make him itch.

"What you doin'?" he asked the young woman in front of the courthouse.

"I'm parked illegally up the block," she said, hurrying down the concrete stairs. "I didn't know it would take so long to give them the money and get you out."

Socrates tried to ask again, *why*, but Dolly kept running ahead of him.

"I hope they haven't towed it," she said.

Her pickup was from the fifties, a Dodge. It was sky-blue with a flatbed back that had an animal cage moored in the center.

"Come on," she said, taking the parking ticket from under the windshield wiper. "Get in."

*

"What's this all about?" Socrates asked as they made their way from downtown.

"I put up your bail." Dolly was redheaded, plain-faced, and she had green eyes that blazed. There were fans of tiny wrinkles around her eyes but she was no more than forty.

"What for?"

"Because of Bruno," she said as if it should have been obvious.

"Who's that?"

"The dog. That's what I called him. I mean you can't take care of somebody if he doesn't even have a name. Most of your best vets always name their patients if they don't get a name from the owners."

"Oh," Socrates said. He was wondering what to do with his liberation. Some men who'd spent as many years behind bars as Socrates had wanted to go back to jail; they liked the order that they found there.

"I'd rather be dead," he said.

"Excuse me?"

"Why'd you get me outta there?"

"Because," Dolly said. "Because I know what you did you did because of Bruno. He was almost dead when you brought him in to me. And when those policemen came to arrest you I just got mad. They think that they can just walk in anywhere."

He hadn't been looking for a fight. It was an early work day because he'd had to help with inventory at the supermarket and that started at four in the morning. He'd worked twelve hours and was tired. A dog, big and black, was nosing around, begging for food and Socrates told him to *git*. The dog got himself into the street and a speeding Nissan slammed him down. The man didn't even hit the brakes until after the accident.

Socrates was already to the dog when the white man backed up and parked. The poor dog was scrabbling with his front paws, trying to rise, and whining from the pain in his crushed hind legs.

Socrates just wanted to help. As far as he was concerned the white man broke his own nose.

"How you know why I did what I did?" Socrates asked Dolly.

"Because I went back to where you told me the accident happened. I wanted to find out if the owner was somewhere nearby. I thought that I'd have to put Bruno to sleep but I didn't want to do that until I talked to the owner.

"But there wasn't an owner. Bruno didn't have a home but I met an old lady who saw what happened. That's what I told your lawyer. You know I don't know if Miss Marsh would have gone down there or not. But I told her about Bruno and Mrs. Galesky and then she told me how I could put up your bail.

"I don't know if I'd want her for a lawyer, Mr. Fortlow."

"Why's that?"

"She was trying to tell me how you were a convicted felon and that this charge against you was tough and you might run if you could. Even after I told her that I knew that you were innocent. I thought you black people helped each other out?"

"Dog gonna live?" Socrates asked.

Dolly's face got harder and Socrates found himself liking her in spite of her youth and race.

"I don't know," she said. "His legs are broken and so's his hip. I don't even think they could do a replacement on a human hip that was that bad. His organs seem fine. No bleeding inside but he'll never use those legs again."

They drove on toward Dolly's Animal Clinic on Robertson near Olympic.

4

Bruno was a biggish dog, sixty pounds or more, and little of that was fat. He was unconscious in a big cage on an examining table in Dolly's clinic.

"I gave him a tranc," she said. "I don't like to do that but he was in so much pain and his crying bothered my other patients."

In a large room connected to the examining room Socrates could see rows of cages that ran from small to large. Most of the "patients" were dogs and cats fitted with casts or bandages or attached to odd machines. But there was also a monkey, three different kinds of birds, a goat, and something that looked like a tiny albino sloth.

"Would he die if you left him alone?" Socrates asked. It was ten o'clock or later. There was only him and Dolly in the small animal clinic. He realized that he was pinching the skin through his pants pockets and stopped.

"I don't know," Dolly said. "I don't think so. His vitals are strong.

You'd have to get his bones set as well as possible and then keep
him immobile for a couple of weeks. All that and he'd live. But he'd
have to crawl."

"Anything's better than prison or death."

"You pick that up in the jail?" Dolly asked.

Socrates realized that he was scratching again.

"My dad used to get that all the time," she said. "He was a political
activist down San Diego in the sixties. I remember they'd bust up
his protests and beat him until he had black blood coming out. But
the only thing he ever complained about was getting crabs in jail.
He used to say that they could at least keep it clean in there." She
smiled a very plain smile and said, "I got some soap'll clear that up
in two days."

Bruno whimpered in his cage.

"I'ma be in a cage if they put me down for assault," he said.

"But I gave your lawyer Mrs. Galesky's number. I'm sure she'll
straighten it out."

"You are, huh?"

"Yeah." Dolly's homely smile was growing on him. "I got a house
right in back here," she said. "You could stay in the guest bed."

5

Dolly heated apple cider spiced with cinnamon sticks. Then she
made sandwiches out of alfalfa sprouts, grilled chicken, Gruyère
cheese, and avocado. Socrates had four sandwiches and over a
quart of cider.

Who knew when he'd be eating again?

Dolly had fed, petted, and talked to each patient and then led
Socrates out of the back door of the clinic. There was a yard in back
and a large flowering tree that was dark and sweet-smelling. Past the
tree was a wooden fence. The gate in the fence opened to a beautiful little house.

"Nobody can ever see my house if I don't invite them," Dolly said
to Socrates as she fumbled around for her keys. "I like that."

"Where's your father?" Socrates asked after supper. It was late, past
midnight, and Dolly was folding out the bed in the living room.

"He died," she said. "He was always big and strong but then he just got old one year and passed away."

"Didn't he ever tell you about people like me?"

"He never knew anybody like you, Mr. Fortlow."

"How the hell you know what I'm like?" Socrates said belligerently. "Didn't you hear what they said about me in that courtroom?"

Dolly looked up.

With a stern gaze she said, "I know what you're thinking. You're thinking why would she take a man, a convicted murderer, and take him back here in her house? A man like that could rob me, rape me, kill me." Then her serious face turned into a smile. "But I don't have a choice so I can't be worried about it."

"What you mean you ain't got no choice?"

"Because my father died when I was only twelve and my mother just left," she said. "Because the only one who ever loved me was my dog, Buster. And the only thing I ever knew was how to love him and to take care of him. If I see anyone who cares about animals they're okay with me. I treat them like human beings."

"So you mean that anybody bring a hurt animal to you can sit at your table and sleep in your guest bed?"

"No," Dolly said. She was hurt.

"Then what do you mean?"

"I mean that a dog is a living being just like you'n me. It doesn't matter if there is a God or not. Life is what's important. You're not like one of those rich bitches that shave a dog like he was some kind of fuckin' hedge and then bring him to me so I could castrate him.

"You knocked a man down and then carried that big dog over a mile. You went to jail because that dog has a right. How can I look at that and not do all I can do for you?"

6

Socrates was up late in his foldout bed. It was an old couch and the bed was more comfortable than his own. There was no sound coming through the walls in the house. There was a sweet odor. For a long time Socrates let his mind wander trying to figure out the smell. It was familiar but he couldn't place it.

Finally he realized that the scent was from the tree outside. A

window must have been open. It was the thought of an open window that got Socrates to giggle uncontrollably. He hadn't slept next
to an open window in over forty years.

7

Over the next three weeks Socrates dropped by Dolly's every day
after work. He talked to Bruno and accepted meals in the back
house.

"If Bruno live an' I don't go to jail," he promised Dolly, "I'll take
him home wit' me and keep'im for my pet."

The trial came four weeks after that declaration.

8

"You're with the Public Defender's Office?" the judge, Katherine
Hemp, asked Brenda Marsh.

"Yes, your honor," Brenda replied. "I've just been with them
three months now."

"And how does your client plead, Ms. Marsh?" asked Judge
Hemp, an older woman with gray hair and sad eyes.

"Not guilty, your honor."

"I don't want to drag this thing out, counselor. I have a full
caseload and all we want to know here is if your client assaulted,
um," the judge looked down at her notes, "Benheim Lunge."

"I appreciate the court's time, Judge Hemp. I have only three
witnesses and each of them has less than forty-five minutes of
testimony." Brenda Marsh spoke in her own fashion, as usual,
pronouncing each word separately as if it had come in its own individual wrapper. Socrates wondered if Brenda thought that she
sounded like a white woman talking like that.

"Benheim Lunge," said the tall young man in the witness seat. He
might have been handsome if it wasn't for the sour twist of his lips.

". . . and were you then assaulted by this man?" asked Conrad
MacAlister, the pudgy café-au-lait prosecutor.

"Yes sir. He hit me. I'm in good shape but he must've been boxing in that prison or something."

Socrates' eyes wandered over to the jurors' box. They were
mostly women and he could see that they were appalled by Lunge's
description of his broken nose and whiplash from just one swipe of
the ex-convict's fist.

"Thank you, Mr. Lunge." MacAlister smiled at Brenda Marsh.
"Your witness."

Brenda Marsh got up purposefully and stalked over to Lunge.
"Did you, Mr. Lunge, go up to where the dog lay with a brick in your
hand?"

"No."

"I see. Tell me, Mr. Lunge, what is your profession?"

"I sell sporting goods. My father owns a store on Rodeo Drive and
I run it."

"So," asked Brenda. "Then you don't have a medical background?"

"No."

"But didn't you tell Mr. Fortlow that the dog was done for and
that he should be put out of his suffering? And don't you think it
was likely that the defendant thought that you intended to kill the
dog with the brick you held?"

"Objection," said Prosecutor MacAlister. "Mr. Lunge has already
stated that he didn't have a brick in his hand."

"A stone then?" asked Ms. Marsh. "Did you have a stone, Mr.
Lunge?"

"No."

"Did you have anything in your hands when you approached the
wounded dog and Mr. Fortlow on Olympic Boulevard?"

"Um, well, I don't remember. I, uh, I might have grabbed a, a, a,
you know, a thing, a ten-pound weight I keep in the backseat."

"A ten-pound weight? What was this weight made from?"

"Iron."

"So, you approached Mr. Fortlow with ten pounds of iron in your
hand?"

"How was I to know what would happen? For all I knew it was his
dog. I wanted to help but I wanted to protect myself too. He looked,
well, dangerous. And he was big. I knew I had to stop for hitting the
dog but I wanted to protect myself too."

"And did you say that you'd kill the dog with the weight? Didn't you say that you wanted to stop his pain?"

"Absolutely not. I mean I never said that I wanted to kill the dog. I thought he was going to die, though, I mean you should have seen him. He was a mess."

9

"That man right there," said Marjorie Galesky. She was pointing at Benheim Lunge. Dolly Straight had already testified that Socrates Fortlow came to her clinic with the bleeding and crying black dog in his arms. He'd carried the sixty-two-pound dog eleven blocks to get him care.

". . . I was sitting in my front yard," seventy-nine-year-old Mrs. Galesky said, "like always when it's over seventy-two degrees. It was getting colder and I was about to go in when I see this car run over that poor dog. It hit him and then the tires ran over his legs. This man," she said, pointing at Socrates, "the black one, had gone up to help the dog when the other man, the one driving the car, comes running over with a brick in his hand. At least it looked like a brick. They say it was a weight, whatever that means, but it was big and that man came running over with it. He said something to the black man and then he tried to get at the dog. First off the black man pushed the white one and then he hauled off and hit him." The old woman was a few inches under five feet and slight. She looked like an excited child up there on the stand. There was an ancient glee at the memory of the punch. Socrates tried to keep from smiling.

10

"Socrates Fortlow," he answered when asked to identify himself.

"Yes I did," he said when asked if he struck Benheim Lunge. "He hit the dog and drove off for all I knew. I went up and was tryin' to see what I could do when he come up with a chunk'a metal in his hand. He was lookin' all over an' said that it'd be better to put the dog outta his misery. Then he said that he wanted to take the dog in his car. I said I'd go along but he told me that there wasn't room for me an' the dog too. I told him that I'd seen a animal hospital not

far and that I'd carry the dog there. He said no. Then I said no. He
went for the dog an' he still had the iron in his hand. I put up my
hand to stop'im but he just kept comin'. So I hit him once. You
know I didn't mean to do all that to him but he wasn't gonna take
that dog. Uh-uh."

11

"We find the defendant guilty of assault," the foreman of the jury, a
black woman, said. She seemed sorry but that was the decision and
she stood with it.

12

While waiting for his sentence Socrates would go to visit Bruno
every day. Dolly had made a leash with a basket woven from leather
straps to hold Bruno up from behind. If Socrates could heft the
dog's backside Bruno found that he could propel himself forward
by walking with his front legs.

"You could put a clothesline up around your yard, Mr. Fortlow,"
Dolly said. "And then attach his basket to it with a pulley. That way
he could walk around without you having to help him all the time."

"Yeah," Socrates answered. "Dolly, what you put up behind the
ten percent for my bail?"

"The house," she said.

"Uh-huh."

Bruno was leaping from one paw to the other, yelping a little now
and then because his hip still hurt, and licking the hands of the two
new friends.

"If you run I don't care," Dolly said. "But you have to take Bruno
with you."

13

Before the sentencing Brenda Marsh had a long meeting with Socrates. He cursed her and pounded his fist down on the table in the
little room that the court let them use.

He refused to do what she asked of him.

"You wanna take ev'rything from me?" he asked her.

"I'm trying to keep you out of jail," she said in her annoying way. "Do you want to go to jail?"

"There's a lotta things I don't want. One of 'em is that I don't get down on my knees to no man, woman, or child."

Brenda Marsh did not respond. It was then that Socrates realized that she was probably a very good lawyer.

14

Three days later, after the celebration for Socrates' suspended sentence at Iula's diner, Socrates went to his house with Right Burke, the maimed WWII veteran. They sat in Socrates' poor kitchen while Bruno lay on the floor laughing and licking the air.

"I hate it, Right. I hate it."

"You free, ain't ya?"

"Yeah, but I wake up mad as shit every day."

Brenda Marsh had set up a private meeting with Judge Hemp. She'd pleaded for Socrates' freedom. But the judge said that he'd been found guilty and what could she do?

That's when Brenda revealed her plan for Socrates to apologize to the court, to Benheim Lunge, and to the community. He'd promise to write a letter to be posted on the bus stop where he'd assaulted Benheim and to go to Benheim and ask his pardon. He'd make himself available to the juvenile court to talk to young black children and tell them how he had gone wrong but that he wouldn't do it again.

He'd do an extra fifty hours of community service and for that they could suspend his sentence.

"But you free, Socco. Free, man," said Right, his best friend. "That gal did you a favor. 'Cause you know she musta begged that judge. You know after that big trial they just had the court wanna put ev'ry black man they can in the can. Shit. Guilty? Go *straight* to jail!"

"But you know it's just 'cause'a the dog, Right. It's just 'cause'a the dog I said yeah."

"How's that?"

"He needs me out here. Him and Darryl and you too, brother. I ain't gonna help nobody in that jail cell or on the run. You know I woulda let them take that white girl's house if it wasn't that I had obligations."

The dog barked suddenly and put his nose out to be scratched.

"You just a lucky fool, Socrates Fortlow," Right said.

"You got that right, man. I'm a fool to be who I am and I'm lucky I made it this far. Me an' this black dog here. Shit. Me an' this black dog."

JOYCE CAROL OATES

Faithless

FROM *Kenyon Review*

1

THE LAST TIME my mother Cornelia Nissenbaum and her sister Constance saw their mother was the day before she vanished from their lives forever, April 11, 1923.

It was a rainy-misty morning. They'd been searching for their mother because something was wrong in the household; she hadn't come downstairs to prepare breakfast so there wasn't anything for them except what their father gave them, glutinous oatmeal from the previous morning hastily reheated on the stove sticking to the bottom of the pan and tasting of scorch. Their father had seemed strange to them, smiling but not-seeing in that way of his like Reverend Dieckman too fierce in his pulpit Sunday mornings, intoning the Word of God. His eyes were threaded with blood and his face was still pale from the winter but flushed, mottled. In those days he was a handsome man but stern-looking and severe. Gray-grizzled side-whiskers and a spade-shaped beard, coarse and grizzled too with gray, but thick springy-sleek black hair brushed back from his forehead in a crest. The sisters were fearful of their father without their mother to mediate among them, it was as if none of them knew who they were without her.

Connie chewed her lip and worked up her nerve to ask where was Momma? and their father said, hitching up his suspenders, on his way outside, "Your mother's where you'll find her."

The sisters watched their father cross the mud-puddled yard to where a crew of hired men was waiting in the doorway of the big

barn. It was rye-planting season and always in spring in the Chautauqua Valley there was worry about rain: too much rain and the
seed would be washed away or rot in the soil before it could sprout.
My mother Cornelia would grow to adulthood thinking how bless-
ings and curses fell from the sky with equal authority, like hard-
pelting rain. There was God, who set the world in motion, and
who intervened sometimes in the affairs of men, for reasons no
one could know. If you lived on a farm there was weather, always
weather, every morning was weather and every evening at sundown
calculating the next day's, the sky's moods meant too much. Always
casting your glance upward, outward, your heart set to quicken.

That morning. The sisters would never forget that morning. We
knew something was wrong, we thought Momma was sick. The
night before having heard — what, exactly? Voices. Voices mixed
with dreams, and the wind. On that farm, at the brink of a ten-mile
descent to the Chautauqua River, it was always windy — on the
worst days the wind could literally suck your breath away! — like a
ghost, a goblin. An invisible being pushing up close beside you,
sometimes even inside the house, even in your bed, pushing his
mouth (or muzzle) to yours and sucking out the breath.

Connie thought Nelia was silly, a silly-baby, to believe such. She
was eight years old and skeptical-minded. Yet maybe she believed it,
too? Liked to scare herself, the way you could almost tickle yourself,
with such wild thoughts.

Connie, who was always famished, and after that morning would
be famished for years, sat at the oilcloth-covered table and ate the
oatmeal her father had spooned out for her, devoured it, scorch-
clots and all, her head of fair-frizzy braids lowered and her jaws
working quickly. Oatmeal sweetened with top-milk on the very edge
of turning sour, and coarse brown sugar. Nelia, who was fretting,
wasn't able to swallow down more than a spoon or two of hers so
Connie devoured that, too. She would remember that part of the
oatmeal was hot enough to burn her tongue and other parts were
icebox-cold. She would remember that it was all delicious.

The girls washed their dishes in the cold-water sink and let the
oatmeal pan soak in scummy soapsuds. It was time for Connie to
leave for school but both knew she could not go, not today. She
could not leave to walk two miles to the school with that feeling *something is wrong,* nor could she leave her little sister behind.

Though when Nelia snuffled and wiped her nose on both her hands Connie cuffed her on the shoulder and scolded, "Piggy-*piggy.*"

This, a habit of their mother's when they did something that was only mildly disgusting.

Connie led the way upstairs to the big bedroom at the front of the house that was Momma and Pappa's room and that they were forbidden to enter unless specifically invited; for instance if the door was open and Momma was cleaning inside, changing bed-clothes so she'd call out *Come in, girls!* smiling in her happy mood so it was all right and they would not be scolded. *Come in, give me a hand,* which turned into a game shaking out sheets, fluffing out pillowcases to stuff heavy goosefeather pillows inside, Momma and Connie and Nelia laughing together. But this morning the door was shut. There was no sound of Momma inside. Connie dared to turn the doorknob, push the door open slowly, and they saw, yes, to their surprise there was their mother lying on top of the unmade bed, partly dressed, wrapped in an afghan. My God, it was scary to see Momma like that, lying down at such an hour of the morning! Momma, who was so brisk and capable and who routed them out of bed if they lingered, Momma with little patience for Connie's lazy-tricks as she called them or for Nelia's sniffles, tummyaches, and baby-fears.

"Momma?" — Connie's voice was cracked.

"Mom-ma?" — Nelia whimpered.

Their mother groaned and flung an arm across one of the pil-lows lying crooked beside her. She was breathing hard, like a winded horse, her chest rising and falling so you could see it and her head was flung back on a pillow and she'd placed a wetted cloth across her eyes mask-like so half her face was hidden. Her dark-blond hair was disheveled, unplaited, coarse and lustreless as a horse's mane, unwashed for days. That rich rank smell of Momma's hair when it needed washing. You remember such smells, the sis-ters would say, some of them not-so-nice smells, all your life. And the smell in their parents' forbidden room of — was it talcum pow-der, sweaty armpits, a sourish-sweet fragrance of bedclothes that no matter how frequently laundered with detergent and bleach were never truly fresh. A smell of bodies. Adult bodies. Yeasty, stale. Pappa's tobacco (he rolled his own crude paper cigarettes, he chewed tobacco in a thick tarry-black wad) and Pappa's hair oil and that special smell of Pappa's shoes, the black Sunday shoes always kept polished. (His work-boots, etc., he kept downstairs in the closed-in porch by the rear door called the "entry.") In the step-in closet close by the bed, behind an unhemmed length of chintz, was a blue-speckled porcelain chamberpot with a detachable lid and a rim that curled neatly under it, like a lip.

The sisters had their own chamberpot — their potty, as it was called. There was no indoor plumbing in John Nissenbaum's farmhouse as in any farmhouse in the Chautauqua Valley well into the 1930s and in poorer homes well into the 1940s, and even beyond. One hundred yards behind the house, beyond the silo, was the outhouse, the latrine, the "privy." But you would not want to make that trip in cold weather or in rain or in the pitch-black of night, not if you could help it.

Of course the smell of urine and a fainter smell of excrement must have been everywhere, the sisters conceded, years later. As adults, reminiscing. But it was masked by the barnyard smell, probably. Nothing worse than pig manure, after all!

At least, we weren't *pigs*.

Anyway, there was Momma, on the bed. The bed that was so high from the floor you had to raise a knee to slide up on it, and grab on to whatever you could. And the horsehair mattress, so hard and ungiving. The cloth over Momma's eyes she hadn't removed and beside Momma in the rumpled bedclothes her Bible. Face down. Pages bent. That Bible her mother-in-law Grandma Nissenbaum had given her for a wedding present, seeing she hadn't one of her own. It was smaller than the heavy black family Bible and it was made of limp ivory-leather covers and had onionskin pages the girls were allowed to examine but not to turn without Momma's supervision; the Bible that would disappear with Gretel Nissenbaum, forever.

The girls begged, whimpered. "Momma? Momma, are you sick?"

At first there was no answer. Just Momma's breath coming quick and hard and uneven. And her olive-pale skin oily with heat like fever. Her legs were tangled in the afghan, her hair was strewn across the pillow. They saw the glint of Momma's gold cross on a thin gold chain around her neck, almost lost in her hair. (Not only a cross but a locket, too: when Momma opened it there was, inside, a tiny strand of silver hair once belonging to a woman the sisters had never known, Momma's own grandmother she'd loved so when she was a little girl.) And there were Momma's breasts, almost exposed! — heavy, lush, beautiful almost spilling out of a white eyelet slip, rounded like sacs holding warm liquid, and the nipples dark and big as eyes. You weren't supposed to stare at any part of a person's body but how could you help it? — especially Connie who was fascinated by such, guessing how one day she'd inhabit a body like Momma's. Years ago she'd peeked at her mother's big milk-swollen breasts when Nelia was still nursing, jealous, awed. Nelia was now five years old and could not herself recall nursing at all; would come one day to believe, stubborn and disdainful, that she had never nursed, had only been bottle-fed.

At last Momma snatched the cloth off her face. "You! Damn you! What do you want?" She stared at the girls as if, clutching hands and gaping at her, they were strangers. Her right eye was bruised and swollen and there were raw red marks on her forehead and first Nelia then Connie began to cry and Momma said, "Constance, why aren't you in school? Why can't you let me alone? God help me — always 'Momma' — 'Momma' — 'Momma.'" Connie whimpered, "Momma, did you hurt yourself?" and Nelia moaned, sucking a corner of the afghan like a deranged baby and Momma ignored the question, as Momma often ignored questions she thought nosy, none of your business; her hand lifted as if she meant to slap them but then fell wearily, as if this had happened many times before, this exchange, this emotion, and it was her fate that it would happen many times again. A close sweet-stale blood-odor lifted from Momma's lower body, out of the folds of the soiled afghan, that odor neither of the little girls could have identified except in retrospect, in adolescence at last detecting it in themselves: shamed, discomforted, the secret of their bodies at what was called, invariably in embarrassed undertones, *that certain time of the month.*

So: Gretel Nissenbaum, at the time she disappeared from her husband's house, was having her period.

Did that mean something, or nothing?

Nothing, Cornelia would say sharply.

Yes, Constance would insist, it meant our mother was *not* pregnant. She wasn't running away with any lover because of *that.*

That morning, what confusion in the Nissenbaum household! However the sisters would later speak of the encounter in the big bedroom, what their mother had said to them, how she'd looked and behaved, it had not been precisely that way, of course. Because how can you speak of confusion, where are the words for it? How to express in adult language the wild fibrillation of children's minds, two child-minds beating against each other like moths, how to know what had truly happened and what was only imagined! Connie would swear that their mother's eye looked like a nasty dark-rotted egg, so swollen, but she could not say which eye it was, right or left; Nelia, shrinking from looking at her mother's bruised face, wanting only to burrow against her, to hide and be comforted, would come in time to doubt that she'd seen a *hurt eye* at all; or whether she'd been led to believe she saw it because Connie, who was so bossy, claimed she had.

Connie would remember their mother's words, Momma's rising desperate voice, "Don't touch me — I'm afraid! I might be going somewhere but I'm not ready — oh God, I'm so afraid!" — and on and on, saying she was going away, she was afraid, and Connie trying to ask where? where was she going? and Momma beating at the bedclothes with her fists. Nelia would remember being hurt at the way Momma yanked the spittle-soaked corner of the afghan out of her mouth, so roughly! Not Momma but *bad-Momma, witch-Momma* who scared her.

But then Momma relented, exasperated. "Oh come on, you damn little babies! Of course 'Momma' loves you."

Eager then as starving kittens the sisters scrambled up onto the high, hard bed, whimpering, snuggling into Momma's arms, her damp snarled hair, those breasts. Connie and Nelia burrowing, crying themselves to sleep like nursing babies, Momma drew the afghan over the three of them as if to shield them. That morning of April 11, 1923.

And next morning, early, before dawn. The sisters would be awakened by their father's shouts, "Gretel? Gretel!"

2

. . . *never spoke of her after the first few weeks. After the first shock. We learned to pray for her and to forgive her and to forget her. We didn't miss her.* So Mother said, in her calm judicious voice. A voice that held no blame.

But Aunt Connie would take me aside. The older, wiser sister. *It's true we never spoke of Momma when any grownups were near, that was forbidden. But, God! we missed her every hour of every day all the time we lived on that farm.*

I was Cornelia's daughter but it was Aunt Connie I trusted.

No one in the Chautauqua Valley knew where John Nissenbaum's young wife Gretel had fled, but all knew, or had an opinion of, why she'd gone.

Faithless, she was. A *faithless woman.* Had she not *run away with a man: abandoned her children.* She was twenty-seven years old and too young for John Nissenbaum and she wasn't a Ransomville girl, her people lived sixty miles away in Chautauqua Falls. Here was a wife who'd committed *adultery,* was an *adulteress.* (Some might say a *tramp,* a *whore,* a *slut.*) Reverend Dieckman, the Lutheran minister, would preach amazing sermons in her wake. For miles through the valley and for years well into the 1940s there would be scandalized talk of Gretel Nissenbaum: a woman who left her faithful Christian husband and her two little girls with no warning! no provocation! disappearing in the middle of a night taking with her only a single suitcase and, as every woman who ever spoke of the episode liked to say, licking her lips, *the clothes on her back.*

(Aunt Connie said she'd grown up imagining she had actually seen her mother, as in a dream, walking stealthily up the long drive to the road, a bundle of clothes, like laundry, slung across her back. Children are so damned impressionable, Aunt Connie would say, laughing wryly.)

For a long time after their mother disappeared, and no word came from her, or of her, so far as the sisters knew, Connie couldn't seem to help herself teasing Nelia saying "Mommy's coming home!" — for a birthday of Nelia's, or Christmas, or Easter. How many times Connie thrilled with wickedness deceiving her baby sister and silly-baby that she was, Nelia believed.

And how Connie would laugh, laugh at her.

Well, it *was* funny. Wasn't it?

Another trick of Connie's: poking Nelia awake in the night when the wind was rattling the windows, moaning in the chimney like a trapped animal. Saying excitedly, *Momma is outside the window, listen! Momma is a ghost trying to get YOU!*

Sometimes Nelia screamed so, Connie had to straddle her chest and press a pillow over her face to muffle her. If they'd wakened Pappa with such nonsense there'd sure have been hell to pay.

Once, I might have been twelve, I asked if my grandfather had spanked or beaten them.

Aunt Connie, sitting in our living room on the high-backed mauve-brocade chair that was always hers when she came to visit, ignored me. Nor did Mother seem to hear. Aunt Connie lit one of her Chesterfields with a fussy flourish of her pink-frosted nails and took a deep satisfied puff and said, as if it were a thought only now slipping into her head, and like all such thoughts deserving of utterance, "I was noticing the other day, on TV, how brattish and idiotic children are, and we're supposed to think they're cute. Pappa wasn't the kind to tolerate children carrying on for a single minute." She paused, again inhaling deeply. "None of the men were, back there."

Mother nodded slowly, frowning. These conversations with my aunt seemed always to give her pain, an actual ache behind the eyes, yet she could no more resist them than Aunt Connie. She said, wiping at her eyes, "Pappa was a man of pride. After she left us as much as before."

"Hmmm!" Aunt Connie made her high humming nasal sound that meant she had something crucial to add, but did not want to appear pushy. "Well — maybe more, Nelia. More pride. After." She spoke insinuatingly, with a smile and a glance toward me.

Like an actress who has strayed from her lines, Mother quickly amended, "Yes, of course. Because a weaker man would have succumbed to — shame and despair —"

Aunt Connie nodded briskly. "— might have cursed God —"

"— turned to drink —"

"— so many of 'em *did*, back there —"

"— but not Pappa. He had the gift of faith."

Aunt Connie nodded sagely. Yet still with that strange almost-teasing smile.

"Oh indeed, Pappa did. That was his gift to us, Nelia, wasn't it? — his faith."

Mother was smiling her tight-lipped smile, her gaze lowered. I knew that, when Aunt Connie left, she would go upstairs to lie down, she would take two aspirins and draw the blinds, and put a damp cold cloth over her eyes and lie down and try to sleep. In her softening middle-aged face, the hue of putty, a young girl's face shone rapt with fear. "Oh yes! His faith."

Aunt Connie laughed heartily. Laugh, laugh. Dimples nicking her cheeks and a wink in my direction.

Years later, numbly sorting through Mother's belongings after her death, I would discover, in a lavender-scented envelope in a bureau drawer, a single strand of dry, ash-colored hair. On the envelope, in faded purple ink *Beloved Father John Allard Nissenbaum* 1872-1957.

3

By his own account, John Nissenbaum, the wronged husband, had not had the slightest suspicion that his strong-willed young wife had been discontent, restless. Certainly not that she'd had a secret lover! So many local women would have dearly wished to change places with her, he'd been given to know when he was courting her, his male vanity, and his Nissenbaum vanity, and what you might call common sense suggested otherwise.

For the Nissenbaums were a well-regarded family in the Chautauqua Valley. Among the lot of them they must have owned thousands of acres of prime farmland.

In the weeks, months, and eventually years that followed the scandalous departure, John Nissenbaum, who was by nature, like most of the male Nissenbaums, reticent to the point of arrogance, and fiercely private, came to make his story — *his side of it* — known. As the sisters themselves gathered (for their father never spoke of their mother to them after the first several days following the shock), this was not a single coherent history but one that had to be pieced together like a giant quilt made of a myriad of fabric-scraps.

He did allow that Gretel had been missing her family, an older sister with whom she'd been especially close, and cousins and girl-friends she'd gone to high school with in Chautauqua Falls; he understood that the two-hundred-acre farm was a lonely place for her, their next-door neighbors miles away, and the village of Ransomville seven miles. (Trips beyond Ransomville were rare.) He knew, or supposed he knew, that his wife had harbored what his

mother and sisters called *wild imaginings,* even after nine years of
marriage, farm life, and children: she had asked several times to be
allowed to play the organ at church, but had been refused; she
reminisced often wistfully and perhaps reproachfully of long-ago
visits to Port Oriskany, Buffalo, and Chicago, before she'd gotten
married at the age of eighteen to a man fourteen years her senior
. . . in Chicago she'd seen stage plays and musicals, the sensational
dancers Irene and Vernon Castle in Irving Berlin's *Watch Your Step.*
It wasn't just Gretel wanting to take over the organ at Sunday
services (and replacing the elderly male organist whose playing,
she said, sounded like a cat in heat), it was her general attitude
toward Reverend Dieckman and his wife. She resented having to
invite them to an elaborate Sunday dinner every few weeks, as the
Nissenbaums insisted; she allowed her eyes to roam the congregation during Dieckman's sermons, and stifled yawns behind her
gloved hand; she woke in the middle of the night, she said, wanting
to argue about damnation, hell, the very concept of grace. To the
minister's astonished face she declared herself "not able to *fully*
accept the teachings of the Lutheran Church."

If there were other more intimate issues between Gretel and
John Nissenbaum, or another factor in Gretel's emotional life, of
course no one spoke of it at the time.

Though it was hinted — possibly more than hinted? — that John
Nissenbaum was disappointed with only daughters. Naturally he
wanted sons, to help him with the ceaseless work of the farm; sons
to whom he could leave the considerable property, just as his married brothers had sons.

What was generally known was: John woke in the pitch-dark an
hour before dawn of that April day, to discover that Gretel was
gone from their bed. Gone from the house? He searched for her,
called her name, with growing alarm, disbelief. "Gretel? Gret-el!"
He looked in all the upstairs rooms of the house including the
bedroom where his sleep-dazed, frightened daughters were hud-
dled together in their bed; he looked in all the downstairs rooms,
even the damp, dirt-floor cellar into which he descended with a
lantern. "Gretel? Where are you?" Dawn came dull, porous and
damp, and with a coat yanked on in haste over his night clothes,
and his bare feet jammed into rubber boots, he began a frantic yet
methodical search of the farm's outbuildings — the privy, the cow

barn and the adjoining stable, the hay barn and the corncrib where rats rustled at his approach. In none of these save perhaps the privy was it likely that Gretel might be found, still John continued his search with growing panic, not knowing what else to do. From the house his now terrified daughters observed him moving from building to building, a tall, rigid, jerkily moving figure with hands cupped to his mouth shouting, "Gretel! Gret-el! Do you hear me! Where are you! Gret-el!" The man's deep, raw voice pulsing like a metronome, ringing clear, profound, and, to his daughters' ears, as terrible as if the very sky had cracked open and God himself was shouting.

(What did such little girls, eight and five, know of God — in fact, as Aunt Connie would afterward recount, quite a bit. There was Reverend Dieckman's baritone impersonation of the God of the Old Testament, the expulsion from the Garden, the devastating retort to Job, the spectacular burning bush where fire itself cried *HERE I AM!* — such had already been imprinted irrevocably upon their imaginations.)

Only later that morning — but this was a confused, anguished account — did John discover that Gretel's suitcase was missing from the closet. And there were garments conspicuously missing from the clothes rack. And Gretel's bureau drawers had been hastily ransacked — underwear, stockings were gone. And her favorite pieces of jewelry, of which she was childishly vain, were gone from her cedarwood box; gone, too, her heirloom, faded-cameo hairbrush, comb and mirror set. And her Bible.

What a joke, how people would chuckle over it — Gretel Nissenbaum taking her Bible with her!

Wherever in hell the woman went.

And was there no farewell note, after nine years of marriage? — John Nissenbaum claimed he'd looked everywhere, and found nothing. Not a word of explanation, not a word of regret even to her little girls. *For that alone we expelled her from our hearts.*

During this confused time while their father was searching and calling their mother's name, the sisters hugged each other in a state of numbness beyond shock, terror. Their father seemed at times to be rushing toward them with the eye-bulging blindness of a runaway horse — they hurried out of his path. He did not see them except to order them out of his way, not to trouble him now. From the rear entry door they watched as he hitched his team of horses to his buggy and set out shuddering for Ransomville along the winter-rutted Post Road, leaving the girls behind, erasing them from his mind. As he would tell afterward, in rueful self-disgust, with the air of an enlightened sinner, he'd actually believed he would overtake Gretel on the road — convinced she'd be there, hiking on the grassy shoulder, carrying her suitcase. Gretel was a wiry-nervous woman, stronger than she appeared, with no fear of physical exertion. A woman capable of anything!

John Nissenbaum had the idea that Gretel had set out for Ransomville, seven miles away, there to catch the mid-morning train to Chautauqua Falls, another sixty miles south. It was his confused belief that they must have had a disagreement, else Gretel would not have left; he did not recall any disagreement in fact, but Gretel was after all an *emotional woman,* a *highly strung woman;* she'd insisted upon visiting the Hausers, her family, despite his wishes, was that it? — she was lonely for them, or lonely for something. She was angry they hadn't visited Chautauqua Falls for Easter, hadn't seen her family since Christmas. Was that it? *We were never enough for her. Why were we never enough for her?*

But in Ransomville, in the cinderblock Chautauqua & Buffalo depot, there was no sign of Gretel, nor had the lone clerk seen her.

"This woman would be about my height," John Nissenbaum said, in his formal, slightly haughty way. "She'd be carrying a suitcase, her feet would maybe be muddy. Her boots."

The clerk shook his head slowly. "No sir, nobody looking like that."

"A woman by herself. A —" a hesitation, a look of pain, "— good-looking woman, young. A kind of a, a way about her — a way of —" another pause, "— making herself known."

"Sorry," the clerk said. "The 8:20 just came through, and no woman bought a ticket."

It happened then that John Nissenbaum was observed, stark-eyed, stiff-springy black hair in tufts like quills, for the better part of that morning, April 12, 1923, wandering up one side of Ransomville's single main street, and down the other. Hatless, in farm overalls and boots but wearing a suit coat — somber, gunmetal-gray, of "good" wool — buttoned crooked across his narrow muscular torso. Disheveled and ravaged with the grief of a betrayed husband too raw at this time for manly pride to intervene, pathetic some said as a kicked dog, yet eager too, eager as a puppy he made inquiries at Meldron's Dry Goods, at Elkin & Sons Grocers, at the First Niagara Trust, at the law office of Rowe & Nissenbaum (this Nissenbaum, a young cousin of John's), even in the Five & Dime where the salesgirls would giggle in his wake. He wandered at last into the Ransomville Hotel, into the gloomy public room where the proprietor's wife was sweeping sawdust-strewn floorboards. "Sorry, sir, we don't open till noon," the woman said, thinking he was a drunk, dazed and swaying-like on his feet, then she looked more closely at him: not knowing his first name (for John Nissenbaum was not one to patronize local taverns) but recognizing his features. For it was said the male Nissenbaums were either born looking alike, or came in time to look alike. "Mr. Nissenbaum? Is something wrong?" In a beat of stymied silence Nissenbaum blinked at her, trying to smile, groping for a hat to remove but finding none, murmuring, "No ma'am, I'm sure not. It's a misunderstanding, I believe. I'm supposed to meet Mrs. Nissenbaum somewhere here. My wife."

Shortly after Gretel Nissenbaum's disappearance there emerged, from numerous sources, from all points of the compass, certain tales of the woman. How rude she'd been, more than once, to the Dieckmans! — to many in the Lutheran congregation! A *bad wife. Unnatural mother.* It was said she'd left her husband and children in the past, running back to her family in Chautauqua Falls, or was in Port Oriskany; and poor John Nissenbaum having to fetch her home again. (This was untrue, though in time, even to Constance and Cornelia, it would come to seem true. As an elderly woman Cornelia would swear she remembered "both times" her mother ran off.) A shameless hussy, a tramp who *had an eye* for men. *Had the hots* for men. *Anything in pants.* Or was she *stuck-up, snobby.* Marrying into the Nissenbaum family, a man almost old enough to be her father, no mystery there! Worse yet she could be sharp-tongued, profane. Heard to utter such words as *damn, goddamn, hell.* Yes and *horseballs, bullshit.* Standing with her hands on her hips fixing her eyes on you, that loud laugh. And showing her teeth that were too big for her mouth. She was *too smart for her own good,* that's for sure. She was *scheming, faithless.* Everybody knew she flirted with her husband's hired hands, she did a hell of a lot more than flirt with them, ask around. Sure she had a *boyfriend,* a *lover.* Sure she was an *adulteress*. Hadn't she run off with a man? She'd run off and where was she to go, where was a woman to go, except *run off with a man?* Whoever he was.

In fact, he'd been sighted: a tower operator for the Chautauqua & Buffalo railroad, big red-headed guy living in Shaheen, twelve miles away. Or was he a carpet sweeper salesman, squirrelly little guy with a mustache and a smooth way of talking, who passed through the valley every few months but, after April 12, 1923, was never seen there again.

Another, more attractive rumor was that Gretel Nissenbaum's lover was a thirty-year-old Navy officer stationed at Port Oriskany. He'd been transferred to a base in North Carolina, or was it Pensacola, Florida, and Gretel had no choice but run away with him, she loved him so. *And three months pregnant with his child.*

There could have been no romance in the terrible possibility that Gretel Nissenbaum had fled on foot, alone, not to her family but simply to escape from her life; in what exigency of need, what despondency of spirit, no name might be given it by any who have not experienced it.

But, in any case, where had she *gone?*

Where? Disappeared. Over the edge of the world. To Chicago, maybe. Or that army base in North Carolina, or Florida.
We forgave, we forgot. We didn't miss her.

The things Gretel Nissenbaum left behind in the haste of her departure.

Several dresses, hats. A shabby cloth coat. Rubberized "galoshes" and boots. Undergarments, mended stockings. Knitted gloves. In the parlor of John Nissenbaum's house, in cut-glass vases, bright yellow daffodils she'd made from crepe paper; hand-painted fans, tea cups; books she'd brought with her from home — *A Golden Treasury of Verse,* Mark Twain's *Joan of Arc,* Fitzgerald's *This Side of Paradise,* missing its jacket cover. Tattered programs for musical shows, stacks of popular piano music from the days Gretel had played in her childhood home. (There was no piano in Nissenbaum's house, Nissenbaum had no interest in music.)

These meager items, and some others, Nissenbaum unceremoniously dumped into cardboard boxes fifteen days after Gretel disappeared, taking them to the Lutheran church, for the "needy fund"; without inquiring if the Hausers might have wanted anything, or whether his daughters might have wished to be given some mementos of their mother.

Spite? Not John Nissenbaum. He was a proud man even in his public humiliation. It was the Lord's work he was thinking of. Not mere *human vanity*, at all.

That spring and summer Reverend Dieckman gave a series of grim, threatening, passionate sermons from the pulpit of the First Lutheran Church of Ransomville. It was obvious why, what the subject of the sermons was. The congregation was thrilled.

Reverend Dieckman, whom Connie and Nelia feared, as much for his fierce smiles as his stern, glowering expression, was a short, bulky man with a dull-gleaming dome of a head, eyes like ice water. Years later when they saw a photograph of him, inches shorter than his wife, they laughed in nervous astonishment — was that the man who'd intimidated them so? Before whom even John Nissenbaum stood grave and downgazing.

Yet: that ringing, vibrating voice of the God of Moses, the God of the Old Testament, you could not shut out of consciousness even hours, days later. Years later. Pressing your hands against your ears and shutting your eyes tight, tight.

"'Unto the WOMAN He said, I will GREATLY MULTIPLY thy sorrow and thy conception; IN SORROW shalt thou bring forth children: and thy desire shall be to THY HUSBAND, and he shall RULE OVER THEE. And unto Adam He said, Because thou hast harkened unto the voice of THY WIFE, and has eaten of THE TREE, of which I commanded thee, saying, THOU SHALT NOT EAT OF IT: cursed is the ground for thy sake; in sorrow shalt thou eat of it all the days of thy life: THORNS ALSO AND THISTLES shall it bring forth to thee; and thou shalt eat the herb of the field; in the SWEAT OF THY FACE shalt thou eat bread, till thou return to the ground; for out of it thou wast taken: for DUST THOU ART, and UNTO DUST SHALT THOU RETURN.'" Reverend Dieckman paused to catch breath like a man running uphill. Greasy patches gleamed on his solid face like coins. Slowly his ice-eyes searched the rows of worshipers until as if by chance they came to rest on the upturned yet cowering faces of John Nissenbaum's daughters, who sat in the family pew, directly in front of the pulpit in the fifth row, between their rigid-backed father in his clothes somber as mourning and their Grandmother Nissenbaum also in clothes somber as mourning though badly round-shouldered, with a perceptible hump, this cheerless dutiful grandmother who had come to live with them now that their mother was gone.

(Their other grandparents, the Hausers, who lived in Chautauqua Falls and whom they'd loved, the sisters would never see again. It was forbidden even to speak of these people, *Gretel's people*. The Hausers were to blame somehow for Gretel's desertion. Though they claimed, would always claim, they knew nothing of what she'd done and in fact feared something had happened to her. But the Hausers were a forbidden subject. Only after Constance and Cornelia were grown, no longer living in their father's house, did they see their Hauser cousins; but still, as Cornelia confessed, she felt guilty about it. Father would have been so hurt and furious if he'd known. *Consorting with the enemy* he would deem it. *Betrayal.*)

In Sunday school, Mrs. Dieckman took special pains with little Constance and little Cornelia. They were regarded with misty-eyed pity, like child-lepers. Fattish little Constance prone to fits of giggling, and hollow-eyed little Cornelia prone to sniffles, melancholy. Both girls had chafed, reddened faces and hands because their Grandmother Nissenbaum scrubbed them so, with strong gray soap, never less than twice a day. Cornelia's dun-colored hair was strangely thin. When the other children trooped out of the Sunday school room, Mrs. Dieckman kept the sisters behind, to pray with them. She was very concerned about them, she said. She and Reverent Dieckman prayed for them constantly. Had their mother contacted them, since leaving? Had there been any . . . hint of what their mother was planning to do? Any strangers visiting the farm? Any . . . unusual incidents? The sisters stared blankly at Mrs. Dieckman. She frowned at their ignorance, or its semblance. Dabbed at her watery eyes and sighed as if the world's weight had settled on her shoulders. She said half-chiding, "You should know, children, it's for a reason that your mother left you. It's God's will. God's plan. He is testing you, children. You are special in His eyes. Many of us have been special in His eyes and have emerged stronger for it, and not weaker." There was a breathy pause. The sisters were invited to contemplate how Mrs. Dieckman with her soft-wattled face, her stout-corseted body and fattish legs encased in opaque support hose, was a stronger and not a weaker person, by God's special plan. "You will learn to be stronger than girls with mothers, Constance and Cornelia —" (these words *girls with mothers* enunciated oddly, contemptuously). "You are already learning: feel God's strength coursing through you!" Mrs. Dieckman seized the girls' hands, squeezing so quick and hard that Connie burst into frightened giggles and Nelia shrieked as if she'd been burnt, and almost wet her panties.

Nelia acquired pride, then. Instead of being ashamed, publicly humiliated (at the one-room country schoolhouse, for instance: where certain of the other children were ruthless), she could be proud, like her father. *God had a special feeling for me. God cared about me. Jesus Christ, His only son, was cruelly tested, too. And exalted. You can bear any hurt and degradation. Thistles and thorns. The flaming sword, the cherubims guarding the garden.*

Mere *girls with mothers,* how could they know?

4

Of course, Connie and Nelia had heard their parents quarreling. In the weeks, months before their mother disappeared. In fact, all their lives. Had they been queried, had they had the language, they might have said *This is what is done, a man, a woman — isn't it?*

Connie, who was three years older than Nelia, knew much that Nelia would not ever know. Not words exactly, these quarrels, and of a tone different from their father shouting out instructions to his farm hands. Not words but an eruption of voices. Ringing through the floorboards if the quarrel came from downstairs. Reverberating in the windowpanes where wind thinly whistled. In bed, Connie would hug Nelia tight, pretending Nelia was Momma. Or Connie was herself Momma. If you shut your eyes tight enough. If you shut your ears. Always after the voices there came silence. If you wait. Once, crouched at the foot of the stairs it was Connie? — or Nelia? — gazing upward astonished as Momma descended the stairs swaying like a drunk woman, her left hand groping against the railing, face dead-white and a bright crimson rosebud in the corner of her mouth glistening as she wiped, wiped furiously at it. And quick-walking in that way of his that made the house vibrate, heavy-heeled behind her, descending from the top of the stairs a man whose face she could not see. Fiery, and blinding. God in the burning bush. God in thunder. *Bitch! Get back up here! If I have to come get you, if you won't be a woman, a wife!*

It was a fact the sisters learned, young: if you wait long enough, run away and hide your eyes, shut your ears, there comes a silence vast and rolling and empty as the sky.

There was the mystery of the letters my mother and Aunt Connie would speak of, though never exactly discuss in my presence, into the last year of my mother's life.

Which of them first noticed, they couldn't agree. Or when it began, exactly — no earlier than the fall, 1923. It would happen that Pappa went to fetch the mail, which he rarely did, and then only on Saturdays; and, returning, along the quarter-mile lane, he would be observed (by accident? the girls weren't spying) with an opened letter in his hand, reading; or was it a postcard; walking with uncharacteristic slowness, this man whose step was invariably brisk and impatient. Connie recalled he'd sometimes slip into the stable to continue reading, Pappa had a liking for the stable which was for him a private place where he'd chew tobacco, spit into the hay, run his callused hands along a horse's flanks, think his own thoughts. Other times, carrying whatever it was, letter, postcard, the rarity of an item of personal mail, he'd return to the kitchen and his place at the table. There the girls would find him (by accident, they *were not* spying) drinking coffee laced with top-milk and sugar, rolling one of his clumsy cigarettes. And Connie would be the one to inquire, "Was there any mail, Pappa?" keeping her voice low, unexcited. And Pappa would shrug and say, "Nothing." On the table where he'd dropped them indifferently might be a few bills, advertising flyers, the *Chautauqua Valley Weekly Gazette*. Nelia never inquired about the mail at such times because she would not have trusted her voice. But, young as ten, Connie could be pushy, reckless. "Isn't there a letter, Pappa? What *is* that, Pappa, in your pocket?"

And Pappa would say calmly, staring her full in the face, "When your father says *nothing*, girl, he means *nothing*."

Sometimes his hands shook, fussing with the pouch of Bugler and the stained cigarette-roller.

Since the shame of losing his wife, and everybody knowing the circumstances, John Nissenbaum had aged shockingly. His face was creased, his skin reddened and cracked, finely stippled with what would be diagnosed (when finally he went to a doctor) as skin cancer. His eyes, pouched in wrinkled lids like a turtle's, were often vague, restless. Even in church, in a row close to Reverend Dieckman's pulpit, he had a look of wandering off. In what he called his earlier life he'd been a rough, physical man, intelligent but quick-tempered; now he tired easily, could not keep up with his hired men whom he more and more mistrusted. His beard, once so trim and shapely, grew ragged and uneven and was entirely gray-grizzled, like cobwebs. And his breath — it smelled of tobacco juice, wet, rank, sickish, rotted.

Once, seeing the edge of the letter in Pappa's pocket, Connie bit her lip and said, "It's from *her,* isn't it!"

Pappa said, still calmly, "I said it's *nothing,* girl. From *nobody.*"

Never in their father's presence did either of the sisters allude to their missing mother except as *her, she.*

Later when they searched for the letter, even for its envelope, of course they found nothing. Pappa had burned it in the stove probably. Or torn it into shreds, tossed into the garbage. Still, the sisters risked their father's wrath by daring to look in his bedroom (the stale-smelling room he'd moved to, downstairs at the rear of the house) when he was out; even, desperate, knowing it was hopeless, poking through fresh-dumped garbage. (Like all farm families of their day, the Nissenbaums dumped raw garbage down a hillside, in the area of the outhouse.) Once Connie scrambled across fly-buzzing mounds of garbage holding her nose, stooping to snatch up — what? A card advertising a fertilizer sale, that had looked like a picture postcard.

"Are you crazy?" Nelia cried. "I hate you!"

Connie turned to scream at her, eyes brimming tears. "Go to hell, horse's ass, I hate *you!*"

Both wanted to believe, or did in fact believe, that their mother was not writing to their father but to them. But they would never know. For years, as the letters came at long intervals, arriving only when their father fetched the mail, they would not know.

This might have been a further element of mystery: why the letters, arriving so infrequently, arrived only when their father got the mail. Why, when Connie, or Nelia, or Loraine (John's younger sister, who'd come to live with them) got the mail, there would never be one of the mysterious letters. *Only when Pappa got the mail.*

After my mother's death in 1981, when I spoke more openly to my Aunt Connie, I asked why they hadn't been suspicious, just a little. Aunt Connie lifted her penciled eyebrows, blinked at me as if I'd uttered something obscene — "Suspicious? Why?" Not once did the girls (who were in fact intelligent girls, Nelia a straight-A student in the high school in town) calculate the odds: how the presumed letter from their mother could possibly arrive only on those days (Saturdays) when their father got the mail; one day out of six mail-days, yet never any day except that particular day (Saturday). But as Aunt Connie said, shrugging, it just seemed that that was how it was — they would never have conceived of even the possibility of any situation in which the odds wouldn't have been against them, and in favor of Pappa.

5

The farmhouse was already old when I was first brought to visit it: summers, in the 1950s. Part red brick so weathered as to seem without color and part rotted wood, with a steep shingled roof, high ceilings, and spooky corners; a perpetual odor of woodsmoke, kerosene, mildew, time. A perpetual draft passed through the house from the rear, which faced north, opening out onto a long incline of acres, miles, dropping to the Chautauqua River ten miles away like an aerial scene in a movie. I remember the old wash room, the machine with a hand-wringer; a door to the cellar in the floor of that room, with a thick metal ring as a handle. Outside the house, too, was another door, horizontal and not vertical. The thought of what lay beyond those doors, the dark, stone-smelling cellar where rats scurried, filled me with a childish terror.

I remember Grandfather Nissenbaum as always old. A lean, sinewy, virtually mute old man. His finely cracked, venous-glazed skin, red-stained as if with earth; narrow rheumy eyes whose pupils seemed, like the pupils of goats, horizontal black slats. How they scared me! Deafness had made Grandfather remote and strangely imperial, like an old almost-forgotten king. The crown of his head was shinily bald and a fringe of coarse hair bleached to the color of ash grew at the sides and back. Where once, my mother lamented, he'd been careful in his dress, especially on Sundays, for church-going, he now wore filth-stained overalls and in all months save summer long gray-flannel underwear straggling at his cuffs like a loose, second skin. His breath stank of tobacco juice and rotted teeth, the knuckles of both his hands were grotesquely swollen. My heart beat quickly and erratically in his presence. "Don't be silly," Mother whispered nervously, pushing me toward the old man, "— your grandfather *loves you*." But I knew he did not. Never did he call me by my name, Bethany, but only "girl" as if he hadn't troubled to learn my name.

When Mother showed me photographs of the man she called Pappa, some of these scissored in half, to excise my missing grandmother, I stared, and could not believe he'd once been so handsome! Like a film actor of some bygone time. "You see," Mother said, incensed, as if the two of us had been quarreling, "— this is who John Nissenbaum really *is*."

I grew up never really knowing Grandfather, and I certainly didn't love him. He was never "Grandpa" to me. Visits to Ransomville were sporadic, sometimes canceled at the last minute. Mother would be excited, hopeful, apprehensive — then, who knows why, the visit would be canceled, she'd be tearful, upset, yet relieved. Now, I can guess that Mother and her family weren't fully welcomed by my grandfather; he was a lonely and embittered old man, but still proud — he'd never forgiven her for leaving home, after high school, just like her sister Connie; going to the teachers' college at Elmira instead of marrying a local man worthy of working and eventually inheriting the Nissenbaum farm. By the time I was born, in 1951, the acreage was being sold off; by the time Grandfather Nissenbaum died, in 1972, in a nursing home in Yewville, the two-hundred acres had been reduced to a humiliating seven acres, now the property of strangers.

In the hilly cemetery behind the First Lutheran Church of Ransomville, New York, there is a still-shiny black granite marker at the edge of rows of Nissenbaum markers, JOHN ALLARD NISSENBAUM 1872-1957. Chiseled into the stone is *How long shall I be with you? How long shall I suffer you?* Such angry words of Jesus

Christ's! I wondered who had chosen them — not Constance or Cornelia, surely. It must have been John Nissenbaum himself.

Already as a girl of eleven, twelve, I was pushy and curious, asking my mother about my missing grandmother. *Look, Mother, for God's sake where did she go? Didn't anybody try to find her?* Mother's replies were vague, evasive. As if rehearsed. That sweet-resolute stoic smile. Cheerful resignation, Christian forgiveness. For thirty-five years she taught high school English in the Rochester public schools, and especially after my father left us, and she became a single, divorced woman, the manner came easily to her of brisk classroom authority, that pretense of the skilled teacher of weighing others' opinions thoughtfully before reiterating one's own.

My father, an education administrator, left us when I was fourteen, to remarry. I was furious, heartbroken. Dazed. *Why? How could he betray us?* But Mother maintained her Christian fortitude, her air of subtly wounded pride. *This is what people will do, Bethany. Turn against you, turn faithless. You might as well learn, young.*

Yet I pushed. Up to the very end of her life, when Mother was so ill. You'd judge me harsh, heartless — people did. But for God's sake I wanted to know: what happened to my Grandmother Nissenbaum, why did nobody seem to care she'd gone away? Were the letters my mother and Connie swore their father received authentic, or had he been playing a trick of some kind? And if it had been a trick, what was its purpose? *Just tell me the truth for once, Mother. The truth about anything.*

I'm forty-four years old, I still want to know.

But Mother, the intrepid schoolteacher, the good-Christian, was impenetrable. Inscrutable as her Pappa. Capable of summing up her entire childhood *back there* (this was how she and Aunt Connie spoke of Ransomville, their pasts: *back there*) by claiming that such *hurts* are God's will, God's plan for each of us. A test of our faith. A test of our inner strength. I said, disgusted, what if you don't believe in God, what are you left with then? — and Mother said matter-of-factly, "You're left with yourself, of course, your inner strength. Isn't that enough?"

That final time we spoke of this, I lost patience, I must have pushed Mother too far. In a sharp, stinging voice, a voice I'd never heard from her before, she said, "Bethany, what do you want me to tell you? About my mother? — my father? Do you imagine I ever knew them? Either of them? My mother left Connie and me when we were little girls, left us with *him,* wasn't that her choice? Her selfishness? Why should anyone have gone looking for her? She was trash, she was *faithless.* We learned to forgive, and to forget. Your aunt tells you a different story, I know, but it's a lie — *I* was the one who was hurt, *I* was the youngest. Your heart can be broken only once — you'll learn! Our lives were busy, busy like the lives of us grown women today, women who have to work, women who don't have time to moan and groan over their hurt feelings, you can't know how Connie and I worked on that farm, in that house, like grown women when we were girls. Father tried to stop both of us going to school beyond eighth grade — imagine! We had to walk two miles to get a ride with a neighbor, to get to the high school in Ransomville; there weren't school buses in those days. Everything you've had you've taken for granted and wanted more, but we weren't like that. We hadn't money for the right school clothes, all our textbooks were used, but we went to high school. I was the only 'farm girl' — that's exactly what I was known as, even by my teachers — in my class to take math, biology, physics, Latin. I was memorizing Latin declensions milking cows at five in the morning, winter mornings. I was laughed at, Nelia Nissenbaum was *laughable.* But I accepted it. All that mattered was that I win a scholarship to a teachers' college so I could escape the country, and I did win a scholarship and I never returned to Ransomville to live. Yes, I loved Pappa — I still love him. I loved the farm, too. You can't not love any place that's taken so much from you. But I had my own life, I had my teaching jobs, I had my faith, my belief in God, I had my destiny. I even got married — that was extra, unexpected. I've worked for everything I ever got and I never had time to look back, to feel sorry for myself. Why then should I think about *her?* — why do you torment me about *her?* A woman who abandoned me when I was five years old! In 1923! I made my peace with the past, just like Connie in her different way. We're happy women, we've been spared a lifetime of bitterness. *That* was God's gift to us." Mother paused, breathing quickly. There was in her face the elation of one who has said too much, that can never be retracted; I was stunned into silence. She plunged on, now contemptuously, "What are you always wanting me to admit, Bethany? That you know something I

don't know? What is your generation always pushing for, from ours?
Isn't it enough we gave birth to you, indulged you, must we be
sacrificed to you, too? What do you want us to tell you — that life is
cruel and purposeless? that there is no loving God, and never was,
only accident? Is that what you want to hear, from your mother?
That I married your father because he was a weak man, a man I
couldn't feel much for, who wouldn't, when it came time, hurt me?"

And then there was silence. We stared at each other, Mother in
her glisten of fury, daughter Bethany so shocked she could not
speak. Never again would I think of my mother in the old way.

What Mother never knew: In April 1983, two years after her death,
a creek that runs through the old Nissenbaum property flooded its
banks, and several hundred feet of red clayey soil collapsed overnight into the creek bed, as in an earthquake. And in the raw,
exposed earth there was discovered a human skeleton, decades old
but virtually intact. It had been apparently buried, less than a mile
behind the Nissenbaum farmhouse.

There had never been anything so newsworthy — so sensational
— in the history of Chautauqua County.

State forensic investigators determined that the skeleton had
belonged to a woman, apparently killed by numerous blows to the
head (a hammer, or the blunt edge of an ax) that shattered her
skull like a melon. Dumped into the grave with her was what appeared to have been a suitcase, now rotted, its contents — clothes,
shoes, underwear, gloves — scarcely recognizable from the earth
surrounding it. There were a few pieces of jewelry and, still en-
twined around the skeleton's neck, a tarnished-gold cross on a
chain. Most of the woman's clothing had long ago rotted away and
almost unrecognizable too was a book — a leatherbound Bible? —
close beside her. About the partly detached, fragile wrist and ankle
bones were loops of rusted baling wire that had fallen loose, coiled
in the moist red clay like miniature sleeping snakes.

PETER ROBINSON

The Two Ladies of Rose Cottage

FROM *Malice Domestic 6*

IN OUR VILLAGE, they were always known as the "Two Ladies of Rose Cottage": Miss Eunice, with the white hair, and Miss Teresa with the gray. Nobody really knew where they came from, or exactly how old they were, but the consensus held that they had met in India, America, or South Africa, and decided to return to the homeland to live out their days together. And, in 1939, they were generally believed to be in or approaching their nineties.

Imagine our surprise, then, one fine day in September, when the police car pulled up outside Rose Cottage, and when, in a matter of hours, rumors began to spread throughout the village: rumors of human bones dug up in a distant garden; rumors of mutilation and dismemberment; rumors of murder.

Lyndgarth is the name of our village. It is situated in one of the most remote Yorkshire dales, about twenty miles from Eastvale, the nearest large town. The village is no more than a group of limestone houses with slate roofs, clustered around a bumpy, slanted green that always reminded me of a handkerchief flapping in the breeze. We have the usual amenities — grocer's shop, butcher's, newsagent's, post office, school, two churches, three public houses — and proximity to some of the most beautiful countryside in the world.

I was fifteen in 1939, and Miss Eunice and Miss Teresa had been living in the village for twenty years, yet still they remained strangers to us. It is often said that you have to "winter out" at least two years before being accepted into village life, and in the case of a remote place like Lyndgarth, in those days, it was more like ten.

As far as the locals were concerned then, the two ladies had served their apprenticeship and were more than fit to be accepted as fully paid-up members of the community, yet there was about them a certain detached quality that kept them ever at arm's length.

They did all their shopping in the village and were always polite to people they met in the street; they regularly attended church services at St. Oswald's and helped with charity events; and they never set foot in any of the public houses. But still there was that sense of distance, of not quite being — or not *wanting* to be — a part of things.

The summer of 1939 had been unusually beautiful despite the political tensions. Or am I indulging in nostalgia for childhood? Our dale can be one of the most grim and desolate landscapes on the face of the earth, even in August, but I remember the summers of my youth as days of dazzling sunshine and blue skies. In 1939, every day was a new symphony of color — golden buttercups, pink clover, mauve crane's-bill — ever-changing and recombining in fresh palettes. While the tense negotiations went on in Europe, while Ribbentrop and Molotov signed the Nazi-Soviet pact, and while there was talk of conscription and rationing at home, very little changed in Lyndgarth.

Summer in the dale was always a season for odd jobs — peat-cutting, wall-mending, sheep-clipping — and for entertainments, such as the dialect plays, the circus, fairs, and brass bands. Even after war was declared on the third of September, we still found ourselves rather guiltily having fun, scratching our heads, shifting from foot to foot, and wondering when something really warlike was going to happen.

Of course, we had our gas masks in their cardboard boxes, which we had to carry everywhere; streetlighting was banned, and motor cars were not allowed to use their headlights. This latter rule was the cause of numerous accidents in the dale, usually involving wandering sheep on the unfenced roads.

Some evacuees also arrived from the cities. Uncouth urchins for the most part, often verminous and ill-equipped for country life, they seemed like an alien race to us. Most of them didn't seem to have any warm clothing or Wellington boots, as if they had never seen mud in the city. Looking back, I realize they were far from home, separated from their parents, and they must have been scared to death. I am ashamed to admit, though, that at the time I didn't go out of my way to give them a warm welcome.

This is partly because I was always lost in my own world. I was a bookish child, and had recently discovered the stories of Thomas Hardy, who seemed to understand and sympathize with a lonely village lad and his dreams of becoming a writer. I also remember how much he thrilled and scared me with some of the stories. After "The Withered Arm," I wouldn't let anyone touch me for a week, and I didn't dare go to sleep after "Barbara of the House of Grebe" for fear that there was a horribly disfigured statue in the wardrobe, that the door would slowly creak open and . . .

I think I was reading *Far from the Madding Crowd* that hot July day, and, as was my wont, I read as I walked across the village green, not looking where I was going. It was Miss Teresa I bumped into, and I remember thinking that she seemed remarkably resilient for such an old lady.

"Do mind where you're going, young man!" she admonished me, though when she heard my effusive apologies, she softened her tone somewhat. She asked me what I was reading, and when I showed her the book, she closed her eyes for a moment, and a strange expression crossed her wrinkled features.

"Ah, Mr. Hardy," she said after a short silence. "I knew him once, you know, in his youth. I grew up in Dorset."

I could hardly hold back my enthusiasm. Someone who actually *knew* Hardy! I told her that he was my favorite writer of all time, even better than Shakespeare, and that when I grew up I wanted to be a writer, just like him.

Miss Teresa smiled indulgently. "Do calm down," she said, then she paused. "I suppose," she continued, with a glance toward Miss Eunice, "that if you are really interested in Mr. Hardy, perhaps you might like to come to tea someday?"

When I assured her I would be delighted, we made an arrangement that I was to call at Rose Cottage the following Tuesday at four o'clock, after securing my mother's permission, of course.

That Tuesday visit was the first of many. Inside, Rose Cottage belied its name. It seemed dark and gloomy, unlike ours, which was always full of sunlight and bright flowers. The furnishings were antique, even a little shabby. I recollect no family photographs of the kind that embellished most mantelpieces, but there was a huge gilt-framed painting of a young girl working alone in a field hanging on one wall. If the place sometimes smelled a little musty and ne-glected, the aroma of Miss Teresa's fresh-baked scones more often than not made up for it.

"Mr. Hardy was full of contradictions," Miss Teresa told me on one occasion. "He was a dreamer, of course, and never happier than when wandering the countryside, alone with his thoughts. But he was also a fine musician. He played the fiddle on many social occasions, such as dances and weddings, and he was often far more gregarious and cheerful than many of his critics would have imag-ined. He was also a scholar, head forever buried in a book, always studying Latin or Greek. I was no dullard, either, you know, and I like to think I held my own in our conversations, though I had little Latin and less Greek." She chuckled, then turned serious again. "Anyway, one never felt one really *knew* him. One was always look-ing at a mask. Do you understand me, young man?"

I nodded. "I think so, Miss Teresa."

"Yes, well," she said, staring into space as she sometimes did while speaking of Hardy. "At least that was *my* impression. Though he was a good ten years older than me, I like to believe I got glimpses of the man behind the mask. But because the other villagers thought him a bit odd, and because he was difficult to know, he also at-tracted a lot of idle gossip. I remember there was talk about him and that Sparks girl from Puddletown. What was her first name, Eunice?"

"Tryphena."

"That's right." She curled her lip and seemed to spit out the name. "Tryphena Sparks. A singularly dull girl, I always thought. We were about the same age, you know, she and I. Anyway, there was talk of a child. Utter rubbish, of course." She gazed out of the window at the green, where a group of children were playing a makeshift game of cricket. Her eyes seemed to film over. "Many's the time I used to walk through the woodland past the house, and I would see him sitting there at his upstairs window seat, writing or gazing out on the garden. Sometimes he would wave and come down to talk." Suddenly she stopped, then her eyes glittered, and she went on. "He used to go and watch hangings in Dorchester. Did you know that?"

I had to confess that I didn't, my acquaintance with Hardy being recent and restricted only to his published works of fiction, but it never occurred to me to doubt Miss Teresa's word.

"Of course, executions were public back then." Again she paused, and I thought I saw, or rather *sensed* a little shiver run through her. Then she said that was enough for today, that it was time for scones and tea.

I think she enjoyed shocking me like that at the end of her little narratives, as if we needed to be brought back to reality with a jolt. I remember on another occasion she looked me in the eye and said, "Of course, the doctor tossed him aside as dead at birth, you know. If it hadn't been for the nurse, he would never have survived. That must do something to a man, don't you think?"

We talked of many other aspects of Hardy and his work, and, for the most part, Miss Eunice remained silent, nodding from time to time. Occasionally, when Miss Teresa's memory seemed to fail her on some point, such as a name or what novel Hardy might have been writing in a certain year, she would supply the information.

I remember one visit particularly vividly. Miss Teresa stood up rather more quickly than I thought her able to, and left the room for a few moments. I sat politely, sipping my tea, aware of Miss Eunice's silence and the ticking of the grandfather clock out in the hall. When Miss Teresa returned, she was carrying an old book, or rather two books, which she handed to me.

It was a two-volume edition of *Far from the Madding Crowd,* and, though I didn't know it at the time, it was the first edition, from 1874, and was probably worth a small fortune. But what fascinated me even more than Helen Paterson's illustrations was the brief inscription on the flyleaf: *To Tess, With Affection, Tom.*

I knew that Tess was a diminutive of Teresa, because I had an Aunt Teresa in Harrogate, and it never occurred to me to question that the "Tess" in the inscription was the person sitting opposite me, or that the "Tom" was any other than Thomas Hardy himself.

"He called you Tess," I remember saying. "Perhaps he had you in mind when he wrote *Tess of the d'Urbervilles?*"

Miss Teresa's face drained of color so quickly I feared for her life, and it seemed that a palpable chill entered the room. "Don't be absurd, boy," she whispered. "Tess Durbeyfield was hanged for murder."

*

We had been officially at war for about a week, I think, when the police called. There were three men, one in uniform and two in plainclothes. They spent almost two hours in Rose Cottage, then came out alone, got in their car, and drove away. We never saw them again.

The day after the visit, though, I happened to overhear our local constable talking with the vicar in St. Oswald's churchyard. By a great stroke of fortune, several yews stood between us and I was able to remain unseen while I took in every word.

"Murdered, that's what they say," said P.C. Walker. "Bashed his 'ead in with a poker, then chopped 'im up in little pieces and buried 'em in t' garden. Near Dorchester, it were. Village called 'igher Bockhampton. People who lived there were digging an air-raid shelter when they found t' bones. 'Eck of a shock for t' bairns."

Could they possibly mean Miss Teresa? That sweet old lady who made such delightful scones and had known the young Thomas Hardy? Could she really have bashed someone on the head, chopped him up into little pieces, and buried them in the garden? I shivered at the thought, despite the heat.

But nothing more was heard of the murder charge. The police never returned, people found new things to talk about, and after a couple of weeks Miss Eunice and Miss Teresa reappeared in village life much as they had been before. The only difference was that my mother would no longer allow me to visit Rose Cottage. I put up token resistance, but by then my mind was full of Spitfires, secret codes, and aircraft carriers anyway.

Events seemed to move quickly in the days after the police visit, though I cannot be certain of the actual time period involved. Four things, however, conspired to put the murder out of my mind for some time: Miss Teresa died, I think in the November of that same year; Miss Eunice retreated into an even deeper silence than before; the war escalated; and I was called up to military service.

The next time I gave any thought to the two ladies of Rose Cottage was in Egypt, of all places, in September 1942. I was on night watch with the 8th Army, not far from Alamein. Desert nights have an eerie beauty I have never found anywhere else since. After the heat of the day, the cold surprises one, for a start, as does the sense of endless space, but even more surprising is the desertscape of wrecked tanks, jeeps, and lorries in the cold moonlight, metal wrenched and twisted into impossible patterns like some petrified forest or exposed coral reef.

To spoil our sleep and shatter our nerves, Rommel's Afrika Corps had got into the routine of setting up huge amplified speakers and blaring out "Lili Marleen" over and over all night long. It was on a night such as this, while I was trying to stay warm and awake and trying to shut my ears to the music, that I struck up a conversation with a soldier called Sidney Ferris from one of the Dorset regiments.

When Sid told me he had grown up in Piddlehinton, I suddenly thought of the two ladies of Rose Cottage.

"Did you ever hear any stories of a murder around there?" I asked, offering Sid a cigarette. "A place called Higher Bockhampton?"

"Lots of murder stories going around when I was a lad," he said, lighting up, careful to hide the flame with his cupped hand. "Better than the wireless."

"This would be a wife murdering her husband."

He nodded. "Plenty of that and all. And husbands murdering their wives. Makes you wonder whether it's worth getting married, doesn't it? Higher Bockhampton, you say?"

"Yes. Teresa Morgan, I believe the woman's name was."

He frowned. "Name don't ring no bell," he said, "but I do recall a tale about some woman who was supposed to have killed her husband, cut him up in pieces, and buried them in the garden. A couple of young lads found some bones when they was digging an air-raid shelter a couple of years back. Animal bones, if you ask me."

"But did the villagers believe the tale?"

He shrugged. "Don't know about anyone else, but I can't say as I did. So many stories like that going around, they can't all be true, or damn near all of us would be murderers or corpses. Stands to reason, doesn't it?" And he took a long drag on his cigarette, holding it in his cupped hand, like most soldiers, so the enemy wouldn't see the pinpoint of light.

"Did anyone say what became of the woman?" I asked.

"She went away some years later. There was talk of someone else seen running away from the farmhouse, too, the night they said the murder must have taken place."

"Could it have been him? The husband?"

Sid shook his head. "Too slight a figure. Her husband was a big man, apparently. Anyway, that led to more talk of an illicit lover. There's always a lover, isn't there? Have you noticed? You know what kind of minds these country gossips have."

"Did anyone say who the other person might have been?"

"Nobody knew. Just rumors of a vague shape seen running away. These are old wives' tales we're talking about."

"But perhaps there's some tru —"

But at that point I was relieved of my watch, and the next weeks turned out to be so chaotic that I never even saw Sid again. I heard later that he was killed at the battle of Alamein just over a month after our conversation.

I didn't come across the mystery of Rose Cottage again until the early 1950s. At that time, I was living in Eastvale, in a small flat overlooking the cobbled market square. The town was much smaller and quieter than it is today, though little about the square has changed, from the ancient market cross, the Queen's Arms on the corner, the Norman church, and the Tudor-fronted police station.

I had recently published my first novel and was still basking in that exquisite sensation that comes only once in a writer's career: the day he holds the first bound and printed copy of his very first work. Of course, there was no money in writing, so I worked part-time in a bookshop on North Market Street, and on one of my mornings off, a market day, as I remember, I was absorbed in polishing the third chapter of what was to be my second novel when I heard a faint tap at my door. This was enough to startle me, as I rarely had any visitors.

Puzzled and curious, I left my typewriter and went to open the door. There stood a wizened old lady, hunch-shouldered, white-haired, carrying a stick with a brass lion's head handle and a small package wrapped in brown paper, tied with string.

She must have noticed my confused expression, because, with a faint smile, she said, "Don't you recognize me, Mr. Riley? Dear, dear, have I aged that much?"

Then I knew her, knew the voice.

"Miss Eunice!" I cried, throwing my door open. "Please forgive me. I was lost in my own world. Do come in. And you must call me Christopher."

Once we were settled, with a pot of tea mashing beside us — though, alas, none of Miss Teresa's scones — I noticed the dark circles under Miss Eunice's eyes, the yellow around the pupils, the parchmentlike quality of her skin, and I knew she was seriously ill.

"How did you find me?" I asked.

"It didn't take a Sherlock Holmes. Everyone knows where the famous writer lives in a small town like Eastvale."

"Hardly famous," I demurred. "But thank you anyway. I never knew you took the trouble to follow my fortunes."

"Teresa would have wished it. She was very fond of you, you know. Apart from ourselves and the police, you were the only person in Lyndgarth who ever entered Rose Cottage. Did you know that? You might remember that we kept ourselves very much to ourselves."

"Yes, I remember that," I told her.

"I came to give you this."

She handed me the package and I untied it carefully. Inside was the Smith, Elder & Co. first edition of *Far from the Madding Crowd*, complete with Hardy's inscription to "Tess."

"But you shouldn't," I said. "This must be very valuable. It's a fir —"

She waved aside my objections. "Please take it. It is what Teresa would have wished. And I wish it, too. Now listen," she went on. "That isn't the only reason I came. I have something very important to tell you, to do with why the police came to visit all those years ago. The thought of going to my grave without telling someone troubles me deeply."

"But why me? And why now?"

"I told you. Teresa was especially fond of you. And you're a writer," she added mysteriously. "You'll understand. Should you wish to make use of the story, please do so. Neither Teresa nor I have any living relatives to offend. All I ask is that you wait a suitable number of years after my death before publishing any account. And that death is expected to occur at some point over the next few months. Does that answer your second question?"

I nodded. "Yes. I'm sorry."

"You needn't be. As you may well be aware, I have long since exceeded my three score and ten, though I can hardly say the extra years have been a blessing. But that is God's will. Do you agree to my terms?"

"Of course. I take it this is about the alleged murder?"

Miss Eunice raised her eyebrows. "So you've heard the rumors?" she said. "Well, there was a murder all right. Teresa Morgan murdered her husband, Jacob, and buried his body in the garden." She held out her tea cup and I poured. I noticed her hand was shaking slightly. Mine was, too. The shouts of the market vendors came in through my open windows.

"When did she do this?" was all I could manage.

Miss Eunice closed her eyes and pursed her cracked lips. "I don't remember the exact year," she said. "But it really doesn't matter. You could look it up, if you wanted. It was the year the Queen was proclaimed Empress of India."

I happened to know that was in 1877. I have always had a good memory for historical dates. If my calculations were correct, Miss Teresa would have been about twenty-seven at the time. "Will you tell me what happened?" I asked.

"That's why I'm here," Miss Eunice said rather sharply. "Teresa's husband was a brute, a bully, and a drunkard. She wouldn't have married him, had *she* had any choice in the matter. But her parents approved the match. He had his own small farm, you see, and they were only tenants. Teresa was a very intelligent girl, but that counted for nothing in those days. In fact, it was a positive disadvantage. As was her willfulness. Anyway, he used to beat her to within an inch of her life — where the bruises wouldn't show, of course. One day she'd had enough of it, so she killed him."

"What did she do?"

"She hit him with the poker from the fireplace and, after darkness had fallen, she buried him deep in the garden. She was afraid that if the matter went to court the authorities wouldn't believe her, and she would be hanged. She had no evidence, you see. And Jacob was a popular man among the other fellows of the village, as is so often the case with drunken brutes. And Teresa was terrified of being publicly hanged."

"But did no one suspect her?"

Miss Eunice shook her head. "Jacob was constantly talking about leaving his wife and heading for the New World. He used to berate her for not bearing him any children — specifically sons — and threatened that one day she would wake up and he would be gone. Gone to another country to find a woman who could give him the children he wanted. He repeated these threats in the ale-house so often that no one in the entire county of Dorset could fail to know about them."

"So when he disappeared, everyone assumed he had followed through on his threats to leave her?"

"Exactly. Oh, there were rumors that his wife had murdered him, of course. There always are when such mysteries occur."

Yes, I thought, remembering my conversations with Sid Ferris one cold desert night ten years ago: rumors and fancies, the stuff of fiction. And something about a third person seen fleeing from the scene. Well, that could wait.

"Teresa stayed on at the farm for another ten years," Miss Eunice went on. "Then she sold up and went to America. It was a brave move, but Teresa no more lacked for courage than she did for beauty. She was in her late thirties then, and even after a hard life, she could still turn heads. In New York, she landed on her feet and eventually married a financier, Sam Cotter. A good man. She also took a companion."

"You?" I asked.

Miss Eunice nodded. "Yes. Some years later, Sam died of a stroke. We stayed on in New York for a while, but we grew increasingly homesick. We came back finally in 1919, just after the Great War. For obvious reasons, Teresa didn't want to live anywhere near Dorset, so we settled in Yorkshire."

"A remarkable tale," I said.

"But that's not all," Miss Eunice went on, pausing only to sip some tea. "There was a child."

"I thought you said —"

She took one hand off her stick and held it up, palm out. "Christopher, please let me tell the story in my own way. Then it will be yours to do with as you wish. You have no idea how difficult this is for me." She paused and stared down at the brass lion's head for so long I feared she had fallen asleep, or died. Outside in the market square a butcher was loudly trying to sell a leg of lamb. Just as I was about to go over to Miss Eunice, she stirred. "There was a child," she repeated. "When Teresa was fifteen, she gave birth to a child. It was a difficult birth. She was never able to bear any other children."

"What happened to this child?"

"Teresa had a sister called Alice, living in Dorchester. Alice was five years older and already married with two children. Just before the pregnancy started to show, both Teresa and Alice went to stay with relatives in Cornwall for a few months, after it had been falsely announced that Alice was with child again. You would be surprised how often such things happened. When they came back, Alice had a fine baby girl."

"Who was the father?"

"Teresa would never say. The one thing she did make clear was that no one had forced unwanted attentions on her, that the child was the result of a love match, an infatuation. It certainly wasn't Jacob Morgan."

"Did she ever see the child again?"

"Oh, certainly. What could be more natural than visiting one's sister and seeing one's niece grow up? When the girl was a little older, she began to pay visits to the farm, too."

Miss Eunice stopped here and frowned so hard I thought her brow would crack like dry paper. "That was when the problems began," she said quietly.

"What problems?"

Miss Eunice put her stick aside and held out her tea cup. I refilled it. Her hands steady now, she held the cup against her scrawny chest as if its heat were the only thing keeping her alive. "This is the most difficult part," she said in a faint voice. "The part I didn't know whether I could ever tell anyone."

"If you don't wish —"

She waved my objection aside. "It's all right, Christopher. I didn't know how much I could tell you before I came here, but I know now. I've come this far. I can't go back now. Just give me a few moments to collect myself."

Outside, the market was in full swing, and during the ensuing silence I could hear the clamor of voices selling and buying, arguing over prices.

"Did I ever tell you that Teresa was an extremely beautiful young girl?" Miss Eunice asked after a while.

"I believe you mentioned it, yes."

She nodded. "Well, she was. And so was her daughter. When she began coming by herself to the house, she was about twelve or thirteen years of age. Jacob didn't fail to notice her, how well she was 'filling out' as he used to say. One day, Teresa had gone into the village for firewood and the child arrived in her absence. Jacob, just home from the ale-house, was there alone to greet her. Need I say more, Mr. Riley?"

I shook my head. "I don't mean to excuse him in any way, but I'm assuming he didn't know the girl was his step-daughter?"

"That is correct. He never knew. Nor did *she* know Teresa was her mother. Not until much later."

"What happened next?"

"Teresa came in before her husband could have his way with the struggling, half-naked child. Everything else was as I said. She picked up the poker and hit him on the head. Not once, but six times. Then they cleaned up and waited until after dark and buried him deep in the garden. She sent her daughter back to her sister's and carried on as if her husband had simply left her, just as he had threatened to do."

So the daughter was the mysterious third person seen leaving the farm in Sid Ferris's account. "What became of the poor child?" I asked.

Miss Eunice paused again and seemed to struggle for breath. She turned terribly pale. I got up and moved toward her, but she stretched out her hand. "No, no. I'm all right, Christopher. Please sit."

A motor car honked outside and one of the street vendors yelled a curse.

Miss Eunice patted her chest. "That's better. I'm fine now, really I am. Just a minor spasm. But I do feel ashamed. I'm afraid I haven't been entirely truthful with you. It's so difficult. You see, I was, I *am*, that child."

For a moment my mouth just seemed to flap open and shut and I couldn't speak. Finally, I managed to stammer, "You? *You* are Miss Teresa's daughter? But you can't be. That's not possible."

"I didn't mean to shock you," she went on softly, "but, really, you only have yourself to blame. When people see two old ladies together, all they see is two old ladies. When you first began calling on us at Rose Cottage fifteen years ago, Teresa was ninety and I was seventy-six. I doubt a fifteen-year-old boy could tell the difference. Nor could most people. And Teresa was always remarkably robust and well-preserved."

When I had regained my composure, I asked her to continue.

"There is very little left to say. I helped my mother kill Jacob Morgan and bury him. And we didn't cut him up into little pieces. That part is pure fiction invented by scurrilous gossip-mongers. My foster-parents died within a short time of one another, around the turn of the century, and Teresa wired me the money to come and live with her in New York. I had never married, so I had no ties to break. I think that experience with Jacob Morgan, brief and inconclusive as it was, must have given me a lifelong aversion to marital relations. Anyway, it was in New York where Teresa told me she was really my mother. She couldn't tell Sam, of course, so I remained there as her companion, and we always lived more as friends than as mother and daughter." She smiled. "When we came back to England, we chose to live as two spinsters, the kind of relationship nobody really questions in a village because it would be in bad taste to do so."

"How did the police find you after so long?"

"We never hid our identities. Nor did we hide our whereabouts. We bought Rose Cottage through a local solicitor before we returned from America, so it was listed as our address on all the official papers we filled in." She shrugged. "The police soon recognized that Teresa was far too frail to question, let alone put on trial, so they let the matter drop. And to be quite honest, they didn't really have enough evidence, you know. You didn't know it — and Teresa would never have told you — but she already knew she was dying before the police came. Just as I know I am dying now."

"And did she really die without telling you who your father was?"

Miss Eunice nodded. "I wasn't lying about that. But I always had my suspicions." Her eyes sparkled for a moment, the way a fizzy drink does when you pour it. "You know, Teresa was always unreasonably jealous of that Tryphena Sparks, and Mr. Hardy did have an eye for young girls."

Forty years have passed since Miss Eunice's death, and I have lived in many towns and villages in many countries of the world. Though I have often thought of the tale she told me, I have never been moved to commit it to paper until today.

Two weeks ago, I moved back to Lyndgarth, and, as I was unpacking, I came across that first edition of *Far from the Madding Crowd*.

1874: the year Hardy married Emma Gifford. As I puzzled again over the inscription, words suddenly began to form themselves effortlessly in front of my eyes, and all I had to do was copy them down.

Now that I have finished, I suddenly feel very tired. It is a hot day, and the heat haze has muted the greens, grays, and browns of the steep hillsides. Looking out of my window, I can see the tourists lounging on the village green. The young men are stripped to the waist, some bearing tattoos of butterflies and angels across their shoulder blades; the girls sit with them, in shorts and T-shirts, laughing, eating sandwiches, drinking from pop or beer bottles.

One young girl notices me watching and waves cheekily, probably thinking I'm an old pervert, and as I wave back I think of another writer — a far, far greater writer than I could ever be — sitting at his window seat, writing. He looks out of the window and sees the beautiful young girl passing through the woods at the bottom of the garden. He waves. She waves back. And she lingers, picking wild flowers, as he puts aside his novel and walks out into the warm summer air to meet her.

DAVE SHAW

Twelve Days Out of Traction

FROM *South Dakota Review*

I WAS twelve days out of traction in a 7-11 outside Poughkeepsie cradling Slim Jims and a six-pack of RC's, pretending to ponder the price of a three-week-old loaf of Wonder while I was deciding how to slip on the freshly mopped floor so that the unhidden video camera behind the front counter might give me the best possible out-of-court settlement, when in comes this hoss wearing a ski mask and sombrero, waving a .22 and telling everybody freeze or we'll be having our heads blown off. I'd just about settled on a basic ass-first prat, which would've been risky because sometimes they're unbelievable when they replay it slow frame, but I didn't really have my heart in one of those realistic, wrenching, twisting falls that actually does hurt when you land on a shoulder or something, because my left wrist and lower right leg were still casted and my back was still sore from the traction and the memory of the Honda's bumper I had stepped into three and a half months before outside an Acme in Binghamton. Some old bat had decided to give me a love tap with the gas instead of braking and that laid me up a little longer than it should have and gave me black outs for a while and six total broken or fractured bones, not to mention fusing vertebrae numbers 7 and 8. It's a living, or so I thought. Then into the Poughkeepsie 7-11 came the Bandit and his .22, which meant no falls for me that day with all the cops that'd be crawling around the place in a matter of minutes, all of them disturbed about missing the "Mexican Bandito" as everyone was calling him even though he had a Canadian accent, and none of them having time to fill out a report on a guy who might have permanent back pain as a result of a slip on the negligently wet floor by the Wonderbread. It was too bad because by the time Prudential would have figured out that most of my injuries were old ones, I would have turned the settlement check into small bills and gotten a new p.o. box.

Next thing I know after the Poughkeepsie 7-11, I'm thinking about retiring at the ripe old age of 41. When you think about it, there are a lot of disincentives to working your chosen profession in this country. Chief among them in my case being the occasional competition for attention with Mexican-Canadian gun-waver types, and the complete lack of benefits, too, such as health care. For instance, with the Acme run-in with the bumper the whole hospital thing came to damn near forty-seven thou, and the settlement was only for sixty, which meant I would have only netted thirteen K for three months of sucking pureed chicken out of rubber bags. I say would have, because when you don't have health care, you learn to tiptoe out of the hospital at midnight before everything's completely done healing and the blue suit guy drops in to see about settling up. I'm sure in the end they'll just mail the bill to me, Earl Lester, Binghamton. Unfortunately for them, today I'm Lester Earl, Ithaca, living off sixty grand in twenties.

I do have to share some of the pie. My lawyer is any number of men named Homer Pierce. They all go by Homer Pierce because of a little joke of ours, having originated six years ago from a newspaper story about a lawyer in Utica named, you guessed it, Homer Pierce, who had been cited by the State Bar for seventeen ethics violations and only been placed on probationary status. One night in Troy while we played a little seven card with twos, fours, nines, one-eyed jacks and suicide kings wild, I and three of the eleven future Homer Pierces decided why risk inadvertently tarnishing a good lawyer's name by using an alias other than Homer Pierce for all our lawsuits. The joke, of course, was that we knew full well there weren't any "good" lawyers.

So far Homer Pierce has represented me on seventy-eight suits. He's been victorious in procuring settlements in fifty-nine of these, a pretty nice rate of return for a lawyer, but you got to have someone who knows how to fall, too. Homer Pierce's height varies from suit to suit, from 5'6" to 6'3", his weight from about 165 to 310. Like his size, his settlements vary, too, from the paltry $500 dust-yourself-off money to the big rips, like the Acme gastapper and the time the cop inadvertently ran into me last year on a sidewalk outside a bank in Schenectady after I had advertently gotten in his way while he was chasing a burglar, bank bells clanging and everything. The burglar, of course, was wearing a sombrero, but he wasn't famous yet, and the police and everybody made time to pay me some attention while he got away. You should have seen me moaning about my back on that one. Homer Pierce had to do damn near nothing for the check from the bank's insurance company. None of the Homer Pierces have any real licenses to practice anything, but they're good at the verbal muscle game and making official looking stationery, and they've got a rudimentary knowledge of law which is more than is needed, I assure you. I can assure you because once in a pinch I had to be my own Homer Pierce after a tractor ran over my toe during a free tour of a dairy farm outside Herkimer.

The clincher, of course, is that in reality I am no victim and in reality I am sick to death of all the victim talk sweeping the damn country. No wonder the Mexican-Canadian has been coming down (or up) here to do all his damage. He probably thought the money would practically jump into his hands, this countryful of victims we got just waiting to give it away, and so far it practically has. Kills me, really. The way I see it, if you don't have your own scam, that doesn't make you a goddamn victim; it only makes you a goddamn idiot. Case in point: Newt Gingrich. Genius. And since the Poughkeepsie episode, I've been thinking that this is at the root of what I think will make retirement a little harder to handle — worrying about eventually feeling like the rest of the average ducks out there, blending in and not giving a damn, whining my ass away. I'd rather somebody just blow my goddamned head off if it comes to all that. Damn these back pains.

The guy who certifies my injuries as one hundred percent bona fide and worth the price of settlement is Dr. Richard Greggson, who got his degree through mail order from the Pacific Coast Institute of Medicine and Pharmacology. He's got two diplomas because, on occasion, circumstances arise which dictate him being Greg Richardson. Essentially it's the same service either way, although sometimes Greg Richardson will throw a free twenty-one day Valium prescription into the deal, whereas Richard Greggson, who got a Certificate of Ethics via mail while I was in the hospital waiting for the clock to tick, will usually raise objection to the pills.

Both Richard Greggson and Greg Richardson were delighted

about the Acme gastapper incident because there were actual broken bones involved. The two of them have so many repros of the
hospital x-rays filed away that every settlement from here on out
would start negotiations at a decent five figure minimum. Neither
Richard Greggson, Greg Richardson, or Homer Pierce are happy,
though, about my thinking about retiring. I am the key man in our
little industry.

But there have been aggravations, and not just what happened
after the Bandit walked into the Poughkeepsie 7-11. For instance
Homer Pierce has been acting more like a real lawyer lately, always
greed greed greed, where's my cut?, never any respect for the art of
the fall. I get laid up and everybody gets delusions of seriousness. I
met with the original three of him in a Burger King in Spectator the
day before the Poughkeepsie incident, and it was all I could do to
stop myself from punching his goddamn noses in. We sat at a
window table and discussed why we were not going to actually
litigate anything, even though that was where the "big money" was.
Our primary problem was, of course, that none of him had any
kind of license to litigate jack, and unlike the field of medicine,
they do actually check things like that, especially when you actually
take a case to trial.

Why let that stop us? One of him snapped, his mouth full of
Whopper. Nothing's stopped us yet, blah blah blah. Yeah, said another of him, we can beat some of these bastards big.

I suggested that maybe we hadn't been stopped by anything because we had a proven method. Then I reminded each of him of
that one time when I was him in Herkimer, and it'd be just as easy to
do that from now on, cut out the middle action. You could see who
really needed who in his darting little eyes then. I also told him that
the three of him were acting like real lawyers. To which each of him
sort of looked at me like yeah, well, what's your point?

I had in fact forgotten the point, although I began to wonder if it
might have something to do with why my goddamn lawyer couldn't
have driven to visit me in the Binghamton's County Memorial.
Then all of a sudden the Arby's next door was being robbed by a
gun-toting guy in a big sombrero, and people were standing around
out front like they were thinking about clapping. Then they parted
for him like the Red Sea when he darted for his car. That Mexican-
Canadian must not ever sleep.

Deep down I'm sure Homer Pierce knew I wasn't going to leave him dry. There'd be too many ways for everything to fall apart if each fall was a one-man operation, and, hell, what was I going to do, go back to hustling pool? I'd had my fill of that in Niskayuna, and it was the most boring predictable depressing thing in the world. Got so bad playing dumbass Hubris-filled make-pretend sharks I had to start giving people breaks like, okay, if this asshole doesn't act like he knew he was going to hit this shot that he's never made before in his whole life, I won't run the table on him; or okay, if this pretender doesn't act pissed off after he's missed a three banker, I won't take all of his money. Goddamn if most of the time the assholes didn't keep puffing out their chests and kissing away cash. It's like the ear-benders were all caught in raccoon traps, you know, where you put a treat inside a can with a hole only big enough for a raccoon to get an unclenched paw in through and when he grabs the treat he's stuck, not knowing all he's got to do is let go of the treat and he can get his paw out. Raccoons don't ever have the wherewithal to let go. Same thing hustling pool suckers in Niskayuna. I had to get out.

I'd always been good at taking a fall, ever since I used to go tumbling down the stairs just to get my father to glance up from his numbers. After a while he got so used to my careening from step to step that he'd just say, "Earl, cut it out," without even raising his eyes. Sometimes I'd even lie in one place at the bottom of the stairway for ten or fifteen minutes, pretending I was paralyzed with my eyes stuck crossing toward my nose. Nothing, not a peep from him. My mother found me that way once and nearly had a heart attack. "Lester! Lester, speak!" I was a natural making a living doing it. That is until Poughkeepsie.

It was after I met with Homer Pierce at the Burger King that day before Poughkeepsie that I first realized I was still in quite a bit of goddamn back pain from when the damn Honda had rolled me. I was hoping to find Dr. Greg Richardson in Albany to make me feel better, but instead Dr. Richard Greggson was in, who suggested, instead of Valium, maybe a steam bath or a whirlpool might do me a world of good, and he'd also read up on some new balms which could do miracles. He said this with a straight face, even crinkling up his high forehead as if he'd been born to practice medicine all his life. I wondered if I should give him a black eye. Instead, I patiently asked him when Dr. Richardson might be back. He assured me it would not be for some time, his blue eyes dancing behind his fake non-prescription glasses. The IRS was looking for him.

The drive to Poughkeepsie was a long, unpleasant, stiff one. I thought maybe I should start making a little book to tide me over until it would be easier to do proper falls; but if you think hustling's like setting raccoon traps, you haven't seen anything compared to taking bets. Then whizzing toward me down two lane Route 46 came a brown Ford Escort that switched back to its side of the road just in time. The driver, of course, was wearing a sombrero. I started questioning what had happened to my work ethic.

In Poughkeepsie I got a room at a trap and went for a six-pack at the 7-11 I was going to fall in the next day. It was around 9:30, and I commented to the young greaser behind the counter that the floors could use a mopping. They do it in the mornings, he said, it wasn't his business. Right, I said, nothing he could do. Then he asked had I heard the Bandito had hit a Safeway on the other side of town that evening and wasn't this guy something?

"It's a little blatant," I said to him, feeling my jaw jut a little, "isn't it? All this stealing with a gun?"

The greaser had no idea what I was talking about. "He's the Bandit, man." He said this like it answered all arguments, his eyebrows bunching into an earnest sense of purpose. He couldn't wait to get robbed.

And, sure enough, the next day I did get to see the Bandit, man, live and in person, ruining what would have been a perfectly functional prat. When he burst into the 7-11 waving the .22, my first instinct was to try to do whatever I could to speed the whole thing up because the floor was drying fast, and I still had to discreetly nudge out of view the "Wet Floor" stand-up sign, to secure the full prize. If the warning isn't clearly displayed, the store insurer basically has to start negotiations mid-twenties.

But the Mexican-Canadian was a bit of a showman, a charmer, taking his time with things, and all of a sudden, realizing the situation, I was feeling like the gatecrasher. He spoke slowly through the black ski mask like he was everybody's friend, nodding the big sombrero in everybody's directions as he spoke, peppering his phrases with "okays" and "ays" and an occasional French word.

When he said the words "heads blown off" to the duchess behind the counter and the five or six of us scattered around the store, it was like he meant taking a quiet nap in the woods. Then all of a sudden everyone was down on the floor except for him and me.

"Please," he said to me, "you, too." From about ten feet away he fixed the .22 between my eyes, and I realized that the easiest, least painful way for me to get my casted self down actually would have been for me to do a nice safe fall, but I couldn't risk getting pumped because some sudden jerky-ass landing on the linoleum startled him. "Please," he said again, this time with a little less charm, "down."

I struggled to get down on one knee, focusing on his faceless ski mask, big nails of pain tearing up my back, when it dawned on me he might take my slowness as defiance.

"I've been in an accident," I said to him. "I'm still in pain."

"Yes," he said, following his outstretched .22 toward me, "I'm sure you are. Get down."

I dropped to all fours, felt myself grimace, felt a tendon rip in the casted wrist. Then finally I was doing a dead man's float on the cool damp linoleum, ammonia clearing a space behind my eyes. My back was spasming as he stepped over me and stood with a foot on each side of my ribs, still pointing the gun, I was sure, at my head.

I tried to talk myself through it. Told myself that that very day Homer Pierce and I would file suit against the 7-11 for having such a blatantly insecure store. Sure, a settlement was iffier, taking it that route, but the potential payout was higher. Hell, look at the trauma I was going through. Maybe we'd even litigate this one.

But I was fooling myself. Instead of thinking about a nice thick settlement check, I found myself reaching for my wallet out of my back pocket, and blindly handing it up to him. Then I slid my Rolex off the uncasted wrist and easily handed that back, too, without turning my head. Maybe it was the ammonia working me over. Everything in my body loosened up there for a moment. Hell, for a moment, even the muscles in my back relaxed.

HELEN TUCKER

The Power of Suggestion

FROM *Ellery Queen's Mystery Magazine*

IT WAS getting weird. Downright scary, in fact.

At first he had thought it was a trick, some kind of practical joke she was playing on him. But he soon realized that was a stupid idea, because in the fifteen years they had been married, he'd never known her to play a joke on him or anyone else, practical or otherwise. Nelda was not the joking type. For that matter, more often than not, she didn't even get the point of a joke *he* told. She would give that little artificial laugh, but he could tell by the vacant look in her pale blue eyes that she simply didn't *get* it.

After deciding it wasn't a joke, he was positive that it must be some kind of fad or craze going around that he hadn't heard about. After all, he worked all day and didn't have time to waste on finding out what sort of nonsense currently occupied the minds of women. He was forty-two years old, one of the leading designers in Beldon and Nelms Architectural Company, and before the year was out, he expected to be made a partner in the firm. Sometimes he even worked at night (and sometimes he didn't, but Nelda thought he did). You didn't get to be a partner by staying home day and night to see what your wife was up to or what kind of crap she was reading. Before all this weird stuff began, he'd never known Nelda to read anything but fashion magazines and books about the beautiful people, whoever the hell they were.

He figured Nelda was pretty typical of the average forty-year-old housewife. She had a rinse put on her blond hair, which she wore in a Dutchboy cut, every so often to keep it that color, her skin was still pretty good (probably thanks to whatever that stuff was she slapped on at regular intervals), and she didn't need a lot of makeup. She was tall, five-eight, and her figure was still good, though she had thickened a bit in the middle. She dressed sensibly, but always in style, and spent just about all the money he gave her on clothes. She could pass for . . . oh, maybe thirty-five, if you stretched your imagination a bit. She was interested in buying nice things for the house, trying out new recipes, her weekly bridge game with "the girls," and lunching twice a week with some of her old college friends who lived in the city. To his knowledge, she had never been interested in occult mumbo jumbo or reading books about same.

The weird stuff started about six weeks ago and showed no signs of stopping or even letting up. It was, in fact, getting worse. Actually, it might have been going on for a while before he noticed. He first became aware of the spooky undertones one night after dinner when he sat down on the sofa, on the end by the three-way lamp, to catch up on the latest *Architectural Digest*. On the table, under the lamp, was a pile of books. The title of the top book was *Psychic Experiences Through the Ages*. What the hell was Nelda doing with a book like that? He took the second book off the pile. *Early Spiritualism*. The third book, *Psychical Research*. And the fourth, *Telepathy in Everyday Life*. Beneath that book was a bunch of brochures and pamphlets on clairvoyance, extrasensory perception, precognition, and altered states of consciousness.

"Jehovah's Jaguar, Nelda! Where'd you get this stuff?"

She looked up briefly from her Queen Anne chair by the fireplace. "The library." Then she was buried again in the book she held, the title of which was *Hypnosis and Dream Telepathy*.

"Why're you reading this junk?"

She looked up again, the epitome of patience. "I don't think it's junk, Hugh. They were all written by experts in their field."

"Whatever. Why're you reading it?"

She lowered the book again. "A couple of the girls think I may have ESP or something like it, and I thought if I read up on the subject, I could find out for sure."

"So now you're going to start telling fortunes?"

"Hardly." She gave him a condescending smile. "Some rather . . . odd things have been happening lately, and I confess I've been a bit shaken by them."

"Like what?"

"Well, at a recent bridge game, it occurred to me suddenly that I knew every card that was going to be played before it was played.

When I realized that, I also sensed that I knew what cards were in the other three hands even before the bidding began. Of course, with an advantage like that, I mopped up that afternoon."

He laughed, first uproariously, then derisively. "I'll take you with me to my next poker game."

"It isn't funny, Hugh. It's a little . . . frightening." She paused, then said, "The next thing that happened was a lunch a couple of days later. Ruth and Barb and I were to meet at The Tea Kettle. Ruth arrived at the same time, and I said to her — I don't know where I got the idea — 'Barb isn't coming. She's going to phone and tell the hostess to tell us she's ill.' Sure enough, we had no sooner sat down than the hostess came over and said, 'Mrs. Long just called and said to tell you she's not feeling well and can't make it today.'"

He couldn't think of a word to say. He just looked at her, wondering if his very practical, down-to-earth wife had all of a sudden run mad.

He had planned to go to Sonja's that night. After all, he hadn't seen her for three days. But something about the seriousness of Nelda's expression, her tone of voice, made him decide to stay home. It was easy enough to get away when he wanted to. All he had to say was, "We're having some problems with the Grandy building," or, "That new house on May Avenue, well, the owner has changed his mind about the shape of the deck, so I've got to have it done by tomorrow." And he'd be off for a few hours of bliss with Sonja. Nelda was gullible as hell. She never suspected anything. But tonight — he didn't know why — he thought he'd better not go.

"Anything else?" he asked. "Or is that the sum total of your psychic experiences?"

"Are you making fun of me?" A small frown furrowed her forehead.

"No, of course not. I'm just curious."

"There've been some little things that made me wonder, but nothing as significant as the two I told you about. The thing is, these experiences, as you call them, are happening more often, and each time I get a stronger premonition." She stopped suddenly and looked toward the telephone on the end table. "Like right now. The phone is going to ring."

He waited. A minute, two minutes, three minutes. Nothing happened. And then the phone rang.

"Don't bother to answer it," she said. "It's a wrong number."

An act of Congress could not have prevented him from picking up the phone. "Hello."

"Has Jimmy come in yet?" asked a gruff voice.

He held the phone away from him, looking at it as though it were a hissing viper, then he barked into it, "Wrong number!"

She continued with her reading without looking up and without saying "I told you so," for which he would have been grateful had he not been so befuddled. What the hell was going on here? Had the woman suddenly become possessed with some kind of strange powers? Ditch-water dull Nelda, whom he could read like a child's primer? It couldn't be.

"Has something happened to you, something strange?" he asked. "I mean — do you feel, er, different? Headache or . . . anything?"

"Not at all. I feel the same as I always have."

He couldn't think of anything else to ask, so he just sat staring at her, going over in his mind the horrendous difference it could make in his life if his wife really had suddenly become a seer into the future. But, of course, he didn't believe in that stuff and his first thought had been correct. It was just a fad, a phase she was going through, reading all those crazy books. She'd get tired of it soon enough and go back to being ditch-water dull Nelda whose every move and sentence he could anticipate. And that made him psychic in his own right, didn't it?

But that didn't explain the telephone business. How had she known?

It had taken him hours to get to sleep that night, but by the next morning he was ready to pooh-pooh the whole psychic business. If you played bridge with the same people week after week, year after year, you could tell by looking at their expressions what kind of cards they were holding, just as he could tell by the expressions, or lack thereof, on the faces of the members of his poker club. And it was a safe enough guess that Barbara Long wouldn't show up for a lunch date: That hypochondriac canceled half her social engagements because of some imaginary illness. As for the phone, what the hell? They never got any calls at night anyway, so if the phone rang, there was a ninety-five percent chance it was a wrong number.

Nelda was getting ideas from all that crap she was reading. She'd lose interest pretty soon and go back to fashion magazines and the beautiful people, whoever the hell they were.

He scrutinized himself in the mirror extra carefully while shaving. Had it been that long since he'd checked, or had his hairline receded a bit more overnight? And was that puffiness under his eyes the beginning of bags? He worked out at the gym once a week in an effort to keep a flat stomach, but there was nothing the gym could do about eyes and hair. He couldn't afford to let himself go in any way, not if he wanted to keep Sonja. She was a beaut: statuesque brunette, heart-shaped face with sexy, pouty lips, skin that almost glowed in the dark, and she was fifteen years younger than he. He'd already invested a fortune in her: all that jewelry, lingerie, champagne, and room-service dinners (he couldn't afford to take her out and be seen by someone who knew him; it would jeopardize his partnership). So he paid her rent in the hotel suite on the twelfth floor, and he hoped that he was the only one who visited her there. Had to be, he kept telling himself, because she was always available for him, even on the spur of the moment.

Tonight he would see her for sure. Nelda could predict ringing phones, sick friends, card games, or the end of civilization as we know it; his own prediction was that he'd have one hell of a night with Sonja.

It was about a week, possibly ten days, later that he had to go home unexpectedly in the middle of the morning. He'd left plumbing estimates for the Grandy building in a folder on the bureau, just walked right out that morning without seeing it. The house was quiet when he entered — no TV or radio talk shows or CDs playing golden oldies — and his first thought was that Nelda wasn't home, but then he remembered seeing her car in the driveway.

He found her sitting at her little antique desk in a corner of the living room. She was studying something, her concentration so great that she did not even hear him as he approached. As he bent over her, he saw what she was studying so intently. A sheet of white paper, completely blank.

"What . . ." he began, but at the sound of his voice, she started violently, let out a little scream, and turned in her chair.

"Good Lord, Hugh, what are you doing home now? You just about scared me into apoplexy."

"Sorry," he said, "I forgot that folder on the bureau. Had to come back for it. What are you doing?" he added, although it was perfectly obvious she wasn't doing a damn thing.

"I — I was just thinking." She had a guilty look about her, as though she had been caught doing something underhanded.

"About what?"

She hesitated a second or two, then, looking down at the Oriental rug as though counting figures in the design, said, "It's gotten worse, Hugh. Much more prevalent."

He really didn't have time to stand there and jaw with her about the trivialities of her life. "What are you talking about, Nelda?"

"The ESP . . . clairvoyance, or whatever you want to call it."

He didn't want to call it anything; he'd prefer to ignore it, forget it altogether. She was still reading those stupid books all the time, and he'd certainly done a good job of ignoring that. "What now?" he asked with as much civility as he could manage. "You see something written on that blank paper?"

She nodded, then shook her head. "Not really, but when I first saw this piece of paper, it came to me that I'm going to get a letter today from someone I haven't heard from in years. Someone I'd completely forgotten about. When you came in, I was trying to figure out who it could be."

He laughed at her. "Why waste time? Just wait till the postman comes and you will know." He laughed again. "It's just your imagination working overtime because of those lunatic books you read. You're turning into a real loony tune, you know that?"

He didn't wait for an answer. He went up to the bedroom, got his folder, and went back down to the living-room door. "I may be a little late coming in tonight," he told her. "There's a dinner meeting, followed by some business. May be eleven or after before it breaks up."

She didn't look around, just nodded.

As he was getting in his car, he saw the postman's red, white, and blue jeep turn the corner. Ha! He would wait for the mail, take it to her, and convince her that this ESP she thought she had was nothing but pure, unadulterated rubbish.

He took the handful of mail from the postman, and without even looking through it, rushed back into the house and dropped it on the desk in front of her. "There," he said, "show me the letter from your long-lost friend, or whoever."

She went through the mail slowly: bills, advertisements, an envelope of coupons, and a letter addressed to her in a strange, circular handwriting. She looked up at him, a somewhat frightened expression on her face, then opened the letter. He leaned over her shoulder and read as she did:

Dear Nelda,

It's been years, and you probably don't even remember me, but we were acquainted in college (I hesitate to say friends, because we didn't see that much of each other). My husband and I have just moved here from Kansas City, and I would like very much to see you again and get reacquainted. We don't know any people here yet except those Jack works with. I would appreciate it so much if you would call me sometime.

Sincerely,
Nita Conway Delahan

There was a P.S. which gave the phone number.

He couldn't get it out of his mind. Had his average, dull, ordinary wife really become possessed of some kind of psychic powers? Impossible! He didn't believe it for a minute. And yet . . . What else could explain the strange goings-on?

That night when he went to his dinner meeting (with Sonja), he was still trying to find some logical explanation.

"What's the matter with you?" Sonja complained after she had rolled the room-service dinner trolley out into the hall. "You haven't spoken a dozen words since you came in. I ordered your favorite meal, your favorite wine, and I'm wearing the negligee you brought me last week. You haven't commented on anything or even noticed anything."

He knew if there was anything Sonja couldn't stand, it was being ignored. He'd had some disappointing evenings — she had sent him home after about thirty minutes — when she'd been convinced she did not have his absolute and unconditional attention.

"My dear, beautiful girl," he said quickly, pulling her down beside him on the small flowered-chintz sofa, "forgive me if I sometimes take all this perfection for granted. You see, I've come to expect nothing less from you. The way you look, the things you do . . . you are the ideal in every way."

The words were so far removed from his usual pattern of conversation or compliments that he felt he was speaking a foreign
tongue. It was almost funny, a joke, but it seemed to satisfy, even
please her, for she smiled and snuggled closer to him. "Problems
at work?" she asked. That, too, was unusual, because they always
talked about her, not him.

"No, nothing like that," he said, and then he decided to tell her.
"Nelda has been acting . . . I don't know . . . sort of strange lately.
Well, not strange, maybe, but bizarre things have been happening."

"She's found out about us?"

"Oh, no. No way that could happen. I'm too careful." And then
he told her about the phone call and the letter and about all the
books Nelda had been reading.

Anything Sonja didn't understand was dismissed with a little
shrug and a change of subject. As was this. "All those crazy books,"
she said. "That would send anybody around the bend. How do you
like my new perfume? Do I smell like Elizabeth Taylor?"

"I don't know how Elizabeth Taylor smells," he said, laughing,
and from then on, they had an exemplary evening.

It was almost eleven-thirty when he went home. He expected to
find Nelda fast asleep in her twin bed, possibly with the bedside
lamp still on and one of those nutty books lying open beside her.
What he found was Nelda sitting up in bed, her fingers pressed
against her temples, her eyes closed.

"What's the matter?" he asked. "You got a headache or something?"

She opened her eyes slowly and looked around as though coming out of a trance or regaining consciousness after a coma. He
almost expected her to say, "Where am I?"

For a long time she didn't say anything, and then: "Hugh, I have
been seeing the oddest thing: a series of pictures in my mind, all in
still-life."

"Nelda, what the hell are you talking about?"

He sat down on his bed and removed his shoes. Kee-rist, he
hoped she wasn't going to start her loony-tune business now. He
was wiped out. Sonja had had the agility of an Olympic gymnast
tonight. He smiled, remembering.

"I was trying to read," she said, "but these pictures kept flashing
across my mind. Then, I'm not sure what happened, but I seemed

to go outside myself. Maybe it was an altered state of consciousness. The pictures became much clearer. Much."

He'd be damned if he'd ask her what kind of pictures. He didn't even want to know.

She told him anyway. "I saw a room. It was like a hotel room, a suite, maybe, but it was furnished better than the average hotel room. There were some pictures, family pictures I suppose, on a table, and there was a little sofa or love seat with flowered upholstery, and you were sitting there. You were by yourself, but your mouth was moving as though you were talking to someone. That picture faded and another came on — exactly as though it were being shown on a screen — and you were not alone anymore. There was a woman sitting beside you on the sofa, a very pretty dark-haired woman. Hugh, am I going crazy, or is it . . . is it the ESP again?"

He was staring at her, his mind in turmoil. "What — what are you talking about?" His voice came out scarcely above a whisper.

"I'm not sure. I saw it so clearly, but I'm not sure what it was I was seeing. Where was your meeting tonight?"

"At the Baxter Hotel. We met in the suite of a visiting architect." He thought it best to get at least a remnant of truth in his answer.

"That explains it then." She let out a sigh of relief. "I was seeing the meeting. But I wonder why I didn't see more than just two people."

He didn't answer; he couldn't.

She plumped her pillow several times and lay down. When he came out of the bathroom, she was either asleep or pretending to be.

But it was nearly dawn before he closed his eyes.

The first thing he did when he got to his office that morning was to call Sonja and tell her she would have to move from the Baxter to the Cromley on the other side of town.

"In your dreams, buster," she said, furious at having been awakened and even more furious at being told she would have to leave her deluxe digs. "I'm not going to some second-rate fleabag."

"The Cromley is a first-class apartment hotel, and I'll see that you have as much space there as you have at the Baxter. I'll make the arrangements this morning and you can move this afternoon." He hung up before she could protest further.

He didn't have a clue what had happened to Nelda or what was going on in *her* mind, but obviously she didn't know (or hadn't seen pictures) of his intimate moments with Sonja. It seemed to be a good idea to move Sonja farther away from Nelda (maybe proximity had something to do with the pictures she saw) before Nelda caught on.

No matter what was happening in her mind, it had made a wreck out of his own. He couldn't concentrate on work, or even Sonja. All he could do was stare at Nelda when he was with her and wonder and wonder. And when he was away from her he wondered even more . . .

He was going bat crazy. He was obsessed with it, couldn't get his mind on anything else. He had never believed in all that psychic stuff; it was a hoax, a ripoff, like fortunetellers at a county fair. There *had* to be some logical explanation for the things that had happened rather than the psychological mumbo jumbo that Nelda kept mouthing. Extrasensory perception, altered states of consciousness, precognition. Horse hockey!

Yet he couldn't come up with *any*thing that even partially explained how Nelda knew the phone was going to ring, that it would be a wrong number, or that the postman was going to deliver a letter from someone she hadn't heard from in years, or how — and this was the really scary one — she could describe a hotel room she'd never been in and even see him sitting beside Sonja on the sofa.

Could she have followed him that night, peeped through the keyhole? Common sense said no, that he was becoming paranoid. Nevertheless, he began seeing Sonja at lunchtime on the days when he knew Nelda was either playing bridge or meeting someone for lunch.

For a while, maybe a week, nothing unusual happened — except that Nelda kept reading those damn books. She would sit in her chair by the fireplace, a book in her hands, and every so often she'd look up with a strange little smile on her face, as though she knew an amusing joke on him which he wasn't privy to.

Then one night the phone thing happened again. He was watching the Bulls go down in inglorious defeat (what could they expect without Air Jordan?) and she was reading a book entitled *Authentic Witchcraft*. Witchcraft, for God's sake! Wouldn't you know?!

The phone rang and he reached for it, but she said, "Don't

bother, it's for me. Sheila wants to tell me that our bridge game has been postponed until next week because her daughter's just been taken to the hospital. The baby will be born tonight."

He froze, his hand extended in midair, while she picked up the phone.

"Hello, Sheila," she said at once. "Yes, as soon as the phone rang, I knew it was you. You're going to the hospital to be with Linda, aren't you? Uh-huh, just my ESP at work." She gave a little laugh. "Give Linda my love. No, I can't tell you if it will be a boy or a girl, but it will be perfect. Yes, see you next week. Bye."

He turned the TV off. He couldn't focus on the game anymore. All he could do was stare at Nelda, his mind going round and round like a carousel, round and round and round in the same dizzying circle, getting nowhere.

She was bending over the bed, shaking him. "Hugh, wake up. Wake *up!* It's almost nine o'clock. You've overslept."

He turned over and groaned, opened his eyes then closed them again. "Go away," he mumbled.

"You're already late," she persisted. "Get up."

"I'm not going to the office today."

"Are you sick?"

Instead of answering, he pulled the sheet up over his head. He was sick, yes. Sick of all the craziness that had taken over his life. He felt that last night had been the ultimate blow to what was left of his sanity. He wasn't sure at this moment whether he could distinguish reality from fantasy anymore.

Yesterday he had decided that he was being overly cautious in seeing Sonja only during lunch, so after he left the office at five, he dropped in on her at the Cromley. It was nearly eight when he got home and Nelda met him at the door. "Hugh, the most peculiar thing . . ." she began. "Maybe you can explain it for me."

"What?" He was totally enervated and the last thing he wanted right now was conversation.

"When you didn't get home at the usual time, I started worrying, and then suddenly, my mind went blank for a second or two, and after that I started seeing those still-life pictures again. I saw a hotel room, not the same one I saw before, but — and this is what's peculiar — there were the same family pictures around the room that I saw in that other room where you had the meeting. And the same woman was there, that dark-haired woman, and . . ."

He didn't listen to any more. He started trembling and knew that if he didn't get out of her sight at once, she would notice that he was having an acute attack of anxiety. He rushed upstairs, calling as he went, "I've already eaten, so don't make any dinner for me." He went straight to bed.

The trembling lasted a long time; it was as though he were having a hard chill. Finally it stopped and he took long, deep breaths. Something had to be done. Things couldn't continue this way. He didn't want to give up Sonja, but he couldn't afford any scandal in his life right now (and Nelda would sure as hell divorce him if she found out) because Jim Beldon and Harry Nelms were both strong family men and absolute Puritans about practically everything. He'd have to stop seeing Sonja until after he made partner. Then he could relax a little and resume the relationship.

Nelda sat down on her bed and leaned toward his. "Hugh, I had the most peculiar dream last night."

Kee-rist, please! He didn't want to hear about her dream.

"You were in that room — the one I told you about with the pictures and the dark-haired woman — and all of a sudden a man came bursting in wearing a mask and with a gun in his hand. He said, 'You don't belong here, this is my territory,' and he shot you right through the heart. Then he took the mask off and went to the dark-haired woman and said, 'If I ever catch you fooling around again, I'll kill you too.' Then he kissed her and took her into a bedroom and . . ."

He came out from under the cover. "Nelda, for God's sake, have you lost your mind completely? That's the craziest thing I ever heard."

"I thought so too," she said calmly, smiling. "That's why I told you about it, so we could both have a good laugh."

Instead of laughing, he got out of bed and headed for the shower. "I'm going to work after all," he said.

His first thought had been to go to Sonja at lunchtime to tell her he couldn't see her again for a while, but then he decided he'd wait until the middle of the afternoon. He didn't call ahead, just went at three o'clock. Sonja seemed only mildly surprised to see him. "Gee,

Hugh, I never know when to expect you anymore. You've gotten to be a real drop-in visitor."

He was trying to think of some way to break it to her gently that he was going to have to drop out for a while. "Sonja, baby, look, I've got something to tell you. I've got to . . ."

At that moment the door to the hall was thrown open and a man came in quickly and closed the door behind him. Hugh's first thought was, He's not wearing a mask; that's a stocking over his head. And then he saw the pistol in the man's hand, and he began shaking. "No!" he screamed. "Don't shoot. For God's sake, don't shoot."

"You don't belong here," the man said. "This is my territory."

He was going to be shot, killed. He had to get out. How? The man was between him and the door, and it would do no good to go to the bedroom because the man would follow. Sonja had backed against the far wall and was cringing there like a terrified animal. The hell with Sonja; her other lover wouldn't shoot her. Nelda had said as much.

He remembered the fire escape just under the balcony. If he could make it to that before the man pulled the trigger . . . He ran to the balcony and was climbing over when he saw the man coming out on the balcony, the gun aimed at his head. "Don't shoot, *please* don't shoot," he cried, reaching for the fire escape.

His foot slipped on the first rung and he tried to catch hold of the balcony rail but missed. He fell fourteen stories, landing on the concrete beside the Cromley's pint-sized swimming pool. The last sound he heard was Sonja's scream . . . or was it his own?

He was already sitting in the back booth when she arrived at The Tea Kettle. His name was Ivan. He was forty years old, had blond hair turning gray which looked the color of pale sand, brown eyes, a mottled complexion which probably was a result of teenage acne, and he was tall and skinny as a telephone pole. He had been a private investigator until his license was revoked three years ago. Now he clerked part time in a furniture store and took on "special jobs" investigating whenever one turned up, which was infrequently.

She slid in the booth across from him and, without a word, took a long white envelope out of her pocketbook and slipped it across the table to him.

Without opening the envelope, he pocketed it. "Gee, Nelda, it was so much fun, I should be paying you."

She knew this was a bit of fawning, not truth. "You'll find a little bonus in there, along with your fee."

"I wasn't expecting that," he said, obviously pleased.

"That last episode may have been a little hairy," she said. "You deserve something extra."

"I'd have settled for a few explanations from you about how you managed it all." He looked at her admiringly.

"I couldn't have done it without your help," she told him. "Not just any P.I. would have suited. Did I tell you I interviewed three before someone recommended you?"

"I get most of my jobs word of mouth. What'll you have?" he asked as a waitress stopped at the booth. "My treat today. Shall we celebrate?"

"I'll just have a cup of tea and an English muffin," she said. "They don't have the wherewithal for celebrations here."

He ordered coffee and a pastry and as soon as the waitress left said, "Now tell me how you did it with what little information I gave you."

"Easy," she said. "Almost too easy. First I took home an armload of books on everything pertaining to psychology and boned up on all phases of it. Also, I made a point of reading the books constantly whenever Hugh was home. Then I started making up things to tell him. I told him about a fictitious bridge game in which I knew in advance every card that would be played. Then I made up something about a friend not joining another friend and me for lunch after I predicted she wouldn't. That was the same night I had you call at nine on the dot and ask if Jimmy had come in yet. I had predicted that the phone would ring and that it would be a wrong number. I think that call shook Hugh up a little. The second time I had you call — that was when I chatted on about Sheila and her daughter's expected baby — well, Sheila had called that afternoon with the information that her daughter had just been taken to the hospital."

"Yeah," he said, grinning. "I just listened and marveled. You should have been an actress."

"There was some luck involved also," she admitted. "I wrote a letter to myself from someone who never existed, someone I supposedly hadn't seen in ages, and then predicted the letter would arrive in the mail and what it would say. It was sheer luck that Hugh was home when the letter came, otherwise I would have had to wait until he came home to open the letter, and that wouldn't have been nearly as effective."

He broke out in a big laugh. "You didn't really need to hire a P.I., Nellie, my girl."

"Oh yes, I did. You were the one who found out who the woman was, where she lived, and all the vital information. All I had was a suspicion that he was seeing another woman. Also, getting into her two suites was a stroke of genius. I couldn't have done that. Knowing what her places looked like was really what did the trick."

"Simple," he said. "All I had to do was tip the room-service guy into letting me wheel in the trolley."

They were both quiet as the waitress returned with their orders. Then he said, "I'll miss our little sessions. Do you think we could see each other now and then?"

She was thoughtful for a minute. "Not right away. I'm going to do some traveling for a month or two. I always wanted to go to Paris for shopping, but Hugh was too busy to get away and too tight to let me go. Also, I thought a cruise would be nice, maybe to somewhere like Alaska. But after that . . ." She gave him her one-hundred-watt smile. "Yes, Ivan, I think we should keep in touch."

He sipped his coffee, looking at her over the rim of the cup. "I'm not sure but what you really *are* psychic. How did you know your husband was going to rush out to the balcony and fall and kill himself when I went in there with a stocking over my head and a gun in my hand? All I said was what you told me to: "This is my territory, you don't belong here."

"I didn't know," she said. "I thought he might have a heart attack, or maybe a stroke. It never occurred to me he'd try to get away."

"But I never would have shot him, or the woman. Murder's not my thing. What made him panic like that?"

She gave a little shrug, then laughed. "It must have been the power of suggestion."

DONALD E. WESTLAKE

Take It Away

FROM *Mary Higgins Clark Mystery Magazine*

"NICE NIGHT for a stakeout."

Well, *that* startled me, let me tell you. I looked around and saw I
was no longer the last person on line. Behind me now was a goofy-
looking guy more or less my age (thirty-four) and height (six feet)
but maybe just a bit thinner than me (190 pounds). He wore
eyeglasses with thick black frames and a dark-blue baseball cap
turned around backward, with bunches of carroty-red hair sticking
out under it on the sides and back.

He was bucktoothed and grinning, and he wore a gold-and-pur-
ple high school athletic jacket with the letter X hugely on it in
Day-Glo white edged in purple and gold. It was open a bit at the
top, to show a bright lime green polo shirt underneath.

His trousers were plain black chinos, which made for a change,
and on his feet were a pair of those high tech sneakers complete
with inserts and gores and extra straps and triangles of black
leather here and there that look as though they were constructed to
specifications for NASA. In his left hand he held an *X Men* comic
book folded open to the middle of a story. He was not, in other
words, anybody on the crew, or even *like* anybody on the crew. So
what was this about a stakeout? Who *was* this guy?

Time to employ my interrogation techniques, which meant I
should come at him indirectly, not asking "Who are you?" but
saying "What was that again?"

He blinked happily behind his glasses and pointed with his free
hand. "A stakeout," he said, cheerful as could be.

I looked where he pointed, at the side wall of this Burger Whopper, where it was my turn tonight to get food for the crew, and I saw the poster there advertising this month's special in all twenty-seven hundred Burger Whoppers all across the United States and Canada, which was for their Special Thick Steak Whopper Sandwich, made with U.S. government–inspected steak guaranteed to be a full quarter-inch thick.

I blinked at this poster, with its glossy color photo of the special Thick Steak Whopper Sandwich, and beside me the goofy guy said, "A steak out, right? A great night to come out and get one of those steak sandwiches and take it home and not worry about cooking or anything like that because, who knows, the electricity could go off at any second."

Well, that was true. The weather had been miserable the last few days, hovering just around the freezing point, with rain at times and sleet at times, and at the moment — 9:20 P.M. (2120 hours) on a Wednesday — outside the picture windows of the Burger Whopper, there was a thick, misty fog, wet to the touch, kind of streaked and dirty, that looked mostly like an airport hotel's laundry on the rinse cycle.

Not a good night for a stakeout — not my kind of stakeout. All the guys on the crew had been complaining and griping on our walkie-talkies, sitting in our cars on this endless surveillance, getting nowhere, expecting nothing, except maybe we'd all have the flu when this was finally over.

"See what I mean?" the goofy guy said, and grinned his buck-toothed grin at me again and gestured at that poster like the magician's girl assistant gesturing at the elephant. See the elephant?

"Right," I said, and I felt a sudden quick surge of relief. If our operation had been compromised, after all this time and energy and effort, particularly given my own spotty record, I don't know what I would have done. But at least it wouldn't have been my fault.

Well, it hadn't happened, and I wouldn't have to worry about it. My smile was probably as broad and goofy as the other guy's when I said, "I see it, I see it. A steak out on a night like this — I get you."

"I'm living alone since my wife left me," he explained, probably feeling we were buddies since my smile was as moronic as his. "So mostly I just open a can of soup or something. But weather like this, living alone, the fog out there, everything cold, you just kinda feel like you owe yourself a treat, know what I mean?"

Mostly, I was just astonished that this guy had ever *had* a wife, though not surprised she'd left him. I've never been married myself, never been that fortunate, my life being pretty much tied up with the Bureau, but I could imagine what it must be like to have *been* married, and then she walks out, and now you're not married anymore. And what now? It would be like if I screwed up *real* bad, much worse than usual, and the Bureau dropped me, and I wouldn't have the Bureau to go to anymore — I'd probably come out on foggy nights for a steak sandwich myself and talk to strangers in the line at the Burger Whopper.

Not that I'm a total screwup — don't get me wrong. If I were a total screwup, the Bureau would have terminated me (not with prejudice, just the old pink slip) a long time ago; the Bureau doesn't suffer fools, gladly or otherwise. But it's true I have made a few errors along the way and had luck turn against me, and so on, which in fact was why I was on this stakeout detail in the first place.

All of us. The whole crew, the whole night shift, seven guys in seven cars blanketing three square blocks in the Meridian Hills section of Indianapolis. Or was it Ravenswood? How do I know? — I don't know anything about Indianapolis. The Burger Whopper was a long drive from the stakeout site — that's all I know.

And we seven guys, we'd gotten this assignment, with no possibility of glory or advancement, with nothing but boredom and dyspepsia (the Burger Whopper is not my first choice for food) and chills and aches and no doubt the flu before it's over, because all seven of us had a few little dings and dents in our curricula vitae. Second-raters together, that's what we had to think about, losing self-esteem by the minute as we each sat alone there in our cars in the darkness, waiting in vain for François Figuer to make his move.

Art smuggling: has there ever been a greater potential for boredom? Madonna and Child, Madonna and Child, Madonna and Child. Who cares what wall they hang on, as long as it isn't mine, those cow-faced Madonnas and fat-kneed Childs? Still, as it turns out, there's a lively illegal trade in stolen art from Europe, particularly from defenseless churches over there, and that means a whole lot of Madonnas *und Kinder* entering America rolled up in umbrellas or disguised as Genoa salamis.

And at the center of this vast illegal conspiracy to bore Americans out of their pants was one François Figuer, a Parisian who was now a resident of the good old U.S. of A. And he was who we were out to get.

We knew a fresh shipment of stolen art was on its way, this time from the defenseless churches of Italy and consisting mostly of the second-favorite subject after M&C, being St. Sebastian — you know, the bird condo, the saint with all the arrows sticking out of him for the birds to perch on. Anyway, the Bureau had tracked the St. Sebastian shipment into the U.S. through the entry port at Norfolk, VA, but then had lost it. (Not us seven — some other bunch of screwups.) It was on its way to Figuer and whoever his customer might be, which is why we were there, blanketing his neighborhood, waiting for him to make his move. Meanwhile, it was, as my goofy new friend had suggested, a good night for a steak out.

Seven men, in seven cars, trying to outwait and outwit one wily art smuggler. In each car we had a police radio (in case we needed local backup); we had our walkie-talkie; and we had a manila folder on the passenger seat beside us, containing a map of the immediate area around Figuer's house and a blown-up surveillance photo of Figuer himself, with a written description on the back.

We sat in our cars, and we waited, and for five days nothing had happened. We knew Figuer was in the house, alone. We knew he and the courier must eventually make contact. We watched the arrivals of deliverymen from the supermarket and the liquor store and the Chinese restaurant, and when we checked, they were all three the normal deliverymen from those establishments. Then we replaced them with our own deliverymen and learned only that Figuer was a lousy tipper.

Did he know he was being watched? No idea, but probably not. In any event, we were here, and there was no alternative. If the courier arrived with a package that looked like a Genoa salami, we would pounce. If, instead, Figuer were to leave his house and go for a stroll or a drive, we would follow.

In the meantime we waited, with nothing to do. Couldn't read, even if we were permitted to turn on a light. We spoke together briefly on our walkie-talkies, that's all. And every night around nine, one of us would come here to the Burger Whopper to buy everyone's dinner. Tonight was my turn.

*

Apparently everybody in the world felt thick fog created a good night to eat out, to counteract a foggy night's enforced slowness with some fast food. The line had been longer than usual at the Burger Whopper when I arrived, and now it stretched another dozen people or so behind my new friend and me. A family of four (small, sticky-looking children, dazed father, furious mother), a young couple giggling and rubbing each other's bodies, another family, a hunched fellow with his hands moving in his raincoat pockets, and now more in line beyond him.

Ahead, however, the end was in sight. Either the Whopper management hadn't expected such a crowd on such a night, or the fog had kept one or more employees from getting to work; whatever the cause, there was only one cash register in use, run by an irritable fat girl in the clownish garnet-and-gray Burger Whopper costume. Each customer, upon reaching this girl, would sing out his or her order, and she would punch it into the register as if stabbing an enemy in his thousand eyes.

My new friend said, "It can get really boring sitting around in the car, can't it?"

I'd been miles away, in my own thoughts, brooding about this miserable assignment, and without thinking I answered, "Yeah, it sure can." But then I immediately caught myself and stared at the goof again and said, "*What?*"

"Boring sitting around in the car," he repeated. "And you get all stiff after a while."

This was true, but how did *he* know? Thinking, What is going *on* here? I said, "What do you mean, sitting around in the car? What do you mean?" And at the same time thinking, Should I take him into protective custody?

But the goof spread his hands, gesturing at the Burger Whopper all around us, and said, "That's why we're here, right? Instead of four blocks down the street at Radio Special."

Well, yes. Yes, that was true. Radio Special, another fast-food chain with a franchise joint not far from here, was set up like the drive-in deposit window at the bank. You drove up to the window, called your order into a microphone and a staticky voice told you how much it would cost. You put the money into a bin that slid out and back in, and a little later the bin would slide out a second time with your food and your change.

A lot of people prefer that sort of thing because they feel more secure being inside their own automobile, but us guys on stakeout find it too much of the same old same old. What we want, when there's any kind of excuse for it, is to be *out* of the car.

So I had to agree with my carrot-topped friend. "That's why I'm here, all right," I told him. "I don't like sitting around in a car any more than I have to."

"I'd hate a *job* like that, I can tell you," he said.

There was no way to respond to that without blowing my cover, so I just smiled at him and faced front.

The person ahead of me on line was being no trouble at all, for which I was thankful. Slender and attractive, with long, straight, ash-blond hair, she was apparently a college student and had brought along a skinny green loose-leaf binder full of her notes from some sort of math class. Trying to read over her shoulder, I saw nothing I recognized at all. But then she became aware of me and gave a disgusted little growl, and hunched farther over her binder, as though to hide her notes from the eavesdropper. Except that I realized she must have thought I was trying to look down the front of her sweater — it would have been worth the effort, but in fact I hadn't been — and I suddenly got so embarrassed that I automatically took a quick step backward and tromped down squarely on the goof's right foot.

"Ouch," he said, and gave me a little push, and I got my feet back where they belonged.

"Sorry," I said. "I just — I don't know what happened."

"You violated my civil rights there," he told me. "That's what happened." But he said it with his usual toothy grin.

What *was* this? For once, I decided to confront the weirdness head-on. "Guess it's a good thing I'm not a cop, then," I told him, "so I *can't* violate your civil rights."

"To tell you the truth," he said, "I've been wondering what you do for a living. I know it's nosy of me, but I can't ever help trying to figure people out. I'm Jim Henderson, by the way. I'm a high school math teacher."

He didn't offer to shake hands and neither did I, because I was mostly trying to find an alternate occupation for myself. I decided to borrow my sister's husband's. "Fred Barnes," I lied. "I'm a bus driver. I just got off my tour."

"Ah," he said. "I've been scoring math tests. Wanted to get away from it for a while."

Mathematicians in front of me and behind me — another coincidence. It's all coincidence, I told myself, nothing to worry about.

"I teach," Jim Henderson went on, "up at St. Sebastian's."

I stared at him. "St. Sebastian's?"

"Sure. You know it, don't you? Up on Rome Road."

"Oh, sure," I said.

The furious mother behind us said, "Move the line up, will ya?"

"Oh, sorry," I said, and looked around, and my girl math student had moved forward and was now second on line behind the person giving an order. So I was third, and the goof was fourth, and I didn't have much time to think about St. Sebastian's.

Was something up, or not? If I made a move and Jim Henderson was merely Jim Henderson, just like he'd said, I could be in big trouble, and the whole stakeout operation would definitely be compromised. But if I *didn't* make a move, and Jim Henderson actually turned out to be the courier or somebody else connected to François Figuer, and I let him slip through my fingers, I could be in big trouble all over again.

I realized now that it had never occurred to any of us that anybody else might listen in on our walkie-talkie conversations, even though we all knew they weren't secure. From time to time, on the walkie-talkies, we'd heard construction crews, a street-paving crew, even a movie crew on location, as they passed through our territory, talking to one another. But the idea that François Figuer, inside his house, might have his own walkie-talkie, or even a scanner, and might listen to us had never crossed our minds. Not that we talked much, on duty, back and forth, except to complain about the assignment or arrange for our evening meal. . . .

Our evening meal.

Who was Jim Henderson? What was he? I wished now I'd studied the picture of François Figuer more closely, but it had always been nighttime in that damn car. I'd never even read the material on the back of the picture. Who was François Figuer? Was he the kind of guy who would do . . . whatever this was?

Was all this — please, God — after all, just coincidence?

The customer at the counter got his sack of stuff and left. The math girl stood before the irritable Whopper girl and murmured her order, her voice too soft for me to hear — on purpose, I think. She didn't want to share *anything*, that girl.

I didn't have much more time to think, to plan, to decide. Soon it would be my turn at the counter. What did I have to base a suspicion on? Coincidence, that's all. Odd phrases, nothing more. If coincidences didn't happen, we wouldn't need a word for them.

All right. I'm ahead of Jim Henderson. I'll place my order, I'll get my food, I'll go outside, I'll wait in the car. When he comes out, I'll follow him. We'll see for sure who he is and where he goes.

Relieved, I was smiling when the math girl turned with her sack. She saw me, saw my smile and gave me a contemptuous glare. But her good opinion was not as important as my knowing I now had a plan, I could now become easier in my mind.

I stepped up to the counter, fishing the list out of my pants pocket. Seven guys and we all wanted something different. I announced it all, while the irritable girl spiked the register as though wishing it were *my* eyes, and throughout the process I kept thinking.

Where did Jim Henderson live? Could I find out by subtle interrogation techniques? Well, I would say to him, we're almost done here. You got far to go?

I turned, "Well," I said, and watched the mother whack one of the children across the top of the head, possibly in an effort to make him as stupid as she was. I saw this action very clearly because there was no one else in the way.

Henderson! Whoever! Where was he? All this time on line and just when he's about to reach the counter, he *leaves*?

"That man!" I spluttered at the furious mother, and pointed this way and that way, more or less at random. "He — Where — He —"

The whole family gave me a look of utter, unalterable, treelike incomprehension. They were going to be no help at all.

Oh, hell, oh, damn, oh, gol*darn* it! Henderson, my eye! He's, he's, he's either Figuer himself or somebody connected to him, and I let the damn man escape!

"Wenny-sen fory-three."

I started around the family, toward the distant door. The line of waiting people extended almost all the way down to the exit. Henderson was nowhere in sight.

"Hey!"

"Hey!"

The first "hey" was from the irritable Whopper girl, who'd also been the one who'd said "Wenny-sen fory-three," and the second "hey" was from the furious mother. Neither of them wanted me to complicate the routine.

"You gah *pay* futhis."

Oh, God, oh, God. Time is fleeting. Where's he gotten to? I grabbed at my hip pocket for my wallet, and it wasn't there.

He'd picked my pocket. Probably when I stepped on his foot. Son of a *gun*. Money. ID. . . .

"Cancel the order!" I cried, and ran for the door.

Many people behind me shouted that I couldn't do what I was already doing. I ignored them, pelted out of the Burger Whopper, ran through the swirling fog toward my car, my face and hands already clammy when I got there, and unlocked my way in.

Local police backup, that's what I needed. I slid behind the wheel, reached for the police-radio microphone and it wasn't there. I scraped my knuckles on the housing, expecting the microphone to be there, and it wasn't.

I switched on the interior light. The curly black cord from the mike to the radio was cut and dangling. He'd been in the car. *Damn* him. I slapped open the manila folder on the passenger seat and wasn't at all surprised that the photo of François Figuer was gone.

Would my walkie-talkie reach from here to the neighborhood of the stakeout? I had no idea, but it was my last means of communication, so I grabbed it up from its leather holster dangling from the dashboard — at least he hadn't taken *that* — thumbed the side down and said, "Tome here. Do you read me? Calling anybody. Tome here."

And then I noticed, when I thumbed the side down to broadcast, the little red light didn't come on.

Oh, that bastard. Oh, that French —

I slid open the panel on the back of the walkie-talkie, and of course the battery pack that was supposed to be in there was gone. But the space wasn't empty, oh no. A piece of paper was crumpled up inside there, where the battery pack usually goes.

I took the paper out of the walkie-talkie and smoothed it on the passenger seat beside me. It was the Figuer photo. I gazed at it. Without the thick black eyeglasses, without the buckteeth, without the carroty hair sticking out all around from under the turned-around baseball cap, this was him. It was *him.*

I turned the paper over, and now I read the back, and the words popped out at me like neon: "reckless," "daring," "fluent, unaccented American English," "strange sense of humor."

And across the bottom, in block letters in blue ink, had very recently been written: "THEY FORGOT TO MENTION 'MASTER OF DISGUISE.' ENJOY YOUR STEAK OUT. — FF"

STEVE YARBROUGH

The Rest of Her Life

FROM *Missouri Review*

THE DOG was a mixture of God knows how many breeds, but the vet had told them he had at least some rottweiler blood. You could see it in his shoulders, you could hear it when he barked, which he was doing that night when they pulled up at the gate and Chuckie cut the engine.

"Butch is out," Dee Ann said. "That's kind of strange."

Chuckie didn't say anything. He'd looked across the yard and seen her momma's car in the driveway, and he was disappointed. Dee Ann's momma had told her earlier that she was going to buy some garden supplies at Western Auto and then eat something at the Sonic, and she'd said if she got back home and unloaded her purchases in time, she might run over to Greenville with one of her friends and watch a movie. Dee Ann had relayed the news to Chuckie tonight when he picked her up from work. That had gotten his hopes up.

The last two Saturday nights her momma had gone to Greenville, and they'd made love on the couch. They'd done it before in the car, but Chuckie said it was a lot nicer when you did it in the house. As far as she was concerned, the major difference was that they stood a much greater chance of getting caught. If her momma had walked in on them, she would not have gone crazy and ordered Chuckie away, she would have stayed calm and sat down and warned them not to do something that could hurt them later on. "There're things y'all can do now," she would have said, "that can mess y'all's lives up bad."

Dee Ann leaned across the seat and kissed Chuckie. "You don't smell *too* much like a Budweiser brewery," she said. "Want to come in with me?"

"Sure."

Butch was waiting at the gate, whimpering, his front paws up on the railing. Dee Ann released the latch, and they went in and walked across the yard, the dog trotting along behind them.

The front door was locked — a fact that Chuckie corroborated the next day. She knocked, but even though both the living room and the kitchen were lit up, her momma didn't come. Dee Ann waited a few seconds, then rummaged through her purse and found the key. It didn't occur to her that somebody might have come home with her momma, that they might be back in the bedroom together, doing what she and Chuckie had done. Her momma still believed that if she could tough it out a few more months, Dee Ann's daddy would recover his senses and come back. Most of his belongings were still here.

Dee Ann unlocked the door and pushed it open. Crossing the threshold, she looked back over her shoulder at Chuckie. His eyes were shut. They didn't stay shut for long, he was probably just blinking, but that instant in which she saw them closed was enough to frighten her. She quickly looked into the living room. Everything was as it should be: the black leather couch stood against the far wall, the glass coffee table in front of it, two armchairs pulled up to the table at forty-five degree angles. The paper lay on the mantelpiece, right where her momma always left it.

"Momma?" she called. "It's me and Chuckie."

As she waited for a reply, the dog rushed past her. He darted into the kitchen. Again they heard him whimper.

She made an effort to follow the dog, but Chuckie laid his hand on her shoulder. "Wait a minute," he said. Afterwards he could never explain to anyone's satisfaction, least of all his own, why he had restrained her.

Earlier that evening, as she stood behind the checkout counter at the grocery store where she was working that summer, she had seen her daddy. He was standing on the sidewalk, looking in through the thick plate glass window, grinning at her.

It was late, and as always on Saturday evening, downtown Loring was virtually deserted. If people wanted to shop or go someplace to eat, they'd be out on the highway, at the Sonic or the new Pizza Hut. If they had enough money, they'd just head for Greenville. It had been a long time since anything much went on downtown after dark, which made her daddy's presence here that much more unusual. He waved, then walked over to the door.

The manager was in back, totalling the day's receipts. Except for him and Dee Ann and one stock boy who was over in the dairy aisle sweeping up, the store was empty.

Her daddy wore a pair of khaki pants and a short-sleeved pullover with an alligator on the pocket. He had on his funny-looking leather cap that reminded her of the ones policemen wore. He liked to wear that cap when he was out driving the MG.

"Hey, sweets," he said.

Even with the counter between them, she could smell whiskey on his breath. He had that strange light in his eyes.

"Hi, Daddy."

"When'd you start working nights?"

"A couple of weeks back."

"Don't get in the way of you and Buckie, does it?"

She started to correct him, tell him her boyfriend's name was Chuckie, but then she thought *Why bother?* He'd always been the kind of father who couldn't remember how old she was or what grade she was in. Sometimes he had trouble remembering she existed: years ago he'd brought her to this same grocery store, and after buying some food for his hunting dog, he'd forgotten about her and left her sitting on the floor in front of the magazine rack. The store manager had carried her home.

"Working nights is okay," she said. "My boyfriend'll be picking me up in a few minutes."

"Got a big night planned?"

"We'll probably just ride around a little bit and then head on home."

Her daddy reached into his pocket and pulled out his wallet. He extracted a twenty and handed it to her. "Here," he said. "You kids do something fun. On me. See a movie or get yourselves a six-pack of Dr. Pepper."

He laughed, to show her he wasn't serious about the Dr. Pepper, and then he stepped around the end of the counter and kissed her cheek. "You're still the greatest little girl in the world," he said. "Even if you're not very little anymore."

He was holding her close. In addition to whiskey, she could smell after-shave and deodorant and something else — a faint trace of perfume. She hadn't seen the MG on the street, but it was probably parked in the lot outside, and she bet his girlfriend was in it. She was just three years older than Dee Ann, a junior up at Delta State, though people said she wasn't going to school anymore. She and Dee Ann's daddy were living together in an apartment near the flower shop he used to own and run. He'd sold the shop last fall, just before he left home.

He didn't work anymore, and Dee Ann's momma had said she didn't know how he aimed to live, once the money from his business was gone. The other thing she didn't know — because nobody had told her — was that folks said his girlfriend sold drugs. Folks said he might be involved in that too.

He pecked her on the cheek once more, told her to have a good time with her boyfriend and to tell her momma he said hello, and then he walked out the door. Just as he left, the manager hit the switch, and the aisle lights went off.

That last detail — the lights going off when he walked out of the store — must have been significant, because the next day, as Dee Ann sat on the couch at her grandmother's house, knee to knee with the Loring County sheriff, Jim Wheeler, it kept coming up.

"You're sure about that?" Wheeler said for the third or fourth time. "When your daddy left the Safeway, Mr. Lindsey was just turning out the lights?"

Her grandmother was in bed down the hall. The doctor and two women from the Methodist church were with her. She'd been having chest pains off and on all day.

The dining room table was covered with food people had brought: two hams, a roast, a fried chicken, dish upon dish of potato salad, cole slaw, baked beans, two or three pecan pies, a pound cake. By the time the sheriff came, Chuckie had been there twice already — once in the morning with his momma and again in the afternoon with his daddy — and both times he had eaten. While his mother sat on the couch with Dee Ann, sniffling and holding her hand, and his father admired the knickknacks on the mantelpiece, Chuckie had parked himself at the dining room table and begun devouring one slice of pie after another, occasionally glancing through the doorway at Dee Ann. The distance between where he was and where she was could not be measured by any known means. She knew it, and he did, but he apparently believed that if he kept his mouth full, they wouldn't have to acknowledge it yet.

"Yes sir," she told the sheriff. "He'd just left when Mr. Lindsey turned off the lights."

A pocket-sized notebook lay open on Wheeler's knee. He held a ball-point pen with his stubby fingers. He didn't know it yet, but he was going to get a lot of criticism for what he did in the next few days. Some people would say it cost him re-election. "And what time does Mr. Lindsey generally turn off the lights on a Saturday night?"

"Right around eight o'clock."

"And was that when he did it last night?"

"Yes sir."

"You're sure about that?"

"Yes sir."

"Well, that's what Mr. Lindsey says too," Wheeler said. He closed the notebook and put it in his shirt pocket. "Course, being as he was in the back of the store, he didn't actually see you talking with your daddy."

"No," she said. "You can't see the check-out stands from back there."

Wheeler stood, and she did too. To her surprise, he pulled her close to him. He was a compact man, not much taller than she was.

She felt his warm breath on her cheek. "I sure am sorry about all of this, honey," he said. "But don't you worry. I guarantee you I'll get to the bottom of it. Even if it kills me."

Even if it kills me.

She remembers that phrase in those rare instances when she sees Jim Wheeler on the street downtown. He's an old man now, in his early sixties, white-haired and potbellied. For years he's worked at the catfish plant, though nobody seems to know what he does. Most people can tell you what he doesn't do. He's not responsible for security — he doesn't carry a gun. He's not front-office. He's not a foreman or a shift supervisor, and he has nothing to do with the live-haul trucks.

Chuckie works for Delta Electric, and once a month he goes to

the plant to service the generators. He says Wheeler is always outside, wandering around, his head down, his feet scarcely rising off
the pavement. Sometimes he talks to himself.

"I was out there last week," Chuckie told her not long ago, "and
I'd just gone through the front gates, and there he was. He was off
to my right, walking along the fence, carrying this bucket."

"What kind of bucket?"

"Looked like maybe it had some kind of caulking mix in it —
there was this thick white stuff sticking to the sides. Anyway, he was
shuffling along there, and he was talking to beat the band."

"What was he saying?"

They were at the breakfast table when they had this conversation.
Their daughter Cynthia was finishing a bowl of cereal and staring
into an algebra textbook. Chuckie glanced toward Cynthia, rolled
his eyes at Dee Ann, then looked down at the table. He lifted his
coffee cup, drained it, and left for work.

But that night, when he crawled into bed beside her and
switched off the light, she brought it up again. "I want to know what
Jim Wheeler was saying to himself," she said. "When you saw him
last week."

They weren't touching — they always left plenty of space between them — but she could tell he'd gone rigid. He did his best to
sound groggy. "Nothing much."

She was rigid now too, lying stiffly on her back, staring up into
the dark. "Nothing much is not nothing. Nothing much is still
something."

"Won't you ever let it go?"

"*You* brought his name up. You bring his name up, then you get
this reaction from me, and then you're mad."

He rolled onto his side. He was looking at her, but she knew he
couldn't make out her features. He wouldn't lay his palm on her
cheek, wouldn't trace her jawbone like he used to. "Yeah, I brought
his name up," he said. "I bring his name up, if you've noticed, about
once a year. I bring his name up, and I bring up Lou Pierce's name,
and I'd bring up Barry Lancaster's name too if he hadn't had the
good fortune to move on to bigger things than being DA in a
ten-cent town. I keep hoping I'll bring one of their names up, and
after I say it, it'll be like I just said John Doe or Cecil Poe or
Theodore J. Bilbo. I keep hoping I'll say it and you'll just let it go."

The ceiling fan, which was turned off, had begun to take shape. It looked like a big dark bird, frozen in mid-swoop. Three or four times she had woken up near dawn and seen that shape there, and it was all she could do to keep from screaming. One time she stuck her fist in her mouth and bit her knuckle.

"What was he saying?"

"He was talking to a quarterback."

"What?"

"He was talking to a quarterback. He was saying some kind of crap like 'Hit Jimmy over the middle.' He probably walks around all day thinking about when he was playing football in high school, going over games in his mind."

He rolled away from her then, got as close to the edge of the bed as he could. "He's just like you," he said. "He's stuck back there too."

She had seen her daddy several times in between that Saturday night — when Chuckie walked into the kitchen murmuring, "Mrs. Williams? Mrs. Williams?" — and the funeral, which was held the following Wednesday morning. He had come to her grandmother's house Sunday evening, had gone into her grandmother's room and sat by the bed, holding her hand and sobbing. Dee Ann remained in the living room, and she heard their voices, heard her daddy saying, "Remember how she had those big rings under her eyes after Dee Ann was born? How we all said she looked like a pretty little raccoon?" Her grandmother, whose chest pains had finally stopped, said, "Oh, Allen, I raised her from the cradle, and I know her well. She never would've stopped loving you." Then her daddy started crying again, and her grandmother joined in.

When he came out and walked down the hall to the living room, he had stopped crying, but his eyes were red-rimmed and his face looked puffy. He sat down in the armchair, which was still standing right where the sheriff had left it that afternoon. For a long time he said nothing. Then he rested his elbows on his knees, propped his chin on his fists, and said, "Were you the one that found her?"

"Chuckie did."

"Did you go in there?"

She nodded.

"He's an asshole for letting you do that."

She didn't bother to tell him how she'd torn herself out of Chuckie's grasp and bolted into the kitchen, or what had happened when she got in there. She was already starting to think what she would later know for certain: in the kitchen she had died. When she saw the pool of blood on the linoleum, saw the streaks that shot like flames up the wall, a thousand-volt jolt hit her heart. She lost her breath, and the room went dark, and when it relit itself she was somebody else.

Her momma's body lay in a lump on the floor, over by the door that led to the back porch. The shotgun that had killed her, her daddy's Remington Wingmaster, stood propped against the kitchen counter. Back in what had once been called the game room, the sheriff would find that somebody had pulled down all the guns — six rifles, the other shotgun, both of her daddy's .38's — and thrown them on the floor. He'd broken the lock on the metal cabinet that stood nearby and he'd removed the box of shells and loaded the Remington.

It was hard to say what he'd been after, this man who for her was still a dark, faceless form. Her momma's purse had been ransacked, her wallet was missing, but there couldn't have been much money in it. She had some jewelry in the bedroom, but he hadn't messed with that. The most valuable things in the house were probably the guns themselves, but he hadn't taken them.

He'd come in through the back door — the lock was broken — and he'd left through the back door. Why Butch hadn't taken his leg off was anybody's guess. When the sheriff and his deputies showed up, it was all Chuckie could do to keep the dog from attacking.

"She wouldn't of wanted you to see her like that," her daddy said. "Nor me either." He spread his hands and looked at them, turning them over and scrutinizing his palms, as if he intended to read his own fortune. "I reckon I was lucky," he said, letting his gaze meet hers. "Anything you want to tell me about it?"

She shook her head no. The thought of telling him how she felt seemed somehow unreal. It had been years since she'd told him how she felt about anything that mattered.

"Life's too damn short," he said. "Our family's become one of those statistics you read about in the papers. You read those stories and you think it won't ever be you. Truth is, there's no way to insure against it."

At the time, the thing that struck her as odd was his use of the word *family*. They hadn't been a family for a long time, not as far as she was concerned.

She forgot about what he'd said until a few days later. What she remembered about that visit with him on Sunday night was that for the second time in twenty-four hours, he pulled her close and hugged her and gave her twenty dollars.

She saw him again Monday at the funeral home, and the day after that, and then the next day, at the funeral, she sat between him and her grandmother, and he held her hand while the preacher prayed. She had wondered if he would bring his girl-friend, but even he must have realized that would be inappropriate.

He apparently did not think it inappropriate, though, or unwise either, to present himself at the offices of an insurance company in Jackson on Friday morning, bringing with him her mother's death certificate and a copy of the coroner's report.

When she thinks of the morning — a Saturday — on which Wheeler came to see her for the second time, she always imagines her own daughter sitting there on the couch at her grandmother's place instead of her. She sees Cynthia looking at the silver badge on Wheeler's shirt pocket, sees her glancing at the small notebook that lies open in his lap, at the pen gripped so tightly between his fingers that his knuckles have turned white.

"Now the other night," she hears Wheeler say, "your boyfriend picked you up at what time?"

"Right around eight o'clock." Her voice is weak, close to break-ing. She just talked to her boyfriend an hour ago, and he was scared. His parents were pissed — pissed at Wheeler, pissed at him, but above all pissed at her. If she hadn't been dating their son, none of them would have been subjected to the awful experience they've just gone through this morning. They're devout Baptists, they don't drink or smoke, they've never seen the inside of a night-club, their names have never before been associated with unseemly acts. Now the sheriff has entered their home and questioned their son as if he were a common criminal. It will cost the sheriff their votes come November. She's already lost their votes. She lost them when her daddy left her momma and started running around with a young girl.

"The reason I'm kind of stuck on this eight o'clock business,"

Wheeler says, "is you say that along about that time's when your daddy was there to see you."

"Yes sir."

"Now your boyfriend claims he didn't see your daddy leaving the store. Says he didn't even notice the MG on the street."

"Daddy'd been gone a few minutes already. Plus, I think he parked around back."

"Parked around back," the sheriff says.

"Yes sir."

"In that lot over by the bayou."

Even more weakly: "Yes sir."

"Where the delivery trucks come in — ain't that where they usually park?"

"I believe so. Yes sir."

Wheeler's pen pauses. He lays it on his knee. He turns his hands over, studying them as her daddy did a few days before. He's looking at his hands when he asks the next question. "Any idea why your daddy'd park his car *behind* the Safeway — where there generally don't nothing but delivery trucks park — when Main Street was almost deserted and there was a whole row of empty spaces right in front of the store?"

The sheriff knows the answer as well as she does. When you're with a woman you're not married to, you don't park your car on Main Street on a Saturday night. Particularly if it's a little MG with no top on it, and your daughter's just a few feet away, with nothing but a pane of glass between her and a girl who's not much older than she is. That's how she explains it to herself anyway. At least for today.

"I think maybe he had his girlfriend with him."

"Well, I don't aim to hurt your feelings, honey," Wheeler says, looking at her now, "but there's not too many people that don't know about his girlfriend."

"Yes sir."

"You reckon he might've parked out back for any other reason?"

She can't answer that question, so she doesn't even try.

"There's not any chance, is there," he says, "that your boyfriend could've been confused about when he picked you up?"

"No sir."

"You're sure about that?"

She knows that Wheeler has asked Chuckie where he was between seven-fifteen, when several people saw her mother eating a
burger at the Sonic Drive-in, and eight-thirty, when the two of them
found her body. Chuckie has told Wheeler he was at home watching TV between seven-fifteen and a few minutes till eight, when he
got in the car and went to pick up Dee Ann. His parents were in
Greenville eating supper at that time, so they can't confirm his
story.

"Yes sir," she says, "I'm sure about it."

"And you're certain your daddy was there just a few minutes
before eight?"

"Yes sir."

"Because your daddy," the sheriff says, "remembers things just a
little bit different. The way your daddy remembers it, he came by
the Safeway about seven-thirty and hung around there talking with
you for half an hour. Course, Mr. Lindsey was in the back, so he
can't say yea or nay, and the stock boy don't seem to have the sense
God give a betsy bug. Your daddy was over at the VFW drinking beer
at eight o'clock — stayed there till almost ten, according to any
number of people, and his girlfriend wasn't with him. Fact is, his
girlfriend left the country last Thursday morning. Took a flight
from New Orleans to Mexico City, and from there it looks like she
went on to Argentina."

Dee Ann, imagining this scene in which her daughter reprises
the role she once played, sees Cynthia's face go slack as the full
force of the information strikes her. She's still sitting there like that
— hands useless in her lap, face drained of blood — when Jim
Wheeler tells her that six months ago, her daddy took out a life
insurance policy on her momma that includes double indemnity in
the event of accidental death.

"I hate to be the one telling you this, honey," he says, "because
you're a girl who's had enough bad news to last the rest of her
life. But your daddy stands to collect half a million dollars because
of your momma's death, and there's a number of folks — and I
reckon I might as well admit I happen to be among them — who
are starting to think that ought not to occur."

Chuckie gets off work at Delta Electric at six o'clock. A year or so
ago she became aware that he'd started coming home late. The first

time it happened, he told her he'd gone out with his friend Tim to have a beer. She saw Tim the next day buying a case of motor oil at Wal-Mart, and she almost referred to his and Chuckie's night out just to see if he looked surprised. But if he'd looked surprised, it would have worried her, and if he hadn't, it would have worried her even more: she would have seen it as a sign that Chuckie had talked to him beforehand. So in the end she nodded at Tim and kept her mouth shut.

It began happening more and more often. Chuckie ran over to Greenville to buy some parts for his truck, he ran down to Yazoo City for a meeting with his regional supervisor. He ran up into the north part of the county because a fellow there had placed an interesting ad in *National Rifleman* — he was selling a shotgun with fancy scrollwork on the stock.

On the evenings when Chuckie isn't home, she avoids latching onto Cynthia. She wants her daughter to have her own life, to be independent, even if independence, in a sixteen-year-old girl, manifests itself as distance from her mother. Cynthia is on the phone a lot, talking to her girlfriends, to boyfriends too. Through the bedroom door Dee Ann hears her laughter.

On the evenings when Chuckie isn't home, she sits on the couch alone, watching TV, reading, or listening to music. If it's a Friday or Saturday night and Cynthia is out with her friends, Dee Ann goes out herself. She doesn't go to movies, where her presence might make Cynthia feel crowded if she happened to be in the theater too, and she doesn't go out and eat at any of the handful of restaurants in town. Instead she takes long walks. Sometimes they last until ten or eleven o'clock.

Every now and then, when she's on one of these walks, passing one house after another where families sit parked before the TV set, she allows herself to wish she had a dog to keep her company. What she won't allow herself to do — has never allowed herself to do as an adult — is actually own one.

The arrest of her father is preserved in a newspaper photo.

He has just gotten out of Sheriff Wheeler's car. The car stands parked in the alleyway between the courthouse and the fire station. Sheriff Wheeler is in the picture too, standing just to the left of her father, and so is one of his deputies. The deputy has his hand on her father's right forearm, and he is staring straight into the camera, as is Sheriff Wheeler. Her daddy is the only one who appears not to notice that his picture is being taken. He is looking off to the left, in the direction of Loring Street, which you can't see in the photo, though she knows it's there.

When she takes the photo out and examines it, something she does with increasing frequency these days, she wonders why her daddy is not looking at the camera. A reasonable conclusion, she knows, would be that since he's about to be arraigned on murder charges, he doesn't want his face in the paper. But she wonders if there isn't more to it. He doesn't look particularly worried. He's not exactly smiling, but there aren't a lot of lines around his mouth, like there would be if he felt especially tense. Were he not wearing handcuffs, were he not flanked on either side by officers of the law, you would probably have to say he looks relaxed.

Then there's the question of what he's looking at. Lou Pierce's office is on Loring Street, and Loring Street is what's off the page, out of the picture. Even if the photographer had wanted to capture it in this photo, he couldn't have, not as long as he was intent on capturing the images of these three men. By choosing to photograph them, he chose not to photograph something else, and sometimes what's outside the frame may be more important than what's actually in it.

After all, Loring Street is south of the alley. And so is Argentina.

"You think he'd do that?" Chuckie said. "You think he'd actually kill your momma?"

They were sitting in his pickup when he asked her that question. The pickup was parked on a turnrow in somebody's cotton patch on a Saturday afternoon in August. By then her daddy had been in jail for the better part of two weeks. The judge had denied him bail, apparently believing that he aimed to leave the country. The judge couldn't have known that her daddy had no intention of leaving the country without the insurance money, which had been placed in an escrow account and wouldn't be released until he'd been cleared of the murder charges.

The cotton patch they were parked in was way up close to Cleveland. Chuckie's parents had forbidden him to go out with Dee Ann again, so she'd hiked out to the highway, and he'd picked her up on

the side of the road. In later years she'll often wonder whether or
not she and Chuckie would have stayed together and gotten married if his parents hadn't placed her off-limits.

"I don't know," she said. "He sure did lie about coming to see me.
And then there's Butch. If somebody broke in, he'd tear them to
pieces. But he wouldn't hurt Daddy."

"I don't believe it," Chuckie said. A can of Bud stood clamped
between his thighs. He lifted it and took a swig. "Your daddy may
have acted a little wacky, running off like he did and taking up with
that girl, but to shoot your momma and then come in the grocery
store and grin at you and hug you? You really think *anybody* could
do a thing like that?"

What Dee Ann was beginning to think was that almost everybody
could do a thing like that. She didn't know why this was so, but she
believed it had something to do with being an adult and having ties.
Having ties meant you were bound to certain things — certain people, certain places, certain ways of living. Breaking a tie was a violent act — even if all you did was walk out door number one and
enter door number two — and one act of violence could lead to
another. You didn't have to spill blood to take a life. But after taking
a life, you still might spill blood, if spilling blood would get you
something else you wanted.

"I don't know what he might have done," she said.

"Every time I was ever around him," Chuckie said, "he was in a
nice mood. I remember going in the flower shop with Momma
when I was a kid. Your daddy was always polite and friendly. Used to
give me free lollipops."

"Yeah, well, he never gave me any lollipops. And besides, your
momma used to be real pretty."

"What's that supposed to mean?"

"It's not supposed to mean anything. I'm just stating a fact."

"You saying she's not pretty now?"

His innocence startled her. If she handled him right, Dee Ann
realized, she could make him do almost anything she wanted. For
an instant she was tempted to put her hand inside his shirt, stroke
his chest a couple of times, and tell him to climb out of the truck
and stand on his head. She wouldn't always have such leverage, but
she had it now, and a voice in her head urged her to exploit it.

"I'm not saying she's not pretty anymore," Dee Ann said. "I'm

just saying that of course Daddy was nice to her. He was always nice
to nice-looking women."

"Your momma was a nice-looking lady too."

"Yeah, but my momma was his wife."

Chuckie turned away and gazed out at the cotton patch for several seconds. When he looked back at her, he said, "You know
what, Dee Ann? You're not making much sense." He took another
sip of beer, then pitched the can out the window. "But with all
you've been through," he said, starting the engine, "I don't wonder
at it."

He laid his hand on her knee. It stayed there until twenty minutes later, when he let her out on the highway right where he'd
picked her up.

Sometimes in her mind she has trouble separating all the men. It's
as if they're revolving around her, her daddy and Chuckie and Jim
Wheeler and Lou Pierce and Barry Lancaster, as if she's sitting
motionless in a hard chair, in a small room, and they're orbiting
her so fast that their faces blur into a single image which seems
suspended just inches away. She smells them too: smells after-shave
and cologne, male sweat and whiskey.

Lou Pierce was a man she'd been seeing around town for as long
as she could remember. He had red hair and always wore a striped
long-sleeved shirt and a wide tie that was usually loud-colored. You
would see him crossing Loring Street, a coffee cup in one hand, his
briefcase in the other. His office was directly across the street from
the courthouse, where he spent much of his life — either visiting
his clients in the jail, which was on the top floor, or defending those
same clients downstairs in the courtroom itself.

Many years after he represented her father, Lou Pierce would
find himself up on the top floor again, on the other side of the bars
this time, accused of exposing himself to a twelve-year-old girl. After
the story made the paper, several other women, most in their twenties or early thirties, would contact the local police and allege that
he had also shown himself to them.

He showed himself to Dee Ann too, though not the same part of
himself he showed to the twelve-year-old girl. He came to see her at
her grandmother's on a weekday evening sometime after the beginning of the fall semester — she knows school was in session because

she remembers that the morning after Lou Pierce visited her, she had to sit beside his son Raymond in senior English.

Lou sat in the same armchair that Jim Wheeler had pulled up near the coffee table. He didn't have his briefcase with him, but he was wearing another of those wide ties. This one, if she remembers correctly, had a pink background, with white fleurs-de-lys.

"How you making it, honey?" he said. "You been holding up all right?"

She shrugged. "Yes sir. I guess so."

"Your daddy's awful worried about you." He picked up the cup of coffee her grandmother had brought him before leaving them alone. "I don't know if you knew that or not," he said, taking a sip of the coffee. He set the cup back down. "He mentioned you haven't been to see him."

He was gazing directly at her.

"No sir," she said, "I haven't gotten by there."

"You know what that makes folks think, don't you?"

She dropped her head. "No sir."

"Makes 'em think you believe your daddy did it."

That was the last thing he said for two or three minutes. He sat there sipping his coffee, looking around the room, almost as if he were a real estate agent sizing up the house. Just as she decided he'd said all he intended to, his voice came back at her.

"Daddies fail," he told her. "Lordy, how we fail. You could ask Raymond. I doubt he'd tell the truth, though, because sons tend to be protective of their daddies, just like a good daughter protects her momma. But the *truth,* if you wanted to dig into it, is that I've failed that boy nearly every day he's been alive. You notice he's in the band? Hell, he can't kick a football or hit a baseball, and that's nobody's fault but mine. I remember when he was this tall —" He held his hand, palm down, three feet from the floor. "— he came to me dragging this little plastic bat and said, 'Daddy, teach me to hit a baseball.' And you know what I told him? I told him, 'Son, I'm defending a man that's facing life in prison, and I got to go before the judge tomorrow morning and plead his case. You can take that bat and you can hitch a kite to it and see if the contraption won't fly.'"

He reached across the table then and laid his hand on her knee. She tried to remember who else had done that recently, but for the moment she couldn't recall.

When he spoke again, he kept his voice low, as if he were afraid he'd be overheard. "Dee Ann, what I'm telling you," he said, "is I know there are a lot of things about your daddy that make you feel conflicted. There's a lot of things he's done that he shouldn't have, and there's things he should have done that he didn't. There's a bunch of *shoulds* and *shouldn'ts* bumping around in your head, so it's no surprise to me that you'd get confused on this question of time."

She'd heard people say that if they were ever guilty of a crime, they wanted Lou Pierce to defend them. Now she knew why.

But she wasn't guilty of a crime, and she said so: "I'm not confused about time. He came when I said he did."

As if she were a sworn witness, Lou Pierce began, gently, regretfully, to ask her a series of questions. Did she really think her daddy was stupid enough to take out a life insurance policy on her mother and then kill her? If he aimed to leave the country with his girlfriend, would he send the girl first and then kill Dee Ann's momma and try to claim the money? Did she know that her daddy intended to put the money in a savings account for her?

Did she know that her daddy and his girlfriend had broken up, that the girl had left the country chasing some young South American who, her daddy had admitted, probably sold her drugs?

When he saw that she wasn't going to answer any of the questions, Lou Pierce looked down at the floor. "Honey," he said softly, "did you ever ask yourself why your daddy left you and your momma?"

That was one question she was willing and able to answer. "He did it because he didn't love us."

When he looked at her again, his eyes were wet — and she hadn't learned yet that wet eyes tell the most effective lies. "He loved y'all," Lou Pierce said. "But your momma, who was a wonderful lady — angel, she wouldn't give your daddy a physical life. I guarantee you he wishes to God he hadn't needed one, but a man's not made that way . . . and even though it embarrasses me, I guess I ought to add that I'm speaking from personal experience."

At the age of thirty-eight, Dee Ann has acquired a wealth of experience, but the phrase *personal experience* is one she almost never uses. She's noticed men are a lot quicker to employ it than women are. Maybe it's because men think their experiences are somehow more personal than everybody else's. Or maybe it's because they take everything personally.

"My own personal experience," Chuckie told Cynthia the other day at the dinner table, after she'd finished ninth in the voting for one of eight positions on the cheerleading squad, "has been that getting elected cheerleader's nothing more than a popularity contest, and I wouldn't let not getting elected worry me for two seconds."

Dee Ann couldn't help it. "When in the world," she said, "did you have a *personal* experience with a cheerleader election?"

He laid his fork down. They stared at one another across a bowl of spaghetti. Cynthia, who can detect a developing storm front as well as any meteorologist, wiped her mouth on her napkin, stood up, and said, "Excuse me."

Chuckie kept his mouth shut until she'd left the room. "I *voted* in cheerleader elections."

"What was personal about that experience?"

"It was my own personal vote."

"Did you have any emotional investment in that vote?"

"You ran once. I voted for you. I was emotional about you then."

She didn't even question him about his use of the word *then* — she knew perfectly well why he used it. "And when I didn't win," she said, "you took it personally?"

"I felt bad for you."

"But not nearly as bad as you felt for yourself?"

"Why in the hell would I feel bad for myself?"

"Having a girlfriend who couldn't win a popularity contest — wasn't that hard on you? Didn't you take it personally?"

He didn't answer. He just sat there looking at her over the bowl of spaghetti, his eyes hard as sandstone and every bit as dry.

Cynthia walks home from school, and several times in the last couple of years, Dee Ann, driving through town on her way back from a shopping trip or a visit to the library, has come across her daughter. Cynthia hunches over as she walks, her canvas backpack slung over her right shoulder, her eyes studying the sidewalk as if she's trying to figure out the pavement's composition. She may be thinking about her boyfriend or some piece of idle gossip she heard that day at school, or she may be trying to remember if the fourth president was James Madison or James Monroe, but her posture and the concentrated way she gazes down suggest that she's a girl who believes she has a problem.

Whether or not this is so Dee Ann doesn't know, because if her daughter is worried about something she's never mentioned it. What Dee Ann does know is that whenever she's out driving and she sees Cynthia walking home, she always stops the car, rolls her window down, and says, "Want a ride?" Cynthia always looks up and smiles, not the least bit startled, and she always says yes. She's never once said no, like Dee Ann did to three different people that day twenty years ago, when, instead of going to her grandmother's after school, she walked all the way from the highway to the courthouse and climbed the front steps and stood staring at the heavy oak door for several seconds before she pushed it open.

Her daddy has gained weight. His cheeks have grown round, the backs of his hands are plump. He's not getting any exercise to speak of. On Tuesday and Wednesday nights, he tells her, the prisoners who want to keep in shape are let out of their cells, one at a time, and allowed to jog up and down three flights of stairs for ten minutes each. He says an officer sits in a straight-backed chair down in the courthouse lobby with a rifle across his lap to make sure that the prisoners don't jog any farther.

Her daddy is sitting on the edge of his cot. He's wearing blue denim pants and a shirt to match, and a patch on the pocket of the shirt says *Loring County Jail*. The shoes he has on aren't really shoes. They look like bedroom slippers.

Downstairs, when she checked in with the jailer, Jim Wheeler heard her voice and came out of his office. While she waited for the jailer to get the right key, the sheriff asked her how she was doing.

"All right, I guess."

"You may think I'm lying, honey," he said, "but the day'll come when you'll look back on this time in your life and it won't seem like nothing but a real bad dream."

Sitting in a hard plastic chair, looking at her father, she already feels like she's in a bad dream. He's smiling at her, waiting for her to say something, but her tongue feels like it's fused to the roof of her mouth.

The jail is air conditioned, but it's hot in the cell, and the place smells bad. The toilet over in the corner has no lid on it. She wonders how in the name of God a person can eat in a place like this. And what kind of person could actually eat enough to gain weight?

As if he knows what she's thinking, her father says, "You're probably wondering how I can stand it."

She doesn't answer.

"I can stand it," he says, "because I know I deserved to be locked up."

He sits there a moment longer, then gets up off the cot and shuffles over to the window, which has three bars across it. He stands there looking out. "All my life," he finally says, "I've been going in and out of all those buildings down there and I never once asked myself what they looked like from above. Now I know. There's garbage on those roofs and bird shit. One day I saw a man sitting up there, drinking from a paper bag. Right on top of the jewelry store."

He turns around then and walks over and lays his hand on her shoulder.

"When I was down there," he says, "scurrying around like a chicken with its head cut off, I never gave myself enough time to think. That's one thing I've had plenty of in here. And I can tell you, I've seen some things I was too blind to see then."

He keeps his hand on her shoulder the whole time he's talking. "In the last few weeks," he says, "I asked myself how you must have felt when I told you I was too busy to play with you, how you probably felt every time you had to go to the theater by yourself and you saw all those other little girls waiting in line with their daddies and holding their hands." He says he's seen all the ways in which he failed them both, her and her mother, and he knows they both saw them a long time ago. He just wishes to God *he* had.

He takes his hand off her shoulder, goes back over to the cot, and sits down. She watches, captivated, as his eyes begin to glisten. She realizes that she's in the presence of a man capable of anything, and for the first time she knows the answer to a question that has always baffled her: why would her momma put up with so much for so long?

The answer is that her daddy is a natural performer, and her momma was his natural audience. Her momma lived for these routines, she watched till watching killed her.

With watery eyes, Dee Ann's daddy looks at her, here in a stinking room in the county courthouse. "Sweetheart," he whispers, "you don't think I killed her, do you?"

When she speaks, her voice will be steady, it won't crack and break. She will display no more emotion than if she were responding to a question posed by her history teacher.

"No sir," she tells her daddy. "I don't think you killed her. I *know* you did."

In that instant the weight of his life begins to crush her.

Ten-thirty on a Saturday night in 1997. She's standing alone in an alleyway outside the Loring County Courthouse. It's the same alley where her father and Jim Wheeler and the deputy had their pictures taken all those years ago. Loring is the same town it was then, except now there are gangs, and gunfire is something you hear all week long, not just on Saturday night. Now people kill folks they don't know.

Chuckie is supposedly at a deer camp with some men she's never met. He told her he knows them from a sporting goods store in Greenville. They all started talking about deer hunting, and one of the men told Chuckie he owned a cabin over behind the levee and suggested Chuckie go hunting with them this year.

Cynthia is out with her friends — she may be at a movie or she may be in somebody's back seat. Wherever she is, Dee Ann prays she's having fun. She prays that Cynthia's completely caught up in whatever she's doing and that she won't come along and find her momma here, standing alone in the alley beside the courthouse, gazing up through the darkness as though she hopes to read the stars.

The room reminds her of a Sunday school classroom.

It's on the second floor of the courthouse, overlooking the alley. There's a long wooden table in the middle of the room, and she's sitting at one end of it in a straight-backed chair. Along both sides, in similar chairs, sit fifteen men and women who make up the grand jury. She knows several faces, three or four names. It looks as if every one of them is drinking coffee. They've all got styrofoam cups.

Down at the far end of the table, with a big manila folder open in front of him, sits Barry Lancaster, the district attorney, a man whose name she's going to be seeing in newspaper articles a lot in the next twenty years. He's just turned thirty, and though it's still warm out, he's wearing a black suit, with a sparkling white shirt and a glossy black tie.

Barry Lancaster has the reputation of being tough on crime, and he's going to ride that reputation all the way to the Mississippi attorney general's office and then to a federal judgeship. When he came to see her a few days ago, it was his reputation that concerned him. After using a lot of phrases like "true bill" and "no bill" without bothering to explain precisely what they meant, he said, "My reputation's at stake here, Dee Ann. There's a whole lot riding on you."

She knows how much is riding on her, and it's a lot more than his reputation. She feels the great mass bearing down on her shoulders. Her neck is stiff and her legs are heavy. She didn't sleep last night. She never really sleeps anymore.

"Now Dee Ann," Barry Lancaster says, "we all know you've gone through a lot recently, but I need to ask you some questions today so that these ladies and gentlemen can hear your answers. Will that be okay?"

She wants to say that it's not okay, that it will never again be okay for anyone to ask her anything, but she just nods.

He asks her how old she is.

"Eighteen."

What grade she's in.

"I'm a senior."

Whether or not she has a boyfriend named Chuckie Nelms.

"Yes sir."

Whether or not, on Saturday evening, August 2nd, she saw her boyfriend.

"Yes sir."

Barry Lancaster looks up from the stack of papers and smiles at her. "If I was your boyfriend," he says, "I'd want to see you *every* night."

A few of the men on the grand jury grin, but the women keep straight faces. One of them, a small red-haired woman with lots of freckles, whose name she doesn't know and never will know, is going to wait on her in a convenience store over in Indianola many years later. After giving her change, the woman will touch Dee Ann's hand and say, "I hope the rest of your life's been easier, honey. It must have been awful, what you went through."

Barry Lancaster takes her through that Saturday evening, from the time Chuckie picked her up until the moment when she walked into the kitchen. Then he asks her, in a solemn voice, what she found there.

She keeps her eyes trained on his tie pin, a small amethyst, as she describes the scene in as much detail as she can muster. In a round-about way, word will reach her that people on the grand jury were shocked, and even appalled, at her lack of emotion. Chuckie will try to downplay their reaction, telling her that they're probably just saying that because of what happened later on. "It's probably not you they're reacting to," he'll say. "It's probably just them having hindsight."

Hindsight is something she lacks, as she sits here in a hard chair, in a small room, her hands lying before her on a badly scarred table. She can't make a bit of sense out of what's already happened. She knows what her daddy was and she knows what he wasn't, knows what he did and didn't do. What she doesn't know is the whys and wherefores.

On the other hand, she can see into the future, she knows what's going to happen, and she also knows why. She knows, for instance, what question is coming, and she knows how she's going to answer it and why. She knows that shortly after she's given that answer, Barry Lancaster will excuse her, and she knows, because Lou Pierce has told her, that after she's been excused, Barry Lancaster will address the members of the grand jury.

He will tell them what they have and haven't heard. "Now she's a young girl," he'll say, "and she's been through a lot, and in the end this case has to rest on what she can tell us. And the truth, ladies and gentlemen, much as I might want it to be otherwise, is that the kid's gone shaky on us. She told the sheriff one version of what happened at the grocery store that Saturday night when her daddy came to see her, and she's sat here today and told y'all a different version. She's gotten all confused on this question of time. You can't blame her for that, she's young and her mind's troubled, but in all honesty a good defense attorney's apt to rip my case apart. Because when you lose this witness's testimony, all you've got left is that dog, and that dog, ladies and gentlemen, can't testify."

Even as she sits here, waiting for Barry Lancaster to bring up that night in the grocery store — that night which, for her, will always be the present — she knows the statement about the dog will be used to sentence Jim Wheeler to November defeat. The voters of this county will drape that sentence around the sheriff's neck. If Jim Wheeler had done his job and found some real evidence, they will say, that man would be on his way to Parchman.

They will tell one another, the voters of this county, how someone saw her daddy at the Jackson airport, as he boarded a plane that would take him to Dallas, where he would board yet another plane for a destination farther south. They will say that her daddy was actually carrying a briefcase filled with money, with lots of crisp green hundreds, one of which he extracted to pay for a beer.

They will say that her daddy must have paid her to lie, that she didn't give a damn about her mother. They will wonder if Chuckie has a brain in his head, to go and marry somebody like her, and they will ask themselves how she can ever bear the shame of what she's done. They will not believe, not even for a moment, that she's performed some careful calculations in her mind. All that shame, she's decided, will still weigh a lot less than her daddy's life. It will be a while before she and Chuckie and a girl who isn't born yet learn how much her faulty math has cost.

Barry Lancaster makes a show of rifling through his papers. He pulls a sheet out and studies it, lets his face wrinkle up as if he's seeing something on the page that he never saw before. Then he lays the sheet back down. He closes the manila folder, pushes his chair away from the table a few inches, and leans forward. She's glad he's too far away to lay his hand on her knee.

"Now," he says, "let's go backwards in time."

Contributors' Notes

David Ballard was born and raised in Middletown, Ohio, the son of two teachers. He majored in English at Miami University, and he received his law degree from the Ohio State University. He lives in South Bend, Indiana, with his wife, Jeanne, and his son, Jack. "Child Support" is his first published story.

▪ I am addicted to games. I also love reading suspense stories where a character encounters some sort of contest or wager, whether by choice or coercion, and naturally the stakes are high. My earliest influences are the stories of Roald Dahl, Richard Matheson, and the early nonsupernatural stories of Stephen King.

"Child Support" is that kind of suspense story. The idea began as a "what if" scenario while I was throwing Frisbee in the park with Jake, our black Labrador, and Jack was watching in his stroller. I began playing a mental game of how many Jake could catch in a row, and then it struck me just how secluded we really were in that park as it was getting darker.

I listen to movie soundtracks as I write. I'll pick a certain one to set the right mood for a particular story, and then I'll play it over and over until the story is finished. For "Child Support," I must have listened to the soundtrack for *Pulp Fiction* at least three hundred times.

Charles Raisch at *New Mystery Magazine* accepted my story and published it as an "author debut," something he tries to accomplish in each issue. I cannot imagine any better care and handling of a new writer than what the folks at that magazine gave me.

Scott Bartels is a graduate of the University of North Florida, where he won the North Florida Young Writers Award. This is his first published piece. He doesn't use the "F word" nearly as often as this story might lead you to believe.

▪ "Swear Not by the Moon" started with nothing more than a title ("Creole the Killer") and the last sentence. Then I set about crossing the twain that separated the two. It was never a matter of wanting to see how the title and that last line intersected, but a matter of needing to. I paced the streets of the Quarter with Creole, rattled about in his empty house, traversed I-10 on a shared pilgrimage.

So you can imagine my consternation when *Tamaqua* offered to publish the piece but asked me to change the title to "almost anything else." For whatever it says about me, I agonized over this as much as I did the names of my children. I finally settled on Juliet's admonition about pinning one's love to things variable, although I ultimately disagree with her since we all wax and wane.

This story is about a number of things, among them, reconciling obligations with addictions. Creole's is heroin, and I'd like to think that he beats it. Mine is writing, and I hope I never do.

Born in Buffalo, **Lawrence Block** has lived in New York City most of his adult life — though he travels almost as much as Keller, if to less purpose. His fifty-plus books range from the urban noir of Matthew Scudder to the urbane effervescence of Bernie Rhodenbarr, and include four volumes of short stories. An MWA Grand Master, Block has won a slew of awards, including three Edgars, and been presented with the key to the city of Muncie, Indiana.

▪ Short stories, I've come to feel, ought to speak for themselves; writers, on the other hand, probably shouldn't. I'll just say that Keller first saw the dark of day in a short story called "Answers to Soldier." I never thought I'd have more to say about him, but what do I know? A few years later I wrote "Keller on Horseback" and "Keller's Therapy" and realized I was writing a novel on the installment plan. The novel, *Hit Man*, consists of ten short stories, of which "Keller on the Spot" is the eighth. It is, like its fellows, a variation on a theme.

And it was written by hand, with a ball-point pen and a yellow pad, aboard the SS *Nordlys* off the coast of Norway. I don't know that Norway got into the story at all, and the only water's in the swimming pool, salt-free but heavy on the chlorine. But it seemed like an interesting thing to mention.

Mary Higgins Clark is the author of fifteen novels, beginning with *Where Are the Children?*, and three short story collections, each of which has been an international best-seller. She is the mother of five and lives in Saddle River, New Jersey.

▪ I took my first writing course when I was twenty-one. The professor gave our class the best advice I've ever heard. "Take a dramatic situation, one that appeals to you, ask yourself two questions, 'Suppose?' and 'What if?' and turn that situation into fiction.

That was a long time ago, and I've been doing it ever since. I did add a third question, "Why?" because a strong motive is vital.

Last year when I was doing publicity for my newly released book, I was in the Midwest and read about a man who had been arrested for breaking into his neighbor's home by cutting the cinderblocks in the common basement wall between his townhouse and hers.

The situation made me feel creepy, and I began to ask myself the three questions. Suppose? What if? Why?

"The Man Next Door" is my answer.

Merrill Joan Gerber has published five novels, among them *King of the World*, which won the Pushcart Editor's Book Award for "a book of literary distinction," and *The Kingdom of Brooklyn*, which was awarded the Ribalow Prize from *Hadassah* magazine "for the best English-language book of fiction on a Jewish theme." She has also published four volumes of short stories; the most recent, *Anna in Chains*, was published in 1998 by Syracuse University Press. Her stories have appeared in *The New Yorker, The Atlantic, Redbook, The Sewanee Review, The Chattahoochee Review, The Virginia Quarterly Review*, and elsewhere. "I Don't Believe This" was included in the O. Henry Prize Stories, 1986. A recent essay was published in *Commentary* magazine. She studied writing with Andrew Lytle at the University of Florida, held a Wallace Stegner Fiction Fellowship at Stanford, and now teaches writing at the California Institute of Technology. (More about Merrill Joan Gerber can be seen on her website at *http://www.cco.caltech.edu/~mjgerber.*)

▪ There are all kinds of mysteries in life and one of the most puzzling to me is the failure of friendship, or worse, the betrayal of friendship. In "This Is a Voice from Your Past" I examine the circumstances of such a failure and its terrifying consequences.

Edward D. Hoch, past president of the Mystery Writers of America and winner of its Edgar Award for best short story, is a native of Rochester, New York, where he still lives with his wife, Patricia. He is the author of some eight hundred published short stories and has appeared in every issue of *Ellery Queen's Mystery Magazine* for more than twenty-five years.

For twenty years Hoch edited *Best Detective Stories of the Year* and its successor, *Year's Best Mystery and Suspense Stories*. He has published forty-two books in all, including his two most recent collections, *Diagnosis: Impossible* and *The Ripper of Storyville*.

▪ Just thinking about writing a story like "The Old Spies Club" makes me feel old. My former British code expert, Jeffrey Rand, was introduced to readers of *EQMM* back in 1965, and for many years I made the mistake of aging him along with the calendar. Though he took early retirement from British Intelligence in 1976, he still manages to find mystery and intrigue just about everywhere.

And happily he isn't aging nearly as fast these days as he once did.

Pat Jordan is a freelance writer living in Fort Lauderdale, Florida. He is the author of hundreds of magazine articles (*New York Times Magazine, GQ, Playboy, Men's Journal, Los Angeles Times Magazine, Life,* etc.) and nine books. "Beyond Dog" continues the adventures of Sol, Bobby, and Sheila, all of which have been published in *Playboy.*

▪ Sol, who was the inspiration for my story "The Mark," which was selected for last year's *Best American Mystery Stories,* was again the inspiration for this year's selection, "Beyond Dog." Before Sol was sent to prison on a marijuana smuggling conviction, he lived in the apartment next door to mine and my wife's. When I took my dog, Hoshi, for a walk I often stopped first at Sol's apartment to talk about his latest scam. One day, Hoshi was annoyed that Sol was delaying his walk, so he raised his leg and pissed on the chair Sol was sitting on.

Sol was very amused. It appealed to his perverse sense of humor, and after that he took a liking to Hoshi, whom he called either "The Hosh" or "My Man."

Then Sol went away on his "sabbatical" to a prison in Georgia. Often, my wife, Hoshi, and I would visit him. Hoshi had to remain in the car while we talked to Sol in the prison visitors' room. When we returned to the car Sol would already be walking across a field to his dormitory, so we would let Hoshi out of the car. Hoshi would smell Sol off in the distance and begin to howl pitifully while Sol waved to him.

After Sol returned from his sabbatical, he would often go with me to Hoshi's obedience classes. One day, Hoshi's trainer tried to introduce him to a 130-pound rottweiler. Hoshi took a distinct dislike to the rotty and leaped at him with a great gnashing of teeth. The trainer pulled back the rotty and just looked at my 40-pound Hoshi in disbelief. Sol was looking at Hoshi, too, with a smile.

"Heh, you should make that little fella look in the mirror," the trainer said. "Let him see what a little dog he is."

Sol, not smiling now, snapped at him. "Heh, Slick. Don't ever call him a dog, ya hear. The Hosh is Beyond Dog."

Hence, the story.

Stuart M. Kaminsky lives, survives, and thrives in the sunshine and rain of Sarasota, Florida, where his story in this collection is set. Nominated five times for Edgar awards, he has written a dozen works of nonfiction and more than forty novels, including series books about Toby Peters, Porfiry Petrovich Rostnikov, Abraham Lieberman, and Jim Rockford. His film work includes writing credits for *Once Upon a Time in America*, *Hidden Fears*, *Enemy Territory*, and *A Woman in the Wind*. Kaminsky has a B.S. in journalism and an M.A. in English from the University of Illinois and a Ph.D. in speech (film, theater) from Northwestern University, where he taught for two decades. He is currently on leave from Florida State University.

• I've been writing short stories since I was fourteen and long ago found that the effort was relatively easy for me. I learned early that there was no correlation, however, between how long a story took to write and how good it might be. My short story writing was influenced by Jesse Stuart, Anton Chekhov, Raymond Chandler, and a brilliant teacher at the University of Illinois named George Scoufas. Now everything I read influences me. This morning I read about Arthur Ashe on my box of Wheaties and the legend of Dundee Marmalade on the familiar white jar on the breakfast table. Both were fascinating.

The story in this collection features Lew Fonesca, who has settled in Sarasota as a result of his car breaking down. Lew is a process server, a finder of people, and an easy mark for a sad story. This is neither the first nor the last of my stories about Lew and his friends.

Janice Law lives with her sportswriter husband in rural northeastern Connecticut. She has taught extensively at all levels, from junior high school to college, and is currently an instructor at the University of Connecticut. She has published fourteen books, ten of them mysteries, plus short stories and both popular and scholarly articles. She has been nominated for an Edgar.

• The germ of "Secrets," as of so many of my short mystery stories, came from a newspaper brief: the unconventional weapon disposal method used in the story was a gift from the press. Characters to go with the plot emerged only when I thought of setting the story in an immigrant neighborhood like the ones on the west side of Hartford, Connecticut, familiar to me after many years of living in a neighboring town.

As the child of immigrants myself, I was especially sympathetic to the mother and daughter in "Secrets," and it was a pleasure to put this story of violent emotions and remarkable self-control amid the mundane streets, triple-deckers, and small businesses of Connecticut's capital city.

In stories like "Secrets," I am chiefly interested in the surprises afforded by characters, in their unexpected capacities for good and evil, and in their ability to cope with disaster and opportunity.

John Lescroart (Less-kwa) has published ten novels. The first, *Sunburn*, was a paperback original that won the Joseph Henry Jackson Award for Best Novel by a California Author.

The following two books, *Son of Holmes* and *Rasputin's Revenge*, are historical mysteries set in World War I featuring master sleuth Auguste Lupa, the son of Sherlock Holmes (who was perhaps the young Nero Wolfe).

The Dismas Hardy novels include *Dead Irish* (nominated for the Shamus Award for Best Novel), *The Vig, Hard Evidence, The 13th Juror* (a *New York Times* best-seller, nominated for the Anthony Award for Best Novel), and *The Mercy Rule.*

Lescroat's other novels are urban thrillers and include *A Certain Justice*, which explores the themes of race and politics in America, and *Guilt*, the story of a successful and cultured man who is also a killer.

All of Lescroat's thrillers have been selected by various book clubs, and all his books since *Dead Irish* have been translated and published extensively abroad. He lives in northern California and is working on his next Dismas Hardy novel.

▪ Years after first reading Watson's delightful tease about the "missing" story of the Giant Rat of Sumatra, and after I'd already enjoyed a couple of the humorous takes (Firesign Theatre, etc.) on this most famous of the apocryphal Holmesian titles, suddenly one day it came to me. I simply *knew* the story. It was amazing to me that it hadn't already been written, for what else could a Holmes rat story be about except for the plague? It has to be the plague, a missing (or found) serum, and, of course, Professor Moriarty.

I was far from being in "Holmes mode," as the last Holmesian thing I'd written was about a decade ago, but this one hit me in a bolt. The idea was so grandly obvious — surely it was floating around in the ether that day — that I was afraid somebody else would pluck it out and grab it before I did, so I started writing as fast as I could. This was one of the times that really felt almost as if someone were dictating the words to me (Watson?) (Doyle?) and I were a mere conduit. I started writing around ten in the morning, and by four o'clock that same day I'd finished it.

Sometimes they write themselves, and this was one of those times.

John Lutz's first short story was published in 1966, and he's been writing ever since. The author of over thirty novels and two hundred short stories and articles, Lutz is a past president of both Mystery Writers of America and Private Eye Writers of America. He won the Mystery Writers of America Edgar Award in 1986, and the Private Eye Writers of America Shamus Award in 1982 and 1988. He is also a recipient of the Private Eye Writers of America Life Achievement Award. Lutz's work has been translated into virtually every language and adapted for foreign radio and television. His novel *The Ex* was produced as a film of the same title, and his *SWF Seeks Same* was made into the hit movie *Single White Female*. He divides his time between St. Louis, Missouri, and Sarasota, Florida.

■ I've long been a fan as well as a writer of Florida mystery fiction. One of the main reasons for this is that it has a special relationship with one of the most primal environments in the country. The lush foliage, teeming animal life, the sultry climate with its brilliant, revealing sunlight, pervade Floridians' lives as well as their fiction. The heat is always on and getting hotter. In writing "Night Crawlers," I wanted to make maximum use of that unique Florida atmosphere. Originally I was going to title the story "Primal," because my object was to appeal to the primal part of the reader's mind, the dark and merciless area where simple survival rules. Some researchers call it the crocodile part of the brain. I hope this story provides a path to that dim and desperate arena, but only for a brief visit.

Born and raised in eastern North Carolina, **Margaret Maron** lived "off" for several years before returning to her family's homeplace. In addition to a collection of short stories, she's also the author of fifteen mystery novels featuring Lt. Sigrid Harald, NYPD, and District Court Judge Deborah Knott of Colleton County, North Carolina. Her works have been nominated for every major award in the American mystery field and are on the reading lists of various courses in contemporary southern literature. In 1993 her North Carolina–based *Bootlegger's Daughter* won the Edgar Allan Poe Award and the Anthony Award for Best Mystery Novel of the Year, the Agatha Award for Best Traditional Novel, and the Macavity for Best Novel — an unprecedented sweep for a single novel. She is a past president of Sisters in Crime, current president of the American Crime Writers League, and a director on the national board for Mystery Writers of America.

■ The best thing about short stories is that they're short, which is why I spent the first twelve years of my career writing them. I was too intimidated by the novel's length even to attempt one. My first book (Sigrid Harald's first appearance) started out as a short story that kept growing, and Deborah Knott also began as a character in a short story. Although I've managed to fill three hundred consecutive manuscript pages fifteen times now, I think I'll always prefer the shorter form.

Gardenias are the smell of summer in North Carolina, and for anyone who grew up with huge bushes of those fleshy white blossoms planted beneath every open window, they evoke a tangled web of memories. "Prayer for Judgment" details a young child's memory-in-the-making.

Jay McInerney is still recovering from the tumult occasioned by the publication of his first novel, *Bright Lights Big City*, in 1984. To date, *Bright Lights* has been translated into twenty languages. McInerney accepts full blame for the screenplay of the United Artists movie, starring Michael J. Fox and Jason Robards. His subsequent novels include *Ransom* (1985), *Story of My Life* (1988), *Brightness Falls* (1992), and *The Last of the Savages* (1996). He is a frequent contributor to *The New Yorker* and writes a monthly wine column for *House and Garden*. His new novel, *Model Behavior,* will be published by Alfred A. Knopf in the fall of 1998. With his wife, Helen Bransford, and their twins, Maisie and Barrett, McInerney oscillates between New York City and Franklin, Tennessee.

▪ "Con Doctor" has its origins in a trip to a privately run prison outside of Nashville, Tennessee. A friend of mine, who was the prison doctor, invited me to spend a day making the rounds with him. I posed as an intern. It was an eye-opening and stomach-turning experience. The maladies and injuries described in the story were those we encountered over the course of the day. Whether I have done justice to the brooding malevolence of the place I can't say.

Walter Mosley is the author of six best-selling Easy Rawlins mysteries, the first of which, *Devil in a Blue Dress*, was filmed with Denzel Washington in the titular role. His work has been translated into twenty languages. Much of *Always Outnumbered, Always Outgunned*, in which "Black Dog" first appeared, was initially published in *Black Renaissance Noir, Buzz, Emerge, Esquire, GQ, Los Angeles Times, Mary Higgins Clark Mystery Magazine, Story,* and *Whitney Museum*. The central character and some elements of that book were converted into a filmscript by Mosley and televised by HBO. Born in Los Angeles, he now lives in New York City.

Born and raised in upstate New York, the setting for "Faithless" and much of her fiction, **Joyce Carol Oates** now lives in Princeton, New Jersey, where she is a professor of humanities at Princeton University and co-edits the *Ontario Review* with her husband, Raymond Smith. She is the author of a number of works of fiction, poetry, drama, and criticism, and a member of the American Academy of Arts and Letters.

Under the pseudonym Rosamond Smith, she has published six mystery-suspense novels, including, most recently, *Double Delight*. A number of her stories have appeared in *Ellery Queen's Mystery Magazine*, and a story of hers was reprinted in *The Best American Mystery Stories 1997*.

▪ "Faithless" was originally imagined as a mysterious tale in which a family is haunted by the absence of a woman who, it eventually turns out, has never really been "absent." For years in my notes I would come across this enigmatic situation. In time, it evolved into "Faithless," which I've thought of as a miniature novel. At the heart of mystery is the profoundly obdurate, utterly stubborn and implacable refusal of certain individuals to see what is staring them in the face; and, if they're forced to see, to deny it. This is called "faith" — "blind faith." My alliance is with the doomed but defiant heroine of my story — and with "faithlessness."

Peter Robinson was born in Castleford, Yorkshire. His first novel, *Gallows View* (1987), introduced Detective Chief Inspector Alan Banks, who has since appeared in eight more books and three short stories. *Past Reason Hated*, his fifth, won the Crime Writers of Canada's Arthur Ellis Award for Best Novel in 1992. *Wednesday's Child*, the sixth, was nominated for an Edgar in 1995, and *Innocent Graves*, the eighth, also won the CWC Arthur Ellis Award. His short story "Innocence" won the CWC Award for Best Short Story. A collection of his short stories, *Not Safe After Dark*, is to be published by Crippen & Landru in the fall of 1998. He now lives in Toronto, where he occasionally teaches writing courses.

▪ Because I spend most of my time writing the Inspector Banks series, I find it especially liberating once in a while to try something different, and short stories provide the perfect outlet for this impulse. Though part of "The Two Ladies of Rose Cottage" takes place in Eastvale, Banks's patch, it takes place in the fifties, before Banks was born, and it is far from being a police procedural. I have been a great Thomas Hardy fan for some years now, and this story has its origins in a visit my wife and I paid to the house in Higher Bockhampton, Dorset, where Hardy was born and lived on and off until shortly after his marriage to Emma Gifford in 1874. We stood in the room where Hardy was cast aside as dead by the doctor who delivered him, only to be revived by a quick-thinking nurse. We also looked out on the same view he saw as he wrote his early books, up to *Far from the Madding Crowd*, and somehow the idea for a story about someone who actually *knew* Hardy began to form. It didn't have a murder at that point — the crime came later — but it did have the two elements that most of my stories have in their early stages: a sense of place and an interesting character to explore. As it turned out, "The Two Ladies of Rose Cottage" became my first *historical* mystery.

Dave Shaw spent his youth playing baseball on a small field near his house in Loudonville, New York. He received his M.F.A. from the University of North Carolina at Greensboro, and since then his stories have appeared in *The Southern Anthology*, *The Quarterly*, *Southern Exposure*, and many other magazines throughout the United States and abroad. His work has been awarded the Southern Prize for Fiction, a Pushcart Prize nomination, and a Wurlitzer Foundation Grant. He lives with his wife in Pittsboro, North Carolina, where he plays on a slow-pitch softball team and is completing *Cures for Gravity*, a collection of stories.

▪ The best satire, I think, leaves us naked in a room with our clothes at our feet — clothes which, we suddenly realize, were see-through all along. In "Twelve Days out of Traction" I found a narrator and situation which I liked a great deal: a con-man whose crimes have more to do with anarchy and identity than with any willful cruelty. I also found a happy marriage between humor and anarchy. Laughter, I think, often *is* anarchy, an open acknowledgment of personal and societal foibles. At the same time, laughter also can be an acknowledgment that each of us perhaps desires, to some extent, that which is the object of our ridicule. I hoped "Twelve Days" ultimately would work as a story about surrender, in the process describing some of those odd transparent garments to which we all cling. If the story fails to achieve these aspirations, though, I hope it will at least make the reader laugh.

Helen Tucker grew up in Louisburg, North Carolina. A former newspaper reporter and writer for radio, she also worked in the editorial department of Columbia University Press in New York and as director of publicity and publications at the North Carolina Museum of Art in Raleigh.

She is the author of eighteen novels and a number of short stories. In 1971 she became the first woman to receive the Distinguished Alumni Award from Wake Forest University, and in 1992 the Franklin County (North Carolina) Arts Council named her Artist of the Year for outstanding service in the field of literary arts.

She and her husband, William Beckwith, live in Raleigh, where she writes fiction full-time.

▪ Included on my "beat" as a newspaper reporter was Superior Court, and I was completely fascinated, not only by the machinations of the lawyers and the court system, but also by the criminals. Studying them, their motives, and exactly how their crimes were committed became almost second nature to me.

I think probably the idea for "The Power of Suggestion" first came to me as I watched one of those TV commercials for psychics, and I began to solve the mystery in my mind of how a woman could convince her husband that she was psychic.

Donald E. Westlake was born many years ago in the dorp of Brooklyn, New York, but was raised in exile in Albany, also in the great state of New York. He began telling lies at an early age, then figured out how to do so at a profit, and has never looked back. Telling lies for money, he has published over seventy novels, been credited (or debited) with five produced screenplays, and filled the interstices with short stories, criticism, and the occasional essay (aka occasional occasional). The only flaw in his happy existence is that he now finds it impossible to lie for free.

▪ It was a dark and stormy night. Fortunately, I was indoors, at a party that had something to do, as I recall (or, more accurately, do not recall), with the Mystery Writers of America. As in uffish thought I stood, Mary Higgins Clark approached to say that she and Liz Smith were assembling a collection of original short stories to be published in a book called *The Plot Thickens* to raise money in aid of literacy. Now, if it weren't for a general run of literacy in this world I have no idea what would have become of me (farmhand, perhaps, losing limbs one at a time), so that was a charity I felt I could wholeheartedly support. Also, I have been grateful to Mary for some time for her having wrested the annual Edgar Awards dinner out of its church-basement-supper era and brought it to a height of splendid occasion. So I said yes. So she told me the gimmick: All the stories had to contain a thick book, a thick fog, and a thick steak. So I went away and mused, and wondered if I could do a switcheroo with one of those elements: "Stake" instead of "steak," for instance, as in "through the heart." But then it came to me to use "stake" in another way, and do the switcheroo on a different requirement. Thus the story pratfell into existence, and here it is. And isn't it nice that we are all literate.

A native of Mississippi, **Steve Yarbrough** lives in Fresno, California, where he is professor of English at California State University, Fresno. He is the author of the short story collections *Veneer* (due out in the fall of 1998), *Mississippi History,* and *Family Men.* His novel *The Oxygen Man* will be published in 1999. His stories and essays have been published in many journals and magazines, and he has won a Pushcart Prize and a fellowship from the National Endowment for the Arts.

▪ In 1996 Kathleen Kennedy, who produced such movies as *The Color Purple* and *E.T.,* read an essay of mine about southerners and guns and got interested in my work. I went down to L.A. and had a meeting with her, and before too long her production company had optioned an unpublished novel of mine called *The Oxygen Man* and hired me to do the screenplay for it.

The novel has two time frames several years apart, and many of my struggles with the screenplay involved either cutting out material from the past or trying to find a way to work that material into the present action. "The Rest of Her Life" is the first piece of fiction I wrote after finishing the filmscript. The structure of the story, in which most of the action takes place in the past, probably grew out of my impatience with the limitations screenwriting placed on me.

Other Distinguished Mystery Stories of 1997

AGGELER, GEO
The Fire. *South Dakota Review,* Spring
ANDREWS, TOM
Torch Song. *Hardboiled,* no. 23
AXTMANN, FREDERICK
Line of Sight. *Alfred Hitchcock Mystery Magazine,* July/August

BANKIER, WILLIAM
A Gift of Murder. *Ellery Queen's Mystery Magazine,* February
BARNES, ERIC
The Huts. *Greensboro Review,* Summer
BLAIN, W. EDWARD
Driscoll Henley's Last Day. *Ellery Queen's Mystery Magazine,* August
BLOCK, LYNNE WOOD, AND LAWRENCE BLOCK
The Burglar Who Smelled Smoke. *Mary Higgins Clark Mystery Magazine,*
Summer/Fall

CALDWELL, BO
His Moods. *Story Magazine,* Winter
COBEN, HARLAN
Entrapped. *Mary Higgins Clark Mystery Magazine,* Spring
COHEN, STEPHANIE KAPLAN
Lady Luck. *Hardboiled,* no. 23
COMBA, GRETCHEN
The Friction Point. *Greensboro Review,* Summer
CRENSHAW, BILL
Roadkill Poker. *Alfred Hitchcock Mystery Magazine,* April

DEAVER, JEFFREY
Double Jeopardy. *Ellery Queen's Mystery Magazine,* September/October

DEFILIPPI, JAMES
A Fog of Many Colors. *New Mystery,* Summer
DUBOIS, BRENDAN
Trade Wars. *Ellery Queen's Mystery Magazine,* February

FAKO, EDWARD
Drunks. *Antioch Review,* Winter

GALLAGHER, TESS
My Gun. *Kenyon Review,* Spring

HAMILTON, STEVE
The Silence. *Pirate Writings* 5, no. 2

JANCE, J. A.
One Good Turn. *Vengeance Is Hers,* ed. Mickey Spillane and Max Allan Collins (Signet)
JONES, SUZANNE
Shifter. *Ellery Queen's Mystery Magazine,* April
JONES, THOM
Tarantula. *Zoetrope,* Winter

LINK, WILLIAM
The Good Samaritan. *Ellery Queen's Mystery Magazine,* August

McCLINTOCK, MALCOLM
Kelso at the Voodoo Museum. *Alfred Hitchcock Mystery Magazine,* February

NICHOLAS, MARK
A $5,000 Proposal. *Cold Drill,* ed. Kent Anderson (Boise State)
NOVAKOVICH, JOSIP
Crimson. *Manoa,* Winter

OATES, JOYCE CAROL
Lover. *Granta,* Summer

PIKE, EARL C.
The Magician's Wife. *Whiskey Island,* Summer/Fall

SAYLOR, STEVEN
The White Fawn. *Classical Whodunnits,* ed. Mike Ashley (Carroll & Graf)

WEINBERG, ROBERT, AND LOIS H. GRESH
The Adventure of the Parisian Gentleman. *The Mammoth Book of New Sherlock Holmes Adventures,* ed. Mike Ashley (Carroll & Graf)